STAR OF GRAY

By Hubbard J. Tozer

I0660509

Version 1.0

Copyright © 2012 Hubbard J. Tozer

All rights reserved.

ISBN: 978-0-9856654-2-5

First Edition

Dedication

Dedicated to everyone who ever looked into the night sky and wondered. To everyone who ever felt slightly out of step with the rest of the world. To everyone who still dreams of a greater tomorrow, filled with the silence of stars.

You're not alone, and you never will be.

For Linda Robbins-Doyle. Thanks for keeping me funny when I needed to be, romantic when I should have been, and serious when it mattered most. You give me the lines to color in, and for that I am forever grateful.

Chapter One

Taris had only been at the reception for half an hour and already she wanted to leave. The food was lousy, the drinks were *not* free - even though she was assured before she went that they would be - and the wait staff was comprised of Grays which made her really uncomfortable. She considered herself to be something of a liberal-minded woman, especially for a military officer, and being around Grays always made her uncomfortable. She hated the way humans treated them, like little more than property. It revolted her. Still, apart from the occasional rally and petition-signing there was nothing she could do about it anymore except cringe. And drink. She was three whiskey shots deep before Sergeant Gareth Hoble, her trusty noncommissioned officer, found her. He trounced up in his dress black uniform, looking sharp but seriously annoyed. He came to a stop in front of her, carrying an expression of equal parts relief and severe irritation.

"Lieutenant Bodil, I have been looking for you everywhere," he said in an exasperated tone. His Welsh accent was always thicker when he was emotional. "I have spent the last fifteen minutes weaving in and out of the crowd searching for you!"

"Gareth," she said, chomping down a couple of pretzels, "how long have we worked together?"

He blinked, taken by surprise. "Um…oh. Well, that would be three years, two months and eight days, mum. Give or take a day."

"And in that time, do you think you've gotten to know me rather well? You know, my sense of humor? My schedule? What kind of food I like? My habits?"

"Er…well yes, of course mum," he said, giving her a suspicious look.

"Well you haven't gotten to know me as well as you think." She tossed back another shot of whiskey and swiveled around to face him. "If you *really* knew me, you would not have spent the last fifteen minutes looking for me. All you had to do was make a straight line for the bar. I did."

He sighed heavily and sat down next to her, cradling a folder and ceremony schedule in his hands. "I suppose I had hoped you'd be out mingling with the important people, not mucking about at the bar in the back."

She laughed lightly and tossed a few more pretzels in her mouth. "Yeah well, the bar in the front of the building was full."

"I'm sure."

"Care for a drink, Gareth?" she asked.

"You know I don't care for drinking in uniform, mum," he said politely.

"You can put it on my tab," she offered with a wry smile.

His frown gave way to a resigning grin. "Well, in that case I think I would, yes." He looked at the bartender, a young, muscular Gray with a nametag that said Steve. "Um…Steve, is it?"

The Gray looked up, his mirror-like eyes reflecting the world around him with passive interest. He was tall, with chiseled features that carved out the face of an attractive man. The Grays were similar in appearance - at least in the basic form - to humans. This particular Gray appeared to be in his late twenties, with the dimpled smirk of a younger man but the wary almond shaped eyes of an old and wise one. Down his back tumbled the telltale long silvery hair of his race. The Grays never cut their hair. This was a religious principle that they all seemed to abide by, regardless of what tribe they came from. The bartender's skin was pale and his eyes glinted in every light, always with the same expressionless face. All the Grays had the same kind of liquid silver eyes that seemed to move in a way all their own. This particular alien was wearing a very sharp black and white tuxedo for the special banquet occasion. Underneath the blanket of long shimmering hair, she thought she saw the faintest hint of a blue tattoo snaking up the side of his neck. *Well that would help to make him stand out,* she thought. In truth, the

Grays were beautiful, but as much as she hated to admit it, they tended to sometimes look the same to her.

"Yes sir?" Steve the Gray said in the feathery accent they all seemed to have.

"Can I have a whiskey please? Penderyn, if you have it."

"Yes sir. Of course." He poured Gareth's drink quickly and placed it in front of him with a pleasant smile. Gareth reached into his wallet for a tip, but Steve raised a hand in polite protest.

"Oh, thank you sir, but we aren't allowed to accept tips," he said, pointing to the sign above him. It was clearly marked: *Do not tip the Grays. They are here to serve you at your convenience.* With a polite nod, Steve resumed his bartending responsibilities elsewhere, leaving them alone.

Gareth looked at her, eyebrows raised. "Can you believe that?"

She shook her head. "Unfortunately yes. There's some new proposal headed to the Earth World United authority that wants to ban tips and extra wages for Grays. Something about their financial needs not being so high and cost of life being lower because they don't need food and all that. The EWU thinks it will save taxpayer dollars or something. It's total bullshit."

Gareth nodded, sipping his whiskey. "I agree...but that's not what I meant. I meant that they made him wear a nametag that said 'Steve'. As if a Gray would call himself Steve!"

Taris looked over at him to make sure the bartender couldn't hear. "I know what you mean. That assimilation stuff goes too far sometimes. I mean, their words are strange sounding to us I guess but that doesn't mean we have the right to take their names from them. It's awful."

"Yes, I know. It's a real pity," Gareth agreed, swiveling around and grabbing for the pretzel bowl. "Speaking of pity, you look right for some yourself. You might want to straighten yourself up a bit mum, for appearance's sake."

Taris turned back around and met herself in the mirror behind the bar. Forced to evaluate her appearance, she groaned at her own reflection. Strands of her black hair had escaped from the bun and had scattered all over her head in a pathetic, unkempt mess. Her formal black uniform was a little wrinkled - the obligation to attend this event was extremely short notice - and she was apparently missing a button on the side shoulder. Her heart shaped face was frowning unflatteringly as she scrutinized her expression. Her hooded eyes seemed dull and pale, but that might have been from the bad lighting. Her skin was ashen, but lately it seemed to be even more so, highlighting the dusting of freckles on her face. All in all, she'd looked better, but she'd also looked much worse. In this case, she looked every bit of twenty-seven, but she felt so much older than that. Sighing, she decided that the age and the bags under the eyes could not be helped, but at the very least she could do something about the hair. Grumbling about the inconvenience of it all she reached up and * pulled her hair back into a loose but no longer unseemly bun.

Gareth, on the other hand, looked pretty damn terrific. Staff Sergeant Gareth Hoble was a sarcastic Welsh pain in the ass, and she loved him for that. After his father killed himself, Gareth found meaning in the military as a means to escape the forced sympathy and empty words of encouragement from people back home. At only twenty-three, he had somehow managed to become a strapping young man. He was tall and slender, with the traces of his round, childlike face all but gone. He wore his hair tidy and short, and his button nose always seemed a little red. His high cheekbones and small, soft green eyes were always scrutinizing things with the faintest hint of distrust. He seemed to wear a perpetual frown around her, making his wide mouth and pouty lips pursed and tense-looking. Still, in spite of his dour attitude, he was the closest thing she had to a friend, and the most trusted NCO on their small but mighty ship: The Intrepid.

They worked together on board the Intergalactic Spaceship - or ISS - Intrepid. It was a stealth military ship designed to be fast, quiet and effective. It was that ship, and their service to it, that brought them that night to Emissary Hooper's palatial mansion for the annual military recognition awards. It was more of a political meet-and-greet, but she went where she was ordered, and she was ordered to be there. The civilians acted like it was the most amazing and reverent event that they would attend the whole year. They glided around the brightly-lit ballrooms in sequined gowns and expensive tuxedos, clutching their hearts in feigned gratitude for the service members in attendance. Taris truthfully couldn't care less. She was there on orders from the captain, not to rub elbows with the wealthy elite. Their fake smiles and dispassionate military appreciation was about as transparent as their sympathies toward the Grays, who were treated like cattle in tuxedos.

She noticed that the Grays in the emissary's employment wore their brand on the backs of their hands. She could see the round silver mark on Steve's hand, glistening when the light caught it. A circle with a giant H stamped in the middle. The brand wasn't more than a scar that was painfully burned into flesh. She felt sorry for him, and in a way she understood. Perhaps more than any other human being. Absently she traced the scars on her palms. *Well at least mine are not on the front of my hands*, she thought with a bitter frown.

She hated when they branded the Grays. She always thought that was taking it too far. Making them slaves was bad enough, but stamping them as property? That was just low. Now she was swimming in a sea of people who obviously didn't care one way or the other. She hated people who didn't care about others, and that was exactly the kind of people filling the rooms of the enormous house. They stood in small circles, laughing about pithy jokes and stuffing their faces with mini crab cakes. All meaningless dribble. She couldn't wait for it all to be over. Besides, if she was going to sit through an entire reception filled with tiny dinner portions and boring speeches from rich people, she was going to do it drunk. Cash bar be damned. She was just about to turn that declaration into a reality when the dinner bell rang, startling everyone out of pleasant conversation.

Taris frowned. It couldn't be dinner time already, could it? That meant she'd been drinking a lot longer than she had anticipated. She looked down at her wristband to confirm the time, doubting the annoying dinner bell. The wristband itself was a piece of technologically advanced machinery that was so complex that she never bothered to learn all of the functions. She used it primarily to tell the time, check the weather, or reference the occasional map. She touched the front panel and the interface sprang to life, but something was wrong. The numbers on the clock's holographic face were fluttering between numbers sporadically. *Damn high-tech device,* she grumbled. *Fine time to fritz out on me.* As of to mock her, the chiming dinner bell rang once more.

"Ladies and gentlemen, if you will please take your seats in the main ballroom, dinner is about to be served," the Gray host announced in a delicate breathy voice.

"Show time," Gareth said, gulping down his whiskey with a grimace.

Taris paid her tab and together she and Gareth joined the procession of people that filed into the dining hall. The Gray in the front was holding a registry list, ticking names off as they went in. His name tag said Bill. It was a name that didn't fit him well at all.

"Name?" he asked politely.

"Gareth Hobble and Taris Bodil, of the ISS Intrepid," Gareth answered for them.

"Tickets, please," Bill asked, not looking up from his list.

"Oh!" Taris exclaimed, reaching into her pocket. She fumbled around for a bit before she finally found her dinner tickets. "Here you go," she said, handing them to him.

As the host reached down to take them from her, he caught sight of her palms. The inside of both her hands had the same thing: three lines, one vertical and two that crossed it horizontally in the middle. This was inside the shape of a box inside a triangle. She was often embarrassed of her unfortunate scars. Especially when they were noticed by a Gray. His motions stopped entirely. Caught off guard, the Gray dropped the tickets and grabbed her hand, turning her palms up. She felt her pulse quicken, the embarrassment rising to the surface. Before he could get a better look, she yanked her hands back and shoved them deep into her pockets. The Gray looked up and met Taris in the eye.

"*Camme sans supre Adulo?*" he asked quietly in his language. She sighed. This did not surprise her. That reaction happened more often than she could count with Grays. She didn't speak Adulo, but she understood that question very well. It was something that Grays had been asking her since she was a child, and every time she had the same answer.

"It's not what you think," she said amiably. "I'm not one of you."

"Your hands," he said quietly. "But you are branded."

"A burn," she answered quickly, feeling her cheeks blush in embarrassment. "Just an unfortunate burn from when I was a kid. That's it."

Bill frowned. "But…your eyes. They're silver, are they not? You are an Adulo?"

Anticipating this response, she smiled politely and shook her head. "No, no. My eyes are not silver, they're light blue. I'm human I'm afraid. Not a Gray."

His expression fell just slightly, almost like he was disappointed, but it took him only the smallest of moments to compose himself. He reached down to pick up the tickets. When he stood up, his unreadable face had glossed over any hint of emotion from before. "Sorry to misunderstand, ma'am."

"It's okay," she said waving her hand dismissively, "it happens all the time."

The Grays often mistook her unfortunate scars or extremely pale blue eyes to indicate that she was one of them. She always thought that strange, because barring those two random and explainable things there was nothing else about her that resembled a Gray. Her hair was black and theirs was silver, her skin was slightly pink and theirs was the color of gray rock. She wasn't nearly as tall as a Gray - the average was about six foot three - even though at five foot ten she was pretty close. However, her eyes were an unusual color; that much was sure. Mistaking her for an alien was an assumption that people have been making for as long as she could remember. It used to offend her as a child, especially when kids made fun of her, but over the years she'd grown to accept it with grace. Besides, being mistaken for a Gray could not possibly be as bad as actually being one. Bill the Host cleared his throat and looked down on his list.

"Intrepid crew, you are at table eight, to the right of the stage. The steward will escort you."

The steward was another Gray in a white suit standing next to him. His silver hair was braided tightly and roped down his back. He smiled an empty smile and gestured a gloved hand into the ballroom. Taris gave Bill a polite and slightly embarrassed murmur of thanks and followed the steward to her seat. The ballroom was lavishly decorated for the occasion. Round tables were covered with white tablecloths, with the green and blue symbol of the Earth World United Space Fleet emblazoned on the top. The lighting was soft, impersonating candle light, and there were murmurs of light conversation at all the tables. The steward led them to a table slightly in the back of the room, to the right of the stage. She noticed that there were already two other people sitting at the table and she tried to hide her disappointment. She loathed small talk, but it was especially tiresome during dinner. She positioned herself on the other side of the table and put Gareth between her and the strangers. She hoped that it would be enough to keep them from talking to her.

It wasn't.

Chapter Two

"Hi!" said the first man, reaching his whole body over the table to shake her hand. "I'm Matt Conner, and this is my partner in crime, Dave Schuler." He gestured to the man sitting next to him, who looked about as happy to be at the event as she was.

"Hello, Matt, Dave," Gareth said politely, extending a hand. "I'm Sergeant Gareth Hoble and this is Lieutenant Taris Bodil. We're from the ISS Intrepid."

Matt raised his eyebrows over his glasses. "Ooh! Military members! What a coincidence!"

Dave scoffed. "Well of course they are in the military. You didn't get that from their uniforms?" Taris stifled a laugh. He was sarcastic, disgruntled, clearly not in a talking mood. She liked him already. Matt shot him a dirty look and then sat down, smoothing his sandy hair back.

"Wait. Bodil..." he mused. "Hey! I know that name. You aren't by chance related to Murphy Montgomery Bodil, are you?"

Taris nodded. She knew where this was going. "As a matter of fact I am. That's my father."

Matt clasped his hands together in excitement. "Oh my god that's amazing! Your father is a legend in the scientific community! I did my thesis on his genetic adaptation and biological conversion theory. The Neros Effect is one of the greatest genetic evolutionary theories of our time, you know. Oh he's brilliant. What a treat this is! To be seated with a real Bodil!"

"Yes, my father is quite the genius," she agreed politely. Her father was a rock star in the scientific community and she knew it, but she didn't often like to talk about it. While she adored her father, she sometimes found his brilliance to cast a professional shadow that she could never hope to crawl away from. She knew how revered he was in many prominent circles, so she let Matt prattle on about her father's work with genetics for a few minutes. After all, he wasn't the first Dr. Murphy Bodil fan she had ever met. She was used to this kind of conversation by now.

She was also a master of pretending to listen to it.

"…which is why I didn't even think it was possible until your dad proved me wrong! I mean, can you imagine that kind of amalgamation? What could be done with that? Amazing. I'm especially impressed with his genetic observations and discoveries involving Gray anatomy. Oh, my god I just realized…Gray anatomy! Ha! How funny!"

"Yeah," Dave said with a scoff, "everyone loves a good medical joke."

Matt glared at him. "David, you're being an asshole. This is Dr. Bodil's daughter here, not just *anyone*."

"She's not the problem," said Dave, casting a grouchy look around the room. "It's this place and these people. I hate it here."

"Well you don't have a choice. We're here and that's that. Can you at least *pretend* not to hate it for two seconds? Please?"

He sighed. "I know, I know. I'm sorry Matt. I'll play nice."

Taris cleared her throat politely. Now was the perfect time to switch subjects. "So, what do you and Dave do?" she asked.

Matt smiled and rubbed his hands together. "Excellent question. My partner David and I are the dual heads of the scientific research department at the Wayneward Institute in New York. We're engineers."

"Engineers of what?" she asked a little more tersely than she had expected.

Matt frowned. "What do you mean?"

She rolled her eyes. *Academic types. Always trying to make things more complicated.* "Well the term 'engineer' is rather ubiquitous, don't you think? That was so broad a statement as to be meaningless. What kind of engineers are you?"

"Oh the regular type," he responded, shoving a dinner roll in his mouth casually.

"What? What the hell does that mean? What do you specialize in? What is your specific area of expertise? Are you actual experts, or is this some sort of monster-in-the-attic Doctor Frankenstein deal?"

Dave laughed gutturally. "Did I hear that wrong, or did you just compare us to mad scientists?"

"Hey I like that," Matt said, straightening up in his chair. "We're the mad scientists of New York, Dave."

"We should get t-shirts."

"Or at the very least some sort of catch phrase," Matt added with a smile.

Taris groaned. This was getting nowhere.

Gareth stepped in politely. "So, engineers for Wanyeward, eh? Well, that's quite impressive."

Dave ran his hands through his thick mass of auburn curls. "Eh, it's not as impressive as you would think. It's all work in large rooms with no natural sunlight. I have pretty much no life outside of work. They've got us holed up in labs six days a week doing tests, examining materials, building green monsters from spare human parts..." he trailed off with a smirk.

"Haha," she said, staring disapprovingly into her empty wine glass.

"They only let us out today because they needed someone to accept this military science award and our supervisor didn't want to go," he added.

Taris nodded in understanding. "Yeah, that's why we're here too. Wait, did you say military? You're in the fleet?"

Dave shook his head. "Not the fleet. We're in the Army Science Corps."

She looked them both over with a scrutinizing expression. "Really?"

"The Wayneward Institute is a military run organization, lieutenant," Matt explained. "They carry the banner of a civilian brand, but the core is military. The whole building is filled with either service members or government contractors."

"Yes, I knew that. I meant...*you two* are in the military?" she asked suspiciously.

Matt looked to be in his late twenties, but he had to be older than that. He was tall to the point of lanky, with long sandy brown hair and a five o'clock shadow on his face. He wore large, black rimmed glasses with a small blinking light on the side that looked handcrafted, or at the very least enhanced. He had a little sly smile that seemed permanently etched on his pleasant oval-shaped face. His ill-fitting brown suit was spotted with little buttons that had pictures or phrases on them that she couldn't make out in the dim light. He looked like an overgrown teenager as he folded his napkin into the shape of a boat, tossing his unkempt hair to the side in irritation.

Dave, in contrast, was sitting back in his chair with his arms folded in disapproval. He was in his mid thirties, average height and build, with dark brown eyes and a mop of curly reddish-brown hair on his head. His blue suit fit well and he was clean-shaven, but he seemed genuinely unhappy to be where he was. He gave the impression of a disgruntled genius who begrudged his own genetics for the burden of his intellect.

"Yep, Matt and I are in the service if you can believe it," he said in his raspy New York tone. "We're both serving our country through scientific exploration. Not a bad gig, really, unless you count the dog-and-pony shows like this banquet." He looked around the room in blatant disapproval. She knew the feeling. She watched him rock an empty tumbler back and forth with one slender finger.

"What do you drink?" she asked.

He stopped rocking the glass. "Scotch."

Taris flagged down a female Gray waiter holding an empty tray. "Could we have a scotch and a whiskey here, please? Better make them both doubles." The Gray nodded and returned with the order quickly. Dave took a sip of his drink and a smile crept across his lips. Taris thought the smile made him seem far more attractive. She wondered if he knew that, or if he even cared about that sort of thing.

"Mmm. That's good."

"I thought you might like it," she said, sipping her own drink generously. "It's the only thing that makes this whole event even remotely tolerable."

"Ha! Well said. I think I'm going to like you, lieutenant," he said in appreciation, "and believe me when I tell you I don't say that to many people."

"I believe it. The same goes for you, Mister Schuler," she said.

"Major," he corrected amiably, "but it's not a big deal. We hardly wear the uniform these days. We're always in the lab."

"So you're both majors in the Army Science Corps?" Gareth asked. "But this is a military function. Why aren't you wearing your uniforms tonight, as specified?"

Matt shrugged and touched the blinking light on his glasses. "No one told us we had to."

Gareth didn't know how to respond to that. He was a bit of a stickler for protocol and always got a little flummoxed when things didn't quite go right. "Well, then. Blimey."

Matt pointed a finger at him. "Hey sergeant, you're Welsh, right? From Cardiff?"

Gareth looked at him, pleasantly surprised. "Why yes I am, actually. My god sir, how the hell did you know that?"

Matt smiled and tapped his glasses. "My scanning spectacles. They're my own little invention. They save time and energy when you're trying to get a reading on something. Anyway, the specialty buttons on your uniform bear your initials. That means that they were a special order, and they are made by a unique company called Blaidd Drwg. It's a small Welsh company and the only factory is in Cardiff. Really the town was more of a guess, but the buttons were a dead giveaway."

Gareth stared at him in shock. "Wh…what? Wow. You got all of that from scanning my uniform?"

Matt blushed. "Yes. Of course. I mean, they wouldn't put us in charge of a research department if we weren't geniuses, right?"

"Or he just recognized your accent and put two and two together," Dave said dryly.

Matt pushed his hair off of his forehead and glared at his friend. "Thanks a lot, Dave."

"You're welcome, Sherlock of Science," he retorted.

Taris laughed. "Oh it's okay, Major Conner. Accent or no accent, I thought that was impressive all the same."

"Well *thank you*, lieutenant," he said, jabbing Dave in the ribs.

Dave chuckled under his breath and took another generous sip of his scotch. "Matt's scanning spectacles are pretty awesome, actually. They're capable of serving almost any vision purpose. It's really helpful in the lab, too. He can break down elements and dissect the properties of a specimen without ever touching it."

"If they're so great Dave, why aren't you wearing a pair?" Taris asked.

Dave scoffed. "Because some of us don't need to show off our inventions when we go out. Matt uses them in social settings as a chance to explain his brilliant machines to anyone who will listen. He thinks he looks cool."

"I *do* look cool, you grumpy Jew," Matt said, throwing his napkin boat at him. Dave shook his head in feigned irritation, but she could see he wasn't truly offended.

"Excuse me," said a deep voice behind her, "but I think you're sitting in my seat."

She turned around and looked up at a large, massively attractive black man standing behind her.

"Who are you?" she asked, a little tipsy. The man pointed to the nametag on his immaculate black uniform. "Doctor Christian Tomas."

Doctor Tomas was a man with whom the ancient humans would have carved statues in his likeness. He was tall, with broad shoulders and a disposition that assumed authority without having to demand it. He had closely cropped hair and chocolate eyes that were round and alert, absorbing the world around him, constantly analyzing it. His nose was prominent but not dramatic, and his full lips spread between two dimples. His jaw line was strong and jutted, and his uniform pressed up against large, muscled arms. He was staring at her like he expected her to respond to him. Finding her voice, she cleared her throat.

"It's not assigned seating doc, but you're more than welcome to sit next to me," she offered, trying not to stare.

"Uh…it is assigned seating, lieutenant. My place card is right in front of you, see?" he reached over her shoulder and she caught the faint scent of manly cologne. He pulled back and handed her a little title holder that did, indeed, read *Dr. Christian Tomas, ISS Horizon.* She looked up at him, and a wave of embarrassment washed over her.

"I'm so sorry," she said, fumbling to stand up, "I totally didn't pay attention to that."

She stood up to face him, coming much closer than he seemed to care for. He smiled politely. "It's fine. It's okay. Thanks."

She opened her mouth to say something, but all that came out was a high pitched squeal that passed for a giggle. He gave her a strange look but didn't say anything. She was mortified. She read all the place cards at the table before finding her own, which ended up being next to Dave. She schlepped down in her chair, sipping her whiskey to try and keep her embarrassment down. Dave leaned over to her.

"Smooth there, lieutenant," he joked. She glared at him but said nothing. She was starting to think that five drinks in an hour was a bad idea after all.

"So," Gareth said politely as the main course was being served, "what brings you here tonight, Dr. Tomas?"

The doctor looked up at him and swallowed a bite of Beef Bourguignon. "Ah, well. I am accepting the award for my work on the Gray displacement colony on Mars."

"Ah…this isn't vegetarian," Dave complained, staring at the plate of beef in front of him. He flagged down a waiter. "Could I please have a vegetarian plate? I can't eat this. Thanks."

"What sort of work were you doing at the displacement colony, Dr. Tomas?" she asked, hoping to smooth over the misunderstanding from before.

"Well," he said, cutting himself another slice of meat. "I am a member of the ISS Horizon. We're a medical research ship, specializing in diseases and cross-species contamination. A few months ago my team and I helped to contain an illness. There was a virus sweeping through the camp and making not just the Grays, but the humans sick as well. Terrible, nasty thing. Makes you sick for a week, can't eat, all that stuff. It's worse for the Grays. They couldn't sleep, and as you know that is their one and only source of energy, so it was really bad. It actually killed some of them for a want of sleep. We called it the Moss Flu, because of the way it made the skin turn green. I was a part of the team who helped to find a vaccine to prevent it."

Taris whistled in appreciation. "Wow. That's quite impressive, doc."

He nodded, his head down. "Mmm-hmm. And what about you, Lieutenant Bodil? What great achievement do you have to thank for being here today?"

Taris couldn't tell if he was being serious or sarcastic, but she answered anyway. "Um…actually, we haven't done anything."

"We're accepting the award on behalf of our leader, Captain Philip," Gareth explained quickly, shooting her a look that screamed *be nice*. "It's for our work in stopping the trading riots in Sector Two a few months ago."

Dr. Tomas frowned. "Really? I mean, don't take this the wrong way, but crowd control hardly seems like an achievement worthy of an event such as this."

"Tell me about it," she said under her breath.

"What she means," Gareth said, eyeing her carefully, "is that it was unexpected for us as well. The captain told us to come at his behest only a few hours ago. He and Emissary Hooper are good friends and the emissary said that there was no trouble to switch the names at the last minute."

Dr. Tomas nodded. "Ah, so your captain is friends with Boone Hooper? Well that makes sense now."

Taris did *not* like the tone of his voice. She opened her mouth to give him a piece of her mind, when the sound of a microphone turning on interrupted her. She turned to the stage to see Lady Hooper standing at the podium, tapping the microphone with a bejeweled hand.

"Um...hello? Attention? Is this thing on? Oh...it is! Okay! Well hi! Thank you all for coming!" she started as the noise of the crowd ebbed to silence.

Lady Hooper smiled, looking every bit the doting rich man's wife. With well-styled blonde hair, a sequined gold dress and diamonds dripping from everywhere, Lyn Hooper was a trophy wife in her thirties with a wealthy woman's ambitions. She played golf, she held parties, she owned the most expensive personal spaceship on the planet, and she participated in a myriad of charities. People thought this made her generous and altruistic, but Taris had a suspicion that she did it to keep her mind off her cheating, thieving, pig of a husband. If Lyn held any reservations about her husband she hid them well. The welcoming smile and well-manicured nails said that she was there to glitter and shine like a piece of polished metal.

"Well thank you all for joining us tonight," she said, her southern accent dripping on every word. "It's so great to have y'all. I'm Lyn Hooper," she said, pausing as the crowd clapped in appreciation. "Thank you, thank you! I'm Lyn, proud southern mother to three boys and wife to Emissary Hooper." More applause. "Thank you so much! Y'all are so kind! Anyway, before we get started, I thought that we would start the award ceremony off with a moment of silence for the four fleet men who lost their lives in the fight for freedom last week."

Taris resisted the urge to groan. "They didn't lose their lives fighting for freedom," she whispered to Dave, "they got drunk and crashed their ship into the moon."

Dave stifled a laugh. "Hardly something you go to a hero's grave for," he whispered back. "Besides, I heard they were smugglers and thieves who were running an illegal Gray trade off the coast of China."

"Dumbasses," she whispered back.

Both of them snickered, but she caught the eye from Gareth and swallowed her laughs. Finally the moment of silence ended and Emissary Hooper took the stage. Daniel "Boone" Hooper was a good ol' boy from Mississippi. He was also one of the richest men alive. His company, Hooper International, was one of the first to push for laws regulating the buying and selling of branded Grays. In less than ten years, the man went from well-to-do millionaire to powerful multibillionaire. He was even elected emissary to the EWU council for his efforts. His facial hair was shaved into a tidy goatee, cropped as short as the white hair on his head. He had a serious face, slightly rounded, with beady brown eyes and a pointy nose that he used to look down at others. He was overweight but he covered that fact with his tailored white tux. He had a handmade, gold-painted leather sash which looped several times around his generous midsection, fastening in the middle with a round golden medallion with a huge H in the middle. It was his trademark symbol, the same one he burned into the skin of his slaves, marking them his property. Most people thought Boone was an eccentric rich business owner.

Taris thought he was a schmuck.

"Thank you for that lovely opening, Lyn. Isn't my wife lovely?" he asked the crowd, who clapped enthusiastically in response. "Well, I'd like to thank y'all for coming out tonight to be a part of the third annual military recognition awards. It is an honor to serve y'all today, y'all who serve us in so many ways every day. The military is the backbone of the Earth World United sectors and we are forever grateful for everything they continue to do for us. Thirty years ago..."

Taris stopped paying attention right then. She knew the history, and it wasn't a great one. Space travel, Grays, fighting, violence, legislation, liberation blah blah blah. It was all a bunch of political dribble designed to convince the masses that the atrocities committed against other people were for the right reasons. She didn't need to be told how other people thought she should view the world. She looked over in the corner, hoping to flag one of the waitresses to refill her whiskey tumbler. The Grays were standing in the back, quietly lined up in rows. Some of them were wearing wait staff uniforms, others steward or house staff uniforms, and others still wearing uniforms belonging to some of the guests. All the slaves stood in the back, and even in the darkness they seemed otherworldly and strange.

The silver hair still glimmered in the dark, hung loose and low in various degrees of length. They looked like ghosts in the shadows. They stood like statues, unmoving and beautiful, yet they seemed connected somehow. Without having to touch, or look at each other, or even acknowledge each other's presence, they seemed to be content to just be around each other. She had heard rumors that the Grays were telepathic, and that's why they spoke so rarely. She had heard stories since she was a child that the Grays were like fairies; that they could perform magic and talk to each other without speaking and they could disappear and reappear whenever they wanted. She had even heard that some of them had wings, but she'd never seen it. As she grew older, most of this she dismissed as childhood fantasy, but she did notice that the Grays seldom spoke to each other verbally. It was utterly unbelievable to her that they could possibly be contented with a life of servitude on Earth. Taris couldn't imagine what it must be like, to be so far from home, to grapple with their sense of self every day. Away from everything familiar and comfortable. She felt pity for the Grays.

...she feels sad for us, but does nothing...

She heard it. She heard it, but she didn't understand it. She looked around widely, catching strange expressions from Dave and Dr. Tomas, checking to see if anyone overheard that. *I must be drunker than I thought. I didn't say that pity thing out loud.* She stared at her whiskey glass. *Did I?*

She looked up at the Grays and realized, to her shock, that they were all staring directly at her. Her mouth dropped. She felt frozen in place. The Grays typically had unreadable expressions, nothing more than pleasant smiles. Now she found over a dozen of them staring at her with the same shocked expression. If she didn't know any better, she would say they all looked scared.

Are you an Adulo?

"What?" she asked, feeling a little dizzy. "What did you say to me?"

"I said they called your name twice, Lt. Bodil!" Dr. Tomas hissed, gesturing toward the stage. Taris looked up and noticed that the entire room - including Boone Hooper - was now staring at her. She hadn't realized how long she had not been paying attention. She shook her head to clear her thoughts and stood up quickly. A little too quickly, for the motion made her dizzy. She leaned against the table, regaining her balance ungracefully. She straightened the front of her dress black uniform and strode up to the podium, ignoring the looks of irritation from the audience. Boone kept the plastered smile on his face as he held the certificate of appreciation out in front of him, but she could tell he was more than a little irritated with her. He reached out his hand to shake hers, and she tried not to cringe at his clammy, weak handshake. They stood for the obligatory handshake-and-certificate picture, and then he gestured to the microphone, indicating that she say a few words. Gareth was standing at the foot of the stage looking morbidly embarrassed. She tried to give him a look that told him she had it under control, but he seemed to misinterpret that, hanging his head to avoid onlookers.

"Well..." she said, already hating the sound of her voice resonating over the speakers, "um...thanks for this, Emissary Hooper. It's quite an honor."

She felt the sweat dripping off her forehead. She had completely forgotten the fact that she might have to make a speech, and she wasn't so good at thinking-on-her-feet speaking engagements. She looked in the back and noticed that the Grays were still staring right at her. *You're being paranoid,* she told herself. *You're on stage. Of course they're looking at you.*

"I accept this award on behalf of my leader, Captain Tom Philip of the ISS Intrepid. He...deeply regrets that he wasn't here tonight, but he is very thankful...for this."

The audience was still staring at her, expecting her to continue. She had no idea what else to say. "So...I'm so glad that we could be here today...tonight...to make this occasion so special...I mean it is special..." She was floundering. Gareth looking like he wanted to die rather than suffer through any more of her rambling.

Suddenly a woman in the crowd started shrieking.

"*Good god! What's happening*?!" someone else screamed.

"No! No! No!"

"*For the love of god*!" said a large man, standing up so quickly he flipped the table over.

Taris scoffed and leaned on the podium. "Hey shut up! I know it's not the best speech ever but it's not *that* bad."

"It's coming right for us!"

"Run! *It's going to crash*!"

"What are you..."

She realized they weren't shouting at her, but pointing and screaming at the giant ballroom window. Rather, what was coming *toward* the giant ballroom window. Barreling out of the sky, at an intensely fast speed, was a spaceship. It was headed on a collision course for Earth...and it was coming right at them. She heard the screams of people tearing out of the room, but she felt frozen in place as she watched the ship careen toward her. Right for her.

She barely had time to duck when it crashed.

Chapter Three

Taris dragged herself up from under the podium. She could see people screaming and shouting, but her ears were ringing so loudly that it drowned everything out. She was still in shock as she tried to shake her head free of the muddled thoughts. Emergency lights flashed red and sirens wailed, but all she could do was stand there and watch as people scrambled and screamed. It was chaos. Small fires were breaking out in every direction. Debris covered every inch of the floor. The room was uncomfortably dark and she felt the spray of water from the overhead sprinklers, adding to the disorientation. People were running in every direction, but in her head she was the only person there.

This is just like the rebellion, she thought.

Flashes of the war, of chaos, of her fellow rebels dying, it all came back to her. She remembered the screams for mercy, the wailing of the dying, the smell of explosions and dirt and death. *No, not now. I can't lose it now. It was ten years ago*, she told herself, covering her face with her hands. *Ten years. Not now. This is something else. People are injured. Get your shit together, Bodil. Pull yourself together.* She took a deep breath, pushed her disheveled hair back behind her ears, and took a wide look around.

By a stroke of amazing luck, the ship had crashed into the gardens, sliding to a stop into the ballroom. If the ground had not broken the fall, the ship would have dragged its hull through the room and flatted people like ants. As it stood, the only part that actually crashed into the dining hall was the bow. It was also a small transport ship; the smaller personnel carrier type that was used to get from the planet surface to the main ship in orbit. That was fortunate, because a garden would not have broken the fall of a bigger ship. The force of the impact shattered the windows and spread glass and dirt through the dining area like confetti, but Taris considered that lucky. It could have been worse. So much worse. At that moment the emergency lights flickered on and the sprinklers turned off. The entire ballroom was destroyed and scattered with people, although most of the able bodied guests had fled the scene. Dozens had tried to run away from the crash, but from the screaming shouts of horror she assumed that some of them didn't make it.

Taris felt numb, like she wasn't sure how to react. The fog in her head was keeping her from moving or feeling. She didn't know how long she had been standing there, or if anyone noticed. Suddenly she felt a hand on her shoulder. In that moment her mind rushed back into the chaos of reality.

"Gareth! Oh thank god you're all right!" she exclaimed. She wrapped her arms around him, happy that he was still breathing.

"That was horrible," he said, his voice hoarse. "I watched...I mean I saw..."

"I know," she said, cutting him off. "I know. Are you okay?"

He nodded mechanically. "I...I think so. We were on the other side of the ballroom. Everyone at our table was okay. But those people. Those other people..."

He looked like he was on the verge of losing his mind. She didn't blame him, but staying calm was the most important thing for both of them to do at that moment. She needed to be strong for him, which meant it was time for her to pull the leadership card.

"Sergeant Hoble," she said with as much authority as she could, "I need you to get as many people out of here and to safety as you can. Grab Dr. Tomas and start collecting the injured outside. We are service members of the fleet. We're trained for this, remember? We can handle extreme circumstances, but these people can't. I need you to get the civilians to safety."

Gareth looked pale but he nodded. "Yes mum."

He saluted her and started down into the ballroom, helping people to their feet and instructing them to go to the exits. Taris turned and started toward the ship, clomping over the broken glass and overturned tables. She reached the bow and walked around to the starboard side. Sweating profusely, Taris took off her uniform jacket, tucked her ID tags into her blue undershirt and tossed it over the side of a partially overturned table.

"It looks like a military ship," said a familiar voice behind her. She swung around and saw Matt Conner squinting at the ship with his strange little glasses.

"Civilians should be evacuating to the front of the building," she pointed out. "This is a police and military matter."

"We *are* in the military, remember?" grumbled Dave, standing behind his friend with his arms folded. "Besides, we don't have time to wait for emergency crews, lieutenant. There could be people in there, and they could be hurt."

Matt ignored the both of them. "The design of this craft looks to be a transport series L, usually used for the carrying of personnel. This model was recently improved with extra safety modifications…how odd. With the new mods, a crash like this should have been easily avoidable."

"That's what I was thinking," Taris said, turning back to the ship. "Something obviously went wrong. Someone could be injured or dying in there. I can't see through the forward screen." She tried to peer into the shielded bridge, but it was no use. Any ship with the screen on couldn't be penetrated by the sun's rays, let alone human eyesight.

Matt looked up at the front and touched the little light on the edge of his glasses. She heard a strange *whizzing* sound, then he turned to her, eyes wide. "There are bodies in there, lieutenant. One living for sure, but the heart rate is really slow. They're dying."

"Then we have to get in there," she said.

"Let's do it, then," said Dave. He reached into his pocket and pulled out a small cylindrical black device. Taris raised her eyebrows.

"What's that?"

"It's Dave's diffuser," Matt explained proudly. "It allows him to defuse carbon particles. Basically it's like a laser cutter, only so much more precise. He can practically split an atom with that thing if he wanted to."

"Not that I would," Dave pointed out, "unless I have a death wish."

"Why do you have that with you?" she asked.

Dave frowned. "Hey, just because my inventions aren't something you wear doesn't mean they're not something to be proud of. Now hoist me up. We don't have much time."

They turned over a table and hoisted Dave up. He pointed the diffuser at the door seal and adjusted the settings. The laser sparked as it cut through the obsidian metal frame of the ship, and in a couple of minutes the seal was broken. Dave kicked in the door.

"Let's go!" he said.

Taris jumped up onto the table with Matt behind her and the three of them crawled inside the ship. It was a small transport carrier, standard issue, with spots for no more than six passengers excluding the crew. The transport bay was empty of passengers, but the cockpit door was locked.

"*We have to get in there!*" she yelled over the alert noise.

Dave put his hands over his ears. "*Can you turn that damn noise off?!*"

She nodded and ripped the cover off of the computer panel on the side. The alarms were whooping madly as red lights flashed throughout the ship. She reached up to the interface panel, keying in the commands that disabled the warning siren. The sound stopped immediately, to their mutual relief.

"All the safety protocols have been disabled," she said, reading the interface. "The cockpit door is sealed. Dave?"

"I'm on it," he said, pointing his diffuser at the door seal.

"An accident?" Matt asked, scanning the ship.

"No, I don't think so. The safety protocols were off before the ship left orbit. This was intentional."

"Why would anyone intentionally crash a fleet transport ship into the emissary's ballroom?" Matt asked.

Taris looked out into the destroyed dining hall. Boone was switching between screaming outrage and barking orders. The servants were obeying quickly, but she could tell that they feared the backlash of his anger. Emissary Hooper was resting his hand on a weapon on his belt. She didn't need to see it to know what it was. Gray masters often used "compliance" methods on their slaves using a device called a scrathe. The scrathe, ranging from anything as small as the panic-button pen to as big as a multi-blast ray gun, used genetic-specific technology designed to inflict pain only on a Gray. It was completely harmless to humans - and allegedly did no permanent damage to a Gray - but Taris thought even the threat of one was monstrous. Naturally, Boone carried the morally questionable whip model. Electricity shoots out like lightning tentacles and tortures a Gray like a hyper shock collar. She'd never seen it used before, but she'd heard that the whip was monstrous. There were rumors it could even kill.

"I can think of a *few* reasons why someone would wanna crash his parties," she said.

"Got it!" Dave exclaimed, finishing the laser cut. Together the three of them shoved the door open.

The smell of blood was so overpowering that she had to cover her mouth. The co-pilot was dead, that much was certain.

His blood was splattered all over the front of the main screen. Taris swung his chair around and saw that he had been slashed with a blade three times. One slice went down the front and the other two across his chest.

"This was intentional. Whoever killed the copilot sliced him open by carving a calling card into his chest," she said.

"Look at this," Dave said, pointing to the cuts. "It's--"

"A pattern," Matt finished. "It's a symbol. Hey, this looks familiar."

Yeah. I know what you mean," Dave said with a knowing tone. The two scientists exchanged a strange look. She was about to demand answers when she was interrupted with a terrible, guttural noise.

"Unnnnggggg…"

The captain was crumbled up in his chair, bleeding from the head, but still alive. He was wrapped in silver chains which attached to a strange blinking collar around his neck. He was badly beaten and bloodied, but by some miracle still alive.

"Are you all right?" she asked, knowing the answer was no. He lolled head to the side and looked up at her with blackened eyes.

"I…can't…breathe…message…he said…I have to…" He trailed off when he started to sputter blood.

"We have to get him out of here," Dave said urgently.

"The systems are starting to overload," Matt said, scanning the computer. "Holy shit, this thing is set to explode! Why is it set to explode? I mean who *does* that?"

"What's your name?" she asked the pilot urgently.

He looked up at her like he didn't understand at first. "Uh...Roland....my name is Roland Rolf."

"Okay, Roland Rolf. We have to get you out of here. Can you walk?" she asked, pulling on the chains.

He shook his head. "No ma'am. My legs..."

She looked down. He was right. His legs were bashed into two contorted heaps. Since the safety controls were disabled, the impact of the crash shoved his legs into the console with all the g-force of reentry. She looked up at Dave.

"Does that thing cut through chains, Major Schuler?" she asked. He reached up and started keying in specifications on the diffuser.

"It does now, lieutenant," he said. He pointed it at the chains and split them apart in seconds. "What about the collar? Do you want me to--"

"No!" Roland screamed. "Don't touch it! He...he said that...pain...it will kill me if you take it off."

"Lieutenant, the ship is reaching critical levels. We need to go *now*," said Matt, grabbing her arm.

"Roland, you're going to be okay," she assured him. "We're going to get you out of here. Dave, grab his other arm. Matt, get his legs."

Roland screamed in pain as they dragged him out of the cockpit, sobbing with every step they took. They tried to go slowly, but when Matt started hollering words like "explode" and "mere minutes", they had to virtually drag the poor captain out of the doomed ship. They stumbled down out of the cockpit and into the ballroom as fast as they could.

"Medical team!" she screamed over her shoulder. Two officials with medical bags and a hover stretcher appeared. "This man needs help!" They helped Matt and Dave lower Roland onto the stretcher as he screamed in agony.

"*You*!" screamed Boone, stomping toward them with a finger pointed at Roland. "You're the one responsible for this!"

"Sir," Matt said, pointing to the ship.

"Your piss poor excuse for piloting has cost the lives of at least three of my guests!"

"Sir!"

"You murdered three people, and to top it off, you killed one of my translation and dictation Grays! Do you have ANY idea how expensive those things are?!"

"Sir, listen to me, please!" Matt said urgently.

"No, don't try to protect him! I want an explanation and I want it now!"

"Oh for god's sake Emissary Hooper, *shut the hell up*!" Taris exclaimed. He swung around and glared at her, fury dancing in his eyes. His nostrils flared like an animal.

"How *dare* you speak to me like that. In my own house."

"*The ship is going to explode*!" she exclaimed. "That's what he's trying to tell you! We need to get out of here now!"

"Thirty seconds, lieutenant!" Matt screamed. Taris grabbed Boone by the arm and started dragging him out of the room.

"Everyone!" she screamed. *"The ship is about to explode! Get out get out get out! Let's go!"*

People started scrambling for the doors as Taris dragged Boone Hooper through the ballroom, ignoring his insulting protests. She followed the people as they streamed hysterically though the hallways until she saw a way out. She picked up the pace and headed for the door.

As soon as her boots hit the outside stairs, the ship exploded.

Chapter Four

Taris was thrown sharply to her knees and rolled down a few stairs, cursing profusely. Boone fell even farther than she did, bouncing to an ungraceful stop in front of his hysterically screaming wife. *The ship's engine infusion chamber must have ruptured*, she thought, judging by the force of the impact. She had seen it happen before, but never on the ground, and never so close. She sat up and rubbed her head irritably, surveying the scene. Hundreds of people were splayed all over the grand steps of Emissary Hooper's mansion. She saw fire crews and reporters, emergency workers, guests in tattered evening gowns, injured people on hover stretchers and Grays. The Grays were doing more work than any of the humans. They were treating the injured and running for assistance and helping to calm sobbing women. Each one of them, in their own way, was doing their best to control the situation.

The house was a massive inferno. Half the west wing was in flames, with plumes of thick angry smoke funneling into the night sky. She tried to see if the emergency air police were on their way, but looking up made her feel dizzy and a little sick. Groaning, she looked down and resisted the urge to vomit.

"Are you okay, Taris?" She turned and looked up to see Dr. Tomas, holding a hand out to help her up. She smiled weakly and accepted it graciously.

"I'll be okay," she said politely.

"We'll see about that. That's a bad cut you have on your head."

She touched her hairline and felt a wet, sticky spot where her head appeared to be bleeding, and rather intensely at that.

"You're right," she commented, surprised. "When did that happen?"

Dr. Tomas laughed. "It's okay. I'll take care of you." He reached into a medical bag he'd acquired from one of the emergency staff members and started scanning her head for signs of traumatic brain injury. "I saw you drag him out of the house," he said after a couple of moments. "You saved Emissary Hooper's life."

"Hmm. I guess so. Not that he was too thrilled about it at the time," she said, casting a look at the red-faced multibillionaire, bellowing like a blow horn at the late-arriving firefighters.

Dr. Tomas reached into his bag and pulled out a laser suture. "Hold still," he commanded, "this will only take a few seconds." He pointed the laser at her and started to sew up her cut. The sutures stung a little and felt warm, but true to his word, it did only take a few seconds. "There. That will do it." He wiped her head free of excess blood and looked at her with a smile. She reached her hand up to her wound and found it sewed up and dry.

"Thanks," she said with a small smile.

"You're welcome. Hey, has anyone ever told you that your eyes look silver? They kind of look like the Gray's eyes," he said, staring into them intently. She frowned and looked away.

"Yes I know. They're not silver, though. They're light blue. It's just a coincidence."

"No," he said, turning her chin to face him, "don't be embarrassed. Your eyes are lovely." She felt her cheeks grow hot. Dr. Tomas' big brown eyes and gentle touch made her feel girlishly awkward.

"Thank you," she managed to squeak out.

"Doctor! Doctor! Help! *We have a problem*!"

Dr. Tomas turned and ran in the direction of the yelling, Taris trailing shortly behind. Roland was still on the hover stretcher, struggling and shouting as two medics tried to hold him down.

"What's going on?" Dr. Tomas asked, scanning his body.

"I don't know!" the medic exclaimed, fighting to hold Roland down. "He was just lying there whimpering and then all of a sudden that metal collar thing started blinking and he freaked out!" Taris looked at the collar around Roland's bloodied neck. The thing was indeed blinking red, and it was getting faster.

"Get it off! Get it off! It's going to kill me!" Roland shrieked hysterically, grabbing at the collar. Dr. Tomas turned to her.

"Can you get it off?!"

"No!" She searched the crowd frantically. "Dave! David Schuler! *Major Schuler can you hear me*?!"

"Yes! Lieutenant Bodil! Where are you?" His voice cut through the crowd.

"By the fountain in the front of the house!" she screamed. "Hurry!"

Dave and Matt broke through the crowd and came running up the hill. She ran down to meet them halfway.

"The pilot is screaming! He needs his collar off!"

"I'm on it!" Dave said, running past her as he adjusted his diffuser. Matt and Taris ran up behind him.

"*It's going to kill me*!" Roland shrieked. "He said I would be okay! He told me that all I had to do was deliver a message! Why is this happening?!" he exclaimed, sobbing uncontrollably. Dave started sawing through the metal, cursing because it was taking so long. Matt touched the end of his glasses, scanning Roland's collar.

"Oh my god..." he said, putting a hand to his mouth.

Taris looked at him. "What? What is it? What is happening? What is it, Matt?"

"It's..."

Roland looked right at her. "Too late."

She heard the subtle clicking noise, and the sound of bone breaking. Roland convulsed then toppled over, loping off of the edge of the hover stretcher. The only thing that kept him from falling to the ground was the restraining belt around his waist. Taris covered her mouth with her hand.

"The collar snapped his neck in three places," Matt clarified in a quiet voice, "there was nothing we could do."

"God damnit!" Dave cursed, throwing the diffuser in frustration. "I was so close. I almost had it." He rubbed his anguished face, cursing profusely. Matt placed a hand on his shoulder.

"There was nothing you could have done, man."

"What's going on over here?!" Boone's voice boomed as he ambled up the grass, his entourage in toe. Taris noticed that several of the Grays were trailing behind, their expressions taut and uncharacteristically worried. Through the crowd, Taris caught sight of Gareth coming up the hill and breathed a sigh of relief. She tried to catch his eye, but he wasn't looking at her. In truth, he looked pretty worried himself. Boone huffed up the hill and came to a panting stop in front of Taris.

"Was that the pilot? Did he die? Why did you fools let him die?!"

"No one *let him* die sir," Dr. Tomas argued defensively. "The collar he was wearing activated and broke his neck. We were unable to remove it in time."

"Well that's bullshit son," Boone grumbled. "That pilot committed a terrorist act on my property, on my friends and family, and now thanks to your *incompetence* we won't know why."

"Yeah!" chimed in Lyn Hooper from behind a handkerchief, and she looked the worse for wear. Her clothes were covered in black dust, her hair a nest of chaos on her head. "Just look at my house! It looks like Atlanta burnin' up there! Who are we going to hold responsible for this travesty?!"

What a cliché! Taris rolled her eyes. "Oh calm down, Dixieland Princess. As if you couldn't afford to fix or replace all this stuff."

Lyn's mouth dropped, taking a couple of enraged steps toward her. "Excuse me? Stuff? Did *your* house burn down tonight? Because unless it did I don't think you deserve to pass *judgment on ME!*"

"Um, doctor…whatever your name is," Boone said in a strange tone. "I thought you said the man was dead."

Dr. Tomas nodded. "Yes sir. He is."

Boone raised a fat finger at the corpse. "Well then why is he sitting up and lookin' at me?"

Taris swung around and gasped. She had seen Roland's neck break. She had heard it break. She'd seen him die, and yet there he was, sitting right up, and staring right at them.

"Holy mother of moly," she whispered. She took a couple of steps toward him, staring closely at his face. Something was wrong. His face was tense, his eyes were unfocused and he wasn't breathing. He was definitely dead. *The movement is nothing,* she told herself, *an unfortunate nerve reflex.* Then the corpse opened its mouth.

"*Emissary Hooper,*" Roland said. Only it wasn't Roland. It was another man's voice *coming out* of Roland. Taris jumped back about ten feet.

"*Gaaaaah!*" she screamed, nearly leaping into Dr. Tomas' arms.

"Sweet Jesus, did that thing just *speak?*" Dave exclaimed.

"*Emissary Hooper,*" repeated Corpse Roland.

"What in the hell is going on here?!" Taris asked anyone who might answer. Matt daringly peered closer and scanned the body with his spectacles.

"Incredible. Absolutely incredible," he whispered. Taris pushed Dr. Tomas aside and stood in front of Matt.

"Major Conner, is he dead?"

"Well yes, of course he's dead," he answered plainly.

"Then why is he talking?" Lyn asked, dabbing her glistening forehead delicately.

Matt pointed to the collar. "He's not. The collar is playing some sort of message and using the body as a transmitter. It's quite brilliant in design…"

"If it weren't so morbid," Dave finished for him with a disapproving grimace.

"*Emissary Hooper,*" the corpse said again.

"Why does it keep saying that?" Lyn asked, holding her hands to her ears.

Dave cocked his head to the side. "I think it's a voice recognition message."

"It's not going to play until Boone Hooper says he's here to receive it," Dr. Tomas added quickly. "That is, I think."

Boone's eyebrows raised and he cleared his throat. He tried to look brave and undaunted but she could tell he was frightened. Terrified, really. *He has good reason to be,* she figured.

"I am Emissary Daniel Hooper," he said with as much bravado as he could muster. "What is the meaning of this grotesque and unseemly act?"

The corpse was silent for a moment. "*Voice pattern confirmed.*"

Matt patted Dr. Tomas' shoulder. "Good thinking, doc."

"Thanks," he said, looking a little pale.

The Roland corpse turned its head at an inhuman angle, staring directly at Boone. "*This message is for Boone Hooper, Emissary of the Earth World United authority and leader of the American region known as Sector One. This is a recording. Questions cannot be answered or messages returned. You cannot respond to this message. You must listen to the message in its entirety and it will not be repeated. Do you accept the terms of this?*"

Taris looked to Boone. All eyes were on him. She felt her heart thumping quickly in her chest, waiting for him to answer.

"I guess…I guess I have no choice," he said.

"*Answer not recognized.*"

"That means yes, god damnit!" he bellowed, nervous to the point of shaking. The corpse was silent for a minute as the collar blinked several different colors. Finally it stopped, and the light in the front went to a stable green.

"Emissary Hooper," the voice began in a masculine and fluid tone, *"I am sending this message today because I have something that needs to be said. A message if you will, to the whole of the human race. I hope you'll pardon this crass approach, but I fear that anything less dramatic would not have gotten your attention. Before you scream outrage, the human with whom this message was attached to was not a good person. He and his copilot were known illegal slave runner conspirators who were helping to sell children into servitude. They should not be mourned long, and the human race should consider themselves the better for having them gone. In any case, we thought it was about time that someone in your position heard our side of the story."*

"Our side?" Dave whispered to Taris. "What do you think it means?"

Taris took a sidelong look at the Grays. She could see the mutual looks of confusion and fear on their faces. Their eyes were darting between each other in interest and worry, hidden behind their almost-unreadable faces.

"It's them." She nodded to the slaves, who were surreptitiously trying to slink to the back of the crowd. "The voice recording is a Gray."

The corpse recording continued. *"For a long time, opinions have only been one sided. You people think that we hate you; that we've always hated you. Sir, this is profoundly untrue.*

We have not always hated humans. As a matter of fact, it didn't start off as hatred at all. When this all started, we actually considered your race to be friends. Fifty years ago when the humans invented a transgalactic rift manipulator, it allowed you to travel through vast amounts of space instantly. This changed the entire planet as you dawned on a new era of space exploration. Forty-eight years ago you discovered my planet, Caleum. Caleum is filled with a race of people called the Adulos, but you call us the Grays. We were anxious to share our knowledge, wisdom and understanding with the human beings from Earth, who looked so much like us. We thought we were going to join in friendship. We honestly thought you came in peace. We were wrong."

Taris could hear the hurt and betrayal in the voice of the recording. The desperation of the oppressed. She took another look at the Grays, when she realized she wasn't the only one. There were several people eyeing them in the crowd. Some looks were more threatening than others.

"Do you think they planned this?" Matt whispered to her. She slowly shook her head.

"I don't think so," she whispered back. "These Grays look confused and frightened. This seems to be as much news to them as it is to us."

The corpse continued to speak. *"The humans, however, had a different plan in mind for the Adulos. A much different plan. If we only knew of the horror, the tragedy that was to come. Maybe we could have stopped it. It was years before the war was waged, but by then our lands were ripped apart, our families devastated..."*

"What in the cat's canary is he talkin' about?" Lyn Hooper wondered, talking over the voice of the recording. Unfortunately, Taris was closest in proximity.

"The slave trade," Taris explained quickly, trying to listen.

"What about it?" Lyn asked.

Taris furred her brow. "Christ, Lyn, what do you think? After the rebellion, the Earth World United authority made Gray slave trade legal, remember? They defined people as humans and Grays as property."

"So?" she asked, trying to pat her frizzled hair back into some kind of seemly shape. "That was years ago."

"And that makes it somehow less relevant?" she hissed. "Don't you remember the war? I'm sure you do, since you profited so greatly from it."

Lyn turned to her, appalled. "I did no such thing! The war was a terrible time! I lost a third cousin to that dreadful uprising. Those ignorant rebels nearly ruined everything."

Taris felt her blood start to boil. "Those 'ignorant rebels' were fighting against the EWU authority for freedom. They were fighting against oppression and tyranny and the marginalization of others. Trying to give Grays a chance to be seen as people and not property. How dare you talk about the rebels like that."

"I'll talk about them however I please!" she retorted, stomping her foot. "Those bleeding heart idealists were nothing more than dreamers with unrealistic ideals and no real plans for the future."

Taris moved in so close she could see the stained makeup on the edge of Lyn's eyelids. "They gave their lives to standing up against a giant, oppressive industry, Lyn. They were *heroes*. You know nothing about the rebellion, you spoiled little trophy wife, so shut your trap before you get yourself hurt."

Lyn poked her in the chest. "If you think that I am going to let a gutter trash, gin-soaked loser like you talk to me like that-_"

"It's *whiskey*, bitch," Taris interrupted, blowing whiskey breath right in Lyn's face.

"Ugh!" Lyn recoiled, swatting her breath away with her hanky. "Truly appalling!"

"Ladies, please!" Dr. Tomas whispered, irritated. Taris shut her mouth, but not without glaring at Lyn menacingly, wishing she'd burst into flames.

"Caleum is slowly becoming a wasteland. This beautiful world of beautiful people is falling into the hands of the catchers

and the sellers. The unity of our kind is being destroyed. No more. The time has come to fight back. A small but strong group of rebel fighters continues to try and protect and defend the rights and freedoms of my people. This group of warriors is called the Silencium. My name is Vale Teag and I am one of them."

The voice stopped for a moment. It seemed the entire crowd was collectively holding their breath. The Roland corpse stared its dead eyes directly at Boone.

"I am sending this message sir, to tell you that you are officially at war. No one, not human or Adulo, deserves to be oppressed. You force us to live in slavery until our death and that, for us, can be a very long time. You even brand us. Like cattle. Well I tell you this sir, you may burn and scar our skin with your symbol of servitude but it means nothing. We are not property, and we are not inferior."

"Here it comes," Taris whispered under her breath. "Here's the reason for this whole thing. Go on, rebel. Tell him what you want. Make your demands."

"Ten days ago you took something from us. You took an Adulo. A very important Adulo who means a lot to us. His name is Elias. I'm coming to get him back. I know that your first instinct will be to kill him but let me tell you this; if you do that, I will hunt you down, sir. I will hunt you and everyone who holds

meaning to you and I will slaughter them. I will slaughter them...and I will make you watch."

Lyn Hooper squealed in fright and clung to her husband like a cat doused with cold water.

"September 20th is in nineteen days. You have until then to release Elias to us. This is a threat, it is absolute and it is non-negotiable. You have nineteen days. I hope you make the best of them."

With that, the collar around Roland's neck clicked off. The corpse fell back on the table, stone cold dead. With a wailing scream, Lyn Hooper fainted.

Twenty seconds later, all hell broke loose.

Chapter Five

Murder.

That's what the news called it. Murder. Terrorism.
Barbarism. It was everywhere. On every channel. The news
was consumed with the story of what they were calling the
"Hooper Mansion Massacre". Taris sneered at the screen,
flipping through channels, but every story looked the same. The
vehicle crashing into the ballroom, the explosion, the talking
corpse, the look on Boone Hooper's face as he jumped between
different stages of surprise and fury. It was awful. A
sensationalized, melodramatic overreaction that had turned a
tragic event into a reason for full-fledged panic.

In two days people went from normal human beings to
fearful, hyperbolic monkeys, screeching in terror at the sight of
silver hair. It was bad enough to live through it, but to watch
what the news had done to the story was worse. Taris stopped on
a channel that was replaying an interview with Lyn Hooper the
night of the "gruesome attack" that "shook the nation". Lyn was
red faced and frail-looking, dabbing her eyes daintily with a
tissue even though her cheeks were streaked with black runny
makeup. *She must have been mortified when she found that out,*
Taris thought with a self-satisfied grin.

"Oh it was awful!" Lyn professed, touching a hand to her heart dramatically. "All those people! Those service members! I mean, the worst problem I had expected to deal with was, well, that!" She waved her hand in the background where Taris saw herself fighting with what turned out to be a viscount. She was swearing loudly and gesturing profanely at him while Gareth held her back. Lyn turned back to the reporter. "I mean, that was bad enough, but then to watch my house burn and have to deal with some brandy-soaked gutter trash? A woman can only take so much!"

"Oh for god's sake it was *whiskey,* woman!" Taris screamed at the screen, watching herself rip the viscount's bow tie off, taunting him as the authorities tried to chase her down. She barely remembered anything after the corpse collapsed. She remembered draining her flask of its contents but little else. Apparently.

The reporter, a local one she recognized named Mike, politely comforted the teary-eyed Lyn before asking her if she would continue. Lady Hooper bravely obliged. "It's just so tragic. And on the night of the service member recognition awards, of all nights! The banquet was to honor them and instead," she took a moment to dramatically collect herself, "and instead we now have three beautiful, innocent humans to bury! Ooh!" She swooned, and the reporter graciously steadied her so she could continue.

"What do you think of the statement the fugitive known as Vale Teag made to your husband?" the reporter prompted. "Some are saying it was an act of desperation, that the Grays are being unjustly treated. What do you have to say about that?"

Lyn's face hardened. "Statement? Innocent lives were lost because this Gray *criminal* wanted to make a 'statement'. What statement? A statement of violence? Of murder? Now what does that say to you? Does that say this bloodthirsty killer wants peace? I don't think so. What he did was an act of *war*. He declared war on humanity is what he did!"

"Some are saying Vale Teag might be the unspoken voice of the Grays," the reporter continued, goading her for a poignant soundbite. "Some say he's going to lead them out of their slave shackles, if you will."

Lyn pointed a finger at the reporter. "Now you listen here, son. Vale Teag is a vicious, dangerous, angry and unstable Gray and there is *no* honor in that. There is no glory in spilling the blood of innocent people, or setting houses on fire. *Especially* setting innocent people's houses on fire. He is no hero, friends. He's no savior."

"Then what is he?" Taris could practically hear the reporter holding his breath. Lyn Hooper looked directly into the camera just as it closed in on her mascara-stained face.

"He's a terrorist," she responded in a vacant tone. "A monster. He deserves to be shot in the street like a dog. And you know what, Mike? I hope he does. You hear me Vale Teag? I hope you die."

The interview ended abruptly, followed by more footage of the ratings-gold gore and violence. Every now and then Taris caught footage of herself fighting people, knocking over tables, demanding that people stop moping around and "get over it" because "death happens". It was a mess. The different channels did have some creative banners, though. "Shocked Service Members Panic after Becoming Victims of Terrorism Attack" or "Tragedy in Hooperville Causes Hysteria", sometimes variations of the two. Her favorite one was the banner that just said "Tirade of Tragedy" while it showed Christian and Dave dragging her away as she screamed belligerently. *Well at least it's a clever alliteration,* she thought. She was mortified. At one point she actually took a cameraman's equipment and smashed the lens into the ground. She was told the ten thousand dollar replacement bill would be headed her way within the next few days. She didn't even know why she had freaked out like that. The fact that it was on camera only added insult to injury. Deflated, Taris put her face in her hands.

She would have rolled over and gone back to sleep if she wasn't so scared of the nightmares.

Chaos, explosions, injury, death. These were old friends to her. The bad dreams about the rebellion and the prison camp. The war. The visions that seemed like memories, only they weren't. These illusions scared her more than reality. At least in reality she could fight the bad guys, or fight something at least. In the dreams she was powerless. Defenseless. Nightmares seemed to be a part of her life. Her dreams were frequent and rarely ever pleasing.

The nightmares always started off the same. She was standing in a field at night. Large floating stones stood around her in a circle, hovering close but keeping their distance. Her left hand was bleeding, but she could not understand why. In the middle of the circle was a giant ball of blue light. It floated in the air, beautiful and enchanting. Inside the circle were two others, both shrouded in large gray robes with hoods covering their faces. One was a man, she knew, although she could not see his face, and the other she assumed was a woman. She saw curly red hair tumbling out of the hood. It was like the three of them were all waiting for something. Then, like clockwork, the dream would change. It would fill her mind with the battles she couldn't forget. The mangled body parts of her fellow rebels, the faces of the men she killed. All the blood and the misery and the fear of every battle she ever fought regurgitated every night in her dreams. And people wondered why she drank so much.

She woke up in the middle of the night pouring sweat, panicked to the point of hysterical, and turned on the TV to calm herself down.

It didn't help. But then again, nothing really did.

The sun was rising now. She could see it from the window. It gave her a semblance of peace and her heartbeat slowed to a steady, normal rhythm. She pulled her hair back from her face and turned her attention to the news again. The reporter was standing in front of the charred remains of the Hooper ballroom. He was doing a live shot on the scene, looking official and properly respectful. She turned the volume up just as the reporter was in the middle of providing the latest information.

"...still have no leads as to the originator of the attack, but already hundreds of Grays are being pulled in for questioning. As of this morning, though, there have been no new leads on the case, or on the mysterious Elias. As you all know, Emissary Hooper has publicly denied owning a Gray named Elias, or having any prior interaction with the terrorist called Vale Teag, calling both accusations false. I'm told that Emissary Hooper and his family are safe right now and are currently in protective custody. Now, we don't know if this was a specific attack, or the start of more to come, but the EWU president is expected to make an announcement later today. For now, authorities are telling people with Gray branded workers not to panic. Officials did say, however, if people have any suspicions or fears about their Gray worker to call the number on the screen and they will be recalled by the company and handed over to the proper authorities. And remember, if you or someone you know has any information on the suspect named Elias or the terrorist who calls himself 'Vale Teag', please contact authorities immediately. Back to you in the studio, Jeff."

"Well that's good to know Mike, thanks." The reporter turned back to the studio cameras. "Coming up next on Wake Up, World! Ten new ways to use your three-pronged scrathe without draining the battery! You're going to want to stay turned for this one."

She turned the TV off and flung the remote across the room. "This is a *shit show*!" she bellowed to the empty walls.

"You can say that again," said a little voice. She yelped in surprise. At first she saw no one there, but then her senses cleared and she looked down at her wristband.

"Oh," she said sheepishly, staring at the holographic screen. "Hi Dad. I, uh, I didn't see that you called."

"Apparently," he said in a disapproving tone. "Ye seem to be making all sorts of slip ups, love. Some more televised than others."

Her cheeks burned with embarrassment. "Oh. So you saw that, did you?"

"Saw it? The whole bloody planet saw it, Taris! What the hell were ye thinking?"

I was drunk seemed like a lame excuse. "Dad, I know it looked bad, but you know the news. They sensationalize everything, and you know that viscount was a real asshole-"

"That's not what I meant!" he exclaimed, his Irish lift making his voice high and squeaky. "I meant what the hell were you thinking not calling me? Do you have any idea how worried I've been about ye, Taris?"

"Oh," she said again. "I'm sorry dad."

"Well you'd better be," he said, his expression softening. "I've been out of my mind waiting for you to call. Are ye all right?"

She nodded, putting on a brave face. "I'm okay."

He frowned. "I know you better than that, Taris. Ye don't get drunk and smash cameras when you're just okay, love."

"Dad, I swear I'm fine," she said with a groggy, laborious yawn. Her father crossed his arms on the holographic projection screen.

"You say you're fine, love," he said kindly, "but you look like bloody hell, I don't mind telling ye."

She scrunched up her face and glared at him. "Well I've had a rough couple of days, as well you know, and I didn't get much sleep last night. Of course I look like hell, but thanks for saying so." She buried her face in her pillow in defeat and he laughed.

"Ah, don't be like that, Taris," he said, looking over his glasses at her. "You know I'm just giving ye a hard time."

"I know," she muffled through the pillow, "but I'm too tired to fight you."

"I'm not looking for a fight," he said gently. "I just called to see if you were okay is all. After all, it's not every day yer daughter is nearly killed and the news has to tell ye about it."

"Aw dad," she said lifting her head. "Don't be so dramatic. I've been in worse positions than that, you know."

"I don't like to hear about your life from the news, missy. I like to hear it from you first."

She pulled some strands of hair away from her face. "I promise the next time I'm at a banquet that ends with explosions and talking corpses, you'll be the first person I call."

Her dad lifted his arms up, a mischievous twinkle in his eye. "That's all I ask."

She smiled and rested her head on her hand. "So how's the special project coming?"

"Oh fine thanks. I had a bit of trouble this morning when I…wait a minute. How do you know I'm working on my special project?" he asked suspiciously. She gave him a look that was distinctly reminiscent of the one he always gave her as a child.

"I can see you! Your wristband is facing the lab. You called me from your desk."

He was standing in a dark room surrounded by paperwork and computer tablets and screens with code. Dr. Murphy

Montgomery Bodil was a world renowned geneticist in his late fifties. He sported gray hair that showed only the faintest reflection of the black it once was. He had the crescent-shaped smiling eyes of the Irish and the accent to go with it. His white skin was dusted with dark freckles that never seemed to fade with age and his round, bright face held an inquisitive grin that never quite vanished no matter how cross he was. He insisted on wearing glasses, refusing to let laser correction anywhere near his piercing blue eyes. Taris resembled him physically, and for that she was not only proud, but grateful.

He had recently moved from California to the East Coast in Sector One for work, and seemed to be busying himself as only he knew how. Taris hoped it made him happier. He loved to create things. He was always coming up with new ideas and inventions, like the wristband device that she was wearing. It was, amongst other things, a holographic communication device that her father used with her liberally. The thought occurred to her that Matt and Dave would truly love to meet her father. They could compare their brilliant inventions and talk about gene splicing or whatever. She was about to bring up Matt and his spectacles when she realized that he'd been talking for ten minutes and she hadn't heard a word that he said.

"...just to pass the time, can you believe that?" he said, asking her the last half of a question that she didn't hear. She smiled politely and nodded.

"Oh wow, dad. That's…amazing."

His expression dropped. "Ah, but ye haven't heard a word I've been saying, have you?"

She blushed. "Oh dad, I'm really sorry. I've just had a trying few days, that's all."

His frown broke into a resigning smile. "Well that's the truth, that is. Oh I'm so sorry, dear. This has to be hard for you. I hope you're doing okay. You know, with everything. I don't want this experience to drudge up old memories from the war and all that."

She could feel the blood draining from her face. She hoped the holographic projection didn't catch it. "Oh no. No I'm fine. No nightmares or flashbacks or anything," she lied.

"Are ye sure, love?"

"I'm sure, dad," she said. "I'm okay. I'm just looking forward to putting this behind me and getting back to duty on Intrepid."

She wasn't sure he entirely believed her, but he seemed willing to let the matter slide. He shrugged casually. "Well you'll be back on duty soon enough, yeah? Going back today, are you?"

"Yep, today. Looking forward to it."

He crossed his arms again. "Well, next time you get a trip to the home world don't spend it throwing wine bottles at the wealthy elite."

"It was whiskey," she protested, as though that somehow made it better.

"Ah, come on now, come see your old dad from time to time. And not just for birthdays. We can go fishing or something, yeah? I bet it's been a while since you've gone out on a boat that floated on water and not in space."

"I will, dad. I promise. Stay out of trouble. Tell the boys at the pub I said hello," she said with a wave.

"They'll be happy to hear it. Take care of yourself. I love you, Taris."

"Love you too, dad. Bye." The transmission ended and the holographic phone blinked off, leaving the room feeling smaller, more isolating. She closed her eyes and tried to sleep longer, but her mind was already awake, even if her body was exhausted. There would be no more sleep for her, she gathered. Maybe not for some time to come.

It had been a very long, very horrible two days, and Taris could not be happier to put it all behind her. She had been feeling rather like someone who had fallen off a mountain. A mountain that was surrounded by medical people and police and military inquisitions and intrusive journalists and she was just done with it. She was tired of talking about it. Tired of the probing eyes and flippant speculations. Tired of spending days in dirty clothes filling out reports. She was just tired. Finally she pushed herself out of bed and headed to the bathroom. She emerged showered, changed and wearing a clean pair of blue fleet sweat pants with a black tank top. The pants were a little big, but she didn't care. Comfortable clothing was an underappreciated luxury in her mind. She yanked on the drawstring to chinch it up to her waist. As she was pulling her hair into a ponytail she smelled the rich aroma of strong coffee. *Gareth must be up*, she thought with a smile.

She opened the bedroom door and strut out of the guest room of Dr. Tomas' apartment. Well, "apartment" may have been something of an understatement. Dr. Tomas lived in an expansive loft in Maryland that overlooked the Potomac River. The sun glistened off of the water on the clear autumn day, adding ambiance to the already bright living room. Half the wall was filled with windows, the leather furniture and large, simple paintings made modern living look luxurious. It was the first time in forty-eight hours where she finally felt a semblance of happiness. She walked by the window and the morning sun kissed her pale face. It was a nice respite from the glaring lights of police inspection units from the night before.

Currently, a no-fly rule was in effect for the whole American sector. That meant no one but those with special clearance were allowed to fly in and out for at least 72 hours. The thought of spending three more days in hell seemed unavoidable. When Matt and Dave mentioned that they had both a transport and special clearances she was only too happy to accept their invitation to give her a lift to her ship. When Dr. Tomas had offered to let her stay with him so she could rest up before returning to duty, she was even more happy to accept the invite.

So was Gareth.

He had been pretty shaken up after the explosion and the talking corpse, and he was desperate to feel "normal again" as he said. Gareth was younger than she, and hadn't been in the military very long. The mansion crash was the first time he'd experienced real crisis, real death. She planned to speak to him about it when they got back to the ship. Sometimes it helped service members to talk about the things they saw with someone who could understand, and Taris certainly could.

She half expected to see Gareth huddled up in front of the TV with a blank stare, but his impressive ability to assimilate into normalcy seemed to be in full force. The Welshman was in fact sitting at the breakfast nook, sipping his morning tea and reading the newspaper. The news played lightly in the background on the enormous television in the living room. She saw a stack of freshly made pancakes on a plate, along with a bowl of fresh fruit. To her surprise, Gareth looked up from his paper with a smile.

"Wow, that Lyn Hooper really is a twat, isn't she?"

Taris laughed. She needed that. "Yeah, she's a piece of work, that's for sure."

"Did you sleep well?" he asked politely. He too, was wearing the blue fleet sweat pants and a black tank top. These were apparently the only spare clothes that Dr. Tomas had on hand. She shrugged and poured herself a cup of coffee.

"Meh, I've had worse nights I guess."

He looked at her with a knowing expression. "The dreams again?"

She nodded. "Just my luck, huh? The first time I get to sleep in days and I don't even get to enjoy it. Those stupid dreams, they show up at the worst times."

"Well at least they're consistent," he offered with a little smile.

She stifled a laugh, grateful for the levity. "How about you? Are you okay?"

Gareth smiled, taking a bite of his buttered toast. "I'm just bloody happy to have food and tea, honestly."

She nodded and took a sip of coffee. It was warm, strong, and with just a dash of cinnamon. She moaned in appreciation. "Oh wow. I needed that. Thanks for making the coffee, Gareth."

He smiled. "Yeah, not bad, eh? Biscuit?" He offered her the plate of blueberry pastries but she declined, choosing a plate of pancakes and a bowl of fruit instead. She sat down next to him and stared at him until he finally turned the corner of his newspaper and looked at her.

"What?" he asked, slightly annoyed.

"Well…it's just…I mean last night you were so unruffled and now…well, now you're reading the Daily Mail and eating scones."

He raised his eyebrows and fluffed out his newspaper. "I'm British, mum. I carry on." His tone implied that he no longer wanted to speak about it, so she let it go. *He'll talk when and if he wants to*, she decided.

"Where's Dr. Tomas?" she asked, changing the subject.

"He went for a run before you got up," Gareth said, swallowing a mouth full of biscuit. "He said it would help him clear his head."

"Mmm," she responded through a mouth full of food. She chewed and swallowed. "Any more news on the no-fly ban?"

"It's still in effect as of this morning. I've had the news on but I haven't been listening all that much. Just more of the same nonsense. The police are stumped, the people are in utter chaos. Riots in different sectors all over the planet. It's a mess.

The emissary is denying any knowledge of the whole thing with the Ephraim character."

"Elias," she corrected, shoving a large bit of melon in her mouth. Gareth made a sound of polite disapproval.

"Eh, whatever. It's all rubbish if you ask me. Terrorism is terrorism and that should be that."

She nodded silently, but secretly she felt like it wasn't that simple. She felt like the public outcry was a knee jerk reaction to a terrible event, and she worried about what this fear would do on the larger scale. The side of the newspaper that faced her had a hotline where people could call United authority reps twenty-four hours a day and get a replacement Gray - with free warrantee! - if they so chose. The ad was placed right next to the section for podrail loans and custom-collar scrathe carriers. Angry, she pushed the paper away before she remembered that Gareth was on the other side.

"You know, this whole thing is just disgusting," she said abruptly, unprompted. "We could have a real problem on our hands and all these people are worried about is getting their money back. It's bullshit."

"Well good morning to you too, sunshine."

Dr. Tomas was standing right in front of her. He had clearly just come back from his run, as he was all sweaty and shirtless. His cocoa skin glistened in the morning light as he wiped his chest off with a towel. She noticed, with distinct appreciation, that he was exactly as toned and as muscular as she had suspected. She looked up at him and gave him a blushing smile.

"Ah, good morning, Dr. Tomas," she said politely. "Good run?"

He nodded, rubbing his face with the towel around his neck. "Very much so. I feel much better. And we're not in uniform so please, call me Christian."

She felt the blush getting deeper. "Okay. You can call me Christian, too. Oh! No! I mean Taris! You can call me Taris!"

Christian gave her an amused look. "All right then. Well I'm going to jump in the shower, and then I'll be right down, okay?"

"Okay." She watched him bound up the stairs with the same stupid grin on her face. She didn't move until she heard the shower turn on upstairs.

"Well that wasn't obvious or anything," Gareth mumbled sarcastically.

"I don't know what you're talking about," she responded casually, gulping her hot coffee down to avoid eye contact. Gareth folded the edge of his newspaper down.

"Oh don't play coy with me, mum. You would have licked the sweat from his brow if he had asked."

"Mmm," she said in agreement. "And much more, too."

His mouth dropped. "Why you saucy little minx."

She looked up the stairs, listening to the sound of the shower. It had been a long time since she'd seen a man like Christian Tomas without a shirt on. She thought about what it would be like to see that more often. Taking a chapter from her therapy books, she imagined herself on a beach with the good doctor. The sand at her feet, the wind in her hair, his chiseled features glistening with the spray of the sea. They could be drinking daiquiris by the ocean. Perhaps he could massage her shoulders, maybe rub oil on her…

"Good god, what are you thinking about?" Gareth said, disgusted. "You're thinking about snogging the doctor, aren't you?"

She blinked, torn from her daydream with force. "Huh? Snaking? Sooting? Wha?"

He folded the newspaper down in front of him neatly. "I said you were thinking of snogging Christian. And you know what? Good for you. Maybe it would loosen you up. You've been tense lately."

"I don't know what 'snogging' means, but if it means what I think it means you're the one who could use it. You've been all uppity lately as well."

He raised a suspicious eyebrow at her and sipped his tea, making a show of appearing blasé as he looked over the cup at her. "I'm always uppity. And I'm pretty sure you don't know what 'snogging' means."

"Sure I do! It means…you know…touching and stuff right?"

He scoffed. "Ha! No idea. Just what I thought."

"Foreplay?" she guessed.

"No. Wrong!"

"Gareth, don't be a jerk. Tell me what it means!"

"What does what mean?" Christian asked politely.

He walked into the kitchen cleanly washed, shaved and, to Taris' disappointment, wearing a shirt. He was wearing his uniform from the waist down, a blue undershirt on the top, his ID tags dangling from his thick neck. He strolled over to the counter, poured himself a cup of coffee, and sat down next to Taris.

Gareth put his tea down. "Lieutenant Bodil here thinks she knows British vernacular, but she doesn't have a clue as to what 'snogging' means."

Christian frowned. "That's…that's kissing right? Like making out?"

Gareth snapped his fingers. "By jove I think he's got it!" he said, playing up his accent for dramatic effect.

Taris crossed her arms. "Aw, is that it? Well that's a bit of a let down. I mean, 'snogging' is too fun of a word to waste just on kissing."

"Oh I disagree," Christian said. "I think kissing is the best part about getting to know someone."

"How do you figure?" Gareth asked, giving Taris a sidelong look.

Christian put some fruit on his plate and popped a strawberry in his mouth. "Well, it's the first real genuine connection you usually have with someone that's something *more*. A kiss can mean a lot of things. It's a true, honest bond between two people. When you're kissing someone that you're interested in, and there's a spark, it could be the whole reason for something wonderful. When you kiss someone you love, it's a reaffirmation of that wonderful feeling. A kiss can be an amazing thing, you know?"

Taris leaned so far back on her chair that she almost toppled over. Gareth raised his eyebrows and smiled. "Wow. You're deep, doctor. I sort of feel like kissing you myself after that."

"Yeah me, too," Taris breathed. They both looked at her, and she quickly tried to backpedal. "I mean…I too, think you're deep. And what not."

"So, how's a rich, romantic, successful lad like yourself still single?" Gareth asked. "I mean, it seems to me that women would be falling for that kissing bit every day."

Christian laughed and shook his head. "That's the thing, Gareth. Sometimes kisses affirm a love, and sometimes they let you know when the love is gone, you know?"

"Ah. Divorced I see."

Christian nodded. "Twice."

"That must have been some kiss off they gave you then, eh?" he said playfully. Christian smiled wryly.

"You should see the alimony I pay every month."

Taris cleared her throat politely and stood up. "I uh…I think I'm going to get another cup of coffee."

As she was pouring herself another cup, she noticed that the screen interface in the kitchen was blinking.

"Hey Christian?" she said. "I think you're getting a call."

He stood up and looked at the screen with a smile. "I'm getting a phone call from the 'mad scientists', apparently. Well I think we all know who *they* are." Christian pushed the accept button, and on the holographic projection screen popped up two mad scientists. Well, one disgruntled scientist and one eccentric one.

"Helllooooo!" Matt said, wearing a pair of oversized goggles and a lab coat. Dave was standing behind him, goggles on his head and two gloved arms folded tightly.

"Good morning all," Dave said in his raspy, perpetually disapproving tone. "Sorry for the delay, but Matt and I have been up to our eyeballs in work since the crash. Apparently Emissary Hooper thinks we're the only damn laboratory on the planet and sanctioned us to do the grunt work for the investigation. I haven't had a decent smoke or a good cup of coffee in days, thank you very much. Anyway, sorry if we caught you all at a bad time is what I'm trying to say."

"No no!" Taris said quickly. "It was actually very good timing. What's up?"

"Well, we came to tell you that the Stargazer should be up and ready to go in about an hour."

"Stargazer?" she asked.

He stared at her. "Yeah. Our transport ship? The one that's taking you back to Intrepid today? Anyway it's almost done with space flight prep. Is an hour enough time for everyone to get ready?"

Christian nodded. "Absolutely. And thanks again for this, fellas. I know it's a bit of an inconvenience but I think I speak for all of us when we say we appreciate the lift."

Matt smiled, making the glasses on his face seem somehow larger. "Aw, it's no trouble at all. I was just telling Dave how we need to get out into the stars more often. Stretch our scientific legs and all that. We'll be able to drop you and Gareth off first, Lieutenant Bodil. The Intrepid coordinates place her in operational orbit around Saturn's rings, so she's closer. Dr. Tomas I hope you don't mind sitting on the Intrepid for about an hour or so? The Horizon is on a medical run to a settlement colony on one of Caleum's moons, but last transmission they sent to the moon base indicated that they would be rendezvousing with Intrepid later this afternoon."

Christian frowned. "That's odd. I wasn't aware of those plans. Weren't they, er, we, going straight to the moon colony?"

Matt looked down at his computer tablet, frowning. "Well, I talked with the moon colony this morning and the last transmission they said the Horizon was going to meet up with the Intrepid at fifteen-hundred today. Do you think there is a mistake? Would you like me to resend the message?"

"No, no," Christian said dismissively. "It's fine. I am just surprised as all. The plans seemed to have changed."

"A lot has changed since the terrorist attack on Emissary Hooper," Dave said in a sour tone. "Everyone's panicking like it's the end of the damn world. I went to get bagels this morning and I was almost mauled by a lynching mob who were chasing after a group of Grays on messenger bikes. People have lost their damn minds. If you'll pardon my language, ma'am."

She shrugged. "Oh it doesn't matter to me. Curse all you want. The world is a strange place full of stupid people who are just afraid of what they don't understand."

"Yeah. Speaking of not understanding things," Dave said slowly, "do you possibly have any time to come to our lab now? I have something that I'd like to show you."

"What is it?" she wondered.

He frowned, rubbing his chin. "Well it's hard to explain. One of my coworkers found something interesting and she wants you to see it. Actually she is insisting that you see it. It's a long story. She's a nice girl, but she can get a little crazy sometimes."

"A trip to New York in lockdown to hang out with a crazy person? Boy you sure are a great salesman," she said sarcastically.

Christian looked at her. "You can take my personal pod to New York if you'd like."

"Trying to get rid of me, Christian?" she said jokingly.

"No, nothing like that. But if you're going to drive, could you do it sober, please?"

"Why?" she said, realizing that she had, in fact, planned to refill her flask while she was on planet. "I mean, the podrail is automatic; it's not like I'd crash it."

"Oh I'm not worried about that," he said gently. "I just think it's best that you stay dry for a little while. For everyone's sake."

She stared at him. Again, she couldn't tell if he was being sarcastic or serious, but it didn't matter. She shrugged noncommittally. "You got it, doc. No podrail under the influence." *After, however…*

"Give me ten minutes," she said, gulping down her coffee. "Gareth, this really is great coffee."

"Better make it fifteen," Dave said, checking his watch. "The pod tracks are going to be really slow today. The traffic report says that the track from Maryland to New York is being checked for clearance, so be sure to wear your tags."

"Will do," she said. "Anything else?"

"Eh, do you have a spare uniform you can wear? I know yours was destroyed in the explosion, but you can't walk up to the building wearing…*that*."

She looked down. "What's wrong with this?"

He shrugged. "Um, you know, it's just not very…military-looking."

"Oh and you're one to talk? The both of you look like cartoons."

"Cartoons?" Matt scoffed, folding his oversized gloved hands suspiciously. "How so?"

"Really?" she asked dryly. "What with the glasses and the crazy hair and the little buttons all over the lab coats--"

"Yeah yeah yeah, okay. You've made your point," Dave grumbled. "Well at least put on a coat. It's cold today."

She brushed some errant strands of hair from her face and shoved her hands into her pockets. "Anything else you want to complain about? Any more requests?"

Dave pointed to Gareth. "Can you bring him as well? I hear he makes a great cup of coffee."

"Aw I don't want to go to New York right now, sir. Can't she just bring you the coffee?" Gareth whined.

"It will get cold in fifteen minutes and Matt can't make a pot worth a damn."

Matt pulled his goggles up with a frown. "Hey! I've been making coffee in this office for six years!"

"And I've been complaining about it for six years," he responded in the same tone.

"I'll bring Gareth," she said, ignoring his groans of protest. "Anything else, I shudder to ask?"

Dave's face suddenly lost all of its playful sarcasm. "Yeah, be prepared for issues when you come into the city."

She raised an eyebrow suspiciously. "Why?"

"Just...prepare yourself. You're not going to like what you see."

Fifteen minutes later, she knew exactly what he meant.

Chapter Six

She stepped out of the transport pod in an oversized gray military coat with an unwilling Gareth in tow. The pod hummed to a stop and opened the doors with a gentle hiss, before hovering back up and rejoining the pods in the return trip queue. The podrail was effective, fast, and operated on a system of technomagnet railing. It saved trillions of dollars in gas and energy costs. Within thirty years of its creation, podrail lines hovered over the streets of all major cities in all the sectors, gleaming like streaks of white light above the world. It was funny how people could marvel at something so magnificent that was funded exclusively with slave trade dollars. *Everything here was paid for by crooks and thieves*, she thought bitterly.

Dr. Tomas' pod had dropped them off right in front of the Wayneward Institute in downtown Manhattan, only it wasn't downtown Manhattan. Somehow, the streets had been transformed into a military district. People were walking quickly though the crowds with worried expressions. Police and military security hovered over the streets on their pulsar bikes. Camera crews were everywhere, turning anxiety into chaos. Check points were established to weed out any Gray terrorists who may be trying to pass as human.

Taris groaned in protest. "They treat the Grays like they're all terrorists now. Like everyone who ever came from Caleum is in on the terrorist plot. That's just terrible."

"Oh, I dunno," said Gareth with a shrug. "Is it so farfetched? I mean, it's not too removed from logic to assume that they would side with someone who wants to free them."

"They're not all terrorists!" she said defensively. "Holding an entire people responsible for the actions of a madman - or madwoman - is just blind stupidity."

Gareth smiled wryly at her. "Well aren't we the liberal minded sort?"

She looked over at the processing stations. The military separated people into two groups: human and nonhuman. The humans looked scared and self-important. The Grays just looked scared. For a people that rarely showed emotion, that was an unnerving thing. She looked at them, at their silver reflecting eyes and long beautiful hair as they huddled together in silent lines. They seemed so solemn as the police weeded through them, piling dozens into transport pods, sending them through the podrail to god knows where. Her heart went out to them. She had a pained, genuine sympathy toward those with whom injustice was being inflicted upon and it made her sick to see. *They're just accepting it. Just letting it happen. Not even putting up a fight.*

"It's not a liberal-minded thing to hate prejudice," she said quietly, "it's a clear-minded thing to do."

With a lingering sympathetic look she walked past the lines, leading the way to the Institute with Gareth following silently. There was a checkpoint right in front of the building, but she was in no mood to wait in line for twenty minutes in the cold. She looked around and spotted a side door that seemed unguarded, and made her way toward it. She hadn't taken two steps before a giant security guard stood in front of them and held out a hand.

"Identification please," he said in a gruff voice. She looked down at his uniform and groaned. On the front of his uniform was a giant yellow circle with an H in the middle.

"So you're a HALO, then?" she asked with disgust. "I'm surprised the emissary let his precious guards off his property in this delicate time."

"There are more than enough of us to go around," he retorted. "Identification, please."

Emissary Hooper was so rich he actually had his own army at his disposal. The Hooper Authority Law Officers, or HALOs, were the prestigious foot soldiers of Sector One. Boone Hooper paraded his troops around the other sectors like they were warriors, but in reality they were little more than glorified security guards with too many weapons and not enough to do. This one was of massive height and substantial girth, with pale skin and a glistening bald head. He was surprisingly young for his size she realized, maybe no older than twenty, with the face of a boy wanting to be a man. He had the expression of a new soldier who had never seen combat, trying to look as tough and dangerous as possible. She smiled, willing to indulge his ego.

"ID you say? Okie dokie." She fumbled with the large buttons of the oversized coat until she pulled out her ID tags. The guard looked down at her and frowned.

"I meant a photo ID," he said.

"I don't have one," she countered. "It got blown up. It's a long story. Anyway, if you scan these they will bring up my military file and picture ID to prove that I am who I say I am. I'm sure you'll find it all in order Private…Needle?"

"It's Kneed-lay," he corrected, pronouncing his name phonetically. Begrudgingly he held up his scanner and pointed it at her tags. The scanner beeped, reading her information. As he read the results, his eyebrows raised in surprise.

"Huh. You don't look like an officer," he said.

"Uh, thanks?"

"It wasn't a compliment, ma'am," he said gruffly, scanning Gareth's tags as well. After he cleared Gareth, he put his scanner down and eyed them disdainfully.

"Lieutenant Bodil, you say? Okay then. Well lieutenant, you know that this is a military facility and we have protocols. Procedures and dress codes. Why are you not in uniform?"

She balked. Was this kid really trying to lecture her? "I told you, it got blown up."

Private Needle scoffed. "Yeah, like I haven't heard that before. Convenient, don't you think? There are terrorists among us now. Walking the streets like people they say, and suddenly your uniform got blown up. So what, you think you're just going to waltz in here?"

She looked at him, squaring her shoulders and keeping a careful eye on his hands. "Yeah, actually. That's why I'm here."

He sneered at her. "You are about to enter one of the biggest scientific testing facilities on the planet and you just happen to be without identification. Or a fitting set of clothes."

"Like I said, they got blown up. Now, it's been a long couple of days and I'm usually a patient woman, but you'd do some good to remember your place, *private*."

He took a couple of steps closer to her. So close that she could see the beads of dirty sweat rolling off of his glistening head. "Heard that before, too. How do I know that you are who you say you are? How do I know if you're even human? Never seen eyes like yours on a human before."

"Hey!" Gareth shouted defensively. "Do you know who you're talking to here? Don't you watch the news?"

Her eyes widened. *Oh no*, she thought. *Don't bring that up.* Needle furred his brow. "Yeah, 'course I do. What do you mean?"

He seemed interested with that. *Okay*, she thought, *maybe I can use this.* "I was on TV this morning," she said self importantly. "I'm sure you must have seen me."

"What program?" Needle asked suspiciously.

"Wake Up, World!" Gareth put in. Needle seemed impressed by that.

"Yeah. That's right. I'm practically famous," she said, puffing out her chest.

Needle peered closely at her, and slowly realization splashed across his face. "Hey wait a minute. I think I do remember you. You're the drunk girl!"

"Yeah," Gareth said proudly before she could stop him. "That's right. She's crazy. She punched a viscount in the face and broke a ten thousand dollar camera! So you'd better watch out, mate. She could fly off the handle at any moment!"

Oh god, she thought, covering her face with her hands. *If he wasn't going to kill us before, he certainly is now.*

"Phh. So you were on the news. So what? That doesn't prove anything," Needle said, tensing back up.

"It proves I'm not a Gray," she shot back. "Ever seen a Gray get sloppy drunk like that? I didn't think so."

That argument seemed to make sense to him. "Okay, you say you're not a Gray. Well let's put that to the test, shall we?" The HALO took another step closer to her and reached for his holster. She took two steps back and pushed Gareth behind her.

"Needle, don't be stupid," she said gently with one hand up. "Think about what you're doing here."

Needle's eyes grew wide. "Your hand! Oh my god, you're branded!"

Taris groaned, thrusting her hands in her pockets. "Oh my god it's a *scar,* damnit, not a brand. Geez, am I going to have to explain this every time I show my hands now? What is with you people?"

Needle shook his head. "Trap! That's a trap! Stay back, Gray!"

He pulled his hand back from his belt. She had a split second of panic, but when she saw what he was holding she breathed a sigh of relief. The black cylinder with the three pronged metal hooks sticking out of the top was a scrathe. She made the sound of mocking derision in the back of her throat.

"Are you serious? You're going to use your scrathe on us?"

"Hey, this isn't just any scrathe," he said. "This is a three pronged scrathe fork."

"You do realize that using any device on a superior officer with intent to cause harm is treasonous," Gareth said, standing just behind her.

"And do *you* realize that a Gray impersonating a human is treason and it is punishable by death," Private Needle countered defensively.

"Grays can't impersonate humans!" Gareth countered. "That's just myth!"

He shook his head. "It's no myth. I hear that some of them can change their hair and their eyes to look like us. I hear that they can see into our minds and can control us. My cousin told me that he's seen these farm places out west where they're combining human and Gray biology to make them look more like us. Like sleeper agents or something. So, so they could be anyone a-and anywhere."

"Rubbish! Total rubbish!" Gareth said, stepping in front of her and advancing on Needle. Taris wanted to stop him, but her eyes were focused on the scrathe. For the first time in her life, and for some reason she couldn't explain, she was genuinely scared of it. Gareth stood in front of the guard and folded his arms.

"Now I've had enough of this talk and I'm bloody fed up with you. So let's have it then. Let's have a go at it, shall we? You think we're Grays? Well all right then. Electrocute me."

Private Needle hesitated. She took that opportunity. "Yeah," she said with all the authority she could muster. "Go ahead private. Electrocute us."

Even though it was a brisk morning in New York, the sergeant was sweating profusely. She saw his finger flick the charge button, turning it on. She felt alerted, like she could almost feel the electricity from the device. Indeed the air around it seemed to be somewhat charged. The feeling of panic rose in her throat. Slowly Needle pointed the scrathe at her, and she drew a quick breath. She braced herself for whatever was about to happen.

She just hoped it didn't hurt too much.

"*Private Needle*! Christ on a cracker man, what the *hell* are you doing?"

Taris opened her eyes to see Dave running down the front of the steps, his lab coat billowing in the wind like the cape of a geeky superhero. She exhaled in welcome relief, but the tension in her muscles was still holding strong. Dave bounded down the steps and Private Needle jumped to attention. He gave him a hasty salute that Dave returned with none of the same enthusiasm. Dave glared up at the HALO and pointed a finger at the scrathe.

"Were you about to use this on them?"

"I, well, sir, you see, they told us not to be too careful about who we let into the facility--"

"Good god! Too careful? Private, you almost used a scrathe on two superior - and might I add *human* - authorities. Sergeant Hoble is your superior NCO and the lieutenant here is an officer!"

Needle was sweating so much from standing at hasty attention that she could see the sweat dripping into his eyes. She thought about stopping Dave's rant, but her heart was thumping too quickly for her to care about anything else. The scrathe was still on, and she was still nervous.

"Well sir, that is, I mean, well it's not like it would have hurt them or anything. It's harmless to humans." Needle protested weakly.

"I don't give a good god damn what that thing can or can't do, private. The point is that you planned to harm them without provocation and after they'd provided you with adequate identification." Dave put his hands on his hips in a very military-leader manner.

"You know it's against the rules to make a show of force against a superior officer," he said, pointing a threatening finger. "If Lt. Bodil wants to make a case against you, she can. She has more than enough reason to, kid."

"I…" he turned to her with genuine remorse. "I'm so sorry ma'am. I honestly didn't know."

"Yes you did," she argued, the knot in her stomach still twisted horribly, "but you were too afraid to trust your instinct. Never do that as a soldier."

"It's a sure bet you'll live to regret it," Gareth added. "If you're lucky enough to live, that is."

Private Needle was thoroughly unglued at this point, humiliation splotching his skin in angry red groups. He looked like he was close to crying he was so nervous. Taris sighed heavily, rubbing her temple with her fingers. "Look, kid. Calm down. I can tell you're new to the ranks so I'm going to let it go for now, but I want you to remember this. Remember the day that you didn't trust your instinct and learn from it."

He gave her a strange look - like appreciation and confusion in one - but nodded respectfully. "Y-yes ma'am. Thank you ma'am. I appreciate it ma'am."

Dave made a sound in his throat of extreme irritation. "Okay, that's enough of that. Now turn that damn thing off and go inside. And tell your NCO that you're relieved of duty for twelve hours until you've calmed down. I don't want you scrathing every person in sight checking to see if they're human. Got it?"

Needle nodded and pressed the disengage button on the scrathe, shoving the thing back in his holster. As soon as the device turned off, the fear that had been roped around her heart evaporated, leaving her irritated and a little angry. Needle ran up the stairs and hurled apologies but it was no use. She was already too pissed off to care about his remorse. She didn't stop glaring at him until the door to the facility shut behind him. Dave grumbled words of dispassionate excuse and pulled out a small metal case.

"Either of you care for a blue?" he asked, offering his open pack.

Far from the carcinogen-filled death sticks of the past, Cobalts - known as "blues" - were synthesized relaxant chemicals rolled into the shape of a cigarette using blue biodegradable paper. The medicine was designed to relax the user and open the lungs and sinuses, not unlike how an oxygen mask operated. Originally used more to calm the nerves of military service members after a battle, most now people used the blues simply to relax, being more like a cup of tea than anything lethal. However, many still frowned on inhaling anything that wasn't oxygen, and Gareth was no exception. He declined the offer but Taris accepted, taking out a blue cigarette. She held the small indigo-papered roll in her hand and let Dave light it for her. Puffs of billowy blue smoke curled out of her mouth and nose.

"I didn't know you smoked, lieutenant," Dave said, taking a long, luxurious drag.

"She doesn't anymore," Gareth said with a disapproving tone, "but when she has bad days she tends to indulge herself."

"I wouldn't call it indulging," she said, already feeling ten times calmer. "I'd call it a necessity." The blue smoked down quickly. As soon as she put out the butt on the disintegrator ashtray, the feelings of scrathe fear had completely left her.

"Feel better?" Dave asked kindly.

She smiled. "Much."

"Ah good. Me, too. I've been losing my mind up there in the lab and I needed a break."

"Why is that?" Gareth asked. "How'd your lab end up with this esteemed responsibility, sir?"

"Well, the Institute here is a partner with Hooper industries, so they've got every available team member up there working to find a clue about the attack on Emissary Hooper. Pain in the ass." Dave flicked the blue into the disintegrator tray and shoved his hands into his lab coat pockets, grimacing. "My chain of command is acting like he's the most important person on Earth or something. Anyway, Matt and I have had like three hours of sleep in the last two days and I'm starting to go crazy. I had to get some fresh air and have a smoke. Clear my head, you know?"

"Glad you came down when you did I guess," Taris said with a sour tone.

"Oh, that boy Needle is okay but he's jumpy," Dave said with a shrug. "The Grays really scare him now and he's a little trigger happy. He'll get over it."

"I hope so," she said, looking around at the line of silver haired silent people as they filed into transport pods. "I hope everyone does."

Chapter Seven

Walking into the lab, it hardly looked like a laboratory. Or at least, one that had ever been cleaned. Books and papers surrounded blinking machines, various monitors displayed complied data or scientific observations. The LED board was filled with a mix between equations and musical notes, along with scattered words and the occasional doodle. Large digital poster frames hovered close to multiple walls, the images rotating between scenes of space and scenes from various movies. The speakers were blasting loud electronic music that she was unfamiliar with but assumed was from somewhere in the twenty-first century. Cups, plates and strange figurines were taking refuge on the tops of mountains of medical and field journals. These were scattered near computer tablets that were left running, forgotten, on low power. The lights were on low power and flickered from inconsistent maintenance. Carefully she slid around Tessla coils and ropes of electrical wiring, sidestepping what looked like a giant block of ice in a tube.

"This place is your lab?" she said with a doubting tone. "It looks more like a lair."

"Hey!" Dave said with a smile. "I like that. The Lair. Dramatic."

"The lair for the mad scientists," said Gareth. "Seems fitting."

At the epicenter of this chaos was Matt, sitting in a white anti-gravity chair, hovering over a table that was piled high with blackened artifacts from the crash. He was recording notes onto a tablet and humming loudly to the music. His goggles were high on his head, pushing his hair up in all directions. Above him was one very strong white light that projected down onto his table, illuminating his lab coat brightly. For reasons she couldn't begin to understand he was wearing giant rubber oversized gloves. He looked up at them and waved frantically.

"My god," she said under her breath, "you really are the mad scientists in the lair."

"Ah, lieutenant!" he said, turning the little light off on the side of his scanning spectacles. "So great to see you again. All fresh and clean I see!"

"And you Major Conner, all…gloved I see."

He jumped off the chair, which lowered itself to the ground, and wrapped her in a completely unprofessional hug. She tensed until he pulled back. Quizzically she looked at Dave.

"Is he always like this?" she asked.

"Yep. This is one of the reasons why I drink," Dave muttered.

Illustrating his point, he pulled out a flask from his lab coat. A small, unremarkable silver thing, shaped conveniently to fit in his hand. He unscrewed the top, took a strong pull from it, and without even asking he handed the flask to her. She, too, took a generous pull. *Scotch, strong, smooth.* With a nod of thanks she handed it back to him and wiped her mouth with her fingertips.

"So!" she said, rubbing her hands together. "Who is this person that just has to meet me and what do they--"

"Oh! Oh Dave! Is this her? It is really her?"

Taris swung around and nearly collided with a short Japanese woman, almost running her over. Taris came to a stiff stop and held her hands out to steady herself, only to find the woman wrapping her arms around her midsection.

"Oh my gosh ma'am it's so good to meet you!" she said, tightening her grip around Taris' waist. "I've heard so much about you! Matt and Dave have filled me in with most of it. Your service record explained the rest. Oh welcome to the lab!"

"You looked up my service record?" She glanced at Dave. "And what's with all the hugging around here? Are you people breathing mercury or something?"

"Don't look at me," he said, taking another pull from the flask. The woman around her midsection finally pulled back, pushed her short black hair behind her ears and stuck out her hand.

"Oh! Forgive my manners! I got all excited! I'm Major Natsumi Riko, lieutenant. Computer scientist specializing in outer space systems development and communications. Pleasure to meet you."

Standing at no taller than five foot three, Natsumi had an ageless, serious face that seemed pleasantly disrupted by her constant smiling. She had gleaming, straight white teeth and shoulder length brown hair that she kept pulling away from her eyes. Her oval shaped face was complimented with well-formed eyebrows and a pair of techno-glasses. Taris gave her a suspicious look but, fearing another hug, shook the welcome hand generously.

"I'm Lieutenant Taris Leigh Bodil. This is my NCO, Sergeant Gareth Hoble."

"Pleasure," he said kindly. Her face lit up when he spoke.

"Oh! Welsh! You're Welsh!" Natsumi exclaimed. "Wonderful! I love the Welsh! *Sut wyt ti?*"

"Ah…" Gareth said, rubbing his neck with his hand. "While I am Welsh, I'm afraid I don't speak Welsh."

Her mouth dropped. "You don't speak *Welsh*?!"

"Yeah well, you know. English seemed to work so well and all…"

"Matt!" Dave yelled from across the enormous room, "why is the spotlight on but all the house lights are off?!"

"Because it's easier for me to focus on the key elements that way!" he yelled back. "Too much interference with all the lights on!"

"Well tough. I'm turning them all on anyway." At his word, the lights in the entire lair lit up. Taris had to shield her eyes with her hands from the initial shock. Once they adjusted she turned back to Natsumi, who was now staring at her with her hands covering her mouth.

"Oh! Oh my gosh. Your hands. The brand. I didn't know." She reached out, pointing to Taris's face. "And your eyes. Well, the guys didn't tell me that you're an Adulo! Good lord. How did you manage to get a commission?"

"No," Garerth started. "Mum, it's not what you-"

"*Camme sans supre Adulo? Moseu de meta lansure nola? Sercrum fesuia!*"

Taris rubbed her temple with her forehead. She had faced enough mistaken identity for one day. For one lifetime. "No, sorry, it's…it's not what you think."

Natsumi blinked. "Oh, you mean you'd rather speak English? Wow, the both of you favor that dialect, eh?"

"No! Well I mean yes, but…" She sighed heavily. *I should put this on a recording on my wristband and just play it whenever this happens*, she thought. "Nastumi I'm not a Gray. I'm a human. I was born and raised in California by my parents. Human parents. The scars on my hands were from when I was a kid. I was three and I tried to pick up an iron sculpture and the metal was hot and it burned me. It's a scar, not a brand. I'm totally and completely human."

"What? Really? But your eyes--"

"Are just a coincidence I'm afraid," Taris finished for her. "Just an interesting coincidence. That's all."

"They're more of a light blue anyway," Gareth said, trying to be helpful.

Natsumi peered in closer. "Really? Are you sure? Because they look gray to me."

"Yeah. I know. So, how many languages do you speak?" she asked, changing the subject. It worked. Natsumi turned to her and smiled.

"All of them, lieutenant."

Taris burst into laughter. "All of them? That's impossible. All languages, ha!"

Natsumi wasn't laughing. "Well…yes."

Taris stopped laughing. "How in the *hell* have you learned *every* language? How do you even keep them all straight in your head?"

"Well, it's really quite simple. Well no, it's quite complicated, but if you'd like I can show you a little of the fundamental ways that I keep them all in order in my head--"

"What's this?" Gareth asked, pointing to a blinking light on a giant metal platform. Its twin platform was on the other side of the room, holding a series of stacked metal crates.

"Ah that. That's the time travel device," Dave said proudly.

"*Time travel*?" Gareth asked, clearly impressed by the notion. "No. You must be joking. That science fiction stuff can't be real."

"Oh no," Dave said, taking a couple of steps closer to the platform. "This is quite real. We've been trying to perfect time travel technology for years. Can't seem to quite get it right, though."

"What do you mean?" Taris asked, intrigued. Dave made a sound in the back of his throat that indicated disapproval.

"Well," he said, rubbing his neck nervously, "you see, things go one way just fine, but they come back all..."

"Broken," Natsumi finished for him.

Taris raised her eyebrows. "Broken? Like how? Like...in small pieces, broken?"

"Sometimes," he admitted with a frown. "Or inside out. Or mashed together. Or on fire."

"*On fire?!*"

"Only once!" he added quickly. "That was only the one time."

"Wow," Gareth said, pointing to the platform of controls. "This thing is really…whoops."

The platform started making loud whooping noises, the lights blinking various shades of red. Dave's eyes grew wide. "Oh my god, *get out of the way!*"

He had just enough time to yank Gareth to the ground when the smoldering boulder that used to be the metal crates came barreling right at them. Natsumi and Taris ducked as the metallic fireball hurled over their heads and smashed into the wall, creating a three foot crater in the cement. Matt rushed over and switched the device off, and it groaned to a winding stop. He had to scream that the coast was clear several times before Taris could bring herself to believe it. Slowly they all stood back up, Dave glaring at Gareth like he'd accidentally tried to kill him, which wasn't so far from the truth.

"Is everyone okay?" she asked, scanning the room for signs of blood or amputated limbs. Everyone seemed to be in working order, much to her relief. She walked over and touched Gareth's shoulder gently.

"Are you okay?" she asked, genuinely worried. He nodded, dusting his uniform with shaking hands.

"I'm all right, mum," he said quietly. "I'm not hurt. I'll be okay, except--"

"Look what you did!" Dave growled, stomping over to face Gareth directly. "What in the *hell* possessed you to touch the launch button?!"

Gareth looked at him, cheeks flush with embarrassment. "Ah. Um. Sorry about that. Oh god. Um, would you, ah, like some coffee…sir?"

"You crazy, stupid *son of a bitch*!" Dave screamed, face red with anger.

"Hey," she said, standing defensively in front of Gareth. "Don't call him that! It was an accident, Dave."

He ignored her, keeping his eyes fixed on Gareth. "You could have killed us! *You could have set this whole god damn place on fire! What the HELL DID YOU--*"

"Dave," Matt said calmly, placing a hand on his friend's shoulder. "Calm down, buddy. Your heart's going to explode."

"Damnit!" Dave bellowed. "Look at our wall! Good god, look at the transport crates! This ignorant putz just put a *crater in our lab*, Matt!"

"Gareth is *not* an ignorant putz," Taris exclaimed defensively, pushing him farther behind her. Dave looked like he was out for blood. "It was a slip of the hand. Total mistake!"

"It was a molten pile of metal that flew at our heads!" he screamed. Matt stood in front of Dave, blocking his view of the both of them.

"David Schuler, look at me. Dave...it was an accident, okay? It's all good, man. No one is hurt, the equipment is okay, we're all good here." Matt succeeded in calming Dave down eventually, but not without a few more angry and colorful metaphors. Finally, when Dave's face returned to a normal color, Matt smiled and gripped his friend's shoulders gently.

"You good?" he asked.

Dave took a deep breath and let it out slowly. Taris realized why he smoked blues so frequently, although it hardly seemed to be doing him much good. "Yeah. I'm okay. I'm calm."

Matt smiled. "Good. Now you can talk to people again."

Dave clenched his jaw so tightly she was surprised he didn't crack his teeth. "Natsumi?" he said as evenly as he could manage. "Would you please show Taris your findings? Now?"

"Yes," Natsumi said, staring at the molten ball of metal above her. "But didn't you want to come? What will you be doing?"

"Gareth and I have some *accident* reports to fill out," he said stiffly, "and he has some coffee to make. It had better be some damn fine coffee, too."

Gareth shoved his hands in his pockets, a remorseful but enthusiastic expression on his face. "Oh, it will be that, sir. That's the truth. Just ask Lt. Bodil! I am renown for my brilliant coffee making skills. Integral part of the team, I am."

"It's true," she said, trying not to appear as amused as she really was. "He is an incredible coffee maker. When he's not throwing smoldering boulders at you, that is."

He opened his mouth to retort, but took one look at the wall and thought the better of it. Defeated, he turned to Dave. "Oh…just show me to the kitchen, sir."

"I'd like a cup, too. If you don't mind, Gareth," Matt said with a sheepish smile.

"I could murder a cup myself," Taris added.

"Speaking of murder," Natsumi started cautiously. "Lieutenant, there is something I need you to see. And you're really not going to like it."

She took one last look at the hole in the wall. "Terrific," she said dryly. "Lead me to the next catastrophe. Can't wait."

Chapter Eight

"So, let me get this straight," she said slowly, sitting forward in her chair. "You're saying that *Emissary Hooper* killed the corpse pilot?"

They were sitting in a corner of the lair on hover chairs, surrounded by reflecting glass monitors. The lights were dim except for the glow of the screens, surrounding them in the memories from the past. Taris moved her hover chair closer to the big screen in the middle and enlarged the picture with her fingers. It was of Boone Hooper during the night of the crash. He was standing proud and appropriately bereft in the circle of onlookers as his wife wailed about the state of their home. She frowned at the image and sat back in her chair.

"He doesn't look like he's killing anything."

Natsumi gave her a strange look. "Oh. No, no. That's not what I said. I said he was not surprised by the murdered pilot, not that he killed him."

Matt and Dave walked up, holding cups of coffee with mutual expressions of appreciation. Gareth trailed behind, sipping his tea thoughtfully. Dave had apparently forgiven his time travel machine mishap for the time being. He was letting him live, anyway. "How do you mean, mum?"

"Here let me show you," she said, rewinding the footage.

Natsumi had been pouring over notes and logs from the crash. Cameras on the emissary's compound caught every possible angle of the event, from the ceremony, to the crash, to the gruesome talking corpse at the end. It allowed for a more holistic view of everything.

"Here," she said, stopping the footage. "Right here. This is right where the corpse was talking about Elias, remember?"

"Acutely," she responded.

Natsumi continued. "Okay, well look at everyone's faces. Do you see? Everyone has the telltale expressions of their emotions at that exact moment."

Taris frowned. "Not really."

Natsumi looked over her glasses at Taris like a disapproving school teacher forced to try and educate a room full of rambunctious children. "Okay, I'll break it down. All the Grays have the look of surprised worry on their faces. It's minute, of course, since emotion rarely translates to their expressions, so I imagine that even this small reflection of fear must mean utter terror under the surface."

"Huh," Gareth said, sipping his tea thoughtfully. "I hadn't noticed their reaction."

"I don't think many people did," she responded. "Now look here at the group of humans in the crowd. Most people are in a state of confusion or revulsion, do you see?" She pointed to the board and drew her finger across the screen, rolling over the freeze-frame crowd of horrified onlookers. "Everyone looks scared to death and completely confused."

"Except Taris and Lyn," Dave added with a smug smile, pointing to the screen. It was paused right at the moment where Taris blew whiskey breath in Lyn's face. The frozen image of revolution on Lady Hooper's face was priceless.

"Lyn Hooper is an idiot," Taris argued defensively.

"I thought you were going to set her hair on fire," he responded in a tone that implied he would have found that amusing.

"Funny, that's exactly what I was thinking at the time," Taris said with a small smile.

Natsumi cleared her throat politely. "Okay, well that little tiff with Lyn Hooper notwithstanding, there was more going on that a lot of people didn't notice. Look at this."

Taris squinted at the giant screen as it zoomed in on the small crowd in front of the talking corpse. Almost everyone was staring at Roland in a state of revolted horror. Everyone that is, except for Boone.

"Boone is talking," she realized. She watched as the rich man's lips moved almost imperceptibly. "Who is he talking to?"

"Well, when we look closer at his hand, we see it's pressed against his ear, so…"

"An earpiece," she finished. Of course. "Of course the bastard was wired the whole time. Can you make out what he's saying?"

Natsumi frowned. "That's the tricky part. He knew he was being watched, so he covered his mouth with his hands. However! I did manage to make out the words 'hammerhead', 'cleansing', and 'Elias'."

"Well that's random. What do you suppose that means?" she wondered.

"Don't really know unless it's in context," Natsumi said. "But that's what he said. I just thought it was so bizarre, you know? I mean, who makes a phone call during, well, *that*?" She pointed to the screen, where the frozen footage of the grotesque talking corpse was in mid-sentence, jaw open and slack like a wooden puppet in shock.

"Clearly a man with something to hide in a hurry," Taris said.

"So you think he knows about Elias after all?" Gareth asked.

Natsumi nodded. "I believe so, yes. His expression tells me that he's furious and he feels threatened. Not in the conventional sense, but there's something more. He seems to

117

think he's being mocked somehow. I think that call he made was to cover his tracks. Emissary Hooper is hiding something. Something big."

"My god. I think she's right." Gareth said quietly.

"Do you think he could he be a Gray?" Taris wondered. "Like, he's being so cruel to them because secretly he hates himself or something?"

Dave shook his head. "Not unless they've gotten really, really good at disguising themselves, no. Or at least not fully. Matt did a full scan of everyone he met at the party, including Boone and his wife, and the bastard registers as human."

"Well yeah," said Natsumi. "But you did say Matt's readings were strange, Major Schuler."

That got Taris's attention. "What do you mean?"

Dave shot Natsumi a look that could kill. Clearly that information was not something he wanted to share. "All right," he said with the sound of defeat in his tone, "Natsumi is correct. There were some irregularities in the readings. It was probably nothing though."

"That's not what Matt told me," Natsumi said casually, not willing to let it go.

"Okay!" Dave bellowed before she could continue. "Thank you, Natsumi. How about we keep our comments to ourselves for the moment, eh?"

She looked affronted, but when she glanced at Taris and her anger dissolved into a look of guilt. "Oh. Right. Sorry."

"What did you guys find, Dave?" Gareth asked. Taris was pretty invested in finding out the answer herself now.

Matt leaned in on his chair and stared right at her. His eyes were alight with a strange sort of restrained excitement that seemed unusual for him. "Look it's only a guess. A hunch, really. Just a blip on the screen for a moment and then it was gone--"

"What?" Taris demanded, impatient. "Spit it out, guys!"

"Hybrids," Dave finished for him. "Matt and I think there were human-Gray hybrids in the crowd."

She looked at him. "What? That's just crazy. Those don't exist."

"That's what I thought," Dave said with a dismissive shrug, "but stranger things have happened."

She scoffed. "Everyone knows that Grays and humans can't produce offspring together."

"Not to mention it's extremely illegal," Gareth pointed out. "That's like a mandatory life sentence in Sector Two if you're caught coupling with a Gray."

"Same in Sector One," she said quickly, "but that's not the point. The point is that hybrids aren't real. They're just stories you tell your siblings when you want to scare them into thinking that they're not really human. Or adopted."

"Ha!" said Gareth, kicking his feet up on the table. "I used to do that with my sisters all the time."

"I'm telling you, Taris," Dave insisted. "Something was different about this party. Someone wasn't what they said they were."

She folded her army doubtfully. "Okay...do you happen to know which one of the attendees was a hybrid? That could be helpful."

"No...we...didn't," Matt said slowly, his tone sounding odd and forced. "It was just a background scan. I was compiling information throughout the night to look over later."

Dave jumped in. "The explosion damaged his glasses, so a lot of files from that day were corrupted."

Matt's eyes seemed to light up at that. "Right! Yes! Damaged! Very unfortunate, very frustrating. I managed to fix my spectacles, but alas the files were a bit jumbled."

"Well there you go," she said. "It was probably just a glitch. Something that went wrong with the scan. Combined two people into one or whatever."

Dave groaned in stubborn protest. "Taris, hybrids are not a myth. Hybrids are real. I really believe that."

She stared at him. "Major Schuler. You, of all people, believe in hybrids. I mean c'mon! You're a scientist; I shouldn't even have to spell this out for you. The findings have been conclusive on this matter."

"So *far*," he pointed out. "And that's only from knowledge of released testing and information. I mean, there could be experiments all the time that are working toward coming up with a way to bridge the gap."

"You cannot combine Gray and human DNA to make a living being!" she exclaimed, strangely offended at the notion. "It's scientific fact."

"Science is subjective," he argued. "There is no such thing as a scientific fact, just widely accepted theories. Science is in the process of constantly being discovered and disproved."

"Well then I'm disproving you, Dave, because there is no such thing as a Gray-human hybrid. My father is a geneticist, this is his life's work. I grew up surrounded by this stuff and I know this for a fact. Hybrids aren't real."

Dave sighed heavily and lit a blue, regardless of the fact that they were indoors and surrounded by potentially flammable equipment. He took a long luxurious drag, exhaling a puff of bright blue smoke through his nose like a grumpy dragon. "Taris, just trust me on this. Or at the very least give it a chance to be possible."

She folded her arms. "Well of course, Dave. Anything is *possible*."

He pointed the blue at her with a wink. "Exactly. Give it some time, but I think that eventually you will believe me. I have faith that you'll come around."

"I'm sorry, but shouldn't we be alerting someone about this?" Gareth said, staring at all of them like they were crazy. He stood up and put his hands on his hips. "Look, I don't know if Boone Hooper is human or Gray or grown in a lab or whatever, but the truth of the matter is that he's probably dangerous. I mean look at this evidence! Why are we all standing around here talking about him like he's a villain in a TV show when he is very real! He's obviously some sort of mad man. Let's call the police and have him arrested!"

"No," Natsumi said quietly.

Gareth spun around. "No?! Of course we have to tell someone! We're not heroes or detectives! We have to tell someone."

"Who?" Matt prompted. "The HALOs? Boone Hooper owns them and everything else in this sector, man."

"Practically the whole planet," Taris added unhelpfully.

Gareth paused at that. "Well…what about the police, then? The United authority will surely know what to do. We need to let the police manage it!"

"You're talking about the most powerful man on this planet," Dave said carefully. "We can't just march in there with just our accusations and speculations and expect him to lie down and take it. He's rich, he's powerful and he will ruin us if he wants to."

Gareth threw his hands up in the air. "But he could be dangerous, don't you see that? Shouldn't we be striking while the iron is hot before someone suspects us? Who is to say that he doesn't have this whole place wired with cameras?"

"Yes, the building was donated by Emissary Hooper," Dave said. "But we disabled the cameras ages ago. All of them. Even the ones they keep thinking we'll never find."

"The one in the bathroom was the most disturbing," Matt added with an unsettled frown.

Gareth shook his head. "This is mad. This is totally mad. Well, what are you lot going to do then? Just sit around with this information and do nothing about it?"

"No," Matt said. "We're going to do something…eventually."

"Brilliant. Eventually. Well why did you even call us over here then? To share in this horrible discovery so we could all do nothing about it? I mean, do you even have a plan?" Gareth asked, his voice rising with his anxiety.

"We could use the Intrepid," Taris said. Gareth swung around to stare at her.

"What do you mean 'use the Intrepid'?"

"It's a stealth ship," she said, forming the plan as the words came out. "It's designed to fly under the radar. If he's keeping this Elias guy hostage somewhere, knowing that it could instigate another terrorist attack, then he's putting countless lives at risk. Maybe even the whole planet."

"Yes, mum," Gareth said in a worried tone. "I know the circumstances could be dire, but how is the Intrepid going to change any of that?"

"I don't know exactly," she admitted. "Maybe we could trail some of Hooper's ships or fly into his compound and look for clues?"

Gareth scoffed. "Good luck with that, Nancy Drew. The ship is stealth but not invisible. You'll get shot down as soon as you enter crowded Sector One air space. Not to mention the fact that Captain Philip and Boone Hooper are friends. He'll never agree to this!"

"Captain Philip is a good man," she said. "He would do the right thing here and he would expect us to do the same. Look I know it's a crazy plan but I agree with these guys. I think we have an opportunity here to get some real answers before this Vale guy strikes again. Some real solutions."

Gareth looked unconvinced. "And then what? You get proof and then it all just goes away? Boone Hooper goes to jail and the world goes back to the way it should be? I'm so sorry, mum, but I think that's highly unlikely."

"We have to at least try," Natsumi said quietly. "If we don't try, and something bad happens, I'll very much regret it."

Gareth threw his hands up in the air. "I give up. You're going to get yourselves arrested or killed because you want to be heroes," he grumbled. "Well I'm not going. You can all go dancing to your deaths but I'm not going."

Taris stood up and walked over to him, putting a hand on his shoulder. "Gareth, I know it sounds stupid to you, but this might be the best chance we have at saving people. The terrorist gave Boone an ultimatum, but he didn't say whether or not it would *only* be Boone. For all we know, the whole of Sector One could be targeted if the emissary fails to deliver."

"She's right," Dave added. "We don't know how far this Vale guy or this Silencium organization will go to get their friend back. I think the talking corpse was only a taste of what they're willing to do for their cause."

Gareth looked at her with an expression that pleaded for her walk away. She could see it in his face; she knew that expression well. She was hoping to persuade him. She didn't need his permission of course, but she'd been working with

Sergeant Hoble for three years, and she was not about to lose him now.

"Oh for god's sake," Gareth grumbled. "You're always trying to save the world, aren't you?"

She shrugged. "Some people knit. Some people watch TV. I like to kick ass and make a difference. It's my thing," she said with a playful smile. "Come on, Gareth. What do you say? Will you be my wingman here?"

He sighed. "Just try not to get captured, at least. I don't think your daddy will get you out of prison camp this time, and I certainly have no intention of going there."

Dave choked on a mouthful of coffee. "Did he just say prison camp? Why were you in prison camp?!"

"Actually it's an interesting story," Natsumi chimed in. "You see, after the surrender of the rebellion forces, most of the leaders were sent to work camps as penance for their crimes against the United authority. Taris was sentenced to ten years but her father…" she trailed off when she saw the look on Taris' face. "Um…I mean…it's none of my business."

"Taris," Matt said gently, "we had no idea…"

"It's nothing," she said quickly. She wasn't about to have *that* conversation with them. *Damn Natsumi and her due diligence.* Taris pushed her hair back. "Forget about it. It's in the past. Anyway, we have more important things to worry about. Come on, guys. Let's go catch us a criminal."

Chapter Nine

"I cannot believe I let you talk me into this," Gareth whined as they left orbit, eying her aggressively from the other side of the passenger bay.

"A little late to turn back now, don't you think?" she responded mildly. Gareth folded his arms, displeased but out of arguments. They were well beyond the atmosphere of the Earth, headed on a course to rendezvous with the Intrepid. The plan was to take the evidence about Boone Hooper and bring it in front of Captain Philip. From there she planned to plead their case for an investigation. The plan seemed so simple when they'd left, but she couldn't shake the feeling that they were treading in dangerous waters.

The Stargazer was a standard science transport vessel, but this one was not without its strange attributes. There was enough room for ten people to sit comfortably in the white chairs of the main cabin, but the walls were surrounded with strange designs and paintings. Blue swirls and green vines and words that didn't look like words at all were scrawled all over every wall. There were large statues from different time periods everywhere, pushed into the little alcoves and corners. It looked as though the scientists had turned their transport into extra storage. As Taris moved a large crystallized rock off the chair next to her, she realized that wasn't far from the truth. Stranger still was that the entire bay smelled like blueberries. When she asked about it, Matt gave her a long and complicated explanation that she didn't understand, but from what she gathered, the air filtration system was broken and the only freshening scent it would produce was blueberry. It was overwhelmingly pungent, and it was starting to make her dizzy. Matt and Dave were piloting the ship, shutting themselves off in the small cockpit. Taris kicked an unmarked crate over and put her feet up. She turned to Gareth to say something about the horrid smell when she realized he was staring suspiciously at Dr. Tomas. Taris rolled her eyes.

"Stop staring," she whispered to Gareth. "You're making it obvious."

"I can't help it," he whispered back. "He's making me nervous. I'm trying to decide if he's a Gray."

"Oh god, they never should have mentioned that whole hybrid thing," she grumbled.

Ever since they left Earth, Gareth had become increasingly more paranoid that the good doctor was a hybrid and that's why he wanted to go with them. Paranoid was putting it lightly. Gareth had spent the last hour going through the list of every human he knew to decide if they were Gray insurgents. Everyone but his own mother was on the list of possibilities, but Taris figured even dear old mum might be on the list as well.

"He's one," Gareth hissed into her ear. "Christian. He has to be. I know it. I'm looking for the signs. He's got 'hybrid' written all over him, mum."

"Looking for signs? What signs?" she whispered back. "He's not a Gray, Gareth. He doesn't act like one, he doesn't sound like one. He's just a regular guy. Besides, Matt speculated that these hybrids are supposed to look just like humans. If he was one, how could you even tell?"

Gareth shrugged. "I dunno. I just will. I'll let you know when he starts to go Gray."

"You do that."

She wasn't about to sit there and listen to Gareth grow more and more paranoid, and the smell of blueberries was getting to be too much. As soon as the ship passed the moon they entered open space range. They were headed out into the solar system to rendezvous with the Intrepid, and the trip from that point on was likely to be smooth and uneventful. She waited until they passed Mars before she decided she couldn't take it anymore. Gareth was practically screaming at her with his eyes, begging her to sit down, but she waved him off.

"This smell is killing me," she said loud enough for everyone to hear, "I'm going to fix it. Natsumi, where is the air filtration system?"

She pointed to the cockpit. "It's in there, on the right when you walk in the door. Second panel down."

"Thanks." Ignoring Gareth's almost inaudible squeal of disapproval, she breezed past him and rapped on the cockpit door.

"Come," Matt said with a little giggle.

She pushed open the door. The cockpit was small, with a standard bubble front screen that allowed for panoramic star view. The guidance and controls were on a black touch screen panel. Nothing out of the ordinary for a transport. They even had an extra chair for a weapons officer, although she assumed the ship hadn't been armed in a long time. Matt and Dave turned to greet her, but without so much as an explanation she went directly to the filter interface. She pulled the panel door off, exposing the controls.

"Hey!" Matt protested as they glided easily through the asteroid belt. "What are you doing?"

"I'm turning off the scent in your air filter," she explained as she typed commands into the system.

"But why?" he protested. "Blueberries smell nice! I think it's a nice smell."

"It's awful," she said, looking up at him. "It's making me want to vomit."

Dave swiveled his chair around and put his booted feet up on empty chair next to him. He smoothed down the front of his black uniform and scrutinized her in the dim light. Both the mad scientists had taken it upon themselves to dress in uniform for the occasion of going into space, although Taris did notice that their hair was still too long and Matt's scanning spectacles were hardly regulation-standard.

"You know," Dave said casually, picking at his fingers, "they say that the scent of blueberries is repugnant to a Gray."

"Well that's something me and the Grays have in common, then. And why is that?" she asked, working her way around their confusing system.

"No one knows," he shrugged, "but it's the truth. They say that if you want to flush out a Gray insurgent that you only have to make the room smell like blueberries and eventually they won't be able to take it."

"So really, the blueberry smell is a good thing," Matt said a little defensively. "It's Gray-terrorist-proof."

"Yeah well it's Taris-proof too," she grumbled, stealing a look into the main cabin. "And if that's the case Dr. Tomas is not a hybrid, despite Gareth's paranoid assumptions. He seems totally unaffected by this god forsaken putrid stench of…ah-HA! Got it!" Within a few moments the smell of blueberries dissipated. Taris sighed in relief and took a deep breath.

"Ah, there's that good old synthesized air that I know and love," she said.

"Hey! It took me forever to…I mean, I've been trying to turn that thing off for ages!" complained Matt. "How did you do that?"

"I reprogrammed the air freshener to simply cycle and redistribute good air throughout the cabin, rather than just trying to cover up the murky air that exists. It's pretty simple, really."

Dave looked at the interface, impressed. "Wow. You've been on the ship an hour and it only took you two minutes to figure out our systems. Unbelievable."

She smiled and shoved the panel back in place. She kicked his feet off the empty chair and plopped down, swiveling to look at the stars, disrupting the plastic hula girl who was attached to the front of the helm. With a coconut bra and plastic skirt, the little doll seemed whimsically anachronistic.

"And who's this?" Taris tapped the painted black hair and the springy toy danced with the movement.

"That's Hoopa," Matt answered with pride. "Hoopa the Hula Girl."

"Hoopa the Hula Girl?" she repeated. "You named her *Hoopa*?"

"Yeah. You know, because she's hooping her skirts all over the place," he said as though that explained it.

"We found her in a toy shop that sold ancient Earth artifacts," Dave elaborated. "According to the sales lady, hundreds of years ago people put these dolls in their metal automobiles to ward off evil spirits. She's supposed to be good luck."

"Yeah, but *Hoopa*?" she said, fixated. "Why not something sexy like Ramona, or Isabella, or Lola?"

Matt reached over and snatched Hoopa from her perch, bringing her protectively closer to him. "Hey, Hoopa is a great name for her!"

"When you get a good luck skirt dancing girl then you can name her whatever you want," Dave added, looking equally protective. She looked at the half naked plastic doll and shook her head.

"Okay. You win, Hoopa," she said, giving the doll a gentle nudge. "Dance through the stars."

She turned her attention to the screens, taking in the vast brilliance of the universe. She loved the feeling of drifting through space. For so many people it made them feel insignificant, but to her it felt empowering. She loved gliding through the twinkling blackness of the cosmos. It was one of the few things that still made her feel somewhat significant. Feeling at home, she smiled and put her hands behind her head casually.

"So how'd you know how to do that thing you did, with the air filtration?" Matt asked. "That doesn't seem like something most stealth ship XOs would know."

She shrugged. "Hey, you might be the scientific geniuses here, but I know my starships. I've been working on these since I was a kid."

"Oh yeah?" Matt said, turning his head in interest. "Did you used to work on transports with your dad when you were little or something?"

Taris pushed a strand of hair from her face. "No, not dad. With my mom. My mom and I used to rebuild old transport ships together. She was always the handy one around the house. She could fix the leaky pipes or reprogram the computer or get our hover chairs to stop puttering. She needed to I guess. My dad is brilliant but he's totally incapable of performing simple tasks."

"I believe that," Dave said. "He's a geneticist. Building starships doesn't really come with the job."

She smiled at that. "That's true. He was always locking himself in his office or at the lab, slaving away with his latest and greatest project, so my mom was left to take care of me and the house usually. It worked out though; they really balanced each other. My parents were the perfect couple in many ways. Happy, loving, respectful…it was great. She used to always say that she was the tinker and my dad was the thinker."

"You speak about her in the past tense," Matt observed quietly.

"Because she is. My mom died a few years ago. Just me and dad now. He's doing okay, but he's not been the same since she died. Been throwing himself into his work and stuff. Occupying his mind." She touched the wristband on her arm reflexively. "I need to visit him more often."

"My mother says that all the time," Dave said with a wry smile, "although she's doing it to guilt me into coming and seeing my dad's new sword for his collection."

"What?" she asked with amused suspicion. "You mean swords as in, like swords?"

"Swords," Dave repeated, sounding embarrassed. "My dad has decided that he needs a sword collection so he's been spending all his retirement money on ancient metal weaponry. It's awful."

"What kind of swords?" she asked. Dave stared at her.

"Does that matter? The point is that he now looks like he runs the armory for the knights of the round table and my mother is tired of talking about it with him. You know, I have three brothers who all live in Brooklyn in the same neighborhood, yet she wants me to take the podrail every Sunday for dinner so he'll be able to tell me about his new rapier."

"That's really strange," she commented with a teasing smile.

Dave scoffed. "Tell me about it. A progressive Jewish man from Brooklyn with red hair and a sword collection? Trust me, people talk."

"Speaking of talking," Matt said, lowering his voice. "I've got Saturn in my sights and still nothing on the radar. Any luck on transmitting our message to the mother ship?"

"No response?" she asked, worried.

They had been transmitting a coded message since they left Earth's atmosphere, alerting the Intrepid as to their situation. Taris signed the order with her own code. The lack of response was unsettling.

"Better get back to the main cabin," Matt said, nodding to the screen, "we're going to be docking with the Intrepid soon, and it looks like Gareth is going to jump out of his skin back there."

She nodded. "True. What about docking request? The Intrepid is a z-class starship, remember? If it's in stealth mode only authorized ships are allowed to dock with it. I gave you the correct authorization codes, did you use them?"

"We sent it, but we've had no response yet," Matt said with a worried tone. "We haven't had a response from the Intrepid at all, actually."

Taris frowned. "Well it's a heightened alert status," she rationalized, "and the Intrepid is designed not to be detected. I'm sure they have their reasons."

Dave crossed his arms. "Hmmphm. So do we, but that doesn't give us the right to go off the grid. If you didn't know where we were going we'd just be waiting for the Intrepid to peek out of the shadows and wave."

"I guess it's a good thing that I know where I'm going, then," she said, opening the door to the main cabin, "and now if you'll excuse me, I have to return to my seat before my NCO falls apart from suspicion."

Gareth shot her looks of irritation and relief when she returned to her seat. She tried to ignore his I-have-a-theory expression and instead she focused on Natsumi and the doctor, who were currently discussing the Intrepid. Much to her dislike. Not only because they were discussing sensitive material, but because Natsumi got to sit next to the doctor. Taris wasn't so sure that talking about her special ship was necessarily the best of topics, so she sat quietly in front of them, poised to run interference as soon as the topic trended toward classified. She buckled her seat belt and listened as the enthusiastic Major Riko went into the explanation.

"Oh the ISS Intrepid is a fascinating vessel! I read all about it. It's a registered zulu-class, which as you know is the most enigmatic classification. Not much is known about the z-class ships, and with good reason of course. Z-class vessels are known as the 'submarines of space' because of the quiet movements, black exterior, and it's virtually undetectable. It's small, fast, and very effective, isn't that right lieutenant?"

Taris cleared her throat loudly, hoping that Natsumi would get the idea to stop talking, and forced herself to smile. "That's right. She's sleek, silent and deadly. She's a great ship."

"Oh and she's totally self sufficient, too!" Natsumi jumped in, apparently not reading Taris' facial expressions *at all*. "She is designed to redistribute things on an atomic level, like air, water, food, you name it! If they had to, the Intrepid could float in space for over ten years and still not run out of fuel, food or oxygen. That's why they're so small and why the crew is so minimal. I think that the maximum duty station requirement for the Intrepid is twelve, actually. Imagine that! It only takes twelve people to operate the most amazing type of ship in the whole fleet."

"Wow. Very cool. I'm excited to see it up close in person," Dr. Tomas said, peering out the window.

"Me, too!" Natsumi gushed. "That's why I wanted to come along! Well I mean obviously I had other reasons, but to stand inside the hangar deck of a z-class stealth ship is just a dream come true! You know I hear they've improved on the rift manipulators so they can actually travel through time-"

"Okay, that's enough," Taris said blatantly. "It's a z-classification for a reason, right Major Riko? Secrets must be kept. A lady like the Intrepid needs an air of mystery to her, don't you think?"

That time Natsumi got it. "Oh. Oh my gosh, lieutenant. I'm so sorry. I was just blabbing away. I didn't think…"

"Hey, it's okay," Dr. Tomas said with an assuring, handsome smile, "we're all military here. No harm done! We're all on the same side."

You can never be too careful, she thought darkly. "So what's the mission?" she asked, changing the subject.

Dr. Tomas stared at her. "Pardon me?"

"Your mission," she corrected quickly. "I meant what is *your* mission. You know, on the Horizon? Let me start over. So where are you headed next after this, Christian?"

Dr. Tomas gave her a strange and uncomfortable look and turned his eyes away from her. "Ah, um. Well that's a long story."

"Lieutenant?" Matt said over the intercom. She cursed his poor timing and tried to ignore him.

"Go on, doctor. You were just about to tell me all about life on the Horizon--"

"Lieutenant?"

"I'm…sure it's quite fascinating…"

"Lieutenant!"

She swung around and pressed the com button in the interface behind her. "Whaaaat?"

"I...I think you'd better come in here. Something is wrong..."

She was out of her seat and in the cockpit before he could finish his sentence. They were in orbit around Saturn, the rings stretched out into the horizon like ribbons of shimmering majestic rock. The Intrepid was a black blip in space, a shadow cast on the mighty rings. The stealth ship kept low and tight in orbit, just like Taris had left her. Slowly they began their descent into the landing bay. They were on autopilot, following the computer generated docking procedures. The hangar door was open, ready to receive them, but there was something wrong about it. There was something unsettling about the ship, about how it was hovering in space. It felt different. It felt dangerous.

It felt wrong.

"Did you ever get a response?" she asked Matt in a low tone, shutting the door behind her. He shook his head.

"Nothing."

"That's strange," she mused. "Even in stealth mode they should have responded to my recognition codes by now. To send nothing is really wrong. Not to mention rude."

"Maybe they didn't get them," Matt said quietly as they began their descent. Taris shook her head.

"No. They'd never let us board without those codes. They'd fire a warning shot across the bow if that were the case," she said, leaning over him to double-check the transcoding signatures.

"But we're in a fleet ship!" Matt protested. "They'd never fire on us."

She turned to him. "Z-class ships are allowed to fire on any vessel, regardless of origin."

"*What?* Why?"

"Pirates have been stepping up their game lately; stealing fleet cargo ships and masquerading as stranded passengers aboard broken transports. We have to take precautions."

"Well, apparently not too big of precautions," Dave said, nodding to the open hangar bay, "because we're coming in for a landing without so much as a blip on the communication circuit. That's either really stupid or really trustworthy."

The Stargazer began the autopilot docking program for final landing procedures. Silently Taris watched them slink right into the hangar deck. The landing was smooth and procedure standard, but it still felt wrong. They managed to approach and board the ship without any communication whatsoever. As soon as the ship landed, the hangar doors pulled themselves back up and sealed shut.

"We're sealed in," she realized. "The hangar doors just sealed themselves."

"Oh hell, well that's inconvenient," Dave grumbled. "How do you know they didn't just shut the door?"

She pointed up to the hangar door. "See that red mark? That's the emergency lock, it's indicated by a tiny red stripe down the seal. The seal is an emergency protocol."

"Does that mean the ship is in defense mode?" Dave asked. "Well that's not good."

They were sealed off, leaving them inside the hangar deck in total darkness. There were no security guards, no welcome committee, not maintenance team to fuel up the Stargazer for her return home. There was nobody, and that was a very bad sign. For a moment, the three of them didn't move. They sat there silently, with nothing but the lights from the control panel blinking.

"Do you have a weapon on this ship?" she whispered.

Dave nodded. "Top panel above the door. Resonator pistol."

She reached into the dark compartment and her fingers wrapped around the grip of the gun. It was a decent enough handgun, and she wasn't in a position to be picky. She was glad that it was at least a military-standard resonator. She charged the weapon to full and clicked the safety off, walking back out into the main cabin.

"What are you doing?" Gareth asked quietly, eyes darting between her and the resonator. She looked out into the black darkness of the deserted hangar deck.

"Something's wrong on my ship," she said, "and I'm going to go find out what it is."

"Are you crazy, mum?" he said, standing up in protest. "If something is wrong we should leave! We're in a fully capable ship! We should go and get help!"

"Can't," she said. "The bay doors are sealed. The only way to release them is an override code sent from the bridge."

Gareth muttered swear words and slumped back in his chair, peering out the window with a scared expression. Natsumi's eyes grew wide.

"Lieutenant Bodil, if what you say is true then this ship could very well be under attack. Going out there is extremely dangerous. You don't know what's out there waiting for you."

"Yeah," Matt said apprehensively, "I really don't like this."

"Look," she hissed, "either we can stay in here and wait to die or we can go out there and make a fight of it. We can't get the doors open without my code sent from the bridge. If something bad has happened then my crew is in trouble. If they are in trouble I am going to go help them. Understand?"

"Well okay, then," said Christian, the first in the group to speak. The doctor stood up and walked to the corner where he picked up a large, ample female statue. Taris was about to ask why when she noticed he was holding it like a weapon.

"No," she said to him. "You have to stay here, Christian."

"You're not taking them on alone, Taris. You need help."

"If there is a threat on this ship, the last person I want killed is the only medical guy we've got," she explained sternly. "You're staying right here, doctor. That's an order."

He straightened his back. "No. I'm not letting you go out there on your own. It's not happening."

She pointed the resonator in his direction. "I don't remember giving you a choice in the matter, doc. Sorry, but I'm pulling rank. I'm the XO of this ship and this is an order, do you understand? Now is not the time for me to take chances."

He looked like he wanted to fight her, but she simply plucked the round-breasted statue out of his hands and handed it to Dave. Reaching down, she pulled a knife out of the leather sheath in her boot and handed it to Gareth. "Sergeant Hoble, you have field medical training, right?" He nodded hesitantly. "Stay with the doctor. Assist him in any way you can. Barricade yourself in here at the first sign of trouble."

"With only a knife?" he complained, taking the knife with resignation. "Er, that is, why me, mum?"

"Because you can either sit in here with the doctor or you can go out there and face whatever it is that's likely killed the entire crew. Your choice, Gareth."

He sat down next to Dr. Tomas obediently. "Don't worry, mum. I've got everything here under control."

"Lieutenant," Matt said. "My scans are picking up some really mixed signals. If you go out there…you might not come back."

"Major Conner, I'm not going to stay here. No matter what's out there," she said, unlatching the door. He opened his mouth to protest but she held out a hand to stop him. "Look, I have no time for clever remarks, okay? I'm going."

Before anyone could answer, she opened the latch and scaled the outside steps, letting her boots hit the hangar deck with a loud *thump*. She activated the light on the top of the resonator and pointed it in front of her. In only a few steps she reached the side door that led to the main corridor and found it sealed as well. After some difficulty balancing the weapon so the panel could read her palm signature, she managed to activate the manual override on the door. With a light hiss, the door unsealed and swung open, revealing the red blinking hazard lights in the empty corridor. She could feel the wrongness of it. Dread erupted in her mind. Pushing back all the anxiety, she took a deep breath, let it out slowly then turned into the first corner. The stench of death was everywhere.

So was the blood.

Chapter Ten

The first body she found was Arthur Frankel, the chief engineer. He was slumped in the corner, sliced once down the front and twice through the middle. Slashed like an animal and left like a rotted carcass on the side of the road. Covered in his own blood, she could tell he hadn't been dead long. His body was not yet rigid, his blood very newly spilled. The resonator was still clutched in his hand, but the charge had depleted. He'd spent all sixty rounds on something, she realized, and it still wasn't enough. She lowered him down to the ground gently and closed his eyes.

She pulled Arthur's ID tags off of his neck and placed them into the pocket of her coat. Silently she stood up, forcing her thoughts to be on the mission. The time for grieving would come later. When she straightened up, she found that she was no longer standing alone.

"It's just like the copilot from the crash at the mansion," Matt said from behind her. She looked up and saw three people huddled in the corridor. Dave was twisting a wrench in his hand and Matt was holding what looked like a crystal scepter. Natsumi wasn't even armed. Yet they were there, and they were standing by her. She was actually quite relieved that they came -

strength in numbers was an advantage she needed - but said nothing on the matter.

Matt bent down and scanned the body with his glasses. "Actually, it is the same slash, down to the type of blade and movements. It's a tall person, left handed, three strokes. I'm guessing that whoever slashed the copilot and crashed that ship into Emissary Hooper's house is on this ship right now."

"And killing people," she added. "Stay close to me everyone. Whatever's on this ship is clearly in a position to fight. We might have to act quickly so keep your eyes open."

She felt the sweat pour down her face in the hot hallway, lit only by the silent alert lights, blinking an angry red. The ship felt still, rigid. Violated. The Intrepid was quiet usually, as stealth ships are often quiet, but this was different. This was very wrong. She reached the end of the corridor and stopped at the door that led to the stairs. The door was unlocked, so she pushed it open and slipped quietly into the stairwell. The smell was worse in there. It didn't take long to realize why.

"Two more confirmed dead," she said quietly, grabbing their dog tags and putting them into her coat pocket. She reached to the side and grabbed both of their firearms. Both weapons were expelled of their charges. *Damn*, she thought.

"Their names are Gregory Tyrell and Christopher Jenkins. They are…were…navigation specialists. Great guys, the both of them. Greg knew the star charts better than anyone."

"Lieutenant?" Dave asked cautiously. "How many crew are assigned to this vessel?"

"Twelve," she answered in a whisper.

"Including you and Sergeant Hoble?"

"Correct," she said, knowing where he was going.

"So that means…"

"That means that there are either seven more bodies to find, or seven people to rescue. Either way, we need to keep going."

As they crept up the stairs, she felt her heart thumping in her chest. She remembered this feeling, from the war. The feeling of fear and of dread, clouded in a sea of deranged bravery and determination. They reached the fifth deck, and came to the door marked BRIDGE. She knew that whatever managed to infiltrate the ship was likely going to be in there, and was obviously armed and skilled. With only one working resonator, she was going to have to make every shot count.

"Major Conner," she said in a voice barely audible, "scan the bridge. What do you see?"

Matt touched the light on his glasses and then turned to her. "Three life signs. One very faint. Heartbeat barely visible."

"And any dead?" she asked. Matt nodded slowly. She didn't need him to elaborate.

"As soon as the threat is neutralized and the deck is cleared, I will run over to the security panel and deactivate the seal," she said. "From there you all will get back into the Stargazer and go get help."

"What about you?" Natsumi asked.

"I'll stay here and take care of the wounded and keep the ship protected while we wait for help to arrive."

"By yourself?" Natsumi asked. Taris looked over at the door, fearing what she would find on the other end.

"Hopefully not by myself, Major Riko. Major Conner said three life signs." She pointed the resonator at the door. "I'm hoping that all three are on our side. Dave, you still got that little door opener demoleculizer thingy you invented?"

Dave fumbled in his pocket and produced his little device. She nodded. "Good. Major Schuler, if you please, open the door."

It took only a couple of moments for his device to break the seal. Taris pushed the door open and crept into the room, pointing her resonator into the dimly lit bridge. She had expected something bad, but what she found was more than that. It was gruesome. Blood and bodies everywhere, the front screen was splattered in red. Her crew, her *entire* crew, was slashed from stem to stern. Consoles were broken and overturned. Bodies lay flopped over the sides of chairs like forgotten dolls. The bridge had obviously been the place where most of the fighting had taken place. Furniture, equipment, lifeless flesh everywhere, but no enemies that she could see. That made her both worried and scared. Now when she encountered them - if any still lived - it would be a surprise. And she hated surprises. She heard a noise in the corner, buried under a mountain of metal that had once been the security panel. Right under where Matt and Dave were standing.

"There's someone under there." She pointed to the debris at their feet. "Can you get that thing off of them?"

"Yes, lieutenant," they accidentally said in unison, shooting each other an irritated look. With no small amount of effort, they managed to pull a giant piece of the security console away, revealing a man huddled underneath. His right arm was bleeding and he seemed to be unconscious, but very obviously still alive. Matt and Dave managed to drag the unconscious man out from under the rubble.

"That's Lt. Vinny Tyler, chief of security and weapons," she said, smiling in relief. Lieutenant Vincenzo Anthony Tyler was a beast of a man, formidable even when unconscious. His bronzed skin was strained under thick bulging muscles, and his angular, cleanly shaved chin jutted out of his handsome face with prominence. His short brown hair stuck out at all times, like an animal's hide when it sensed danger. Italian roots and American raised, Vinny was loud, strong, forceful and a long time friend of hers. They had served together on one of her early assignments, and since then she and Vinny had become fond drinking and card playing buddies. She was relieved to see that he had survived the tragedy on the bridge. Somehow, she wasn't all that surprised. Matt scanned him quickly and then looked up at her.

"He has a massive brain hemorrhage. If he doesn't get medical care soon he will die. I don't think he'll make it to Dr. Tomas."

"There's a medical kit still hanging on the wall there," she said, pointing to the white box by the door. "It should have all the emergency medical stuff you need, including the equipment needed to treat brain bleeds."

Natsumi snatched it off the wall and fell beside the unconscious man. "What do I need to do?"

"Just follow the directions on the package and everything will be fine," she said. "I need to keep looking for survivors."

Taris left them to tend to Vinny and made her way toward the front of the bridge. At first she saw nothing but red lights and sparking equipment. No more people. No more survivors. Her heart sunk. *I should have been here,* she told herself, *if I was here I never would have let this happen. Damnit, this is all my fault. It's all my fault!* She kicked a piece of console out of her path angrily. The console fragment clamored to the ground. As it did, she caught the sight of the faintest tuft of white hair under the overturned chair.

"Oh my god…"

She fell to her knees and started pulling debris away with all her strength. With one final heave the chair toppled over, revealing a very bloodied, very weak man underneath. He was in his sixties, with white hair surrounded by leathered skin; a side effect from years of running marathons on the surface of Mars. He had the look of a military man who had seen too many wars to find the thrill of them anymore. Captain Tom Philip was bleeding badly from a wound on his forehead, out of his ears, and his breathing was heavy, but he was alive. He was alive, and at that moment, that was all that mattered to her. He looked up at her with his one non-swollen eye and made the attempt at a smile. His movements were awkward and unfocused.

"Lt. Bodil?" he said quietly. "Taris, is that really you?"

"Yes," she said. She dropped the resonator at her side and cradled his head in her hands. "Yes sir, it's me."

"That coat is very nice on you, lieutenant," he said weakly, forcing a strained smile.

Taris felt her words choke in her throat but she kept them down. "Captain, you have to forgive me. I'm so sorry I didn't get here sooner."

"That's all right," he said softly, trying to focus on her face, "It's good to know they didn't…get us all. In the end. And Sergeant Hoble?"

"He's fine, sir. We're both fine," she said, badly masking the emotion in her voice. "Captain Philip, what happened here?"

He looked up at her, his brown eyes bloodshot and unfocused. "The Grays. The Grays came for us. There were three of them. Called themselves religious men…but this is what they did. Three of them…did this to *us*, lieutenant."

"But sir, how did they get on the ship? How did they penetrate our defenses?" she asked, searching the wreckage for signs of silver hair. Her blood was boiling, desperate for answers.

"We answered a distress call," he explained, sputtering as blood seeped out of his mouth. "We were the only ship in range so we answered the call. We thought it was a family ship, run out of fuel. They were begging for help, saying they needed medical assistance. We couldn't let them just…float out there. We let them in the hangar, and then they attacked. Oldest…trick in the book…the fake distress call, and we fell for it…damn…"

"But what did they want?" she asked urgently. "Why did they do this?"

He coughed violently a couple of times before he continued. "They called themselves the…the…Silencium. They said they wanted freedom. They said…they said we were the wicked ones…that we were the devil. They said they want this ship…to help them in the fight…against us. To find their lost…friend…that was the key they said."

"Elias?" she asked, hoping she was wrong. He thought about it and then nodded laboriously.

"Yes...that's the name. They said that they needed this ship, but I wouldn't let them have it. We fought. They fought back, but I won, lieutenant. Took them down...all three..."

He pointed to the corner. There, surrounded by wires and metal, she saw the shimmer of silver hair, lying amongst the rubble. Captain Philip looked proud of himself at that, and then his entire body started to spasm. She tried to hold onto him as well she could, but when he finally stopped shaking he sputtered violently. Globs of blood came up and into his hand. He started to shudder, fading in and out of consciousness.

"It's going to be okay, sir," she said with all the bravery she could muster. "It's going to be okay. We're going to call for help. Everything is going to be okay."

"Don't...don't let them win, Taris," he said softly.

"What do you mean, sir?"

"Keep the Grays at bay. Keep this ship safe. More will come. I know they will come. Whatever you do, you protect this ship. The Intrepid is the best ship I've ever served. She will serve you well, too."

"Captain Philip, don't talk like that."

"No, lieutenant," he insisted. "I have to. This is it. This is all I have left...so I'm going...to make it count. Listen to me,

Taris. Whatever you do…don't let the Intrepid fall into the hands of the enemy. Guide her through the stars with honor. She'll not steer you wrong."

The tears rolled down her face, and she made no effort to stop them. His breathing sounded laborious, his breaths gasping and wet.

"Please sir…please don't leave me…"

Captain Tom Philip smiled weakly, reached up on his uniform, and with no small amount of effort, managed to pull the rank off of his shoulders. She shook her head violently in protest, but he was unwavering. He tucked the rank into her hand, and closed her fingers around it.

"Congratulations, Captain Taris Leigh Bodil," he said, taking a giant, laborious breath. "The ISS Intrepid…is yours."

Captain Philip exhaled loudly, as if the last thread that was keeping him hanging to life had finally frayed. His face drained of life and she felt his body go slack. She watched his life seep out of his broken, bloodied body. She sat there, holding him, clutching her rank in her hand, letting the tears roll off her cheeks. She quietly wept in her overwhelming grief at the loneliness and strange abandonment she felt. Her captain was dead, and at that moment, she felt totally and utterly alone.

A resonator barrel pressed against the back of her neck proved her wrong.

Chapter Eleven

"Don't do anything stupid, Taris," said the familiar voice behind her. "Just stand up and turn around slowly."

She inhaled stiffly, collecting herself as best she could. Gently, she placed the head of her former captain on the ground and pushed the tears out of her eyes. She struggled to control her temper as she stood up slowly, turning to face her gunman.

"I guess we're all learning new things about each other, aren't we, *doctor*?"

"We can learn more if you want," Dr. Tomas said as he stood in front of her, sweat pouring down his face and pointing the resonator at her head. Her resonator. The one she put down to aid Captain Philip in his last moments. A rookie mistake she hated herself for making. Behind him stood Gareth, looking scared and a little sheepish.

"Gareth, what the hell?" she asked, looking over the doctor's shoulder with round, questioning eyes. The Welshman shrugged.

"I thought I didn't have a choice! He told me you'd all die if I didn't let him out. He said something about you guys being killed if he wasn't there to stop it."

Taris surreptitiously looked over at the lifeless, silver-haired bodies in the corner. "I think the good doctor overestimated his necessity."

Dr. Tomas reached out and gently took the captain's rank from her hand. "So you're a captain now, are you?" he said, inspecting the shoulder insignia with a frown. "Well this must be the time for big revelations."

"You win in that category," she grumbled. "The surprise of the day goes to the guy with the gun."

He looked up at her. "Well you have a lot to say for someone who rarely says the right thing at the right time."

"And you presume a lot for a coward who hides behind a gun," she retorted. "You know nothing about me, Christian. Nothing about what kind of person I am, what kind of things I've done. What kind of leader I could be."

He raised his eyebrows. "I should have known you'd be the type to mouth off at gun point. And since you mention it, you're right; I don't know what kind of leader you will be. I have a good idea, though."

She scoffed. "I'm sure you do. You seem full of stupid ideas."

"Oh I wouldn't call them stupid if I were you." He tossed the rank back to her and she caught it in both hands. "Guess you'd better put these on and start proving me right," he said.

She stood in front of him, unflinching. When she didn't move he sighed, affixing the rank to her shoulders himself. She could tell he was serious, but strangely he wasn't vicious, wasn't angry. She'd seen men with murder in their eyes and he was not one of them.

"Why are you doing this?" she asked blatantly.

Christian finished attaching the rank to her shoulders and stood back, pointing the pistol at her forehead. "I wish it didn't have to be this way."

"Then why are you doing this?" she asked again.

He clenched his jaw, trying to work his way around his reasoning without betraying his true intentions. "We have to do what we must for the greater good," he said. "This is the only way."

"Who is this 'we' you're talking about?" she asked. She eyed him closer. "You're not a Gray, are you?"

"Ha!" he laughed. It was a deep, velvety noise in the back of his throat. "Not hardly. I am a human, through and through."

"Okay, then *why are you doing this*?" she asked for the third time. "Aren't we supposed to be on the same side?"

"I don't need to be a Gray to believe in their cause," he retorted. "I have my reasons, Taris. You just have to trust me."

"Trust you. I see. Well if you're so trustworthy then why the *hell* are you holding a gun to my head?!" she screamed. He seemed surprised by her reaction, and immediately she regretting the emotional outburst. She took a deep breath and tried to calm herself down. She did not want to provoke him to kill her, especially not without an explanation.

"Why I'm doing this is my own business Taris," he said.

"Oh it stopped being only your business when you pointed the resonator at me," she said in a calmer tone. "I'm sure it's all quite simple, really. So let me guess. You're a progressive activist dedicated to creating chaos for the sake of making a political statement. No? Okay you're Elias and no one knows it. No? Okay you're a genetically engineered hybrid set on world domination?"

"Taris, don't be ridiculous," he said in a defiant tone. "Hybrids don't exist."

"Yes they *do*," Dave chimed in from the back of the room.

"All right. Not a hybrid, then," she said. "Well I don't know. Maybe you're just a crazy guy with nothing to lose. Maybe you just wanted to make people pay for the pain you endure on a day-to-day basis."

The doctor's expression darkened. "You're half right."

Now she was getting somewhere. "Well which half would that be, doc? Because right now I'm not half of anything. I'm fully and completely, one hundred percent *pissed off.* You'd better start explaining yourself, man."

"Okay," he said, surprisingly accommodating. "I'll answer anything you want to know."

"Really?" She folded her arms. "You're new at this hostile takeover thing, aren't you?"

"This would be my first," he admitted. "And it's not a takeover. It's…an act of desperation I'm afraid."

"I can see that," she said. Well at least she knew what she was dealing with. "Okay then. Let's start with what you're doing here. What is your plan? Who are you working for? Are you even a *doctor*?"

He was letting her have the upper hand in the conversation. That was a good sign. She needed to know what she was up against, if he was part of a larger plot or acting alone and seizing the moment. She needed to know what was motivating him. She needed to know how she could beat him. He was just about to respond when the sound of groaning interrupted him. *Damn it*, she thought, *so close*.

"Ugh. God almighty, my head hurts like a *bitch*," grumbled a grating and familiar voice. Taris looked over the doctor's shoulder and saw Vinny, rolling to his side in front of a triumphant-faced Natsumi. Taris smiled and breathed a sigh of relief.

"Glad to see you're among the living, Vinny," she said from across the room. Vinny lifted his head up and squinted at her.

"Lieutenant Bodil, is that you? Hot damn, how the hell did you get here?" He struggled to stand up. "I thought you were on Earth!"

"Yeah well it's complicated. Quite frankly, it's still that way." She looked down the barrel of the fully charged resonator and her muscles tensed. Vinny, with some help from Natsumi and Matt, managed to pull himself to his feet. He looked around, observing the situation with a pained grimace.

"What the--? What the jumping Jesus juice is going on around here?" he asked incredulously, holding his bleeding arm. "What happened to the bridge? Where's the captain? Did we crash? Where are we? *Who the hell* is this guy with the gun?!"

She furred her brow. "You don't know?" she asked. "Wow. You must have hit your head harder than I thought."

"The affects of the neuroreconstruction might produce mild to moderate aggression, emotional instability, irrational mood swings, hysteria and temporary amnesia," Matt read from the package on the medical device they had used to revive Vinny.

"If any of these symptoms persist for over seventy-two hours, please seek a medical professional for assistance."

Taris rolled her eyes. "Oh good god. Our one witness doesn't remember anything. And he's emotionally unstable. Well that's terrific."

Vinny cast a wary eye at the mad scientists. "And who are *these* pancakes?"

"Pancakes?" Matt asked, scanning him with interest. "Did you just call us 'pancakes'?"

"What kind of an insult is that?" Dave asked, grimacing in dislike. "And besides, it's the guy with the gun you should be more concerned with."

"Yeah, the pancake is right. Who is the asshole pointing a gun at you, LT?" Vinny asked, ignoring the incredulous looks from the scientists.

"My name is Doctor Christian Tomas," the doctor answered, keeping his eyes focused on her. "I am a medical officer on board the ISS Horizon. I'm here on my own volition. The crew of the Horizon has never had any knowledge of my actions or whereabouts."

"Oh I'm sure," she responded. "Like I'm in any position to cross reference that."

"I guess you'll just have to take me at my word," he said.

"Again, not like I have a choice," she said. "So, who do you work for then, doc? You might be acting on your own, but it's clearly on behalf of some cause, right? What, do you belong to some strange group of murdering medics marauding the sky malevolently?"

"Ooh. Nice alliteration, Lt. Bodil," Matt complimented. "Very clever."

"Thanks," she replied with a little smile.

The doctor wasn't grinning. "I am a member of the insurrection group known as the Silencium, Captain Bodil."

"*Captain*? Did he just call you captain?" Vinny's mouth dropped. "What happened to Captain Philip?" At that moment he appeared to fully absorb the scene around him. His expression battled between rage and utter despair. Tears welled in the big man's eyes.

"You son of a bitch," he growled at Christian. "God damn freedom fighters. Gray loving weirdoes with your grand plans to save the universe. You're nothing but a bunch of pirates and terrorists."

"You watch your tongue, lieutenant," Dr. Tomas said, pushing the barrel harder against Taris' forehead, "or this ship will lose two captains today."

Taris found the notion of him pulling the trigger extremely hard to believe, but Vinny's mouth snapped shut.

"So what's your plan here," she said, returning her attention to Dr. Tomas. "You're just going to hold a gun to my head and demand that these people obey you? Then what?"

He seemed to have already thought that part through. "We need this ship, I'm afraid. I had not intended for this to happen, but circumstances being what they are...Anyway, we have no choice but to pilot this ship to the moon colony."

Taris frowned and took a look around at the rubble that was once her bridge. "I don't think you've noticed, but the bridge is really in no shape to be controlled. The helm is damaged, security is on lock down, directional and manual override seem to be inoperable and oh, not to mention the fact that the crew's dead. Who am I going to get to drive this boat, doc? I don't suppose you'd like to take the helm."

"You can use them." He gestured to the crowd standing behind her.

"What, a brain-damaged security chief, three scientists and the engineering NCO? Oh good plan. We're ship shape in Bristol fashion now."

"Would you rather float here in space? On a communications blackout in the middle of nowhere?" he asked.

"No," she said begrudgingly.

"Well, then I guess we will have to fly the ship."

"But I don't want to do that at gunpoint either," she said, holding her ground.

"You don't have a choice right now, Taris. Now let's go."

"Okay, say we actually manage to get this bird flying," she said, playing along. "To what point and purpose? As soon as we get within United air space they'll know something is wrong."

"No, not *this* ship," he protested. "*This* ship is specifically designed to be undetectable. The best part is that even if it does get detected, it registers as a United fleet ship with silent communication clearance."

Crap, she thought. *He's right. This ship can sail straight through the sky on a clear summer's day and no one would give it a second glance.*

"And then what?" she asked. "We get to the moon colony and you'll just...walk off the Intrepid and that's that?"

"I am meeting some friends there. Important people who share in my mission," he said strongly. "I do not stand alone."

"Well you're on your own now, buddy," she said, pointing to the pile of rubble behind her. "Every Gray who came on his ship is dead."

That struck him hard. "Lair."

"See for yourself," she said, holding her hand out.

Keeping the gun pushed firmly against her head, he grabbed her by the arm and made his way toward the bodies. Slowly, he pushed her toward the pile of metal and silver hair. He pulled the debris to the side and gasped. The smell of freshly spilled blood hung heavy in the air. She felt Dr. Tomas tense.

"Oh gods. Oh gods, no."

"It's true," she said quietly. "Maybe next time your little rebel group will think twice about attacking a z-class stealth ship."

He made a desperate noise in the back of his throat, like he was choking back tears. "Oh gods, this is horrible!"

"That's what I've been saying since we got here," she commented.

"How could this happen?" he asked rhetorically. "Why were they even here? This is not how it was supposed to happen at all."

"What, you didn't expect my crew to defend themselves?" she said, hoping her words would sting. "Are you stupid? Of course they were going to stand up and protect themselves. Of course they were going to protect our ship. Truthfully doc, did you honestly think we wouldn't fight?"

He looked at her, his face contorted in anguish. "They weren't supposed to get anywhere near this ship," he said softly.

"They knew it was dangerous. I don't understand. Why did the wicked triumph?"

"I guess the gods are the judge of that, huh?"

"Don't mock a faith you choose not to understand," he countered. "You have no idea what it means to sacrifice for your beliefs."

"Don't get all sanctimonious with me," she said in even tones. "Not while I'm still covered in the blood of my shipmates. The blood that your precious Gray friends spilled. Your people attacked the emissary's mansion and killed people. Your friends murdered my entire crew. This wasn't a sacrifice of faith; this was a slaughter for theatrics. Don't talk to me about religion and fairness, doc. Don't you dare."

She saw his finger clutch the trigger of the resonator. She'd done it. She'd gone too far. Taris was almost certain he was going to shoot her, when she saw movement. It was just for a moment, just a flicker of a moment. It was a movement which turned into a noise that sounded a lot like a man. Swearing in the language of Gray.

"*Gias, et fininis graesthula ii metr de, ughhhh*," said a muffled voice under the toppled helm control panel. Dr. Tomas made a sound of uninhibited relief and swung around.

"Vale. Vale Teag, is that you?" he called out. The top part of the console parted slightly. She saw a pair of reflective eyes peering at her through the darkness. A bloodied hand reached out into the light.

"Christian? Oh thank the gods you found me my friend. What a joy it is to hear your voice and know you are unhurt."

Taris felt the blood drain from her face. "Vale Teag? The terrorist from Emissary Hooper's mansion? Oh sweet fancy Moses. This cannot be happening."

"What? Is one of them terrorists still alive?" Vinny called out from across the room.

Vinny, Matt, Dave, Natsumi and Gareth were standing in the corner. They looked as though they had been talking and were abruptly interrupted. She hoped to god that they were forming a plan. Christian wasn't paying nearly enough attention to them, but then again she could tell he wasn't much of an evil mastermind. Natsumi was wrapping Vinny's bleeding arm slowly, but her lips were moving as she worked. All Taris had to do was keep the doctor distracted long enough for their plan - whatever that was - to work. Luckily, there was a giant, bleeding distraction right in front of her.

"You have to get him out," she told the doctor urgently. "He could die if he's trapped down there too long."

"Let him die," Vinny called out bitterly. "He's just another soulless Gray freak with a sword. Who the hell fights with a sword these days anyway?"

170

"No!" Dr. Tomas exclaimed. "No. We have to get him out. You! Big guy. Vinny, right? You have to help get him out from under this."

Vinny scoffed and crossed his arms. "Pssh. No way. I'm not rescuing that jackass for nothing."

Dr. Tomas pointed the resonator at Taris's temple again. "Help me. Please."

She looked at him. "Do it, Lt. Tyler. Help him get his friend out."

Vinny hesitated for a brief moment, eying the doctor carefully. Finally, after what seemed like far too long of a moment to decide whether or not she ought to live or die, he stomped over to them. Without too much effort, he and Christian managed to toss the console aside. As soon as it was pushed away, Taris saw three bodies. Two dead Grays, and one living one. Dr. Tomas dropped his guard and fell to his knees in front of the living one, helping him to his feet.

"Thank you so much my friend," the wounded man said with an appreciative smile.

What the doctor pulled out of the rubble was a massive and beautiful Gray man. He was of staggering height, about six-foot-six, with shimmering mirror eyes that were round and alert. He was obviously Gray, but his hair was surprisingly short - a rarity. What hair he did have was tussled all over the top of his head, standing up in many different directions, tapered in the back and at the sides. She had never in her life seen a Gray without long hair, but for some reason she thought it made him very attractive, or at least more human-like. He spoke English with only the faintest of accents and seemed well educated; not the ignorant ruffian she had expected.

His full pink lips settled above a dimpled chin, complimenting his angular jaw. His pleasantly shaped physique was like that of a field worker; taught and overworked. His muscles pressed against the dark blue robes that he wore. They looked like the traditional wear of the Gray religious authority. *He must be a priest*, she guessed, *or maybe some sort of shaman*. As Dr. Tomas helped him, Taris noticed the faintest impression of a slave emblem on the outside of his hand. So she had been wrong; he wasn't a religious authority, he was nothing but a runaway slave. *Someone is going to be pissed when they get their traitor slave back*, she thought bitterly.

"Vale, this is Taris Leigh Bodil. She's the new captain of this ship," Dr. Tomas explained. "She brought me here. She thinks we are her enemies."

"Aren't you?" she spat back.

Vale lifted his head slowly and locked his gaze onto hers. His face betrayed no emotion, but his eyes spoke volumes. They flickered with interest, as though he were looking at something mythological for the very first time. His stare was piercing, unnervingly intense. She felt strangely exposed, like he was seeing a part of her that she didn't want anyone to see. She hated it. She wanted to turn away, but something wouldn't let her do it. She found herself staring back at him, equally intrigued. She hated that even more.

As soon as the thought entered her mind, Vale's expression transitioned seamlessly into humble pity.

"Captain, I am sorry for the state of your ship and the loss of the innocent," Vale said in a voice that she recognized from the talking corpse. *What a strange connection to make*, she thought.

"I don't want to hear your feigned pity," she responded. "I don't want your excuses. I don't want to hear anything from you, actually."

"Vale," Dr. Tomas said, holding him up slightly. "What happened? What are you doing here? I thought we were going to rendezvous on the moon colony later tonight?"

"Ah," Vale said with a sorrowful look. "It appears the gods have decided to lead us here instead. Things did not go according to plan."

"You're telling me," Taris said darkly.

"Uh, Dr. Tomas or whatever your name is?" Vinny asked, trying to look as forlorn and lame as he could muster. "Look, the ship is destroyed, I need medical assistance, and your friend there looks like he needs help, too. Can we send for help, please, or go to the nearest starbase?"

"What? No!" Dr. Tomas said incredulously. "I'm sorry Vinny, but time is not on our side. We have to get to the moon base to meet the others."

"No we don't," Vale said sadly. "They have all perished in the fight for freedom. They died valiantly, though. They shall be exalted in their deaths."

Taris took the opportunity to speak before it became a sermon. "Look I know we're taken over, or whatever, but this ship is no good to any of us right now. Unless we make repairs and get medical treatment it's totally pointless. This ship is in no shape to fly."

"Ah, but that is not true," Vale the Gray said. She turned to him.

"What the hell do you mean?"

"I mean that this ship is, at this moment, fulfilling a very real and very working purpose."

Taris gave the bridge a good look around. "I think you and I must have very different opinions of 'working purpose' there, Gray."

"That may be," he said with a strange smile creased on his handsome face, "but before the fight here on the bridge, my tribesmen and I set a plan into motion. My fellow Silencium

174

fighters laid down their lives to make sure the ship received the commands before the consoles were destroyed."

Her heartbeat quickened. "Commands?"

He nodded. "It was all convenient thinking on our part. After your captain captured us and shot down our ship, we knew our lives were forfeit. In our haste, we forged a quick plan. We had only a few moments to act, but we did manage to disconnect communications. Then we programmed your computer with our original coordinates, blocked outside access, and set the ship to autopilot."

"What? Do you mean to tell me that the ship is headed to some unknown destination and we can't communicate with any other ships?" she said. A thought struck her. "Oh my god. That means we're in stealth mode. No one will see us. No one will be able to come help us."

Vale cocked his head to the side. "Yes. This is so, and it was at quite a cost. It was a grave shame that my tribesmen lost their lives. However, I have faith that their sacrifices shall not be in vain."

Taris processed this with a confused expression. "Wait, autopilot? Well that's just a lie. If you did that you would have been hundreds of light years away, not in orbit around Saturn."

"It's no lie," he protested softly. "I speak the truth."

"You must be lying. Otherwise we would have moved by now." As if on command at that very moment the ship rocked, lurching everyone forward. She swung around, forgetting that there was still a gun to her head. Well now they were moving. Seizing the moment, she yanked Vinny's arm and swung him around.

"Well wasn't that convenient timing," she said.

He nodded. "Let's do this!"

Taris lurched forward and threw herself onto Dr. Tomas, knocking him to the ground. Vinny lunged at the Gray and the two of them went crashing into the already destroyed console. Dr. Tomas was temporarily dazed, but managed to recover quickly. Fists flying, he started fighting her with all his strength. Feeling the anger propel her, she snatched the resonator from ground and turned it on him with a whoop of triumph. Vinny managed to get the advantage over Vale and slammed him against the side of the overturned table, holding him in place with his massive forearm. She pried herself off of the doctor and stood up, keeping the weapon pointed carefully at his chest.

"It's not so fun being on the business end of this thing, is it doc?" she taunted.

Vinny reached into his side pocket and pulled out a scrathe whip. The sound of the hiss from the device as it charged made her sick to her stomach. Vale the Gray slid off the overturned table and tried to back up, but only found himself pressed against the wall. He was trapped, and the look on his face said that he knew it. Dr. Tomas looked at her with pleading panic.

"No! Don't do that!" Christian pleaded on behalf of his friend. "He's a good man! The scrathe is torture to them! Please don't do it, Vinny. That device is worse than death to the Grays."

"Yeah well your buddy shoulda thought of that before boarding this boat and killing my friends, traitor," Vinny said, adjusting the frequency of the scrathe. Vale looked pale-faced in his blood splattered blue robes, but his resolution was unrelenting.

"Please," Vale said softly, "you do not know what you do when you wield that weapon."

"This?" Vinny taunted, holding the whip out in front of him. "Oh the scrathe is not a weapon. It's a legal form of compliance encouragement."

Vale inhaled stiffly, his eyes locked on the whip. "A man with a full belly cannot understand the starving man's actions."

Vinny glared at him. "The hell is that supposed to mean?"

"It means that you do not know the pain of the whip because it is of nothing to you," he clarified.

Vinny grinned widely, showing a set of white, perfectly straight teeth. "I guess that makes me a lucky bastard then," he said. "But you're not."

He raised the whip over his head and cracked his wrist forward, releasing the first burst. Blue electric tentacles shot out of the black cylinder, illuminating the dark bridge in an angry indigo light. The scrathe's electrical fingers latched themselves to Vale's body and he screamed with intense pain, collapsing to the ground. The sound was a horrifying, screeching wail unlike any other she had ever heard. It was a true and abject hurting, intensified a thousand times. In her life, she'd never seen a scrathe actually used in front of her. The sound of suffering was almost palpable. After a minute or so the scrathe bolts faded, leaving Vale a quivering heap of a body on the debris-scattered deck, whimpering softly.

"Was that enough for ya, you murderous coward?" Vinny screamed, warming the scrathe back up. Taris shook her head.

"That's enough, Lt. Tyler," she said.

She was surprisingly disturbed by the unsettled anxiety she felt. It's not like she hadn't dealt with this sort of thing before. She'd seen more death and torture in her lifetime than some could ever dream. However, watching Vale quiver in pain, seeing the black scrathe burns on his skin, it was more than she could bear. Lt. Tyler shook his head and raised the whip again.

"No, it's not enough LT," he said in a menacing tone. "It will never be enough."

"Yes it is, Lt. Tyler. Look, he's had enough, okay?"

"No!" he protested. "He killed our crew, LT! He killed the captain! Just once is not enough!"

"Yes it is!" she hollered, reaching for the whip. "Stop! Right now!"

The ship lurched again, throwing everyone to the ground. Lt. Tyler lost his grip, causing the whip to fly in every direction. One of the electric threads hit Vale on the chest directly. The other wrapped itself around her left arm.

The pain was blinding.

It felt like her blood was on fire. Her heart stopped and her mouth closed up. She couldn't breathe. She couldn't function. All she could think about was the pain. It incapacitated her, shook her to her core, turned her muscles into mush. She flopped on the ground in agony for what seemed like an eternity before the pain left, leaving her breathless and sick.

At that moment, the warning red lights turned off. The bridge resumed its normal luminescence, casting a ghostly view of the bloody and destroyed bridge. It took Taris a few muddled moments to clear her head before she would attempt to open an eye. When she did, she saw the stunned, fascinated and confused expressions of the crowd hovering around her. Too weak to stand, she turned her head to the side and found herself staring into the Gray's pale, tortured eyes. Silently, he reached out to take her hand and gave it a quick squeeze. He was trying to comfort her, she realized. The one they called a sociopathic terrorist. He was already injured, already bleeding, yet he was trying to comfort her. When his long fingers touched her palm, his expression changed. Curiously, he turned her hand over. That's when he saw her burn marks. She wanted to explain it, but she lacked the strength to even start. The Gray was looking at her in what she could only describe as relieved amazement. Laboriously, he cleared his throat and raised his head weakly.

"*Gias, es a pilia*," he whispered.

She frowned. "What?"

"*Camme sans supre Adulo*?" he asked.

"No," she said, the pain ebbing away to resentment. "I'm not an Adulo. And I never will be."

Vale's expression was an odd mixture of residual pain and undaunted wonder, almost as if he didn't believe her. Grumbling, she found the strength to move her limbs and pulled herself to an unsteady stand. She turned her head to the side and discreetly wiped the bloody tears from her face. Her eyes met the thunderstruck expression of Lt. Tyler who was staring at the scrathe in genuine confusion.

"Taris," he said, breaking rank protocol in his surprise. "I don't know what happened. These things aren't supposed to do anything to humans. Maybe something went wrong? I don't really know. Oh my god I am so sorry."

She shook her head. She was not going to acknowledge it. No excuses, no explanations, nothing to place fear or doubt in anyone's minds. It was too much to process, too much pain to deal with. Figuring out what had just happened to her would create too many questions, and they had bigger problems. Much bigger problems.

"Lt. Tyler," she instructed, shoving her shaking hands into her pockets, "take Dr. Tomas and Vale Teag to the brig. Lock them up, but *do not* kill them. I need them both alive, you understand me?"

"Yes ma'am."

"Good," she said, masking her confusion with anger. "Shove those bastards in the hole and then get back up here. We have a ship to fix."

Chapter Twelve

It had been over a day and a half of hard work and they still could not find a way to stop the ship from flying on autopilot. They cleaned up the mess, put everything back in place, rebooted the system, but nothing worked. They got all systems back on line, but no matter what they did the doors wouldn't open to release the Stargazer, the pre-programmed path on the helm couldn't be changed, and communication with other ships was apparently impossible. They were just drifting slowly through space at stealth speed, heading to an unknown destination with no way to alter it.

Even Natsumi, the language savant, was no match for the jumbled glyphs that had taken over every computer screen. She had an explanation, something about the written Caleum language being practically telepathic and therefore different from the spoken language, but Taris didn't want explanations. She wanted answers, and she wasn't getting any. Oddly enough, it wasn't the unknown destination or the nine crew members lying on slabs in the morgue that was bothering her. No, the only thing on her mind was the blackened dusting of a scrathe burn on her arm, and how the hell it got there in the first place.

No one had spoken of her scrathing since it had taken place. They didn't talk about it, but she knew they all remembered it. She couldn't stop thinking about it. The memory barely left her mind. No matter how many times she tried to understand it, it seemed to make less sense. She found herself questioning things she'd never questioned before, paranoid from sleep deprivation and anxiety. She felt confused and betrayed and angry. Finally, out of desperation, she decided that she could no longer beat herself up over a freak accident. That's all it was; an accident. A random and unfortunate act and nothing more.

She had to see it that way. She had to put things in perspective. She had a ship that was headed to god knows where, a makeshift crew who was tired and scared, and an international criminal locked up in a holding cell. After trying unsuccessfully for what seemed like the fiftieth time to override the program using her own command codes, she slammed her fist down on the captain's chair and ran her hands over her exhausted face. She was going to have to do something she really didn't want to do. Something she'd been avoiding, but she no longer had a choice. She had tried everything and now it was time to face her fears.

It was time to talk to the prisoner.

"Taris Leigh Bodil...You look terrible," Vale said with a worried expression.

He seemed to have completely recovered from his scrathe thrashing, and for some reason that made her even angrier. She couldn't stop remembering the pain. It haunted her. Meanwhile,

Vale sat in his cell like nothing ever happened. He stood up and placed his hands respectfully in front of him.

"You need sleep," he observed, chastising her. "If an Adulo does not sleep for too long they deplete themselves too much to function. You cannot allow yourself to succumb to such things."

"Where the hell are we going?" she asked bluntly.

They'd tried intimidating, they'd tried demanding, she'd even let Vinny threaten to scrathe him, but in the end this Gray would not budge. He refused to change the computer or relinquish controls to them. Furious, Vinny was ready to throw him out an airlock, but Taris wouldn't have it. She wanted him alive so they could turn in a capture, not a corpse. Somehow a capture just seemed more honorable. Still, she was more than a little frustrated with him. That airlock option was starting to seem more and more appealing. Vale cleared his throat and touched the ends of his tapered hair with a sorrowful expression. He looked almost devastated at the lack of long hair, but recovered quickly. His face went from almost sad to the neutral Gray within moments.

"That is a complicated question, captain. One that would have been better explained by my tribesmen. Had your predecessor not killed them, of course."

"Ha. I bet you didn't plan on your buddies getting killed when you boarded, huh?" she taunted.

He stared at her with an expression so intense that she found herself unable to look him in the eye. "We never meant for any innocent people to die."

"You are sorry for nothing," she retorted. "If you really gave a shit about the lives of innocent people you wouldn't have come here in the first place."

"But that is not true," he said sadly. "We came here against our will. We stayed because we care about the innocent. It is our mission to care for the oppressed and the defenseless."

"Well then your mission is doomed to fail!" she exclaimed irrationally, throwing her hands up in the air.

His eyes flashed with interest. "Your hands. Again I saw it. The mark on your palms. I know that mark. Your energy, it flows through it, Taris. I felt it when I touched your hand on the deck, after the scrathing. That was your first time, wasn't it?"

Her heart was racing. He was right, of course, and the experience left her jarred and confused, but she wasn't about to use that as a way of connecting with a known terrorist. Vale took a cautious step toward her, his eyes filled with sympathy. "The first time is always the hardest. You never expect it to hurt as much as it does."

"Shut up," she snapped, sidestepping the conversation he was trying to have with her. "That ship you crashed into Emissary Hooper's house killed five people. Three humans and two Grays. Do you think they deserved to die? The men and women on my ship that you slashed, do you think *they* deserved to die? Don't talk to me about protecting the innocent when you came in here, guns blazing, and killed my entire crew!"

"We did not do anything with guns blazing," he argued. "We came with no guns. We only had our swords and our faith to protect us. It was *your* men who fired on *us*."

She scoffed loudly. "Ha! That's the worst lie I ever heard! So tell me, if you're so innocent then why did you lure the Intrepid to come help you?"

Vale blinked, confused. "We sent out a distress call because we were in distress. Our engine power had failed. We had been drifting for over a day. The Intrepid offered to help us, until the crew found out what we were. They let us board and then held us captive. They took our ship and shot it down in space. They stranded us here and then they tried to…wrangle us."

Taris was taken aback. Wrangling Grays was not only considered to be inhumane treatment, but also highly illegal. It required the use of scrathe chains and illegal, undocumented branding. The penalties were severe, especially for military members who were caught doing it. To even accuse her crew of that was shocking.

"I've worked with Captain Philip for years," she said slowly. "He was a good man. A man of integrity. A man of the law. He would no more wrangle a Gray than he would sell a child to slavery."

"He's done both, I'm afraid," Vale said quietly. "And much more than that."

"*You lie*," she hissed, feeling the anger begin to surface.

"Ah, but I don't," he said carefully. "I do not have a need to lie. Adulos do not do such things. It serves no purpose."

"That's absolute nonsense," she said bitterly.

"It is no such thing," he said gently. "You should know that. Let me show you, Taris. Let me speak to you through the whispers of the soul."

He was speaking in riddles. The telepathy that Grays were fabled to have, the strange spiritualism, it was drowning her thoughts. He was drowning her thoughts, and she was too tired and too hurt and too confused to handle it. Vale took a cautious step forward and extended an open hand to her.

"Can I see your palm?" he asked.

"You've already seen it. It hasn't changed."

"Taris, please. I know you owe me nothing, but I just. Please."

Maybe it was the way he seemed to stare into her eyes and see her soul. Maybe it was the fact that they shared a brutal and agonizing torture together. Maybe it was just curiosity. Whatever reason was behind it, she decided to indulge him.

Cautiously, she pulled her hands out of her pockets but kept them close to her. She traced the scar tissue of her left palm with her right forefinger. She didn't even know why she was entertaining his idea. He was a fugitive, a dangerous man, a killer. She knew she ought to walk right out of that cell and never look back.

"You're going to read too much into it," she protested. "They're just some scars from childhood. That's all."

"I wish only to glance on them once more," he begged gently. "Please."

She rolled her eyes and conceded. "Ugh, fine. But it's not what you think. See I was a toddler, and my mom was really into iron sculptures at that time-"

"Oh my gods," Vale breathed, grasping her palms. "I thought I saw it before, but I had to be sure. In all my years I never thought it possible. There was a part of me that always thought it might be a myth."

"What? What is it?" she asked. She was curious to see what he saw, in spite of herself. "Does it look like one of your weird little words or something?"

"Oh it's so much more than that, Taris," he said, eying her with new interest. "That symbol is the emblem of the three pillars."

"The emblem of the what?" she asked, looking down. "It doesn't look like a pillar to me."

"That must mean that you are one of the three. The warrior, *a tarischa*. One of the three pillars. My gods, but it's true. I would not have believed this, had my own eyes not seen it."

He looked at her with such reverent intensity that it scared her. She didn't like it. She didn't like the way he made her feel when he looked at her like that. She felt exposed, vulnerable. Uncomfortable, she yanked her hands back defensively and shoved them in her pockets.

"See? I knew you'd read too much into this, damnit."

He cocked his head to the side and blinked. "Don't fight me, Taris. Your hands tell me only a grain of what you really are. You're as much of an enigma to me as you are to yourself."

"Well it's going to stay that way," she said, feeling strangely nervous. He took a step closer to her but she backed up defensively.

"I know we both yearn for answers," he said passionately. "We could learn them together if you would like. Touch my hand. Let us connect with our minds. Let me help you find those answers."

"Shut up! Shut up! *Shut...up!*" she screamed, driving nervousness into irrational hysteria. Before he could respond she jumped up, slammed the chair on the ground and advanced on him. "Now you listen here, Gray," she said, poking him in the chest, "I am done listening to this. You don't know me at all. You think I'm some high and mighty predestined *whatever* but you know what? I'm just a woman with drinking problem and a bad attitude, okay? *Get over it.*"

His eyebrows raised ever so slightly. "If you'd like to continue to labor under that delusion that is your prerogative, but I will not allow you to talk me into believing that you are not important. You, Taris Leigh Bodil, are more significant to me than you will ever know. When you're ready to learn the truth, I'll be waiting for you."

"Don't hold your breath." She leaned in, glowering. "You know what? On second thought, go ahead. Hold your breath. Hold it until you choke, bastard."

She slammed the chair against the wall with all her force and stormed out of the cell.

Chapter Thirteen

Taris paced the hallway for fifteen minutes before her mind stopped racing. Her fists were clenched so tightly she nearly drew blood. She couldn't go back in there. Not yet. She couldn't face him. Vale, with his smug comments and sanctimonious grandstanding and stupid gorgeous face and...

What was she doing? What was he *doing* to her?

"Ugh!" she exclaimed, slamming her fist in the wall. "*God damnit!*"

After a few deep breaths she managed to finally calm down. She leaned against the wall outside of the brig and brought her heart rate down to a normal level. Vale was just trying to psych her out, she told herself. He wanted her to lose her temper and he won. He had managed to avoid talking about the one thing she had gone in there to discuss. She'd dealt with much more formidable foes than Vale Teag, yet every time she talked to him she lost herself in his words. In his voice. In the things he said that were so insane, yet somehow made sense. Embarrassed, she rubbed her face with her hands irritably.

"This is nothing," she said out loud to herself. "He's just a Gray. Just a religious Gray on a mission. No one important."

But if that was the case, then why did she let him hijack the conversation like that?

"Well not anymore." She was going to maintain control of the conversation if it killed her. She stomped back into the cell and found Vale, sitting cross legged on the bed, unmoved from when she last left him.

"I'm not here to talk about me," she said bluntly. "I'm arrogant enough without your goading."

"Fair enough," he agreed with a placid smile.

"Where are we going?" she demanded, folding her arms tightly in front of her.

He had picked up the chair she'd thrown in her tantrum and set it deliberately in front of him. She yanked the chair back a few spaces and lowered herself into it. "Well?"

"We're going to a place called Hammerhead Hold, in Sector One on Earth," he answered calmly, as though that were obvious somehow.

Hammerhead. Why did that seem familiar to her? "Why?"

"There is a landing strip there," he said. "It's unmarked, so we will not be checked. It's the closest unmonitored landing strip to Emissary Hooper's home."

"Why there?" she asked. She could think of a million places she would rather go than a landing pad near Boone Hooper's mansion.

"It is where Jyrisa Ato-Teag, my comrade and connection, said to meet her," he said.

"Teag?" she repeated. "Isn't *your* last name Teag? Is she your sister or wife or something? Is that why you're going through all this trouble?"

Vale shook his head and ran his hands through his hair. "Teag is the country I am from. I guess you could say it is my 'tribe'. Adulos do not have last names."

"Oh," she said, flipping the chair around so she could lean on the back and draped her hands lazily in front of her. "I didn't know that about your people."

"There is a lot that humans do not know about us," he said with an edge in his tone.

"So why is this Jyrisa woman so important? Why risk all of this just to go get her?" she asked.

"Jyrisa used to be a slave at Emissary Hooper's mansion. She knows a lot about the layout, the many buildings, the security codes and much more. She is vital to our mission."

A wave of realization washed over her. "Ah…So this is all about the threat on Emissary Hooper's life. That's what this is all about, isn't it? You're going to assassinate him aren't you?!"

"This is about the Emissary," Vale said in a tense tone, "but it has nothing, nothing to do with his life. The life in question is of much greater importance."

"Elias you mean," she said. "You're doing this for your friend."

"Yes. I do mean Elias."

"What's the big deal with this guy?" she asked, trying not to sound indignant. "Why go through all this trouble for one person?"

He looked at her like he was debating whether or not to tell her something. Finally he sighed and stared at her, intensity rippling in his inhuman eyes. "Elias is the Star of Gray. He must be protected."

She furred her brow. "The what?"

He looked affronted. "My gods, do you really not know what the Star of Gray is?"

"No," she said. "Is that supposed to be common knowledge?"

Vale was stunned, at a loss for words. It took him a moment to gather himself. "Uh, well…I suppose not. I guess I'll say that he is important. Very important."

"Like a prophet?" she guessed.

He frowned. "No. But he is significant to the Grays in the way a prophet is significant to religious people."

That made sense to her. "Well that explains why you're trying so hard to find him."

"Jyrisa is the only slave in existence who made it off of Emissary Hooper's property list with her life in her hands. She is necessary and I trust her. We need to meet her at the complex so she can show us the way."

"The way to what?"

"The way to Elias," he said quietly. She noticed that his voice changed when he spoke Elias' name. There was a respect there, a reverence. "We have to find and free him. That mission starts at the complex."

"What is this complex you keep talking about?" she asked irritably. "I've never even heard of it. Actually, I've never heard of complexes in general."

Vale sighed heavily. "Then you are lucky, but you are also ignorant. The complexes are Earth World United facilities designed to imprison Adulos. They perform experiments on the prisoners. Force them to do unspeakable things in the name of science. That scrathe device that made you scream for mercy was developed in a complex. Imagine the torture that the Adulo test subjects had to endure so they could make that horrible scrathe."

The mention of the event triggered memories of the torture, and she shuddered in spite of herself. She realized that she never actually knew where those devices were created.

Vale continued. "The complexes are big, they're widespread, and they're heavily guarded. They're the place that every Adulo fears, second only to Earth itself. They're in remote locations, so no one can hear the screams, Taris. The screams of the tortured and forgotten are the ones that pierce the soul. These screams cut deeper than that."

"That sounds awful," she said quietly. "But also unbelievable. These torture chamber places can't possibly exist on Earth. If they did, people would have known about them and put a stop to them already."

Vale scoffed, but there was a flicker of sadness in the tone. "So much faith you put in your humans, Taris. You think that the wicked are the few who spread the evil. I disagree. It's the indifference of the many who allow the wicked to endure. Many, many people know about these places, Taris. They know and they do nothing."

She shook her head. "No. I don't believe that. I don't believe any of it."

"You think you know so much, and yet you do nothing. You disagree, and yet you do nothing. You know that the things you own and the clothes you wear and the food you eat are forged on the backs of slaves. Yet you do nothing."

"Hey, I have never agreed with Gray slavery," she retorted, pointing a finger at him. "I've argued against it. Hell I fought against it! I went to war because of my opposition of it for god's sake. I do not support it. Not in any way."

"And yet, you still allow them to serve you food and clean your house and make your clothes. It is not enough."

"That's not true," she argued. "I could scream as loud as I want and it wouldn't affect anything. The Gray trade is far beyond my ability to change it now. There was a chance, during the revolution, but not now." She glared at him. "Look we tried, alright? We tried and we failed. I hate it, and I will never support it, but there's really nothing I can do about it."

"Poor Taris," he said in a tone that surprisingly offered no mockery. "When did they take the fight from you?"

She frowned. "Excuse me?"

"When did you stop trying?" he asked. "When did it no longer matter to you? When did they take the fire from your fury?"

His words hit her harder than she realized. She was shocked to discover that she was unable to come up with a decent response. She had always been a fighter, but after the rebellion and the prison camp, complacency took the place of righteous indignation. And she'd done nothing to stop that. It was just something she'd accepted. She hadn't put up a good fight since the rebellion. Somehow, annoyingly, Vale Teag noticed that before she did.

"No," she said sternly, her resolve shaken. "I'm not doing this. You're not sucking me into this conversation again. I won't let you do it." She stood up abruptly. "I'm leaving."

"No you're not, Taris" he said in a calm voice.

"Ha! And what makes you so sure, Vale?"

"Because you can't leave," he said plainly. "Not yet. Not when I know you need answers more than you need to indulge your temper."

He was right, of course, damn him. She hesitated for a moment, for drama's sake, but finally relented. Slowly she slunk back into the chair, folding her arms in front of her.

"They didn't take the fight from me, by the way," she said obstinately. "Maybe I fight in a different way now. Time has made me a different kind of soldier."

He shrugged and pulled his legs up onto the bed, crossing them slowly. "That is your right, of course, to believe such concessions, but that does not give them validity. Change can be forged from the words of one, or stopped by the silence of many."

"Do you always talk like that?" she complained.

He blinked. "How do you mean?"

"Like a prophet. Do you always talk like you're going to be quoted someday? Seriously, because half the things that come out of your mouth sound like they should be written on the wall of some temple somewhere."

He laughed at that. It was a joyful, mellifluous sound that she was surprised to find enjoyable. She realized that she'd never heard a Gray laugh before. She was starting to realize that she knew very little about Grays in general.

"I shall take that as a compliment," he said. "To have my words written on a temple would be quite an honor."

"So what's your plan, Vale?" she asked, going back on topic. "You're just going to land right next to this super secret facility, take off with your female friend and then what? Walk up to Emissary Hooper and demand that he return Elias?"

He gave her a strange expression. "It is not that simple but yes, essentially."

She shook her head and sighed. "So, let me guess. You're not exactly a man of great soldiering skills, are you?"

"My duty is to my gods and my people," he said evasively. "The Adulos were only recently told to take up arms, but we will fight, if that is what you're asking. We are honor bound to fight for our gods. I will do whatever I am called to do in order to protect our people."

"Yeah, that's what I thought," she said, sighing. "Look Vale, you can fight and die for honor all you want, but you're going to do it a lot sooner than later if you're not trained properly."

"What do you mean?" he asked, cocking his head to one side.

She shrugged. "I mean that you're crazy if you think your plan will work. Getting your friend back from the clutches of Sector One's most powerful man? That's going to take some serious strategy, and I can already tell from the look on your face that you had no idea where to start with that. Not to mention Boone Hooper's house is the most fortified place on the planet right now. You'll be lucky to get a phone call in, let alone a troupe of insurgents with a vendetta. That's total madness. No tactical forethought in that at all."

"We are still unfamiliar with this sort of thing," he explained weakly. She stifled a laugh and stood up, flattening down the sides of her coat.

"You know," she said, smoothing her hair back, "I was going to come here to pump you for information. I thought I was dealing with some serious criminal mastermind. I mean, that talking corpse thing was pretty damn intimidating. I was worried, but you're not an evil genius; you're just an idealist with a fundamental approach to things. You know, we'll be landing in a few hours, and how convenient that we'll be right near a government facility. I'll just turn you over to them when we get there."

His face lost all expression, but eyes rippled with fear. "Taris, please don't do that. You don't understand."

"Oh I understand just fine, Mr. Teag," she said. "These complexes scare the hell out of you. But you hijacked my ship and killed my crew, and I'm afraid you'll have to answer for that. I know it's not what you had in mind but hey, was fun while it lasted, right?"

"You say that you're allowing us to land on Earth as though you have a choice in the matter," he said wryly. Her cheeks flushed red. She did not like to be challenged.

"Now you listen to me," she started, leaning against the chair. "As soon as we get to Earth I will walk off of this ship, find the nearest official and have you arrested. I will hand you off to them like yesterday's trash, and I will personally stand in the front row when they hang you as a terrorist."

Vale sat in front of her, unmoving. His hands were folded in his lap out of respect, but she felt like he was mocking her; that he was entertained rather than frightened.

"Would you like control of your ship back?" he asked calmly.

"Ah, now we're getting somewhere. Good Gray," she said. "That won't stop me from turning you in, of course, but it might help your case."

"It's simple, he said patiently. "It's all in your head, if you will. You could control this ship right now if you wanted to."

"That's a negative there, Gray," she said with a growling sneer. "You and your friends reprogrammed the damn computer systems with your stupid incomprehensible language characters. We don't know how to decipher it. No one ever has. So no; I can't break into the system because it's now operating in *freaking gibberish*."

He shook his head. "It would not be gibberish to you. Not if you accepted it, allowed yourself to understand it."

"*Will you stop saying that?*" she demanded. "I am not an Adulo. I've never been an Adulo. I grew up with normal parents in a normal neighborhood with normal kids, okay? I've had a normal life and I like it like that. Look, I have no problem with you people. Really I don't, but that doesn't mean I'm one of you. I'm just an ordinary woman with an average life."

"You may have had a normal upbringing, Taris," he said, "but you are far from ordinary."

"You don't know a thing about who - or what - I am," she said defensively. He cocked his head to the side, giving her that expression that he seemed to make only for her.

"Neither do you."

She wanted to go get a scrathe and zap him with it. She wanted him to feel pain, to justify her anger by watching him beg for mercy. She wanted to wipe that smug smile off of his face. But she couldn't do it. She couldn't bring herself to use that weapon on him. She could barely stand to think about it.

"You're not going to unlock the computer, are you?"

"No," he said honestly.

"Well, I guess I have no choice but to keep you locked up until we land. After that you become the United authority's problem," she said with resignation. The conversation had not gone as well as she had hoped.

Vale frowned, like she had managed to greatly frustrate him. That probably wasn't far from the truth. "What will you do with Christian?"

Oh, right. The doctor was locked up in the cell across the hallway, and she couldn't very well let him off just because he was human. "Same goes for him too, I guess. Hey, what does all of this have to do with Dr. Tomas?"

Vale's muscles relaxed and he sat back down on the bed. "I think it would be better if Christian himself explained it to you. His story is bound to pique your interest."

"I'm sure," she said. "Well you've been...moderately helpful. I'll see you in a few hours when we land. Hope you enjoy being locked up, because you're going to have to get used to it." She turned to leave, but something stopped her. Vale stood up, but she didn't turn around.

"If you hand me over to the authorities I will not be seeing a jail cell," he said quietly. "I doubt I will live beyond the tree line."

She paused at that. She knew he was right. She wanted to see him brought to justice, not dragged into the woods and shot like a lame animal. That's not to say that she didn't want to watch him die, of course. She hated him. She hated him for what he did to her crew, for the lives he took, for the position she was in and for the confusion about herself that she now faced. She loathed him and all that he did for the sake of his beliefs, but she did not want him killed unjustly. Allowing that would make her no less of a monster than he was. She realized that she had a lot to think about in the next few hours.

"What about my people, captain?" he asked softly after a moment. "The bodies of my dead. What will you do with them?"

"Oh. Well I guess I really haven't given them much thought, actually," she said, turning to face him.

Vale's expression fell, as though he were disappointed in her for that. "On Caleum we have a ceremony. It's a ritual involving cremating the dead and lifting their spirits up to the five heavenly planes. I know you cannot be expected to perform these rituals. However, when we land, if you would be so kind as to give the bodies to a Gray temple authority on Earth that would be most honorable. Regardless of what you think of me or what they did, I hope that you will allow the dead to rest in peace."

"I will make sure that the right thing happens, no matter what," she said honestly.

"I believe that," he said, "but I don't think you're quite sure what the right thing is at the moment. You have so much to learn, *a tarischa*. More than you know."

"Lucky for me I have some time to find out," she said. "Thanks for the help." She turned to go, but something stopped her.

"Taris?" he said gently, like he was looking for an excuse to stop her from leaving. Strangely, she was hoping he would. "Do you know what your name means in my language?"

She shook her head. "I don't know if I want to know."

"It means 'warrior'," he said quietly. "Warrior of the righteous."

"It means 'two paths' in my language," she said with a sad smile. "Huh. That's ironic. I don't suppose they can both be right, eh?"

Vale smiled, an expression that seemed rare on him. "Oh Taris. I have no doubt that they are."

WARNING! WARNING! HULL BREACH, AFT SECTION! ALERT! CAPTAIN TO THE BRIDGE! WARNING!

Hull breach. *Oh god, and we have no control of the ship!* Her thoughts turned entirely to panic. Vale turned to her, eyes wide.

"*What does that mean*?!" he said, yelling over the alert sirens.

"*It means we're all going to die!*" she screamed back.

Without explaining further, Taris tore out of the cell and sprinted down the hallway. She had to make it to the bridge.

She only hoped she could make it in time.

Chapter Fourteen

She tumbled out of the stairwell and onto the bridge, stumbling over her own feet to get to the helm. The Adulo gibberish was still displayed on all the screens, but she understood the warning and blinking angry red lights well enough. She saw the ship schematics on the digital screen. The aft section of the ship was covered in red warning signs. Panicked, she started punching buttons, hoping one of them would tell her what to do. She had to deploy the escape pods, she thought. She had to save the crew. Save the crew. Save Vale. That was all she could think of. Save the crew, save Vale.

No matter what button she touched, nothing changed. Frustrated, she slammed her fists down on the console. *"Sonofabitch! Work, damn you!"*

As soon as the words left her mouth, the warning stopped. The red lights stopped blinking and the console returned to the neutral green. Taris looked down at the console, then back at her hands, confused.

Then something brushed against her leg.

"Holy hell!" she yelped, jumping so high her head nearly hit the ceiling. A startled and red-faced Vinny peeked his head

out from under the helm, looking as frightening and surprised as she was.

"Vinny!" she gasped, trying to keep her heart from bursting out of her chest. "What the hell were you doing under there?!"

"Oh, hey captain," he said innocently. "I was just finishing some of the repairs to the structural damage of the bridge. You know, like you told me to?"

"Oh," she said, starting to calm down. "Right. Well we've got a problem. The ship has a hull breach in the aft section." She scrambled to decipher the interface, pushing keys at random.

He stood up slowly, wiping the grimy sweat from his brow. "No. No, we don't have an aft breach. That was me, actually."

"You?" she asked, freezing in her tracks. "What do you mean?"

Vinny looked sheepish. "Yeah. I was rewiring the central helm to the mainframe grid and…I may have crossed my wires."

"Oh. So we're not about to get sucked into space?" She laughed, mostly out of nerves than anything else. "Well that's a relief."

After she calmed down, she managed to tell Vinny a little about her conversation with Vale. The parts she felt like sharing anyway.

"So, the bastard talked for you, eh?" Vinny asked.

"He talked," she admitted, "but it wasn't all helpful. You know the Grays. They think everything they say is important, even if it doesn't make a damn bit of sense."

He scoffed and reached for a molecular stabilizer tool from his repair kit. "Yeah, I know. My mother had a Gray maid and she was always saying the strangest shit to me about stars and destiny and gods and stuff. They're weird as hell, man. Er, I mean, captain."

She waved off his mistake passively. *Oh yeah. I am the captain now*, she thought. *Huh. That's going to take some getting used to.* She cleared her throat and pushed that thought from her mind. "Wow, Lt. Tyler, this place looks great! Practically back to normal."

She was amazed at how efficient he had been. Despite the smell of death that still lingered in the air, the ship - or at least the bridge - looked just like it always did. Two helm consoles on a large, curved black desk faced the forward screen. The outer walls were lined with computer stations for communications, science scans, security, even a medical alcove for emergencies. In the middle of the room, with a bright touch screen console and a dropdown glass monitor, was the captain's chair. A chair she sat in very rarely. A chair that didn't quite feel as though it belonged to her yet. She touched the armrest gently. The feel of the black leather and hard metal seemed comfortingly familiar. Vinny had made quick work of restoring the ship to working order, but the repairs were entirely physical. They still couldn't access the mainframe or control the ship. He wriggled out from under the helm and she offered him a hand, helping him to his feet.

"Thanks boss," he said, sweat and grime staining his blue undershirt. "Been damn hard, though. I keep forgetting things, not knowing where I am, throwing fits for no reason." He pointed to a fist-sized hole in the wall near the elevator. "I'll uh, I'll fix that right up soon."

She hid a small smile. "Well at least you have an excuse for your outbursts. Mine are a la cart."

He nodded, unsure of how to answer her. "So," he said finally, "do you know how to deprogram that Gray gibberish yet? I'm ready to head to the nearest galactic base so we can execute the bastard. Legally, since you insist."

"Well that will have to wait," she answered. "And the answer to your question is no, I don't. But I do know where we're going at least."

"Well that's good I guess. I haven't been able to figure it out, either. Those symbols and stuff look like swirly nonsense to me."

"I know what you mean," she said. *Despite what some prisoners might insinuate…*

"So where are we headed, boss? Oh god, please tell me it's not to the surface of the sun or something."

"No," she assured him. "It's not that. We're headed to Earth actually. Sector One, if you can believe it."

His eyebrows shot up and he clapped his hands together. "Well hot damn, that's great! I guess we don't have to be too worried about regaining helm control. The eggheads will be thrilled. Apparently it's been really hard to have their brilliant brains be bested by a computer."

Vinny seemed to think it was fun to make fun of the scientists, calling them names and taunting them when things didn't go well. Natsumi thought it was endearing and Matt didn't seem to mind. It sure pissed Dave the hell off though, and she would rather he be in a charitable mood whenever possible.

"Where are the mad scientists right now, anyway?" she wondered.

Vinny started collecting his tools off the deck. "I sent them down to engineering to go tinker with Gareth. They were driving me nuts up here, talking about computer nonsense and being all fascinated with everything. It was making me crazy. I needed to be alone to work."

"Mmm. Personal space. I get you."

She sat down slowly, trying to push away the unsettling feeling that she couldn't seem to shake. The leather was worn and soft, but she still felt strange sitting in Captain Philip's chair. She still called it Captain Philip's chair. She sighed and looked at the screen. A strange feeling of emptiness crept over her as she watched the stars pass her by. The silent, twinkling lights surrounded her, bathed her in the beauty and majesty of space. She could see the blinking lights of other ships in the distance. Ships that she could not reach and could not flag down. She could only watch, screaming internally as they passed by around her, no more noticing her than they would notice a speck of floating dust. It was exasperating. They were a ghost ship. No matter what they did, people wouldn't see them as anything more than a shadow. The ship's ultimate design brilliance was also its downfall. Vinny must have been thinking the same thing, because he slammed his hand down on the console he just fixed.

"Those sons of bitches," he cursed. "They set this all up just to torture us. If we had access to communications we could flag any one of those ships down in seconds, but now? Now we have to mosey on down to Earth because some Gray jackass and some traitor doctor made it happen. Ugh! I'm so freaking pissed right now!"

"It's enough to drive you to drink," she said. He snapped his fingers at the suggestion.

"Exactly. You know, we were going to pick up some supplies when we came to get you, but with the no-fly thing it didn't work out. We don't have a drop of booze on this boat. What bad timing, huh?" he said, leaning against the side of her chair. She looked up at him.

"You people don't know me at all, do you?" She reached into her boot and pulled out a thin, long silver flask. A smile crept across his face.

"Oh Captain Bodil," he said. "I'd kiss you right now, if it doin' that wouldn't be such a huge breach in protocol, anyway."

She laughed. "A simple thanks works for me, LT." She unscrewed the top and the smell of the whiskey hit her nostrils. She sighed in appreciation and took a strong pull, wincing from the impact of the alcohol on her palate. She handed the flask to Vinny and he gulped down a few mouthfuls quickly.

"Whoo," he said, grimacing as he handed the flask back to her. "That's strong stuff."

She smiled. "The strong stuff is the only stuff I carry."

"I can appreciate that," he said, already seeming more relaxed. Together they watched the stars pass by on the screen, letting the whiskey warm their stomachs. Finally, after the alcohol burned away the unease, Taris sat up a little straighter and pulled the edges of her coat out from under her.

"Captain," he said softly, "why are you still wearing that coat?"

She looked down and touched the right cuff with the tips of her fingers. She had showered and was wearing clean clothes; the obligatory black and blue uniform with black boots, ID tags, a blue undershirt, and the fleet symbol on the sleeve. She'd even affixed the captain's rank to the shoulders. However, when she stood in the mirror, something seemed to be missing. The gray coat that she had been wearing called out to her. For reasons she could not explain she put it on and stood in the mirror again. That was when she felt complete. The oversized woolen coat that hung down to her knees, with big metal buttons and deep pockets. The coat that Dr. Tomas had given her on Earth. The coat that still had the blood of Captain Philip on the shoulders.

"I don't know," she said finally. "I guess it serves as a reminder of what I'm doing here. I feel like...I don't know. Like I have to wear it or something. For Captain Philip's sake. Does that make any sense?"

Vinny gave her a look like he didn't quite understand but nodded anyway. "Oh. Okay then, cap."

"Speaking of sentimental," she said, pointing to his overburdened work cart, "what's that pile of strange metal taking up space on your hover platform?" It didn't look like normal debris at all. It was shiny and reflected light, standing out amongst the burned and mangled metal scraps around it.

"Oh yeah. Those." Vinny strutted over to the platform and dragged it over. Upon closer inspection, she realized that it wasn't a pile of rubble at all.

"Are these swords?"

On top of a pile of otherwise useless items were three shiny metal broadswords. The base of the swords were formed strangely, as if smelted and then gripped while piping hot, molded to the exact grip of their owner. They weren't cut perfectly or even symmetrically. Indeed; it seemed as though every sword was a different shape and size from the others. The lengths of the blades were wavy and reflected light like a mirror. They were beautiful, almost like frozen fluid, each one coming to a razor sharp edge. She reached out and grabbed the nearest sone, wrapping her hand around the hilt. As soon as she touched the metal it came to life. It felt warm in her hands and responded to her touch like a ripple on a pond. It was agile to wield, light as a feather, too. And itchy.

Really itchy.

She'd only been holding the sword for a matter of minutes before her hands were red and irritated. Agitated, she tucked the sword in the crook of her arm and scratched her palms rigorously.

"What is this thing made of?" she wondered. "I think I'm allergic to it."

"Holy shit, captain," Vinny gasped. "How the hell did you do that?"

"Do what?" she asked. She managed a really good scratch and sighed in relief, holding the sword out in front of her to inspect it. She was barely gripping the hilt and she could still feel the itch coming on. "I just picked it up and my hands started itching. This sword is Taris-repellent."

Vinny shook his head. "Ma'am you've got some creepy way with Gray technology. I tried playing with those things for like twenty minutes and all it felt like was heavy, bulky metal."

"What?" She tossed the sword between both hands lightly, balancing the holding and the itching with a surprising amount of dexterity. "This thing weighs almost nothing."

His eyes grew wide in insult. "Like hell it does!" To prove this, he reached over and wrapped his paw-sized hands on one of the swords. Then he braced himself, legs apart, shoulders stiff. With one deliberate gesture he heaved the sword off the cart as the tip clanged noisily to the ground. He struggled with the sword as though it weighed a ton. She could actually see the sweat drip down his face as he strained with effort. At first she thought he was embellishing, but after a couple of minutes of watching his muscles nearly bulge out of his skin at the attempt to even raise the sword, she realized he was serious. She stared at the one in her hand. It couldn't be more than three, maybe four pounds at most. Lighter than a resonator pistol. So why the hell was he acting like the sword was made of lead?

Eventually Vinny lost his temper and released his death grip. A little too soon, as the sword clamored to the ground, but not before it slammed down on his foot. Vinny howled in surprise and pain, hopping on one foot as the sword rolled to a stop in front of the cart. Angry, he limped over and kicked the sword for emphasis. That was apparently a bad choice as well, and it sent him reeling into another storm of swears and strained whimpering.

"See?" he said, nursing his right foot. "It weighs like six hundred pounds."

She stifled a laugh and smiled. "Yes…it certainly appears that way."

"Well it does," he said defensively. "So the real question is, how the hell are you holding it like it's nothing?"

Good question. "Could just be this one," she offered. "Maybe that one's just really, really heavy and the one I'm holding isn't."

"Fine," he said, a little hurt that she wasn't taking him seriously. "Pick that other one up, then. I'm not going anywhere near it. Pick up the one on the floor and see for yourself."

"Fine," she said stubbornly. She got up from her chair and replaced one she was holding - she couldn't bear the itching anymore anyway - back on the platform. She could feel Vinny watching her, eyeing her as she bent down and wrapped her fingers around the sword that he couldn't lift. With almost no effort, she raised the sword with ease and placed it on top of the others.

"I told you, captain."

Unable to respond, she walked back to her chair and sat back down, wishing for a plausible explanation. Nothing came to mind.

Vinny, however, was full of opinions. "I knew it. There's something weird with you and Gray stuff. You're strong, but you're not that strong." She looked at him to answer when she saw the look in his eye. The words caught themselves in her throat.

She knew that look.

It was one of confusion and distrust. He was staring at her like he was seeing her for the first time. It was a look she did not appreciate in the slightest. Uncomfortable, and itching her palms to the point of breaking skin, she shot the swords an unwelcome look and decided she'd had enough of Gray stuff ruining her life for one day.

"Lt. Tyler, put those in the armory," she said dismissively. She wanted them out of her sight as soon as possible.

He nodded. "You got it, captain. But do we really need to keep them? What dya think we'll need 'em for?"

"We could need them for something I guess," she said flatly. "We'll be able to study them, maybe? Whatever, I don't know. Perhaps we ought to put them with the bodies of the dead Grays," she mused.

Vinny laughed and gripped the handles of the hover platform that he was using to hold his mountain of tools and salvageable debris. "Well that's going to be hard, ma'am."

"Why?" she asked.

"Because I already put the Gray bodies in the incinerator and tossed the ashes out an airlock."

She jumped up from her chair. "*You did what*?!"

His eyebrows shot up. "Uh…yeah."

"Why did you do that?" she demanded.

Vinny shrugged. "We needed the room. The morgue is filled with our guys, what the hell was I supposed to do?"

"You're *supposed* to consult me first. I would never have allowed that. Those Grays were going to be cremated with their people, not incinerated and jettisoned into space! Christ, Vinny why did you do that?"

"Captain Philip would have *told* me to do that," he argued.

"Yeah well he's not in charge anymore is he? I'm the captain now, and from now on you go though me, do you understand?!"

"Jesus, what is it with you and these Grays?" he snapped. "It's like you're protecting them or something! Taris if I didn't know any better, I'd say you have a soft spot for these terrorists."

"What I do and how I think is my business. It was my choice to honor their dead, Vinny. I am the authority on this ship and I will not have my word or my orders questioned. Oh, and you *will* address me as captain in an official setting. *Do you understand me, lieutenant?*"

Vinny's face burned bright red with anger. Resentfully, he came to attention. "Yes, captain. I'm sorry. Forgive me for speaking out of line," he said stiffly. She wanted to keep yelling at him, but she knew it would do no good. With a resigning sigh she shook her head.

"Lt. Tyler, thank you. And I apologize for snapping at you. It's been a difficult few days." She made a gesture of dismissal and his demeanor relaxed.

"I understand captain. Or I would I guess, if I could remember what happened the last few days," he said sadly.

"Is it because of the emergency neuroreconstruction device?" she asked with a worried frown.

He nodded. "Yeah. I mean, I get that they had to use it, but not knowing what happened to you or how you ended up there? It sucks, captain."

"I'll bet," she said, taking another pull from her flask. "Maybe you should see a doctor."

"Yeah," he agreed. "Too bad the Grays killed the doctor and the only other one on this ship is in the brig."

"Speaking of him," Taris said with resentment in her tone, "he's next on my list of shitty things I have to deal with today."

"Do you think he's ready to talk now?"

She shrugged. "Guess I'll find out." She stood up and stretched, shaking her shoulders clear of anxiety when Vinny's massive frame stood in front of her.

"Captain." He spoke quietly as though to avoid someone hearing him, even though they were alone. "I need to say that I don't like you interrogating the prisoners by yourself."

She sighed. "I'll be fine, Lt. Tyler."

"I only mean," he continued, "that they're tricky. The Gray speaks in strange circles, like he's trying to be honest without being upfront, you know? I don't like that. It's like a lie...only sneakier. And I don't even know what the doctor's deal is. I threatened that guy up and down and he still wouldn't budge. Short of torturing him--"

"Which I will not allow you to do," she pointed out. "Humans aren't tortured on any United authority ship, Vinny. You know that."

"Yeah I know that, cap," he said dismissively, "But I don't think you're going to get him to talk. I couldn't, and I tried everything."

He'll talk for me, she thought. *I know he well.* "Well, I've got to give it a shot."

"I just don't like it, captain. Even if you get them to talk, who knows if they'll even tell you the truth? Plus…" He hesitated.

"Plus?" she repeated.

Vinny winced. "Plus I think they might have done something to you."

She raised her eyebrows. "Done something?"

"I know it sounds crazy," he said in a deep and serious tone, "but think about it. I mean…we all saw the scrathe. We saw that it hurt you, captain. Everyone knows those aliens have some sort of strange magical powers or something. What if the Gray hypnotizes you with his creepy eyes? Made you think the scrathe was burning you? What if he put a spell on you?"

She hid a smile. "I don't think the Grays have magical powers, Lt. Tyler. Especially not the power of hypnosis. That kind of stuff is largely myth--"

"And what about the doctor?" he interrupted, his train of thought unbroken. "He had a hundred opportunities to slip something to you. Make your body respond to the scrathe or whatever. He could have planned this all along, to make you weak and easily controllable."

She frowned. "I don't think that's true. I mean, if he was poisoning me, wouldn't he have poisoned Gareth as well? The scrathe would have hurt him too and it didn't."

"We don't know that," Vinny argued. "It didn't get anywhere close to him. He's a doctor! God knows what kind of medical stuff he has access to, you know?"

"Vinny," she said gently. "I really appreciate the concern, I do, but don't think I was brainwashed, or drugged or anything like that."

His hands dropped to his sides, and a strange look darkened his expression. "Well…what other reason could there be then?"

Vale can give you one, she thought bitterly, *but it's impossible. It has to be.* She thought quickly.

"You know, I think I heard about a defective model of scrathe that was just made," she lied. She didn't even know why she lied, just that she felt like she had to. "I heard that it accidently produces an electromagnetic field that also attacks certain humans. Was the scrathe that you used new?"

Vinny's eyebrows raised in surprise. "Actually yeah."

She shrugged. "Well there you have it. It's probably a defective model. We'll trade it in and get you a new one when we land."

"Okay," he said, sounding more confident in that. "But just to be certain, don't look the Gray in the eyes. Or accept anything from the doctor. Especially food or drink. Just to be safe."

She nodded. "I won't. Thanks, Vinny."

"You got it captain. Oh and um, I'm sorry. You know, for shocking you and everything. I really didn't mean to," he said remorsefully.

"I know," she said quickly. "And don't worry about it. Accidents happen." She didn't want to have that conversation with Vinny just yet. She knew he wasn't saying a lot. She could see it in his eyes when he looked at her. Suspicion. Reservation. Confusion. Even though he didn't dispute her shallow explanations, she knew, deep down, that it wasn't enough. *It would have to be enough for now*, she decided.

After all, she had bigger problems.

Chapter Fifteen

"It's no accident that we met, Taris. I truly believe that everything happens for a reason. Your ship was the ship that I was meant to be on," Christian Tomas said in a deep but serious tone.

She sighed and leaned back in her chair, arms folded in front of her. "Oh you've got to be kidding. When did this become a spiritual thing for you?"

"'The wicked will fold to the warriors of the righteous', as the temple masters say," Dr. Tomas said as though she should know what that meant. "It was fate. Pure and simple. The gods knew I needed to meet you."

There was that headache again. Taris rubbed her temple slowly, trying to push the pain back down. "Oh god. And you looked so normal at the emissary's reception. And what's with this 'gods' thing, as in plural?"

"The gods are the Five Divinities who protect the five tribes of Adulo," he answered gently. "Of course, you would know that if you saw the Grays as anything other than cattle."

"So, you're not a Gray, but you pray to their gods?" she asked.

"The gods aren't just the gods of the Adulos, Taris. They're the protectors of life."

"Okay, whatever," she said dismissively. "Well it was no accident we ended up here, that's true. It's your friend Vale's fault."

"I know," he said with a strange smile. "I knew about the plot to attack the emissary's mansion. I was there to make sure everything went according to plan."

"Of course you were," she said. "So what is your mission?"

"My job was to make sure the message was received. It was a risk, but it was one I was willing to take."

"Well, well. Look who's finally willing to talk?" she said dryly. "Vinny said you were the stone he couldn't squeeze blood from."

Christian folded his arms. "Well of course I'm willing to talk to you. You're important to Vale. That makes you important to me."

She felt her cheeks flush at that. Important to Vale. The idea of it excited her, and infuriated her at the same time. Embarrassed, she tried to push her feelings down, although that seemed to make her cheeks even hotter. She wasn't there to be the object of Vale Teag's eye, she was there to be Captain Bodil.

"Just don't waste my time," she said abrasively. "So why are you doing this? What's in it for you?" She sat forward and rested her arms on her legs. "Really Christian, what kind of dog do you have in this fight?"

He looked up at her, his deep brown eyes filled with pain. "My wife."

She almost fell out of her chair. "Come again? You're *married*?"

"I am married," he said slowly. "To an Adulo."

Married. To an Adulo. Realization washed over her. "Oh, so that's why you didn't flirt with me when we first met."

He scoffed. "Yeah, I'm sure that's the only reason."

She brushed that off. "You do realize that marriage between a Gray and a human is illegal, right? The law clearly states that marriage is between two consenting *human* adults."

"That is an outdated law," he said with an edge in his tone. "It has no basis in modern reality. It was written long before we even knew about the Grays."

"People don't want to change it," she said. "Humans think the laws of marriage need to be defined by our ancestors for some reason, not logic and reality."

"That's a reason, not an excuse," the doctor argued. "And I don't accept it. My wife and I might not be married by Earth standards, but we're married in the eyes of the Five on Caleum, and that's all that matters."

Taris saw the pieces start to fall together. The rendezvous on the moon, being friends with Vale, the big plan for the big Adulo cause. The doctor's story was all starting to make sense. "Let me guess. Your wife's name is Jyrisa."

His eyes grew big. "Well yes, actually. How did you know that?"

Taris sat back in her chair. "Vale told me that you were going to meet her at the complex's unlicensed landing pad. She's putting her life at risk for this rendezvous I hear, even if she is surrounded by dozens of your little Silencium fighters. I understand *Vale's* motivation in all this, but if she is *your* wife--"

"Then I would go to the depths of hell and back to keep her safe," he finished with strength in his tone. "And I swear to the Five that I will, captain."

She saw the sadness that creased his painfully handsome face, the passionate desperation that seeped into every part of him. It reflected a genuine love, wrapped in longing and loss. She knew, in that one look, that he was telling the truth.

"I believe you," she said quietly. A ghost of a smile formed on his lips, but not without reservation.

"You believe me, but do you want to *help* me?" he asked. "Because from here I sit Taris, you're the only one standing between me and saving my wife. I really don't want to have to go through you to get her. But I will."

"Don't make threats to me, Dr. Tomas," she said in even tones, "because I am not the type that hesitates. I'm good at making fast, hard choices."

"Good," he said. "Then maybe you will make the right choice and help me. My wife takes a great risk in coming out into the open to meet with us and I will *not* let her be captured."

"You have no idea the weight of that request," she said seriously. "Helping you means helping Vale, who is currently the most wanted fugitive in the universe. Helping you means putting the remaining few members of my crew - and a few traveling scientists - at greater risk than they already are."

"I know what I'm asking you to do is dangerous," he said. "But would I ask it if I thought there was any other way? No. I'm not asking you to do something you'll regret. I'm asking you to do something that you would regret *not* doing."

"Oh god here we go," she grumbled. "Is this the part where you try to convince me to commit treason just to save your wife? Come on, now."

"You would do it," he said quietly. "If you knew love the way I know love, you would do it."

His words stung her deeply, though he had only meant to illustrate his point. She understood what he was saying more than he knew. Nothing could stop her from protecting the ones she loved. Nothing at all.

"Well I guess it's good for me that I don't have that kind of love, Christian," she said tersely. "Seems like a pain in the ass to me."

He looked up at her. "You use sarcasm to protect yourself, but it's a veil. I can see that. Look, Taris, I know you're a woman of honor. I know that *you* know the slave trade is wrong. You know that these complexes are wrong. You know that turning their planet into our waste dump is wrong. It's all wrong."

She didn't respond. Mostly because he was right and she didn't want to give him the satisfaction of hearing it. She was never really good at hiding her emotions, though. She knew her concession was displayed all over her face.

Christian took that as a sign to go on. "Look, I'm appealing to the humanitarian in you. The one that always stands up for what she thinks is right. Even when she stands alone. The rebel who still fights, even when the odds are not in her favor."

"Words are not enough to get me to abandon my military career and take up arms with terrorists, Christian," she responded. "I can see what you're doing here. It won't work. You're right about a couple of things though. I don't think the slave trade is right, and I am an honorable woman. However, you and I both know that's not enough."

He was silent for a moment, just staring at her. His eyes travelled down to her wrist, still black from the scrathe burn. Embarrassed, she adjusted her wristband to cover it, pushed her sleeves down, and glared at him.

"What?" she said in a challenging tone.

"Don't you want to know, captain?" he asked, pointing to her arm. "Don't you want to know why the scrathe burned your flesh?"

Oh hell no, she thought. *We're not going there, guy. I'm not losing control of this conversation if it kills me.* "No."

"Don't you want to know why they always mistake you for an Adulo?" he pressed. "I heard them speak to you. At the reception, they asked you if you were a Gray. Even Vale asked you. I bet that happens to you all the time, doesn't it?"

"I know what you're doing, and it's not going to work."

He continued, undaunted. "There's a reason for that and you know it. You know you're different. You've always known, but you just deny it. It's easier to lie to yourself."

She'd heard enough. "Don't make me shoot you, doc. I've never been a fan of incapacitating a medical officer, but you should know that I'm not above it."

"You're more than just a spaceship captain," he said, standing slowly. "You're so much more and you don't even know it. You've had the question in front of you the whole time.

Your whole life. But you can't face it, can you? Well it's time to face it. Face the truth. Go on, face it. *Camme sans supre Adulo, Taris?*"

"Okay, that's it." She jumped out of her seat and stood in front of him, pushing him against the wall as she held him by the scruff of his shirt. She was so close that she could see the veins on his temples throbbing.

"Boy, you just don't know how to take a hint, do you?" she said sternly, glaring at him.

"That's the pot calling the kettle black," he responded stiffly.

She rolled her eyes. "Good god. No wonder you've been divorced twice."

"I regret nothing," he said with bravado, "if it keeps my wife from being captured. Those complexes are torture chambers. I will not let her be caught."

"Pissing me off is not the most direct route to helping your wife," she said. "And don't be so dramatic. You don't know they're torture chambers."

"Yes I do," he insisted, emotion rising his tone. "I used to work for a clinic outside of one of them. We had spies sent in. They gave their lives for the intel they got inside that place. The things they're doing in there...it's unspeakable, Taris."

"If you wanted my help you're not going to get it this way," she said. "Driving me into an emotional corner is not going to make an ally out of me."

"You have to do something," he pleaded. "You know it's wrong. You know it. You have to help. Please, Taris."

"Captain," she corrected. "Captain Bodil."

"Please Captain Bodil," he said. "Arrest me, kill me, do whatever you want, but please. Please let me save my wife first."

"Well you should have thought of that, doc," she said calmly. "You crossed a thin gray line just now. I am about two seconds away from kicking your ass for it."

"What did you say?" His tone and his expression changed. He seemed thrown off guard, genuinely surprised by her words. "A thin gray line?" he repeated. "Why did you say it like that?"

That made her pause. She didn't know why she'd said it like that. It seemed normal until he pointed it out. Now she was self-conscious about it. "Don't question me, doc," she spit out.

"Taris, listen to me. Don't turn your back on this, please. Just give me one more chance to plead my case to you. One chance."

"Fine," she said, releasing her grip. "Give me one damn reason why I should even consider helping you. And be quick. I didn't sleep well last night and I'm starting to get a headache. My patience is wearing thin."

As soon as the words left her mouth his entire expression changed. A light went off in his head, like she just inadvertently solved an internal puzzle. "If you help me," he said excitedly, "I can help you find the answers to the dreams you have."

Her breath caught in her throat. "What?"

"You have dreams, don't you?" he said, his gaze locked onto hers. "I hear the Grays talking about it. They say that's a symptom. 'A phantom of the true form', as they say."

She rubbed her temples irritably. "What are you talking about?"

"Do you have crazy reoccurring dreams you can't explain?" he asked.

All the color drained from her face. "How in the *hell* did you know that?" she demanded.

Christian's eyes bored into hers, filled with intensity and urgency. "Vale is a dream walker in trade. He knows all about that."

"You didn't answer my question, doctor."

"Let us go," he countered. "Let me live to save my wife, and I swear to you that you will get the answers to the questions you have about your dreams."

She advanced on him, ready to start demanding answers, her face hard with steely resolve. She was about to start taking things to a more aggressive level when something stopped her. A feeling. No, it was more than that. It was an instinct. Something was wrong. Someone was hurting, scared. Someone needed help. Christian was studying her, eyes wide in interest.

"You can feel it, can't you?" he asked softly. "You can feel the others of your kind. The whispers of the soul. You can feel Vale."

Yes, that was it. It made sense the moment he said it. It was a rumbling, horrifying feeling that crept into her mind. Into her heart. She could feel anguish and pain and fear and righteous anger, and it was all coming from the Gray. It was all so fast and confusing. All she knew was that she was, somehow, impossibly connected to Vale.

And he was in danger.

Chapter Sixteen

She tore out of the doctor's cell, propelled by a desperate need. She crossed the length of the hallway in one leap, pressed her hand against the door and yanked it open. Vale was crumpled in the corner, covered in sweat and black scrathe burns, his silver hair matter to his head. Standing above him, panting from exertion, was Vinny. The scrathe whip was still in his hands, just recently discharged. Vale, covered in a sheet of sweat and shaking from pain, lifted his glinting, pained eyes to her. For the first time, she saw a raw, genuine emotion on his face.

It was relief. *Oh gods, Taris…*

Her heart leapt into her throat. "Vale."

Vinny swung around, eyes wide and crazy. Before he could stop her, she jumped in front of him, shielding Vale with her body. Lt. Tyler's eyes grew wide with confusion and anger. Quickly he raised the whip back up, poised to strike. *Oh no*, she thought, *not again. Please not that again.*

"Vinny, what the *hell* do you think you're doing?" she demanded.

"Step away from him, ma'am!" Vinny said, his voice strained in delirious emotion. "He's a madman! A brainwashing, religious nutjob! Don't look into his eyes! He'll hypnotize you!"

"Lt Tyler, stand back right now." She pushed Vale farther behind her.

"Captain, what are you doing?" His face was red with exertion and emotion. He looked like a madman. She shielded Vale with her body, spreading her coat around him like a cloak. If Vinny was going to scrathe them, she was going to make damn sure that she got the brunt of the hit.

"Fleetman Tyler," she said with severity, "step back and turn your scrathe off immediately, or I will make this your cell and not Vale's. Stand down. Now."

Vinny froze. For a horrifying moment she thought he might defy her. Terrified, she braced for impact. Then, at the last second, a respite from his lunacy broke through. He dropped his hands to his sides and took several steps backward. His face showed nothing but confusion, mistrust, and just a hint of residual anger. Before he could change his mind she yanked the scrathe out of his hand, opened the door and threw it into the hallway.

"I don't want that thing to come into this cell ever again," she told him. "As a matter of fact, I don't want that thing on my *ship*. As soon as we land, you're getting rid of it."

"But captain--"

"I said you're getting rid of it," she said in a tone that did not offer objection. "All of them. There will be no more scrathes on this ship. Period."

Vinny, disoriented and confused, managed to nod mechanically. "Um, yes. Okay, captain. Whatever you say. Sorry, what did you say? I'm having trouble…remembering things…"

"Damn it," she swore, stroking her temples in frustration. "Stupid memory loss. They need to make neuroreconstruction devices with fewer side effects."

"Taris," Vale said in a weak voice. "You came back for me."

She gave Vinny one more glaring look and then fell to her knees by Vale's side. He was badly hurt. He must have taken at least three direct lashes from the whip, she guessed. There were lines of black striping almost all exposed areas of his otherwise perfect skin.

"We've got to get you up," she said, avoiding his gaze. Looking into his eyes would only distract and confuse her, and she couldn't afford to be either of those things at that moment. Quietly, she pulled him up to a sitting position. When he seemed able enough to hold himself up, she yanked the bed sheet off the cot and wiped the sweat - and blood - from his face. He winced only a few times, but she could see he was working fiercely to control his reaction. If it had been her, she would have been sobbing.

"Vale," she said, finally finding her voice through a sea of emotions. His were no longer in her head, but that didn't make it any less confusing. Gently, she dabbed the sweat from his neck with the sheet. "I am so sorry. I had no idea, I swear."

"I know," he said, placing a gentle hand on her hers. Her hand stopped moving, cradled in his touch. She held it there, frozen, unsure of what to do next but unwilling to be the first to break away. "I could sense your surprise. Your confusion," he said.

That made her uncomfortable. It hadn't occurred to her that the emotion-sensing could go both ways. She finished cleaning him up and then wrapped her arm around his waist, helping him to the bed. Relieved, but still shaking, he sat down slowly and leaned against the side of the wall for support.

"Vinny," she barked. "Go to the medic station and get some pain ointment and bandages."

"But captain I--"

"I said now, lieutenant." Without more objection, Vinny walked out of the room mechanically, a befuddled expression on his face.

"If I had known...I would never have let this happen to you," she insisted when they were alone.

Vale gave her a strange smile, like he knew a secret that was too clever to share. "You wouldn't have done this to anyone, my warrior," he said gently. "You never could."

He looked at her, the liquid of his eyes shifting like waves. His lips curved in the smallest of smiles, head cocked ever so slightly to the side. It was that strange expression he gave her, the one that made her feel like he was seeing those things about her that no one could see. With the softest of strokes and the most innocent of intentions, Vale reached up and brushed a strand of her hair away from her face. He tucked it behind her left ear, sweeping one finger down the side of her cheek in the motion. It was such a quick, delicate touch, but in that moment, something changed in her. She felt drawn to Vale, in a strange, complicated, inexplicable way. She was almost ashamed of it, the way he made her feel. Suppressing the enormous smile that threatened to surface, she reached up and touched her cheek where his touch still lingered on her skin.

"Thank you," he whispered, "for walking the thin gray line for me."

"That phrase," she mused. Why did that keep getting brought up? "I said, well that is, I had a conversation with the doctor about that. About the thin gray line."

Vale's eyebrows raised. "Oh? And how did it go?"

"Hard to say," she said. "I got interrupted by this overwhelming sense of dread." She gave him the you-know-what-I-mean look. She did not want to openly admit that she could *sense* Vale's emotions. It was confusing enough to experience, let alone to try and explain it out loud.

Vale took a deep breath and ran his hands through his short silver hair. "Ah yes. That. Well it appears that you have a lot that needs explaining to you."

"She's not the only one," Vinny said from the doorway. He tossed the bandages and ointment at her feet with force. The temporary respite from his irrational anger had apparently ended. Rage Vinny was back, and he was looking for a fight. *Show time*, she thought. She stood up and took several slow, careful steps until she was standing directly in front of him. She positioned herself between Vinny and Vale, blocking Vinny's view of the Gray. Just in case.

"So, you're into coddling the enemy now?" he asked condescendingly. "Or is this a good cop, bad cop thing you didn't tell me about."

"Lt. Tyler," she said in a controlled tone, "would you like to explain what you were doing in here?"

"Scrathing the prisoner, Taris," he answered plainly. "I mean…lieutenant."

Her calm reserve threatened to break with every word he spoke. "Captain," she corrected. "I'm the captain now. I know it's hard for you to remember, but try and keep that in mind."

Vinny's face widened into a feigned apologetic smile. "Oh yes, *Captain* Bodil. I remember now. I keep forgetting everyone's dead. Just like how you seem to keep forgetting *who killed them*." He glanced over her shoulder at Vale, a wicked gleam in his eye.

Taris resisted the urge to punch him square in the jaw. "I don't appreciate your tone *or* your insinuation, lieutenant."

"And I don't appreciate you treating the murderer like a victim!" he countered. "I mean hell, you're willing to sell him, but you're not willing to punish him for killing innocent people? What the hell, cap?"

She put her hands on her hips like she was scolding an unruly child. "What? Sell him? Why would I sell him? What would give you that stupid idea?"

Vinny furred his brow. "Wait…so we're not taking him to the complex to be processed?"

"Ha! No, lieutenant. That's a big negative."

"Then why is he still alive?" Vinny asked, genuinely confused. "I mean, if we're not getting paid then we should throw this silverback out an airlock."

She stood back, appalled. His use of the derogatory word "silverback" for a Gray was exceptionally unsettling. The fact that he had implied they should murder Vale was downright maddening.

"Why would you think that I would want to sell Vale?" she asked suspiciously. "Aside from the fact that you know I'm against the slave trade, it's illegal for anyone in uniform to wrangle Grays. You know that. Using United fleet ships is an even bigger offense."

"I know," he said, "I just thought that you'd finally come around."

"Come around?" she asked. "You think people just 'come around' to the idea of slavery?!"

"Gareth hasn't told you already?" Vinny asked, folding his arms. "Wow. I'm shocked. I really thought he'd have said something to you at this point."

"Told me what?" she prompted.

"About the slave wrangling here on Intrepid," he explained.

She laughed. "That's ridiculous. There's no slave wrangling on this ship. Clearly you're delusional. Must be another effect of the neuroreconstruction."

"I'm not crazy," he argued defiantly. "It's been going on for years. I should know. It was my job to wrangle them."

He was deadly serious. There was no crazy look in his eye, no confusion in his tone. Her smile faded. "What? But that's impossible. I've been working on this ship for over three years and I've never seen a single Gray on this ship until Vale showed up."

"Well yeah," Vinny said with a shrug, "and you wouldn't. We only traded when you weren't around."

She shook her head, restraining her anger. Either he was lying to make her lose her temper, or he was telling the truth and she really would lose her temper. "Why would you do that, Lt. Tyler? It makes no sense."

"Yeah it does. We wanted to make money and you'd never stand for it," he explained. "Your father has some deal with the government that made it impossible for you to be transferred so we just found a way around it."

Her heart started thumping angrily. "And what proof do you have of this, lieutenant?"

"Actually Taris…I am the proof."

She spun around. She'd almost forgotten Vale was there. "When we were taken on board," the Gray said, "your Lt. Tyler here was the one who tried to wrangle me. He happened to mention that I was his twenty-seventh capture. He might have been boasting, but I am sure that number is not far from true."

Vinny brightened. "You're my twenty-seventh? Well hot damn that's great! At thirty I get a special award as a frequent wrangler."

"Wait a minute," she said. "Are you telling me that my crew has been participating in the illegal slave trade? Behind my back? For *years*?"

Vinny nodded. "Proudly, ma'am. We're a top wrangler for the Hammerhead complex, actually. Quite an honor."

Hammerhead. Didn't Vale say they were headed to Hammerhead? "This is unbelievable."

He shrugged. "Ask Gareth. You trust him, right? He'll tell you. I'm shocked that guy actually managed to keep his trap shut about it all this time."

She felt like someone had punched her in the stomach. Blinded by her need for information, she pressed on. "How did you get away with this?" she asked. "How did you do this behind Captain Philip's back?"

"Behind his back?" Vinny repeated, incredulous. "The wrangling was his idea. He commissioned us to the task."

"No," she said quietly. "That is not true."

Vinny raised his hands. "I swear it! He was the one who ran the show! He had a deal with Emissary Hooper. The Hammerhead is owned by Boone's company. He got the Grays for a good price and we made good money. You know the fleet pay isn't terrific. Any little bit helps, you know? This deal has been solid for years."

She balled her fists, but did not lose her cool. He was her fleetman, and she was his captain. She would not show him how much his words angered her. "Captain Philip was a good man," she said through gritted teeth. "He would *never* allow this. He would never treat the Grays like that."

Vinny's anger raged to a boil. "You know, these last few days you've been really damn weird, you know that? You went from a grumpy drunk to some sort of freedom-fighter-loving weirdo, with your band of geeky merry men."

She rolled her eyes. "Are you calling the mad scientists 'merry men'? Have you *met* Dave?"

"Whatever," he said angrily. "My point is that you've changed. You're totally unpredictable, you keep getting emotional, crazy things keep happening around you. I can't even tell which side you're on anymore!"

"I'm one of the good guys," she said calmly. "Do you know which side *you're* on, lieutenant?"

"You think you're on the right side?" he said, eyeing her suspiciously. "Well then how come this silverback is still sitting here after he viciously murdered our whole crew, including your beloved captain? Why isn't he a corpse floating in space by now?"

"Because it is not our place to decide what to do with him," she countered. "I told you, we're not at liberty to execute him. It's not our right or our responsibility. That's something for the United Authority Tribunal to decide."

Vinny's smile grew darker. "Oh yeah? Putting his fate in the hands of the Tribunal, eh? Well that's a crock. You might as well ship him straight to the complex. It will save time."

That was a strange response, even for Rage Vinny. "What do you mean?"

"The Tribunal is responsible for discipline and order in the sectors," he pointed out. "They are in charge of regulating the entire slave population. Who do you think created and commissioned the complexes in the first place?"

Her eyes grew wide. He was right. It all made sense. But that meant… "Oh my god," she gasped. "All those Grays on Earth. The ones being rounded up by the United authority. All those scared people. They're all--"

"Going to the complexes most likely," Vinny said flippantly. "What, you really thought they'd give the Grays due process? They're not even classified as *people*. They fall into the 'property' category. And you can't torture property, now can you?"

She was speechless. Vinny's eyes were full of hate, but his words rang of truth. She thought about how the doctor described the complexes, and the look on Vale's face when he mentions them. Horror. Fear. Hell.

"I don't believe this," she said finally.

Vinny flexed his muscles. "Believe it. The Tribunal will give your buddy here a one way ticket to the cleansing chambers, so if you're not going to kill him, you might as well sell him. That way we get rid of this trash and make some money. I mean, he's nothing but a short-haired silverback. Who the hell cares what happens to him?"

The words left her mouth before she could stop them. "I do."

He glared at her. "Then you're an idiot. He's just property, Taris. A thing. Something to be used and traded but not loved. The sooner you start seeing it that way, the better it will be for everyone."

That did it. "Lieutenant Vincenzo Tyler," she said, standing up straight. "You are hereby relieved of duty."

His mouth dropped. "What?!"

"Effective immediately, you are confined to quarters."

"Confined to quarters?! But that's--"

"Your permission to speak freely is revoked," she said. She reached up and removed his rank from his shoulders in two swift gestures. "You are to remain in isolation until such time as you are authorized release by the ranking officer of this ship. That's me, in case you forgot. Again."

"Captain, you can't--"

"Fleetman Vinny Tyler," she said sternly. "You will now walk out of this cell and report to your quarters and you will not leave unless you are authorized to do so. Is this understood?"

"Yes, but captain. Please. Don't do this," he pleaded.

"You're dismissed, fleetman."

"But--"

"I said *you're dismissed*."

Dumbfounded and speechless, Vinny turned on heel and marched out of the room. She listened to the sounds of his receding footsteps until long after they'd gone. She stood so still and so quiet for so long that she wasn't even sure how much time had passed.

"That was a brave thing you did, *tarischa*," Vale said gently, coming to a strenuous stand. Already the scrathe burns from the whip were starting to fade on his alabaster skin, but he was still shaking. Kindly, he placed a jittery hand on her shoulder. "It could not have been easy to face that kind of deception from someone you trusted so much."

The tears brimmed in her eyes, but they weren't for Vinny. They weren't even about the slave trade. This was something much deeper and more personal. And much angrier.

"My heart isn't broken yet," she whispered. "But it's about to be."

She didn't want to have to explain that. Something told her she didn't have to. She looked over her shoulder at Vale. With the slightest of gestures he nodded, as if to say he understood what she had to do now. That he supported her. That he stood by her. Without further explanation, Taris turned and walked out of the cell. She felt numb. She wasn't even sure what was propelling her feet to move. Mechanically she felt her steps taking her to the person she was searching for. The one she needed to confront.

The person who hurt her most of all.

She opened the door to Engineering, and there he was. Surrounded by friends, laughing and joking. Oblivious, as though nothing was wrong. Natsumi and Dave saw her first, but their friendly expressions dissolved to worry and fear when they saw the look on her face. Matt was clear across the room, absorbed in some sort of junk pile of old spare parts. And there was Sergeant Gareth Hoble. Cradling a cup of tea and looking over some schematic tablets at his desk. Pleasantly, he smiled and waved her in.

She stormed across the length of the room, overturned the desk and slapped Gareth clear across the face.

Chapter Seventeen

"How dare you," she spat out. Gareth stood frozen in front of her, mouth open in terrified shock.

"Captain!" Natsumi gasped.

"What the hell?" Dave said, standing up.

"Did she just hit him?" Matt asked, peeking out from a pile of bolts, shoving his scanning spectacles back up the bridge of his nose. Within seconds she had an audience. She didn't care.

"Captain Bodil," Gareth squeaked out, holding his face with his hand, "what in the bloody hell was that for?"

"Why didn't you tell me this ship was in the slave trade?!" she demanded. His expression changed instantly. It went from one of shock and victimization to that of absolute shame and remorse.

"Oh captain," he said quietly. "I am so very sorry."

"Oh you're sorry? You're sorry?!" She grabbed him by the collar and shoved him against the wall. "You lied to me! You've been wrangling Grays illegally for years? How could you do that, Gareth?"

"No!" he exclaimed. "No, not me! I never participated! I wouldn't even take a cut of the profits!"

"So you just let it happen, then? That's even worse!"

"I wanted to tell you a thousand times but I couldn't!" he said quickly, hands up in surrender. "They made me swear not to! On pain of death I couldn't tell you."

"And you fell for that?" she exclaimed. "It was a scare tactic, idiot! You had a thousand times to tell me what was going on. When we were on away missions. Docked at space ports. For god's sake, you could have mentioned it before we walked into Boone Hooper's mansion!"

"It wasn't just a scare tactic," he said, his voice hoarse. "I tried to tell you. Several times. Remember that time I broke my nose 'falling down a flight of stairs'? Or the time both my arms were crushed in that horrible 'engineering accident'? Or the time a vat of toxic chemicals 'accidentally' fell on my legs?"

That gave her pause. "I thought you were just clumsy."

Tears welled in the Welshman's eyes. "Not hardly. And those were just for the times I had failed at telling you. They said the next time I tried they wouldn't just stop with my legs. I had to stay silent, Captain Bodil. I just had to."

"No," she said, her voice thick with emotion. "You were just too scared to keep trying."

"Taris," Dave said, interjecting from behind her. "Don't do this to him. The boy was scared. You would have been, too."

"I didn't ask for your opinion, Major Schuler," she snapped, keeping her eyes focused on Gareth.

"I know you didn't," he continued, undaunted. "But I think you need to hear it. Sergeant Hoble was in a very bad position in sounds like. Respectfully captain, I don't think you're giving him the chance to defend himself."

"Also you slapped him," Natsumi added. "So I'm thinking you're pretty upset. You probably need to calm down."

"You're damn right I'm pissed!" She swung around and pointed a finger at Gareth. "Do you have any idea what you've done? To me? To the reputation of this ship? To the Grays, for god's sake?"

Gareth hung his head. "I...I don't know what to say, captain. I'm so sorry."

"Sorry isn't good enough!" She struggled to keep from fully losing herself to her temper. She was blinded by anger, shaking from fury and restraint.

She felt a hand on her shoulder. "Taris," Dave said gently. "I think you should let go of him now."

Seething, she turned around, ready to scream at him for interfering. Then she saw the look on his face. The frowning worry, the big brown eyes filled with sympathy, the curly red hair unkempt and tousled all over his head. He looked a little like a torch, white lab coat and all. *A torch of reason*, she thought, finding herself clever. That seemed to bring a semblance of rationality back into her head. She took a deep breath, and the tension subsided slightly. She turned back to Gareth and released her grip on his collar.

He took several steps away from her cautiously. "Oh thank you captain," Gareth said, rubbing his neck.

"Don't thank me yet," she retorted, pacing in front of him like and angry caged animal. *This is far from over.* "I have worked beside you for years, Gareth. Years. I trusted you."

"I trusted you, too, captain," he professed. "I swear I never wanted to have anything to do with the slave trade! I tried to transfer several times to get out of here because of it, but Captain Philip wouldn't let me. He said he was afraid I'd tell the United authority. I was trapped here."

"And now *we're* trapped here," she pointed out, throwing her hands up. "Look at us! If wrangling never happened on this ship we wouldn't be in this mess in the first place!"

"But we are," Dave said gently. "And we're working to correct it."

She'd never wanted a drink more in her life. "Okay, then. Let's say we get control of the ship. Let's say we get everything back in working order and the fleet fixes all the repairs. Then what? Are we going to rescue all the Grays that this ship condemned to those complexes? Are we going to give them their lives back? Are we all going to hold hands and sing show tunes as the sun sets in the horizon? *I THINK NOT*!"

"Captain," Matt said in his ever-present calm tone. "I agree that wrangling is an awful thing. I'm with you on that. And if what you say is true, what the crew members of this ship did was terrible. Criminal."

"But you can't focus on that," Dave added, joining forces with Matt.

"You can't obsess over what you can't change," Matt said. "You can't alter the past, you know?"

"That doesn't make it right!" She could hear the hysteria in her voice, but she made no attempt to correct it. "For years there was slave wrangling going on under my nose and I never knew! All those people, trapped and tortured in those complex places. How could I let that happen?!"

"You didn't," Dave said in soft tones. "Your shipmates did. And they paid dearly for it. All of them."

"Not all of them," she muttered, wondering what Vinny was doing in his restricted quarters. Probably getting drunk. That's what she would have done. Her throat ached for the taste of the whiskey in her flask. She thought about staying within protocol. She thought about steeling a drink when she was alone, able to drink in peace, without scrutiny or judgment.

"Ah screw it." She reached into her pocket, pulled out the flask and downed the contents of it. There wasn't much left, but it was enough to give her palate a shock. She let the whiskey run into her stomach, warming her belly.

"Ah," she said, putting the empty flask back in her boot, "that's better."

"I don't know, captain," Natsumi commented. "I don't think liquor is going to improve the situation any."

"Or your mood," Dave said under his breath.

"Actually, there's a real possibility that will make it worse," Matt added, giving her a worried look.

She ignored them, her steely gaze focused on Gareth. "And what about you, sergeant? Do you have anything to add?"

"No, mum," he said sadly. "That was it."

"You sure? No more surprises? No caveats? No deep dark secrets you're hiding from me? Because if so I'd like to get them all out in the open right now."

"Captain, I swear that's all there is," he said, his words begging forgiveness. "I don't know what else to say."

"Hmm," she said, folding her arms. "Maybe it's best that you don't say anything, then. You seem to be good at that." He looked like she had just slapped him again, except this time the force of the blow hit much harder. Much deeper.

"Oh good god, captain," Dave said. "Ease off on him, all right? You made your point, you had your whiskey. I think you might want to calm down before this conversation gets any more acrid. Before it becomes something you'll regret."

"Ease off?" She turned to him. "What, you think I'm being too hard on the guy? You think I'm being too mean? Maybe you're right, major. Why don't we ask the Grays that he sold how they feel about it. As them if they think I need to ease off." The little bit of whiskey she had in her flask hadn't been nearly enough, she realized.

"I meant that maybe you're being a little harsh to a guy who kept something from you because his life was being threatened," Dave explained in a strained tone.

"Yeah, captain," Matt chimed in. "It's not like you're not keeping secrets of your own or anything."

Now it was her turn to feel like she'd been slapped. She swung around to glare at him, prepared to unleash her anger, but the words would not form. The thoughts would not transform into sentences. She was speechless because he was right.

"That's not the same," she managed to say finally.

"Oh no?" Matt asked, his usual playful tone absent. "It seems to me like there are a lot of things not being said on this ship. Why is Gareth's silence any more dangerous than yours?"

"Or any less significant?" Dave added.

257

They were ganging up on her, she realized. Banding together to oppose her. She felt threatened, like at any moment they were going to turn on her, throw her into a cell, accuse her of being a Gray. Maybe even scrathe her again. They could do all that, she realized, and much more. If they wanted to. She wasn't sure what she was, but she knew she wasn't quite like them. The looks on their faces told her that they knew that, too. Defensively, she took several steps backwards, positioning herself near the door.

"I'm the captain of this ship," she said evenly. "You have no authority over me."

"And we're not implying that," Dave said calmly. "No one's trying to usurp you, Captain Bodil. We just think you're being a little unfair to Sergeant Hoble. Perhaps you're letting your emotions cloud your judgment."

"I am not!" she lied. "And you have no right to say so!"

"Captain," Gareth said, shoulders slumped, arms at his sides, "I would like to surrender myself to you for my actions."

Her mouth dropped. "What?"

"What?" Natsumi asked, placing a hand on his shoulder. "Oh no. You don't have to do that, Gareth."

"No," he insisted. "I do. It's the right thing. The captain is right. I abused her trust and withheld information regarding illegal activity. I have to be held responsible for my actions."

"Dude," Matt said, "don't do this. Not right now. You're not the bad guy here."

Gareth's face was blanched with fear, but he stood up tall. "Thank you all, but I am choosing to do this." He looked at her and came to the position of attention. "I am yours to do with as you will, Captain Bodil."

Even now, even after all that she had said to him, he was still her faithful NCO. She had lashed out at him, hit him even, and he was still committed to her. She was consumed with remorse. What she'd done to him was so unfair, and she was too proud to admit it. She looked at the faces of the rest of them. She could read them like books. Natsumi, emotional and sympathetic, touching Gareth's arm gently, a sign of solidarity. Matt and Dave, standing side-by-side, arms folded identically. Matt looked suspicious, his eyes scanning her behind his blinking spectacles. Dave, disapproval apparent, looked like he had a lot more to say, but was restraining himself. And then there was Gareth. Trusty, kind, young Gareth, with his forlorn face and self-sacrificing stance, prepared to face his punishment. He looked like a hero, ready to throw himself on the cross for his cause. That made her the bad guy. The shame of that enveloped her. She took several more steps backward, easing out into the hallway.

"Just…stay away from me," she said, her voice menacing. She wouldn't cry. Not in front of them. Not now. "All of you. Stay away from me."

Away from them. Away from the moment. Away from the pain and the hurt and the betrayal. She turned on heel, her coat spinning in the movement, and ran through the hallway. Her boots echoed with every step that she put between her and her crew. She had lost all of them. Her friends, her shipmates, the respect for the captain that she had adored. It was all gone. Everything about her life was starting to unravel.

She needed to get away, and there was only one place on the entire ship where she could go.

Chapter Eighteen

Vale was still sitting on his bed as though she had never left. He seemed much recovered, no longer leaning against the wall, hands clasped calmly in his lap. He looked up, and the small smile he reserved just for her spread across his lips.

"I knew you'd come back," he said. She shut the cell door and leaned against it, unable to talk. She wasn't there to talk anyway. She just needed him to be there. To be around him. To be absorbed in the calm that surrounded him. It was the only place on the entire ship that she felt safe. She let the tears roll down her cheeks, allowing herself to give in to the all-consuming grief. It was eating her up inside. He cocked his head to the side and his eyes shimmered with movement. Abruptly, his expression changed from joy to deep sympathy.

"Oh, *tarischa*," he said gently. He stood up and crossed the span of the cell in one stride. "You are so sad."

She nodded, pulling her hair out of her bun and letting it fall around her face. "Yes. I am."

"Your friends," he said, brushing the tears from her cheeks, "they have made you feel vulnerable."

That was the truth. She was not the weepy, depressed type, but she couldn't stop the tears from coming. Not this time, anyway. "They're all turning on me," she said. "They're angry with me, or keeping secrets from me. And the way some of them look at me…it's like they don't trust me anymore."

"They are afraid," he said calmly. "Everyone reacts strangely when they are scared of something."

"But what are they scared of?" she asked, looking down. "Are they really scared of me?"

Vale placed a hand softly on her shoulder and raised her face to look up at his. "They fear the unknown and the unexplained, Taris. They are just as hurt and confused as you are."

"Oh yeah?" she asked. "Can you feel their emotions and stuff, too?"

A small smile spread on his lips. "Ah, no. Adulos cannot feel the emotions of humans, or read their thoughts."

That surprised her. "Not at all? But you can…I mean…I hear you talking in my head. Not just you. I've heard…others. And that strange emotional thing. It was like I knew you were in trouble. How could that have happened?"

Vale looked at her like he always did when she said something that frustrated him. He sighed softly and peered into her eyes. "Taris," he said. "You must have realized by now that you're a little bit different than the average human. Can you at least admit to that?"

She shrugged. "Great," she said, sniffling. "Just another thing that separates me from everyone else."

"There is nothing wrong with feeling confused."

"There is when that confusion could get you killed," she retorted, thinking of the scrathing. The crying subsided, leaving her exhausted, but her thoughts were racing. She was afraid that she'd lost all respect on her ship. Her new friends didn't trust her. Almost the entire crew was now dead. Vinny was as unstable as a time bomb. And Gareth? She couldn't even think about him. Not to mention the fact that the ship had been hijacked by terrorists. One of whom happened the one person she could be around that made her feel somewhat stable. If they land and she turns Vale into the authorities, she'll never forgive herself. If she doesn't turn him in, her crew will never be able to trust her judgment. Vinny will likely lose what little of his mind he has left. The United authority will throw her back in prison camp for sure.

"I...I don't know what to do," she whispered, the realization of that heartbreaking. "No matter what I do, everything is screwed up. I'm all alone."

"No," he said, shaking his head, "you're not."

Without asking, without needed to voice it, he wrapped his arms around her, enveloping her. She should have resisted. He was the enemy. A dangerous freedom fighter with the blood of humans on his hands. He was driven by his own purposes, clever in his words and undaunted in his mission. He could say things to her that would knock the wind from her lungs, or exalt her beyond imagining. He saw her heart and her strengths and vulnerabilities and he would know exactly how to use them to his advantage. He was the last person in the universe she should be trusting. She should have stopped him.

But she couldn't.

She pressed herself into his chest. His body radiated warmth, strength, comfort. He was still shaking a little from the scrathing, but he held her tightly. In a way, they were holding each other up, neither one able to pull away. His arms pulled her closer into him. He rested his head against hers. All the tension, all the fears, all the horror and hopelessness evaporated for that one moment. Right then, right there, it was just him and just her and nothing else. In his arms, nothing else mattered. In his arms, she was perfect. It was the happiest Taris had ever been in her adult life.

So, naturally, it was abruptly taken from her. "You lying, betraying bitch!"

Vinny tore into the cell, whip at the ready. His face was red with emotion and he was sweating profusely. Taris tried to pull away, but Vale grabbed her and held her closer to him protectively.

"Vinny, what are you doing out of your quarters?" she demanded. "Why did you come here?"

"He means to finish the job he started," Vale said, all emotion in his tone evaporated, the unreadable Gray face returned. Vinny pointed at him.

"Oh my god…you're in my head! Do you see that, Taris? He just read my mind!"

"No he didn't," she said, gently untangling herself from Vale's arms. "Grays can't read human minds. Duh."

"And your intentions are rather apparent, considering," Vale said, eying the scrathe hesitantly. He clasped her hand, weaving his fingers in between hers, pulling her back.

Rage Vinny pointed to their interlocked hands accusingly. "What *the hell* is this? You're holding hands now? What has this bastard done to you, Taris?!"

Lecturing him hadn't worked. Ordering him hadn't worked. Yelling at him hadn't worked. It was clear that Rage Vinny was a danger. Not just to herself, but to others. It was time for drastic measures.

"Vinny," she said cautiously, "hand me that whip."

"No!" He clutched it protectively. Taris could hear the hum of the fully charged device in the silence of the room. It terrified her.

"You're hereby ordered to the brig," she said with authority. "You can even have this cell, since you like it so much."

"I don't think so, lady!" he screamed.

"Lt. Tyler, hand me that whip *now*."

He scoffed. "Oh right. You think you can still give me orders."

"I am your captain," she said angrily, "and you will do as I say. Now give me the whip now or I swear to god I will have you court martialed for insubordination."

He straightened his shoulders and glared at her. "I don't take orders from Grays. Or their bitches."

Before she could even respond, Vale leapt in front of her and tackled Vinny. The two of them hit the ground with a loud *crash*. Vinny was a large man but he struggled under Vale, fighting to get control of the scrathe. Taris stood, frozen for a second. Finally, Vale pinned Vinny to the ground and the scrathe slid across the room. She ran over to it and turned it off. Then, for good measure, she opened the panel interface and disassembled the device in a few short strokes. The pieces flew to the ground, scattering around her feet in a shower of metal.

Vale dragged Vinny to his feet and held his head in his massive arms. Vinny struggled, but the more he fought, the tighter Vale's grip got. He looked down at the pile of parts around her boots.

"Hey! I bought that with my own money!" Vinny protested.

"It was a bad investment," she countered.

Vinny struggled under Vale's grasp again, but it was pointless. "So what's your plan then, o'captain my captain?" he demanded. "You and your silverback lover here are going to take over the ship?"

"He's not my lover," she pointed out, "and what we do is none of your business."

"Like hell it isn't," Vinny countered. "I'm still the damn security officer, and from where I stand the security of this ship is in great danger."

"You were relieved of duty," she pointed out.

"I don't think it counts," he shot back, "since you're a Gray spy."

"A what?" she exclaimed. "What makes you think that?" Well, okay. She was in Vale's cell hugging him when Vinny caught them. That question wasn't relevant. "Never mind. But since we're on the topic, what was your plan? To come in here and kill Vale and then what, come after me next?"

A smile crept across his face. "Eh, not exactly."

She rolled her eyes. "Oh Vinny, trust me when I tell you I am in no mood for guessing games right now."

"Okay," he said in a strange tone. "Let's play multiple choice, then. Which one of us in this room has an incapacitator grenade in his pocket? I'll give you a hint. It's not your boyfriend here."

An incapacitator was an effective crowd controller. It knocked anyone out within its radius, leaving them unconscious anywhere from minutes to hours at a time. Panicked, she thrust her hands in his pockets and yanked out the grenade. It was indeed an incapacitator, but it was different. It carried the Hooper, Inc. symbol on the side, along with the words: *For use on Grays only. Will not work on humans.* It was meant for them. And it was live.

Vinny's eyes met hers, the wicked look of self-satisfaction plastered on his crazy face. "Surprise!"

She heard the click of the detonation, and the cloud of smoke enveloped her. She didn't even have time to scream. The last thing she remembered was hitting the ground, just as Vale reached out to catch her.

Then it all went black.

Chapter Nineteen

"Well this is working out well, isn't it, captain?" Gareth whined, struggling against his rope bindings. He was sporting a black eye and his uniform was a bit disheveled as he leaned against the bulkhead, looking agitated and uncomfortable.

"Thanks for that, Gareth," she hissed back, yanking on the the chains around her wrists. "And here I was worried I might be for want of positive morale. I don't need your input right now, okay?"

"Shut up!" Lt. Tyler demanded, pointing the resonator pistol at her. "We're about to land."

Lt. Tyler had made good use of his mutiny in short time. She woke up wrapped in shackles on the hanger deck and linked to Vale. He was sitting in his blue robe, cross legged and calm. As promised, the ship was docking on a hidden landing platform in the tree-covered area in Sector One. Lt. Tyler was in the middle of trying to get the hangar doors unsealed, screaming orders at a terrified-looking Natsumi through the holographic intercom. Dave and Matt were tied up against a bulkhead on the other side of the room, apparently having a whispering argument over something. Dave's arm was bleeding on the side and his hair was matted with dried blood. Gareth was tied up in front of her, bound at his hands and feet with rope, resting against the hull uncomfortably. Dr. Tomas was nowhere to be seen.

Taris struggled against her chains. They seemed abnormally heavy for some reason. She looked down to inspect them further. *Oh shit*, she cursed. *These are no ordinary chains.* They were scrathe-coiled chains, the type used to transport Gray prisoners. The type that would really hurt if the coils were turned on, something that could be accomplished by the touch of a remote. She sighed in frustration, thinking she might be in more trouble that she initially anticipated. Things were definitely not going according to plan.

Natsumi was the real one in trouble. Lt. Tyler had her standing on the bridge by herself, deciphering the seemingly impossible coding language for the hangar bay doors while he made threats over the holocom. Taris could see her, tears in her eyes, frantic expression, typing commands into the computer with fierce speed and determination. Vinny had threatened her on pain of death - the hostages first and then hers - to finish the decoding so he could regain control of the ship. It was a lot of responsibility for one person, and no small task, either. Taris was curious what his motives were. Clearly he wanted the ship, but then what?

She was not about to wait to find out.

"So what's the plan here, Vinny?" she asked. "You're going to just walk up to that complex and sell me?"

"That's exactly what I'm going to do, you betraying bitch," he said gruffly. "Sell you and your little Gray buddy there."

Taris made a sound of derision in the back of her throat. "Well aren't you the criminal mastermind."

"*Shut the hell up!*" he screamed, pointing the resonator at her. "You don't get to call the shots anymore, insurgent."

She furred her brow. "Insurgent?"

"Oh I know your past, Taris. All that stuff with the rebellion? Yeah, I know about it. You're a traitor!"

"I am *not* a traitor," she exclaimed, her blood boiling. "And the rebellion has nothing to do with this."

"Oh I think it does," he countered. "Even then you were fighting the United authority."

"That was a long time ago, before the United authority was ever formed," she pointed out. "Besides, I was absolved of any and all wrongdoing when I was released."

He scoffed. "How convenient for you. So how did you do it, huh? How'd you get pardoned? Mind games? Magic? Used some Gray voodoo to let the prison wardens free you?"

"Politics," she responded dryly. "It's all about who you know."

He stifled a wicked laugh. "Politics. Heh. I'm sure. You probably had this planned from the start, didn't you?

Pretend to be a human, gain our trust, and then kill us all and take control of the ship, right?"

"Vinny what are you talking about?" she asked. He wasn't making sense.

He swung around and glared at her. "All I know is that I'm doing my rounds and I find some random Gray in the brig and you, Taris! You were with him! Collaborating with the enemy!" he bellowed. "The crew's dead, you're in league with this short haired Gray, and the helm's not in our control! On top of that, there's a bunch of civilians running the ship!"

"We're officers in the Army Science Corps!" Matt bellowed from across the room.

"What the hell?" she asked, confused. "*How* have you forgotten everything that's happened…oh." The answer came to her quickly. "The neuroreconstruction device. You're still under the influence of the effects of that thing." Suddenly it all made sense. The memory loss, the aggression, the irrational decisions. "Oh great, he's literally out of his mind and he has us at gunpoint. Brilliant."

"Hey, how'd you even get back on the ship, anyway?" he asked. "Weren't you supposed to be on Earth at some hoity-toity gala? Did you get drunk and forget to go or somethin'?"

She shrugged. "Well you're half right."

"Whatever," he said dismissively. "You're no friend to this ship or to the fleet. The way I heard that Gray talking you're not even *human*. Isn't that right, silverback?"

Vale turned to him but did not answer. Taris was done catering to Vinny's memory loss. Angry, she narrowed her eyes at him. "Well why don't you just kill us then? Why all the chains and grenade nonsense?"

"Um, captain?" Gareth chimed in. "Let's not do anything hasty, yeah?"

"Because," Vinny responded angrily. "I don't want death for you. I want you to pay, and I want to get paid. The complex will make sure that happens. I can guarantee you that."

She believed him. Not wanting to press her luck, especially with scrathe coils around her body, she clamped her mouth shut and stood in silence. Taris's thoughts were flying through her head at a mile a minute. She waited until Vinny went to yell at Natsumi in the holocom before she finally felt compelled to speak.

"Well he's lost it," she said to no one in particular. "He doesn't seem to know at all what's going on. Acting totally on aggression and instinct. Still, that could be a good thing I guess."

"How do you figure?" Gareth asked incredulously. "He managed to take over the entire ship in a matter of minutes. By himself."

"Don't confuse brute strength with brilliance," Vale said seriously. "To conquer is one thing. To control is another."

"Yeah well I would think of anyone here you'd be the one most worried, mate," Gareth said. "He's going to sell you to people who will torture you."

"I thought those places weren't torture chambers, Gareth." she said, trying to swallow her nerves. *I'm getting sold too*, she thought.

"That's not what I meant," Gareth explained. "I mean that Vale is a wanted fugitive. An international terrorist. Complex or no complex, any human with a vengeance would want to torture him."

"Good point," she agreed, worried. "That's probably true. It's okay though. I have a plan."

"Do you?" Vale asked with interest.

"Yes," she said, lowering her voice. "It's easy really. As soon as the people at the complex scan me and find out I'm human there will be some confusion. There's bound to be. So, in that moment of confusion I have a window of opportunity. That's my chance to grab the resonator."

"What resonator?" Gareth asked suspiciously.

She rolled her eyes. "The one closest to me, wherever that is. I've been through this chained prisoner thing before, Gareth. Trust me, there's always a resonator. Anyway, I'll stun

Vinny first and get the scrathe coil detonator from him. Then we'll jog Vinny's memory with a rock or something, or at the very least bring him back here and lock him up." She looked at them, searching for encouragement and approval. She didn't find it.

Vale gave her a thoughtful look. "With confidence like that I hope you have alternative plans."

"What the hell does that mean?" she demanded.

Gareth gave her a panicked look. "He means that it's not going to be that easy! What if Boone's company is in on the complex thing and they try to stop you? What if they kill you and Vale as soon as you go in there, without question? What if there is no resonator? What if they look at you and they think you're a Gray? I mean Grays mistake you for one of them all the time. What makes you think a human will know the difference?"

"Relax, Gareth," she said gently. "That won't happen. None of that. Vinny's plan isn't going to work. He can't sell me. I'm a human! That's so illegal it's not even funny. He'll be in so much trouble for even trying."

"Well, yes..." Gareth trailed off.

"Then it will be fine," she said confidently. "Better than fine. Don't worry, Gareth. We'll be okay. Even in these clothes I'm still the same old me. Nothing will disguise that."

Vinny had draped one of the blue robes from the dead Grays over her military uniform. She didn't know where her oversized coat was. For some reason that fact bothered her above all else. The robes were stained with dried blood. The smell was horrid, but she was not in a position to request a wardrobe change.

"Care for a stand?" she asked Vale. Since they were linked together, movement had to be a joint effort. He nodded, and together they came to their feet. Taris felt the warmth of his touch on her skin, the exciting, jittery feeling she got when they connected in even the smallest of ways. Finally, after far too long of a pause she broke away and stood awkwardly next to Gareth, pretending to inspect her chains for weak links.

Vale stood in stoic silence. He had his head bowed and his eyes closed for so long that she thought he might be praying. She looked up at him, at his strangely peaceful expression, studying his face with the luxury of him not noticing. His face expressed things the way an old man would, yet it was impossibly soft and youthful. Even his silence could speak volumes. She found herself enchanted with him, and slightly ashamed of that fact. Vale raised his head and opened his eyes, breaking her pseudo-trance. She looked away, embarrassed.

"Jyrisa Ato-Teag is close," he said finally in his breathy voice. "I can feel her presence. She is suffering in her heart. There are many suffering here."

"Is she in danger?" she wondered quietly, thinking instantly of poor Christian and his quest to save his wife. "Will you be able to find her, Vale?"

"I know where she is," he said. "She calls to me now. She tells me to run. They all tell me to run. My tribesmen fear for my life."

"I'm sure they do," she said. "You assassinated a human in front a crowd of people and used his body as a puppet. They're using you as a catalyst for riots and civil unrest. Your name is legendary in Sector One. If these humans find out who you really are they will tear you to pieces."

"It is not myself that I worry for," he said quietly. "It's the innocent who sit in cages like animals that I worry for. It's Christian Tomas and his wife I worry for. It's my brothers and sisters who are dying in that complex that I worry for. It's my planet and my race that I worry for. However, on this day, in this place, I worry most for you, Taris Leigh Bodil."

"Me? Why me?" she asked.

"Because," he said, slowly forming the words, "for the person who lives a lie unwillingly, and then is forced to face a deadly truth, they may lose the will to fight. That would be a true tragedy."

She sighed. "Well I don't know what the hell that means but thanks for the encouragement...or whatever that was."

She had the strangest feeling when he looked at her, like he was trying to wiggle himself into her mind. She remembered it from before, when she heard him saying things even though his lips never moved. She closed her eyes and fought his mental invasion as strongly as she could until she felt him relent. Angry, she reached up and grabbed Vale's robes, yanking him down to her level.

"I told you to stay out of my head, bastard," she hissed in his ear.

He didn't even flinch. "You will be forced to face yourself soon, Taris. It's best that you begin that process by starting it with me. I can guide you."

"No more of that," she said, casting a sideways glance at the others. "I'm serious. All I want to do is find a way to get out of this, okay? I have bigger problems than an identity crisis."

His eyes glinted in the darkness like an animal, making him seem much more inhuman. He focused on her intently. "This is true. However, when the time is right, I hope you will consider my offer. I can help you to unlock the secrets of yourself."

"Yeah, yeah," she said, releasing his robes. "For now I just want to get all of this over with."

"Um, let's not rush anything, shall we?" Gareth whined.

The hangar doors unsealed with a hiss and started descending. Vinny whooped in triumph and even Natsumi looked a little excited for a moment, until she realized what she had done. Lt. Tyler stormed over to them and grabbed the end of the chains, yanking them roughly.

"Come on, dogs," he said with a wicked grin. "It's time to go outside and play."

"Good luck guys," Natsumi said, ignoring Vinny. She stared at Taris, pleading apology in her tearful eyes. "Good luck, captain. I'm so sorry."

"It's okay," she said. "Really. It's not your fault. I will be okay."

"*Cespecula modici luach,*" Vale said. "It means 'fight for freedom with valor'. It's what we say to each other before we face conflict."

"Thanks," she said with a brave smile. "The same to you, then."

"Hey shut up the both of you," Vinny said, yanking the chains. "Especially you, Taris."

"Vinny, come on now. Think about this. You're overreacting," she protested.

"I am not!" he screamed. "You're a spy and you killed the whole crew to save your silverback buddy here!"

"I didn't kill the crew!" she retorted. "The crew attacked the Grays and they retaliated! Three of them took the whole ship down!"

"Three?" he repeated. "I don't see three. Where are the other ones?"

"Dead," she responded. "You ejected their bodies out an airlock, remember?"

Vale's stoic expression broke at that. "He…he did what?" he asked, his voice choked with emotion. "He jettisoned them into space?"

She felt her heart sink. She had completely forgotten to tell Vale about that. The look on his face was a mix between horror and devastation. It was hidden behind the Gray mask of calm, but that didn't fool her anymore. "It's the brain damage," she said. "He didn't know what he was doing."

"Don't make excuses for me!" Vinny screamed. "And I didn't shoot no Grays into space. I would have remembered that."

"No, you wouldn't. Apparently." She tried to ration with him. "Look Vinny, I'm not a Gray. I'm not some double agent. I'm Taris! Known each other for years. I beat you at cards all the time. I saved you from the wreckage on the bridge when all of this started! If I was a bad guy, would I have really done that?"

"Saved me?" he said incredulously. "You never saved me! You're the reason we're in this mess!"

She said nothing. All the words that threatened to come out of her mouth were angry, acrid, and nothing she said would make anything any better. He wouldn't remember it, anyway.

Vinny continued. "You know what kills me about all of this? *I trusted you.* Captain Philip trusted you. Everyone trusted you and look what you did to repay that trust. You got the whole damn crew killed. You've been a Gray, secretly, all this time. I can't believe I ever called you a friend. This other Gray at least has the decency to show his true colors but you, Taris? You're nothing but a two-faced liar."

"Vinny, listen to yourself," she insisted. "You sound crazy."

"No I don't!" he protested. "There is no reason for you to have been in that cell, with *that* prisoner, unless you were doin' something dangerous."

"I hug is not really a dangerous act," she argued, regretting the words as they left her mouth. Gareth's eyes grew wide and Vinny threw his hands up in the air.

"See?" he exclaimed. "Turncoat! Right there! You admitted it!"

"I am not," she declared angrily. "But you're a mutineer. A mutineer and a slave selling criminal."

"At least I know what I am," he spat out. "Unlike you. I should have known from the start what you were. Those damn eyes don't look the slightest thing like blue."

"I'm giving you one last chance, Vinny," she said. "Stop this now. Take off the shackles and we will forget this ever happened."

He pulled himself so close to her face she could feel his angry breath on her cheeks. "You don't get to make those kinds of offers. Not to me. Not anymore."

"Fine," she said. "Take me, then. Sell me to the complex, but I warn you, Vincenzo. When they discover I'm human and release me, you will pay dearly for this."

"Ooh. Tough talk coming from an illegal alien," he said. "I don't give a shit what you think. Or your empty threats. Not anymore. Let's go. You too, Sergeant Hoble."

"Me? Why do I have to go?" he asked.

"Insurance," Vinny responded. "I need someone to kill if things go south. You hear me, Natsumi? If you take off in this ship, or in the *Stargazer*, or on foot or whatever, you'll regret it. If you leave *in any way* I will kill Gareth and it will be on your shoulders. You got me?"

Natsumi's holographic image was devastated. "I...understand."

"Good," he growled. "We all understand each other. Let's go."

With an unceremonious yank, he dragged his prisoners down the ramp and into the woods.

Chapter Twenty

"Now these deals are delicate," Vinny said to Gareth, cutting the binds on his hands. "I don't want the client to think our ship is full of wishy-washy loose cannons. You need to act like you're in it with me."

"Ha! I don't think so. Why on Earth would I want to do that?" Gareth asked. Vinny pointed the resonator at him.

"Why do you think? If you don't I'll kill you. Or Taris. Or both. Understand?" he threatened. Gareth looked at her for approval.

"It's okay," she said. "Do it."

Taris was surprised with how quiet the walk seemed to be. She had half-expected to hear the wails and screams of the tortured and dying echoing through the trees. She thought she'd hear crying and hysterics, something like the ambient sounds of a fifteenth century torture chamber. However, to her ultimate surprise, she heard nothing. No screams, no crying, no dying wails for justice. Just the sounds of the forest that surrounded her. The chirping of birds, the scurrying of squirrels, the rustling of the wind through the trees. The only sounds that seemed out of the ordinary were the shuffling of feet and the rattling of the shackles.

They rounded a bend, and abruptly the facility came into view. It was a square white building with twenty feet high walls that offered no one but the birds a peek inside. The front of the building was vacant of anything except for a large metal door which was guarded by only one HALO. Well of course it had to be a HALO, she realized. Would Boone use anything else to protect his assets? She was about to pass judgment for the ineptitude of only having only one guard when she caught sight of the cameras. And the automated turrets. And the laser beams. Her judgment dissolved into apprehension. The lone HALO was garbed in black riot gear with a giant circled H in the front of his vest, a rifle at the ready, two scrathe whips at his side. Taris kept her head down as Vinny forcefully yanked them up the small hill.

"I've got a shipment for Mr. Finnegan," Vinny said gruffly. The guard looked him over with a dubious expression.

"How about a 'hello sergeant' first, Vinny?" he asked. *Oh great, so they know each other*, Taris thought.

"Hello," Vinny said, pouring sweat from his face, his eyes darting around wildly. "I've got a shipment for Mr. Finnegan, *sergeant*."

The HALO frowned. "Hmmphm. You're in a bad mood today, *lieutenant*."

"You have no idea," Gareth commented under his breath.

"Is the Hammer expecting you?" the guard asked, casually looking at a tablet he'd pulled out of his pocket. "Don't see anything on the list for today."

"You know he's expecting us, Charlie," Vinny said.

"I know that he was expecting a shipment two days ago and you never made the delivery. All we got was a straggler who was hanging out by the landing pad. Escapee from the mansion. Not much to brag about. The Hammer wasn't pleased."

Taris discretely caught Vale's eye. *Jyrisa,* she thought. *They got Jyrisa.*

"I was held up."

"How? You look fine to me," the HALO said suspiciously. "And who's this red-faced guy? He new?"

Gareth nearly recoiled at the attention being drawn to him. "Ah...no. I'm no one. I mean I'm not new, I'm just not important. Just a sergeant on the Intrepid. Here to help, apparently. Willingly, of course. On my own volition. Yes, I am here because I want to be and no other reason, I assure you."

Vinny shot him a look that would have killed on sight. "Charlie York, this is Sergeant Hoble. He's a member of my crew."

"Yeah?" Charlie said, eyeing Gareth suspiciously. "What the hell's wrong with him?"

Vinny pressed his lips together. "He's...a little slow."

286

"I see that," he responded, shaking Gareth's outstretched hand mechanically. "Slow seems to be an issue for you fleet guys. But I'm sure you have some great reason as to why you're so delayed in the delivery. As usual."

Vinny yanked on the chains. "It's the truth, Sergeant York. These Gray bastards hijacked my ship. I didn't even have control of my vessel until it landed here."

"Ha! You let your ship get taken over by Grays! What a dumbass!" The HALO was almost doubled over with laughter. Vinny's face reddened with anger.

"Shut up, Charlie. I'm serious! This female pretended to be one of my crew and the male here is…he's…important somehow…"

He couldn't remember. The neuroreconstruction had fried his memory and Vale's name was lost to him. She exhaled in relief. Vinny furred his brow, searching his thoughts for forgotten memories and becoming increasingly more agitated.

The guard stared at him for a moment. He peered up into Vale's face. "I dunno. They don't look that important to me."

"I'm telling you these two are really important for some reason!" Vinny exclaimed, desperation in his voice. "Look they just are, all right. Now, I hope you don't mind but I'm in a hurry, so if we could just speed this up--"

"Not so fast," the HALO said, putting his hand up. "Vinny, you know how this works. You don't get to just stroll on in here and be taken at your word. I need to get a look at the shipment first. Scan them for processing."

Go ahead, she thought smugly. *Let's see how Charlie York likes Vinny Tyler after he tries to sell him a human member of the fleet.*

She heard Gareth make polite protests, but Vinny elbowed him in the ribs so hard he looked like he might pass out. The guard made Taris and Vale line up shoulder to shoulder and he reached into his pocket, pulling out an infoscanner. It was a handheld biological processing device that could determine anything: inebriation, blood type, age, gender, genetic affiliation. She'd seen them many times before. She knew them very well. Vale was first in line. Sergeant York pulled off his hood and burst into laughter.

"A short hair?! You must have *really* messed up before you got captured, silverback. I guess you'd be more of a silverhead, actually."

Vale's gaze was steady, emotionless. "If you say so, sir."

"What did you do to deserve that? Did you sleep with a human? Steal the silver? Set the damn house on fire?" he asked. Tauntingly, he ruffled Vale's hair, even though he had to stand on his tiptoes to do it.

"I'd rather not discuss that sir, if you please," Vale said, looking down.

"Aw, c'mon now, Gray," Charlie said, cocking his head to the side. "Be a good little doggie tell us what you did."

"So he has short hair. Why is that so noteworthy?" Gareth asked, absently picking at a stray thread that had come loose from his cuff. Vinny looked like he was seriously considering clubbing Gareth with the nearest blunt object and leaving him to die in the woods.

"Good god, man!" Charlie exclaimed. "How long have you been in this business?"

Gareth looked up, regretting his comment. "Um, well, I usually stay in the background during these little exchanges. Backstage…and such."

Charlie rolled his eyes. "Okay, British guy, here's the rundown. The Grays think their hair is magical or special or whatever. They never cut it because it never grows back, like it deprives them of power or something. It's all a crock if you ask me."

"Well if that's the case," Gareth said slowly, "if they really believe that, then why would Val…er, the Gray here, why would he want to have his hair cut so short?"

Charlie smiled, revealing a set of crooked, discolored teeth. "I don't think our friend here wanted his hair cut, did you silverback? Someone gave him the trim and taper I think." He looked over at Gareth. "It was probably for punishment. Only the ones guilty of really terrible crimes lose the right to their flowing silver locks."

Gareth looked at Vale with a new hesitation. "Oh."

The HALO laughed. "Yeah, 'oh' is right. So, tell us Gray, what did you do to deserve the haircut?"

Vale's eyes roared with aggression, resentment and hatred, but his face never betrayed one of those emotions. "It was a woman," he said in a dark tone. "It was the price I paid to protect her."

Taris didn't know what to think of that, except that she knew he was telling the truth. She also knew there was a lot more to that story than Vale let on. Charlie whistled in approval, slowly clapping his hands mockingly.

"Bravo. Well done, silverback. Well done. The Hammer hasn't had a short haired criminal to play with in a long time. He'll be pleased with you."

The guard grabbed Vale's left hand and turned it up. She saw the silver outline of his slave brand. It looked like a bird in flight, holding a clover in its talons. He placed the scanner against this symbol and pressed the top button. In less than a minute it blinked green. Charlie looked at the screen.

"Hmm."

Vinny's eyes grew wide. "What? What does it say?"

"It says that your so-called 'important Gray' here is named James Whit. Last known master was from Aukland, New Zealand in Sector Four. Long way from home, then, but nothing significant."

"What?" Vinny said, yanking the scanner out of his hands. "Are you sure about that? I could have sworn he was important somehow."

"Sorry to tell you this, Vinny," Charlie said in a tone that implied he wasn't sorry at all, "but he's just a regular runaway. Standard issue Gray."

Vinny wasn't satisfied. "Can you check again? Maybe you need to look under his tribe name."

"We don't file tribe names," the HALO argued, snatching his scanner back. "We don't keep records of that shit. You know that. What's the matter with you today?"

"No! He's important! I can't, argh, I can't remember why but he is. I know he is." Vinny protested. "Go on, Gray! Tell him! Tell him who you are!"

Vale looked directly at Charlie York. "I am not one to judge the perceptions of my masters. I'm afraid my opinion is invalid."

"What?! That's crap! Charlie, tell me you believe me!"

"Look Vinny, I don't know, okay?" Charlie said. "We can run some more scans, get some more tests done and all that, but for right now I have to go with what the scanner tells me."

"Bullshit," said Vinny, folding his arms. "Total bullshit. Well this better not affect the reward money amount, okay?"

"Fine. Now, back to the Gray here," Charlie said, turning back to Vale. "Hmm. You've been off the grid a few years now. Hellova long time to be on the run. They cut your chair and then you cut them loose, eh?"

Vale nodded noncommittally. The HALO shrugged and stamped the top of Vale's hand like he was approving a slab of meat.

"Ah well, no one will miss you. That's good. The less people come looking for them, the better it will be for everyone."

Taris was next. The guard stood in front of her and yanked the hood off her head. She looked down and started at his scuffed military boots, her breathing slow and steady. If she was going to make a move, the timing had to be just right.

"Well, well, well," Charlie said, scrutinizing her. "Look at this pretty thing. Black hair, white skin. Why you look just like a little chained up princess."

Not hardly, she thought, eying his rifle. *I doubt a princess can shoot 40/40 every time. Bet he can't either.*

"Come on now," he cooed, "let's have a look at you." Before she could protest he grabbed her face, yanking it up to look at him. "Ah, there it is," he said knowingly. "The eyes. You can dye your hair black, you can cover your face, but you can't escape those damn silver eyes, now can you sweetheart? They're always a dead giveaway."

"So you say," she mumbled. The HALO tilted his head to the side and grabbed her hands, looking them over.

"Ever been branded, Snow White?" he asked rhetorically. He turned her palms up and inspected the burn marks on her hands. "Ah there it is. On the palms, eh? You know, I don't think I've ever seen this brand before. Trust me when I say rarely happens in this job. Where did you come from, princess?"

She looked up. "It's not a brand."

He stared at her like she was speaking gibberish. "Uh, no," he said patronizingly, as though he were speaking to a child. "That's your brand, sweetie. That's what happens when you're sold to someone. Okay, so I'll ask again, who were your masters, slave?"

"I am NOT a slave," she spat out.

He gripped her shoulders, pushing his bony fingers into her skin. "Ooh…feisty. I like that in a silverback. So rare."

"Get your hands off me, asshole!" She jerked away from him and kicked him as hard as she could in the shin. He screamed and she staggered back, pushing up against Vale. Strangely, instead of pushing her away she felt him pull her closer.

The HALO pulled himself upright, wincing. "You're going to regret that," he threatened her, holding his injured leg.

"Not as much as you would think," she retorted.

The guard reached up and backhanded her. Hard.

"I don't know where you got off thinking that you're allowed to bite back, but that shit stops now," he growled, letting the spit fly out of his mouth. "You'd better learn obedience quick, unless you're looking for some extra punishment." He stared at her, licking his chapped lips grotesquely with his fat, scratchy tongue. "I can help with that, you know."

She recoiled. "Don't you dare touch me," she warned, "or the next time I won't aim for the leg."

Charlie York hit her with the butt of his rifle, smashing her face with all the force he could muster. Her first thought was that her nose was broken, but quick inspection told her no. It was still extremely painful, intact nose or not. Instead of making any attempt to disentangle himself from her, Vale held her in his arms silently as the blood started to trickle out of her nose. As Sergeant York raised the butt of the rifle again, she felt Vale's arms wrap around her. *Oh my god,* she realized as her blood dripped onto his robes, *he's protecting me.* The guard was just about to go in for another blow when Gareth stepped in front of him.

"Hey!" he shouted with as much bravado as he was capable. "Don't do that…to the merchandise!" He thought quickly. "Because…you haven't paid us! Yes, that's right, there has been no compensation for the capture of these two Grays, and I do not want to be responsible for paying for this assault." He looked to Vinny for assistance. "Don't you agree, sir?"

Lt. Tyler, apparently trying to recall something, broke his concentration. "Um yeah. Right. Exactly. We're not gonna pay for your messes, Charlie."

"You break it you buy it," Gareth added.

Taris wasn't so sure that encouraging this guy to buy her was much of a good thing, but it had stopped him from pummeling her face into hamburger meat. Charlie looked like he might ignore all of that and assault her anyway, but eventually he relented.

"Fine," he said, glaring at her as he lowered his weapon. "You lucked out, princess."

She wanted so very badly to split his face down the middle, but she couldn't. She was defenseless. If she kept it up, it would take more than Gareth - and some brilliantly mentioned financial obligations - to keep her face intact. *Control yourself, Bodil,* she instructed, spitting out a mouthful of blood-filled saliva. Sergeant York, deciding to move the process along, grabbed his scanner and held it to her palm.

"Well now, let's make sure you're of good stock, shall we?" he said.

She felt her heart thumping in her chest so hard it was almost painful. She had never been so nervous about a scan before. The machine blinked yellow a couple of times and made a halting sound. Confused, Charlie scanned her again. *Oh for Christ's sake*, she thought to herself, *let's get this over with.*

"What the hell is taking so long?" Vinny asked after the third try.

"Something's creating interference," the guard mumbled, shaking the scanner. "The readings are mixed. I don't know. It doesn't make any sense."

"Maybe it's broken," Gareth suggested. "Maybe you're doing it wrong."

Charlie glared at him. "I know how to do it, English boy."

"Welsh," Gareth corrected. "I'm not English, I'm Welsh."

"Whatever. Look, it's not the machine. It's *her*," Charlie York said, pointing to her.

"Me? But I haven't done anyt--" He backhanded her again, this time with the end of the scanner. The force was so hard it made her teeth rattle. Blood dripped out of the side of her mouth and her skin felt hot. She pushed back the reaction tears and spat a glob of blood out onto the ground.

"I see you're going to need some extra discipline after all, silverback," he said with a snarl. "But we'll get to that later. Now, how are you creating interference? What are you hiding?"

"Nothing," she said quietly. He brought his face so close to hers she could feel his disgustingly hot breath on her face.

"You had better start cooperating or you're in a world of hurt. You think *I'm* mean? Well you ain't seen nothing yet, Snow White. I've got a guard on my team who is the size of a house. They call him goliath. I think the name speaks for itself. Would you like to meet him, or would you like to be a good little silverback and hand over what you're hiding?"

"I don't know what you mean," she said, truly confused.

"Oh yeah?" he said, pointing to her hands. "Well what's that thing on your wrist, then?"

She almost panicked. She was sure her wristband would go unnoticed. To the untrained eye it looked like a leather strap on her arm. "Oh, it's nothing sir," she protested, touching it instinctually. "It's just a, uh you know, religious decoration."

The HALO glared at her. "Is that so? Well give it to me."

Without the wristband she would be totally defenseless. She couldn't signal for help, and she couldn't locate Jyrisa. Nothing. She had counted on him not noticing. It usually went by unnoticed. Panicked, she clutched the wristband.

"Please sir," she protested, grasping for a lie. "Please don't. This is all I have left. It's a special prayer symbol. It's nothing, really. Just a leather strap!"

Charlie grabbed her arm, digging his fingernails into her flesh. "Damn, you are just *asking* to get the shit kicked out of you, aren't you? Now I'm not going to tell you again. Give me the wristband, or I will shoot your hand off and take it myself."

He pointed the weapon at her hand and charged it to full. The look on the guard's face told her that he wasn't kidding, either. She unlatched the strap and handed the device to him stiffly. With the cover closed, it looked like just a leather strap with a simple metal panel in the front. The guard fiddled with the wristband for a few moments and then shoved it into his pocket.

"There, that's better," he said. "Aw, don't look so sad, Snow White. It was an ugly ass bracelet if you ask me. You should be happy to be rid of it. Go on, now, tell me how happy you are that I took it from you."

I'd like to break your skull in two, she thought. "Yes sir. Thank you, sir."

The HALO nodded. "Good silverback. Now give me your hand again."

She held her breath as she was scanned. She started thinking of all the things she needed to do in order to escape. She'd have to grab the resonator; that much was certain. It wouldn't take more than a second. She would have to shoot the guard and certainly incapacitate Vinny. They could drag him back to the ship long before he came to. She looked up on the wall and saw the security cameras and guns. *If we run through the woods due East in a zig-zag,* she decided, *we could still escape. Vinny might be an issue, but I can't just leave him here. The moment this guy finds out I'm a human--*

"There we go!" Charlie said as the scanner blinked green. "You're a Gray all right."

Her thoughts came to a thundering stop. "Wha…what?"

She stared at his scanner, then back at her hand. On the scanner screen, in block green letters, was one word: GRAY. Her mind went blank. Her heart raced. It didn't make sense.

"No," she whispered, staring at her hand. "But that's impossible."

The guard gave her a strange look. "You act like that's news to you, princess. And I told you it wasn't the machine, English. That bracelet of hers was the problem. It's probably made of that stupid sidus metal. That's all it was."

Gareth was staring at her, all the color in his face drained. "Uh, well, um. Huh. S-sure. Yeah okay, then. Blimey."

"*Ha!*" said Vinny, pointing to her defiantly. "I knew it! You little traitor! Oh my god, we used to play cards with you, and muster with you and…argh! You planned this all along, didn't you? *Didn't you!*"

"Lt. Tyler," Gareth said hesitantly. "Don't do anything stupid, sir. Anything you might remember later and then regret. A lot."

"But she betrayed us! She impersonated an officer in the fleet!"

"I *am* an officer," she protested, still in shock. "I don't know what's going on! Seriously, this is a mistake."

"Liar!" Vinny screamed, lunging at her. "I'll kill you! I swear to god!"

"Then you won't get paid, Vinny!" Gareth argued. It was his only trump card but he was playing it well. It was keeping her alive. "You do want to get paid, don't you?"

"She didn't come up on the register," Charlie York added. "That means she's off the books. An uncharted female will get you double the price of the regular shipment."

Vinny glared at her, the hate raging in his brown eyes. "Fine. Take her. Just promise me that she'll get what she deserves."

The HALO smiled. "Oh trust me, friend. She will."

The guard flipped her hand over, stamping it with a green seal of inspected approval. She felt dizzy. For a moment she thought she might throw up. She looked over at Vale. He was staring at her with a small smile on his face. A smile that was practically undetectable, just slightly curving the right side of his mouth. A smile that made her feel like she didn't understand anything she knew about herself. Horrified, she turned away from him and stared forward, rubbing the spot where her wristband used to be. In that one moment, she lost herself. Everything she knew, everything she was, it was all lost in that one moment.

Her breathing stopped. Then she collapsed.

Chapter Twenty-one

Taris screamed back to consciousness, sprawled on the ground. The scrathe coils burned her skin black and boiled her insides. It was excruciating. All she could think about was the pain, and the agony as she begged for it to stop. When the shocks finally ceased, she realized she was still in front of the complex. Vale was on the ground next to her, thrown down by the shock that coursed through their interlocking links. Charlie the HALO looked horribly displeased.

"Christ, you're not going to faint like that *all* the time are you?" he asked irritably. "The Hammer doesn't like weaklings."

Vale was lying on his back with his eyes closed, his teeth gritted so tightly she thought he might fracture his jaw. With all the strength she could muster she scooted over to him so her head was nearly against his.

"W-w-what t-t-the *hell* just happened t-t-t-to m-me?" she stuttered, the shakes uncontrollable.

"You fainted," Vale whispered matter-of-factly. "You require sleep. I've told you this, Taris."

"T-t-that's not what I meant. I m-m-m-mean why did that thing mark me as a G-g-gray? How did that happen? Did you do something?"

She saw the liquid silver of his eyes shift. "I've done nothing to sway the outcome of that device. That much I can assure you."

"Hey! No talking!" the HALO barked. As soon as the words left his mouth she felt a jolt of pain. She screamed and her muscles seized up, only making it worse. It surged through her veins and then dissipated quickly, leaving an achy dull feeling it its wake.

"You've got it all wrong!" she protested as loudly as she could muster. "I'm not a Gray!"

"Oh no?"

The electricity surged through her again, this time causing her to convulse. Tears flowed from her eyes as she struggled for a breath, for a single respite. Finally, abruptly, the pain abated. The relief made her want to grovel at the guard's feet. She could not fight the scrathing. She could barely move because of it.

"Stop this!" she begged through sobs. "Please stop. I'm a human. I'm from California! My name is Taris Leigh Bodil. I'm an officer in the fleet, if you would just please look at my records--"

"Lies, lies…and more lies."

The torture came again. This time it was stronger. It tore through her, shaking her very core. She couldn't see anything. Nothing mattered. Nothing but the pain. It consumed her thoughts. Eventually she lost the will to even protest. When it finally stopped she curled up in a ball, choking back wracking sobs.

"Taris," Vale wheezed, his whole body covered in sweat and shaking. "I'm begging you. Please stop."

She stopped fighting. She lacked the strength to continue, anyway. All she could do was curl up on the ground and wait for the shaking to subside. She tried to convince herself that it would be okay. That she was not in mortal danger. That she was going to live through this. She told herself this, but she didn't believe it. Even breathing hurt.

"All right, that's enough drama for my tastes. Stand up, silverbacks," Charlie commanded.

Taris painfully gulped in a lungful of air and slowly staggered to her feet. The scrathe pain was still residual, but she found that once the shaking stopped it was easier to regain control of motor functions. Even if it did feel like her muscles were made of lead. Through no small amount of effort, she helped Vale up as well. They were chained together, so standing up - like being shocked - was a joint effort. She felt like she wanted to throw up, but Vale looked stoic and reverent as ever. *It's almost like he's used to this*, she thought to herself. He looked at her out of the corner of his eye.

I am, Taris. Pain is an element of the Adulo life.

Her eyes grew wide with alarm. She knew it was impossible, but she was terrified that somehow the guard would hear him and punish them more. She hated the telepathy. It scared her. She shouldn't be able to hear the thoughts of others. No one should, it was inhuman and wrong. She'd never been able to hear anyone else's thoughts until the day of Boone Hooper's party. That was when all the trouble started.

"Look can we get this over with?" Vinny complained. "I want to get these *things* out of my sight."

"Yeah, yeah." The HALO scanned a charge card and tossed it to him. "Here's the payment for these two."

"And you gave me the bonus for Taris, er, for the female?" Vinny asked.

"Yep. Not that I should have, considering the trouble she's bound to be." Charlie looked at her with a sneering sort of smile that made her want to recoil. "But I guess I'm the generous type."

Vinny stared at the charge card and then back at her. He looked confused, like he couldn't quite process what was going on. "Uh…thanks, Charlie. Yes. Well. I guess that does it then."

She looked at Vinny, hoping that some part of him saw her as Taris, not as a piece of property. She knew he was mad and confused. She knew he wasn't in control of his thoughts and emotions. This wasn't the Vinny she knew. The Vinny that liked to grow tomatoes in his quarters so he can make real spaghetti sauce and cheated at cards and secretly enjoyed Italian opera. The one who never forgets a birthday and always remembered to make the cake. She needed to see if that Vinny was still in there somewhere. When he finally looked at her, it was like she was staring at a ghost. An angry, bitter, distrustful ghost of a person who was being betrayed by his own thoughts. In that moment, her hopes faded.

Gareth grimaced and smoothed his uniform jacket down nervously. Taris could tell he was scared out of his wits, but he seemed to have enough left in him for feigned politeness. "Well, now. Payment. Very good, then. Thanks for that, Sergeant York. And um, it was nice meeting you. Enlightening, to say the least."

"Yep," the guard said, shaking his hand vigorously. "Pleasure's all mine, English."

"Welsh," Gareth corrected again. "I'm from Wales. Christ man, it's a completely different country."

"Whatever," he responded. "It's all the same sector, right?"

Gareth looked like he wanted to explain further, but seemed to find the futility in that idea and gave up. Vinny shook Charlie's hand mechanically, that strange look still plastered on his face. "Okay. Thanks, Charlie. See you next time."

He started to walk away, but she couldn't let it end like that. She wouldn't.

"Vinny!" she said as he started down the hill. He stopped, but didn't turn around. Gareth looked helpless and alarmed, pleading with his eyes that she not speak, not make it worse. Vale didn't look too happy, either.

"What?" he demanded. He sounded violent and furious, but she thought she detected a slight sadness in his voice. At least, so she hoped.

"What will you tell everyone?" she asked softly. "How will you explain where I've gone? What happened to me?" Vinny looked over his shoulder, but didn't meet her in the eye.

"A lot of people died on that ship in the last few days. One more death is not too hard to explain."

"Vinny--"

"Goodbye, Taris."

He started down the hill without looking back. She wanted so badly to tell him that she didn't understand. That the scans were wrong. That is was all a mistake. She wanted to do that, but the look on his face boiled any bravery she had left down to vapor. Gareth trailed behind, keeping his sad eyes on her for as long as he could. She didn't blame him. She wished she could tell him that. She would never blame him.

Despondent, she watched them until they both disappeared out of sight. The moment Gareth turned the bend, he was gone.

She never felt more powerless in her life.

"Okay, that's enough standing around," the guard said, grabbing Vale gruffly by the arm. "Let's go."

He led them to the entrance and keyed in the security code. The door made a metallic grinding noise and then swung open. Charlie York stood back as four armed HALOs in medical uniforms spilled out, scrathes at the ready.

"Welcome to Hammerhead Hold, silverbacks," he said with a snarl. "The last place you'll ever call home."

The complex doors opened into a wide corridor that wrapped around the inside of the square facility. The outside cement walls were lined with thin metal strips of scrathe coils. She was physically repelled by them. She could feel the heat of the painful energy coursing through the wires as they led her down the hall. The HALOs shoved her through the door and into the hallway. Inside, she was escorted past large barred windows that faced what looked like an inner courtyard, although "courtyard" was a generous description. It was an open square area surrounded by the large walls and watched by guards in towers. There was little to no grass to speak of, and the well-worn pathways were mostly mud. Positioned in the muck were ten large metal boxes, big enough to hold one, maybe two people standing up. They were nondescript except for the large grated doors that stood out like protruding teeth around snarling metal lips.

And then there was the Eye.

Of the four watchtowers in the courtyard, only one of them stood out. In the far southern corner of Hammerhead Hold was a giant, revolving black turret. The Eye was an ocular-shaped observatory made of glossy, shielded black metal. It appeared to revolve on command, darting around with movements that resembled a real eye, and observing the courtyard with maniacal scrutiny. It was huge - as big as a two story building if not bigger - and seemed to have an altogether otherworldly quality. The Eye seemed out of place surrounded by the drab cement walls and barbed wire guard posts. As she passed the windows, Taris felt the thing staring at her, watching her every movement. It sent shivers down her spine.

They separated Vale from her then, putting them in two different rooms for processing. The blue-uniformed employees inspected her for diseases, profiled her blood sample, removed her robes and put her in a drab - and ironically gray - prison uniform. As she was dressing herself with the courtesy of several armed guard witnesses, she noticed that the back of her uniform said 8824-SW.

"What does S-W stand for?" she asked the angry, obese female nurse who was processing her. The frowning beast looked down at her chart.

"Says here your name is Snow White, so that would be your initials then," she answered in a disgusted tone.

"Oh really." That was Charlie York's doing, she had no doubt. She expected him to give her trouble, he'd practically promised it, but the fairy tale princess title was just an extra level of spite.

"That's not my name," she said defiantly.

The nurse looked up with large, drooping fake eyelashes that blanketed her muddy brown eyes. "What did ya say?"

"I said that's not my name," she said a little stronger.

"Oh, well aren't you a feisty one," she said with a tone that implied she didn't care for that. "Well too bad. That's the name on the list and that's the name you get."

"I can't change it at all?" she asked, genuinely surprised. "Can't I pay some sort of clerical error fee to get it corrected or something?"

The woman cackled and clicked a few commands on her computer tablet. "Nope. Grays who make corrections are Grays who think for themselves, and we can't have that happen, now can we Ms. White?"

Taris was taken aback. She'd never been treated so callously in her whole life as she had in the last hour. That *included* military prison camp. "I guess not, but I still want to change my name. It's Taris. My name is Taris. Now there has to be someone I can talk to--"

"Sorry honey, it ain't gonna happen," the woman said.

"Well that's unacceptable," Taris pouted.

"Let me give you a piece of advice," the nurse said. "Learn the sit-down-and-shut-up lesson quick, or you'll be in the crates before you know it."

Taris furred her brow. "The crates? What are the crates?"

The woman pointed to the window. "See those big metal boxes out in the courtyard?"

"Yeah," she said, casting a wary look out the window. "What about them?"

A threatening smile spread across the big woman's ruddy lips. "Oh, I'm sure you'll find that out soon enough."

Taris was moved into a new room, absent of objects except for a cabinet on the wall. The fat nurse walked to the cabinet and inserted her key in the lock. Two robotic hands descended from the ceiling and reached into the cabinet, pulling out a collar. It was a shiny metal ring, a half an inch thick, the silver reflective and untarnished. No, she realized, it wasn't silver. It was that strange metal. The kind from the Gray home world that the swords were made out of. *That explains the robotic arms*, she realized. *They can't pick it up themselves*. A smug smile crept across her face. *Weaklings.* The scrathe coil wrapped neatly around the middle of the collar and the whole thing affixed at the back with an electronic clip. The angry lady finished programming the collar and the latch in the back popped open. The mechanical arms reached up and wrapped the collar around Taris's neck roughly. Instantly her neck started to itch, and she reached up to scratch under the collar. *Stupid Gray metal*, she thought bitterly, *itches like hell.*

"Too heavy for you?" she asked the nurse condescendingly.

The woman sneered at her. "But not for you, huh silverback? Don't care though. Wouldn't want to wear that thing if my life depended on it. Yours could though, come to think of it."

The woman laughed as though that were an incredibly clever joke. Taris rolled her eyes and tried not to scratch her neck, shoving the fabric of her prison uniform between her skin and the metal. Without warning, the woman yanked on the collar in the back and pulled out what looked like a little square black box.

"What's that?" Taris asked.

"It's your latch key," she explained. "It's the only thing in heaven and Earth that can take your damn collar off. Every one of the prisoners got one."

"What do you do with them? The keys I mean," she asked.

The woman turned and put her hands on her humongous hips. "You know, I've been doing this job twenty years now and I ain't never heard a Gray talk as much as you during in-processing. Matter of fact, I've never heard a Gray talk this much *period*."

"I'm not a Gray," she responded defensively. She had no other basis of argument. Somehow she knew *take my word for this* wasn't going to cut it.

The woman's badly painted eyebrows raised. "Well that's a first. Never heard that line before." She inspected Taris, staring at her closely as though she was looking for something.

"Well princess, since you ask, all the keys go into the vault in the Hammer's office, but don't think about breaking in there. The keys all go in, but they never, ever come out."

"Well if they never come out then how do the Grays ever get these things off?"

The woman cackled. Years of smoking and bitter attitude echoed in the room. "You don't. The dogs in this pound never get to take the collars off. I think you'd better get used to it," she said, tapping the collar lightly with a long, thickly painted fingernail.

Taris scratched the side of her throat. "Wouldn't bet on it."

She was shuffled though the hallway and into what looked like a cargo elevator, where Vale and two armed guards were waiting for her. His expression was pale and unfocused. For once she was jealous of that. She always wore her expressions so clearly on her face. Having the choice to keep that to herself was something she envied. The HALOs shoved her into the cargo elevator and she looked up at Vale, hoping for some sign of encouragement.

"Eyes straight ahead," the guard said, pointing a scrathe baton at her.

It's going to be okay Taris, she heard him echo in her mind.

Unable to get past her telepathic hesitancy, she turned to look at Vale on instinct. A jolt of electricity shot through her, knocking the wind from her lungs. She doubled over and gasped for air, sucking in small, painful breaths.

"I said eyes forward, silverback!" the guard barked.

It wasn't as excruciating as the whip, but the cattle-prod style scrathe baton delivered enough of a punch to subdue her. Finally regaining her lung capacity, she sucked in a painful gulp of air and straightened back up, staring forward. The elevator descended past what she guessed was at least three stories of earth before it groaned to a stop. The guards opened the large metal doors, revealing an enclosed cement room. Against the wall were cell doors - ten in all - five on each side of the room. There were no windows. Two rows of metal tables lined the large middle area and the dim, cage-covered lights cast a ghastly glow. There was one glass-enclosed wall in the far corner, where an officer was handing out food to a line of silent, silver-haired prisoners. They didn't talk. They didn't even look at each other. They stood around in small, mousy groups, hovering like ghosts in a tomb.

"This is Hammerhead East," the HALO holding the elevator button said. "You'll eat here, sleep here, maybe even die here. Comply with the rules and you'll get to stay here. Disobey and you'll go to the crates. Trust me when I say you don't want to go to the crates. All the testing is done upstairs on the Garden Plaza level. Snow White, you and the short hair here are in group ten. Make sure you're lined up and ready to go by zero-six-hundred every morning. Welcome to your new kennel, silverbacks."

With that, he physically shoved her off the lift.

Chapter Twenty-two

She and Vale hit the cement floor with a wet sounding *smack*. The HALOs laughed, ascending the elevator shaft like boastful hyenas until the doors closed. Exhausted, Taris rested her cheek on the cold ground and closed her eyes. For a moment she considered letting herself stay there, if for no other reason than to just be left alone for a few minutes. Eventually her resolve returned and she pushed herself up to her feet.

"You know, there is a real possibility that we are in way over our heads here," she grumbled, helping Vale up.

"That is certainly a possibility," he replied.

She was irritated at the ill-fitting clothes. Upset with herself for not putting up more of a fight. She grasped the itchy collar around her neck and yanked on it as hard as she could, but nothing she did was going to get it off. Curious, she touched the thin scrathe coil that was slightly depressed in the middle of the collar. It was there, and it was charged. She could feel the hot energy that came from that thin line of electrical wire. One touch from a remote and the collar would activate, burning her insides. She recoiled at the thought, moving her hand away from the coil. Cautiously she reached around and touched the latch in the back.

It felt warm and solid. She needed to get a better look at what she was dealing with.

"Turn around," she instructed Vale.

He did as she asked and she looked at the back of his collar. The latch was indeed a black computerized panel. The front was unremarkable except for a small digital gray square in the middle. On the side was a color scale. At the bottom, the color was gray. At the top, the color was green, with varying colors in the middle. *Hmm, wonder what that means.* Frustrated, she pulled her hair up and tied it into a knot, out of her face. Hijacked Ship. Sold as Slave. Scrathe collar. Underground prison. Trapped. She was on the very fringe of having a full on panic. Vale, on the other hand, seemed unperturbed.

"Something troubles you, Taris," he said calmly, as though making polite small talk.

"Of course something is troubling me!" she hissed. "I've been a captain less than a week and I've already had a mutiny. I just got mistaken for a Gray and sold as property by one of my own deranged shipmates. He's got a makeshift crew hostage on my ship and now I can't help them because I'm a mile underground with a scrathe collar strapped to my neck." She was beyond just angry. There weren't words she could think of to describe the level of ferocity she was feeling. Frustrated, she paced in front of Vale.

"I don't even know why I let this happen, "she said, walking back and forth slowly. "I didn't do anything about it. I just sat there like an idiot and let them put this stupid collar on me. I just froze."

"That's unfair," he said in a quiet tone. "You didn't just freeze. You fought. I have the scrathe burns to prove it."

She stopped pacing and stood in front of him. "No, you're right. I didn't just stand there. I did something worse. I ran my mouth and got us scrathed so much I'm *still* shaking. I injured us both and for what? We ended up here anyway."

"Don't be so angry with yourself," he said kindly. "It's not as though you had a choice in this matter."

She was too busy beating herself up to accept his comforting words. "Oh yeah, I did another thing," she added. "I fainted. What a terrific contribution to the team I am. I'm the one who faints."

He shrugged. "It is not uncommon for people of both planets to succumb to the exhaustion of conscious thought."

She pulled herself closer to him and lowered her voice. "Yeah, I'm sure it is, but I've never fainted in my life. *In my life*, Vale. Now it's practically a defining characteristic. In combat, when I was going on no sleep for three days and waiting for the enemy to blow my freaking head off, even then I never fainted. Now I've fainted for no good reason…And why are you being so calm? You're the most wanted Gray on this planet and we're in a torture chamber. Why aren't you freaking out?!"

His eyes grew wide and he bent down, meeting her at eye level. "Because I do not want to draw attention to myself. Or to you," he said quietly, casting a wary look around. "This is not the time to stand out. Do you understand?"

She did, and that was all she needed to pull herself together. He was very right about that. She might be having a breakdown, but she was by no means going to exacerbate it by getting scrathed to death by some angry HALOs. She'd had enough of that for one lifetime. Taking some deep breaths, she finally calmed down.

"I'm okay now. Assuming I don't just pass out again," she said bitterly.

"As I keep pointing out, you require sleep," he said quietly. "Your body is protecting itself, Taris. We Adulo cannot live without sleep. It is what is most required of us to survive."

"Good thing I'm not an Adulo," she countered. "That must be difficult."

"Taris--"

"No," she said, stopping his train of thought before he had the chance to voice it. "Just...no. Not now. I know what conversation you're trying to have with me and we're not going there, okay?"

"The infoscanner disagrees," he said with the smallest of ironic smiles.

"Look, I know the scanner *said* I was a Gray, but those things are wrong all the time. Scanners malfunction constantly."

Vale frowned. "I know you don't want to address this, but sometimes there are things you just need to accept--"

She grabbed him by the collar and yanked him down to her level.

"No," she hissed, her voice barely over a whisper. "I said *no*, Vale. I know what you're trying to say. You've been hinting at it since you met me, but hear this: I am *not* going to have a heart-to-heart about my background, or my genetics, or my damn bloodline right now. Not when I'm locked in a cement dungeon three stories underground. Not when I have a crew and a ship in danger. Not when lives are at stake. You understand?"

His liquid eyes rippled with his thoughts. "I understand."

She released his collar gently and he straightened up. Uncomfortable, Taris shoved her hands in her pockets and looked around the room.

"Okay then. Well...what the hell are we going to do now?"

Her words bounced off the walls, and she felt the eyes of dozens of people on her. No, not on her she realized, on Vale. He stood more elegantly than she did; regal even. The Grays, who usually wore masked emotions on their faces, were staring at him with discreet and respectful awe. Together the room trembled into silence as groups of Grays started to migrate toward them. There were at least two dozen of them all milling about; hovering in his presence. They seemed as though they merely wanted to be near Vale. They didn't cry out, or speak, or even touch him. They just stood close to him and closed their eyes. It seemed to her that, in that intangible closeness, they found a semblance of peace. Indeed, their smiles, although small, were ones of comfort and safety. Taris felt strangely out of place. She had just been ordering Vale around and here these people were, all but worshipping the guy. Awkwardly, her discomfort gave way to irritation.

"What the hell is going on? Why are they doing that? What are you--"

"Shh," he said, pushing a finger to his lips. His eyes traveled to the glass guard wall and she followed. Cameras were pointed in every direction. They glared at her from behind the glass like little angry black orbs.

"Oh great," she said. "Nothing we say or do is private."

"Taris," he said, standing in front of her. "You must stop talking so much."

"But how are we--"

Use your mind, he instructed, invading her brain with thundering intensity. Now the Grays were all staring at her. She could feel them in her head. She could feel them infringing on her mind. So many voices. Until a few days ago she had never heard the unspoken voices of the Grays. She didn't even know their telepathy was real, she always thought it was a myth. Desperate to communicate, she closed her eyes, focused as hard as she could on the task at hand, and opened her mind.

That was a mistake.

She heard the voices of dozens of Grays all speaking out at once. Speaking to her, about her, around her. All of them, all communicating at elevated tones. It was mentally deafening.

Why is she opening to all of us? a female voice asked.

Why does she fear this, is she mentally incompetent? That sounded like a male, but young.

She needs to stop speaking out loud like the humans do. She looks like a human-- Well that was definitely a woman's voice.

Stop talking! They'll know! What is she doing? She saw a man who looked maybe forty, with a scowl on his face, openly glaring at her.

The lord guardian has come to us, said a sweet voiced woman filled with worry. *The star must be in jeopardy--*

Her hair looks black, scoffed a pretentious male voice. *She cannot be one of us.*

They will kill us all if we don't leave. We lost four just this morning.

Gods be good, please spare my daughters. Please don't let them get my daughters.

"*Enough!*" she screamed, covering her ears. Overwhelmed, she shook her head and backed up out of the crowd. "That is enough I say! Stop it!"

"Taris," Vale said in that strange tone he used with her. It sounded like pride mixed with worry and reverence. It was both flattering and shaming at the same time.

"Nuh-uh. No way. No. I won't," she said, holding her head in her hands. Her temples throbbed. "Too much. It's too much. My brain isn't made like yours; it can't endure that."

"It can. Trust me, but you must control it," he said quietly. "Understand it."

"No. Maybe someday I need to understand that, but not today," she said. "*Not* today. I can't Vale. It hurts. It's too much. Please make it stop."

"Very well," Vale conceded. "*Rethis a tewia-ha.*"

Instantly all the voices in her head ceased screaming. They dissipated into silence. The room was as quiet as it was before, but now she felt as though she had more control. She was going to ask what had changed, but she knew. The words. Vale must have said some sort of command. A command that they all obeyed without question, or one she subconsciously did. Her eyes grew wide. She knew an authority figure when she saw one, and these people treated Vale like some sort of god. She wasn't sure how she felt about that. Power and authority could be a dangerous thing if used in the wrong way. Or by the wrong person.

"Thanks," she said finally. The pain of hearing everyone yelling in her head had ebbed to more of a headache.

"You have no need to thank me," he said amiably. "You weren't ready. In time, I'm sure you'll be able to master that ability. It is a skill, like any other, and it requires time and patience. Neither are luxuries we can afford at the moment I'm afraid."

She scoffed. "I'm not sure time and patience will make it any easier. Look, I don't know if you've noticed but I'm not the same as you."

"Oh? You're not? And what makes you think that?" His expression was stoic and calm, but she caught the hint of a sarcastic smile.

"Oh, so Vale has a sense of humor after all, eh?" she said with a grin. "Well you picked a fine time to put it on display."

She turned around, plopped down on the nearest metal bench. Both were bolted to the floor and had to weigh a ton. *No chair throwing apparently*, she thought. Vale's smile grew. She knew he heard that, but this time it didn't bother her. He sat down in front of her, politely folding his hands on the table. The uninterested HALO behind the wall of thick glass stopped eyeing them. Dispassionately, he went back to watching the small TV on his guard desk. When she felt like it was finally safe to talk - cameras notwithstanding - she tapped Vale's hand gently with her fingertips. He turned his passionate gaze to her, his attention undivided.

"So," she said in a polite tone, "guess we might as well get to know each other a little then."

"If you would like," he responded.

"Okay. Let's start with you," she decided. "What's with your hair? Every time you touch it you act like it reminds you of a dead beloved pet or something."

Whoops. That touched a nerve, she could tell. Still, the anger she saw in his eyes only lived for a moment. He touched the tendrils in question. "Adulo hair is a symbol of pride and strength," he said. "Unlike the humans, our hair does not grow after it is cut. The longer the hair, the older the soul. The oldest souls are the most revered in my culture. It is an honor to wear our hair long."

"Oh," she said. "So when they cut your hair it was like they took a part of you. Like your pride. Your badge of honor."

"More or less," he said, running his fingers through his hair affectionately. "It is more complicated than this, but essentially they reduced me - at least outwardly - to that of an inexperienced, naïve child. One act, in one year, undid over seven hundred Earth years of established honor and elderly nobility."

Her mouth dropped. *"Seven hundred years*? Holy mother of moly you're old."

He frowned at that. "Yes, although you'd never know from the way my hair looks now."

"Oh it doesn't look that bad," she said with a smile. "I think it looks nice."

"Thank you for the encouragement," he said politely, "but I struggle to see it that way. It pains me to feel the shortness of it. I miss the length. It empowered me. I feel…vulnerable without it."

"Vale, I didn't know," she said sympathetically. "I'm so sorry." She was surprised at how much she really meant that.

He forced the smallest of smiles for her benefit. "I thank you for that, but I will be okay. There are worse things in life than a tapered haircut I think."

"That's true." The conversation dulled at that point. She had a lot of things she wanted to talk to him about, but all the thoughts and feelings and emotions she wanted to share weren't safe while surrounded by cameras. Casually, Taris scanned the room. "So, eh, is this, you know, normal to you people? This way of life?"

The Grays were scattered in groups of three or four, apparently having small, quiet conversations around her. Everyone seemed so intensely private. Many who were standing in groups weren't even speaking. In some cases they weren't even looking at each other. It was inhumanly strange behavior, and as much as it embarrassed her to admit it, she felt uncomfortable being the only human there.

"Taris," he said in that exasperated tone. "This prison setting is not a Gray lifestyle. This is not an average social environment for my people. This is captivity. Imprisonment should not be normal to anyone."

"Yeah, you're right," she admitted. "Sorry. I didn't mean to offend."

"I know you didn't."

"I'm not very good at this 'making friends' thing," she explained weakly.

Vale's tiny smile returned. "Oh, I don't know. I've seen worse."

"Huh. I'll bet."

Taris supported her head on her arms and let her mind roll through all her thoughts. Without the wristband they had no way to communicate. She would have to get creative if they had any hope of escaping with their lives, and the window of opportunity was small. She couldn't delay long. Eventually they would find out who Vale was, and there was no telling what unspeakable horrors Boone Hooper would authorize to torture him. Time was already a factor working against them. They still had to find Jyrisa and get to Elias. That is, if the emissary hadn't killed him yet. This complex facility was much larger than she had expected. For all she knew, there were massive compartments in the complex that reached down to the Earth's core, holding thousands of Gray prisoners. Jyrisa could be anywhere.

Frustrated, she slammed her hands down on the table. She was in way over her head and she knew it, but there was nothing she could do about it. She had no weapon, no wristband, no plan of action, and no means of escape. To add insult to injury, the collar had irritated her skin something awful. She scratched her neck gruffly, attempting to convince herself that the situation wasn't actually hopeless.

"Why are you doing that?" Vale asked, tilting his head to one side.

"What?"

"Scratching. You're scratching your neck with your fingernails."

"Oh yeah," she said, digging her pointer finger between the metal and her neck. "This thing itches like hell. What kind of metal is this made out of? Oh where's Matt with his scanning spectacles when you need him."

"It's sidus metal," he answered in a strange tone. "It's the strongest metal from our planet. It's sort of a biological metal I guess you could say, and it's regenerative. It's so strong that it can - and often is - used as an energy source."

"Is it what you make your swords out of?" she guessed.

"Yes. It is. It's a metal completely unique unto Caleum."

"Yeah? Well it itches like hell," she complained.

He frowned. "How bizarre. Adulos have never had a physical reaction to the sidus metal like the one you're experiencing."

"Well that's because I'm not like you, Vale." She finally got a good scratch and sighed in relief. "Ah....god that feels better."

He gave her a proud whisper of a smile. "That's my warrior. Conquering even the smallest of battles with unbounded dedication."

She looked at him. He just paid her a compliment. A strange compliment, but a compliment nonetheless. She hadn't expected that. She felt her cheeks flush, but she didn't allow them to stay pink long. They sat in silence for a few moments. She studied his expression as he glanced around the room. The pain on his face was becoming stronger. He was visibly upset at seeing his fellow Grays imprisoned and collared. She could feel his anxiety and despair. He was containing his strongest feelings, she could tell, but he could not hide them from her completely. The pain was palpable. She didn't blame him. As a matter of fact, she sympathized.

"I understand how you're feeling," she said in a low tone. "You know, with the trapped prison camp thing."

"Oh?"

Her eyes fell to her hands. "In a way I understand that better than most."

He blinked. "And why is that, Taris?"

"Well…let's just say that prison is not unknown to me," she said sadly. "I was in the revolution, you know."

He looked at her, interested. "The one from several years ago?"

She nodded. "That's the one. Do you remember it?"

"I remember. I was here on Earth," Vale said. "The humans were divided across this whole planet. That was when the sectors were assigned and the Earth World United authority was established."

"Right. That's the one," she said. "I was just a teenager, a kid. I wanted to fight for something. I've always had this strange need to fight for things, and the rebellion sure seemed like the cause worth fighting for. The war had been going on for years by then, but I was young and eager to join. As soon as I was old enough, I found some rebels and asked to join their cause."

Vale's eyebrows raised. "You fought for the insurrection forces? What made you do that?"

She sighed and pulled her hair out of its hold, tangling it in her fingers. "Well, I didn't agree with the United agenda. They wanted to change so many things. They wanted to take away our country identities, force us to submit to asinine unification protocols without thinking it through. They wanted to make corporations and not governments the sovereign rulers over the Sectors, removing democracy from our leadership. They wanted to make the slave trade legal, defining 'people' as human life forms *only*. I just didn't think that was right."

"And then what?" he asked.

She gestured around the room. "Well obviously we lost. Miserably. When the armistice was signed and our respective countries submitted to the EWU, the rebels were tried as war criminals and sent to prison camps. I spent nine months fighting the war and two years in prison paying for it. It was rough. I spent every day in a backbreaking hard labor camp while the rest of the world was buying slaves on online auctions. It was tough to swallow."

"So, how did you go from a war criminal to a stealth spaceship captain?" he asked. "That doesn't seem like a logical transition."

"My dad, mostly," she admitted a little sheepishly. "He developed the technology for the genetic detection devices. You know, the infoscanners? The government wanted them so badly they were willing to pay him millions, but he traded them for my freedom instead. In exchange for his genetic detector, the United authority had to free me from prison and send me to military training. A safe place for me, he said. Anyway, they gladly accepted. Anything to save money I guess. They got the machine they always wanted, and I got boot camp at the fleet academy."

"Seems a little extreme, even considering the circumstance, to make you join the fleet that you so recently fought against," Vale commented amiably. "Not to mention a risk on both sides."

She shrugged. "Nah, it wasn't so bad. Two years in a hard labor camp sort of took the insurrection out of me. And don't judge my dad too harshly. He did what he thought was right. He thought it would straighten me out. He was right I guess. Damn him, but he's usually right. And it's okay. Turns out that my rebel training helped me. All that sneaking around and quiet shadow warfare made me a prime candidate for stealth ship training."

"Do you regret what you did?" he asked. "Joining the rebels I mean. Even though it was a failed cause. Do you regret the choice to align yourself with the more difficult side?"

"No," she said without hesitation. "Not at all. The difficult side was the right one. That never changed. Even if it's hard, the right thing is always worth doing. Even if you fail. I'd do it all again, too."

He leaned forward and reached out, touching the side of her face affectionately. "I'm thankful for what you did, Taris. You fought for a cause you believed in against all odds. Win or lose, there is valor in that."

She smiled. "Thank you, Vale. It's genuinely nice to hear that."

He let his hand linger longer than it should have, but she didn't protest. She realized why so many people revered him. His very presence seemed strangely calming. More calming than she would have liked. Realizing how tired she really was, she leaned back on the bench and yawned loudly.

"Oh my god, where do they sleep around here?" she wondered, looking into the small cells. "I could use a nap."

"Taris," he said. "I need to leave you."

She turned back to him sharply. "What?"

"Not abandon you," he clarified. "I mean I need to ask some questions to these tribesmen here with us. I need to see what is happening in this facility. You never know, maybe we'll meet a familiar face." She knew he meant Jyrisa, but their inability to talk openly prohibited him from saying so.

"Go do what you gotta do, man," she said, feigning a dismissive attitude.

"If I leave you here on this metal bench, will you be able to sustain yourself?" he asked, standing up.

She glared at him. "Did you not hear my whole prison camp story? I think I can handle sitting on a bench, thanks. Now go. Find out what you need. I'll try not to cause any trouble while you're gone."

He turned back and gave her a sideways smile. "Now why don't I believe that?"

"Ah, the Vale humor shows itself yet again. Well you've got no choice I guess. Now's not the time to start doubting my word. It's a little late for that."

"I suppose you are correct." He smiled at that and stood up gracefully, sweeping to his feet like a dancer.

"Stay out of trouble," he said.

"Yeah," she replied. "It's a little late for that, too."

Chapter Twenty-three

As it turns out, staying out of trouble was easier than she thought. With the absence of people to speak to, all she could do was sit and do absolutely nothing. Nothing but pace and fret. She had to come up with a plan. Just standing around and waiting for the chance to step outside and flag down a friendly ship wasn't likely, or even feasible. What she really needed was a way to get upstairs and get her wristband back. A quick inspection of the elevator shaft told her that wasn't a good escape. The compartment - like everything else it seemed - was lined with scrathe coils. The thin, hyper-charged electrical lines snaked up the shaft; thin and discreet and painful. Not to mention the fact that she still wouldn't get past the first floor without being shot down. Okay, so sneaking up the elevator wasn't a possibility. She thought about trying to take down the HALO behind the glass, but every option her mind presented was completely impossible. She paced for so long, pondered for so long and cursed herself for so long that she didn't even hear the alarm sound. She wasn't aware of it until everyone started lining up to face the glass guard. It was dinner time, apparently. *Dinner time?* she wondered. *Grays don't eat. Why are they having dinner?*

Trying to blend in, she fell into the queue and patiently waited. She should have been starving, but to her surprise she found that she'd lost her appetite. She was still exhausted, however, and yawned her way all through the line. Finally, she reached the front guard. His beady eyes scrutinized her with a drooping frown. He was very large and sweaty and looked far too young to be so rotund. He also looked like he couldn't give a damn about his job. She didn't blame him. With a grumble she didn't understand, he handed her a small bowl through the open window on the counter.

"What is this?" she asked, sniffing it suspiciously. "It looks like oatmeal and grits got together and had a tasteless baby."

"Lemme guess," he said in condescending tone. "You're the one they call Snow White, am I right?"

"Yup. That's what they call me," she said. "Unfortunately."

The HALO frowned. "Hmmphm. Don't know why. Aside from the hair you don't look like a princess to me."

"Yeah no shit, Sherlock," she responded without thinking.

"Excuse me?" the guard said. Angry and red faced, he attempted to stand up quickly from his too-small chair. He only succeeded in making his dramatic movements awkward and stilted. "What did you say to me?"

Oops. "Um. Oh right. Well it was just a joke."

"At my expense? What are you, some whack-job Gray with a *death wish?*"

"Um," she fumbled haplessly. "That is, sir. I mean, I didn't mean...it just slipped out and--"

"She's new, sir," said a female voice behind her. "She got scrathed earlier today and her brain's still fried. Please forgive her, sir. She meant no harm."

Taris spun around and came face to face with a mature female Gray. She had an oval shaped face with smooth skin that still managed to look wise with age. In truth she looked to be maybe forty, but she could be a hundred for all Taris knew. The woman had a small nose, full red lips and two gigantic silver eyes that stood out like saucers on her face. The most prominent feature was her hair. Her hair was gray, but very unusually, it was also curly. Taris had never seen a Gray with curly hair before. Long and coiled and flowing, her hair bounced down to the middle of her back. Her voice was confident and mighty. She seemed like a woman who was no stranger to a position of authority, and she knew it. Taris liked her immediately.

The HALO lifted his eyes to the curly-haired Gray. "Is that so, Suzy? You standing up for the new dogs now?"

"Only the pups who don't know well enough not to bite the master's hand," she responded wryly.

The guard scoffed. "Well aren't you helpful. Is that the truth, new bitch? Did they fry your brains already?"

Suzy's eyes widened. Taris got the hint. "Ah. Yes. Yep, that's what happened. Got me wee little brains fried outside earlier. I can't think straight...now."

The HALO pursed his lips like he didn't give a damn. "Hmmphm. Okay then. If Suzy says so it must be true. Now take your oatmeal and shut up."

She did as she was told, for no other reason than to avoid losing her temper and getting shot. She grasped the bowl in her hands and sat down at the table farthest from the guard booth. She was right; the oatmeal tasted as bland as it looked. She tried a generous mouthful at first, but it tasted like mushy nothingness. In truth, she was amazed she wasn't so hungry that she gulped the whole thing down. She couldn't really remember the last time she actually had anything to eat. Not to her surprise, she wasn't long for want of company.

"I think he likes you," Suzy said, sliding gracefully to a seat in front of her. "Usually he just throws the bowl at the new ones."

Taris scoffed. "Yeah. He was a real charmer. I think he preferred you to me, though."

The woman shook her head. "Nah. Bobby's not really into the silver hair thing. Don't worry, he's got a big temper but he's mostly harmless. He's more of a barker, not a biter."

"I'd like to see how much he barks with my hands around his neck," Taris said without thinking.

"You're new to all of this, aren't you?" Suzy asked, scrutinizing her. "Taking orders and the authority of the humans I mean. You don't look like you've ever had to bow to them before."

Her accent was distinctly British, which Taris enjoyed. It made her think of Gareth. Even though Suzy's accent was clearly English and not Welsh. She liked the sound of the flowing British vowels as they danced off the tongue. A wave of guilt washed over her at the thought of Gareth. *Oh Gareth…*She made a mental note apologize to him, and to thank him for trying to save her life. If she ever saw him again.

"I guess I am new to this Gray thing," she said, trying to sound casual. "I mean, with the slavery and the bowing and all that. That obvious huh?"

"Yeah," Suzy said, poking at the oatmeal like it was an unknown sea creature. "I could tell by your attitude. The way you treated the HALO, you talked to him like an equal. That's the unequivocal sign of someone who doesn't know how bad they've got it. Not that I'm complaining, mind you; I thought you were brilliant."

"Thanks," she said with a small smile. "I thought you were great, too. You saved my ass, really. I wasn't thinking at all when I opened my mouth. I could have been killed."

"Killed?" Suzy said, shaking her head. "No. You're too valuable for that. Complexes pay wranglers a lot of money for Grays like you. Killing you would be a waste of an investment, and they can't have that now, can they? Count your blessings that you're different, pet. Different will help you here."

"How do you mean?"

"Well, in case you haven't noticed, I have curly hair," she pointed out.

Taris shrugged. "So?"

"So? So? Bloody hell, are we even from the same planet? How many other Adulos have you met who have curly hair? Can you name one?" she asked, the edge in her tone sounding surprisingly more human than Gray.

Taris thought about it. "No, actually."

"I know," she said, calming down. "And it's this stupid crazy hair that's kept me alive so long in this place. I used to hate it, but now it's the one thing I've got that keeps my head on my shoulders. You and I share that good fortune, dear."

She had a moment of panic that Suzy would see her as different. That she would ostracize her, or call her out. Somehow Vale's idea of not drawing attention to herself seemed really wise. "What do you mean?" she asked as casually as she could muster.

Suzy reached over the table and grabbed a handful of her hair, inspecting it appreciatively. "Hmm. That black hair is either a really impressive dye job or it's real," she said, sitting back down. "If it's real you're in luck. They will definitely want to keep you around, and good thing too. The way you run your mouth you'd better thank the gods you're not ordinary."

You have no idea, she thought. "Yeah it's real. Who would have thought that hair would be the reason for living," she joked sarcastically.

Suzy stifled a laugh. "Yeah. Not much for the feminists to brag about, but we'll take what we can get. Different is good. Different means you're more than just a nameless member of the flock. Different means you can get things others can't. You could make a difference."

"Does it mean we can get different food?" she asked. "This tastes like gooey sand."

"Nope," Suzy said, setting her barely touched bowl down dismissively. "Always porridge."

"For every meal?"

"Every single one I'm afraid."

Taris frowned and shoved her bowl away from her. "Well that's great. Just great. At least you don't need to eat. You won't starve or anything."

Suzy gave her a strange look. "It doesn't matter. They force us to eat out of spite. They know we can't stand it so they make us choke down this rubbish. Honestly, I keep hoping I'll get fat and they'll cut me off. I never do, though."

"How long have you been here?" Taris asked, hoping to keep her mind off of the bowl of mush.

"Two years," Suzy answered without skipping a beat.

"Two *years*?" Taris said a little louder than she should have. "For what?"

"Huh, you're a queer one aren't you?" Suzy asked. "What do you mean 'for what'? You think they had a legitimate reason to send me here? My master needed the money and he was offered a high price for me so off I went. Just like the slave I am."

Taris shook her head. "But that's terrible. Two years is way too long to be in a place like this!"

"Oh? You think there's a *right* amount of time to be trapped underground in the world's most inescapable dungeon?"

"I mean, why hasn't anyone done anything?" Taris asked.

"Like whom?" she demanded. "Who's going to come to my rescue, really? The high priests of the Five? No one even knows I'm here."

"Well maybe," Taris said slowly. "But slavery wasn't the first part of your life, was it? I mean, you had to have had a life before you were a slave. Don't you have friends or family? Someone who can vouch for you or get you out?"

Suzy pushed her curls back behind her head and scanned her with her eyes. The liquid ripped in the reflection of the light. It made her look suspicious and angry. "You speak like a human, you know. All idealistic, thinking the world is going to bend to the will of the good and not suffer the injustice of the wicked. Your voice even sounds human. Oh, you've been around them far too long, dear."

"And you didn't answer my question," she said with her arms folded.

Suzy narrowed her eyes at her. "Fine. I had a life on Caleum, sure. We all did. I used to be a pilot. Had my own ship, even. The *Balth'tar* was her title. A powerful, great name for a spaceship, don't you think? Now look at me. Trapped in an underground cinder block dungeon. They force feed me gruel and pump me full of drugs and make my hair turn curly. Now that's the best thing about myself. How sad is that? I went from a starship captain to a curly-haired freak with a stupid name sewn to my shirt."

"Your name isn't Suzy Q?" Taris asked, trying to cut through the tension with a little levity.

Suzy's fierce expression gave way at that and she laughed. "Ha! Not in the slightest. It's Xiana Nerais. And what's your real name? Not Snow White I presume."

"It's Taris…" Taris what? She almost said Bodil, when she remembered that the Grays don't have last names. "Teag," she finished finally. "Taris Teag."

Suzy snapped her fingers together in appreciation. "Ah, a Teag! That doesn't surprise me. Teags are always so sure of themselves, just like you. So you're an empath, then?" she asked.

Taris blinked. Was she supposed to be an empath? She wasn't sure how to answer that correctly. "Um…well, aren't you?"

"No," Xiana said, furring her brow. "I said I was a Nerais, remember? The whole feel-the-emotions-absorb-the-pain stuff is for you tree dwellers."

Tree dwellers? Did the Teags live in trees? Taris was starting to feel like the concept of blending in was going to be harder than she thought. "Well sure," she said nonchalantly, "but don't you…non tree dwellers…have spiritual powers, too?" *I hope.*

"Of course," Xiana said. "Everyone knows that, we just don't like to flaunt it. Nerais tribes never do. We like the hard, gritty action of an actual verbal conversation over the 'I can sense your feelings' nonsense. But we're not as spiritual as your people. You Teags like the old ways. The Nerais want to adapt."

"Hmm, not all of us," Taris said, grateful that she dug her way out of that. "I like having a verbal conversation as well. It feels more real. Has more meaning, you know?"

Xiana smiled. "I think I'm going to like you, Taris Teag."

"Thanks," she said. "I think I'm going to like you, too. You're so different from all the other Grays I've ever met."

"Ha! You're one to talk. You're like a Gray that was raised by a pack of humans. If I didn't know any better I'd assume you *were* human."

"Tell that to the gate guard," Taris grumbled. "The one who scrathed me before I even got though the door."

"The way you run your mouth you're lucky it was just the one time," she said with a cautious expression. "I bet your hair saved you from going straight to the crates."

Hmm. She hadn't thought of that. "Maybe."

"See, I'm telling you, dear," Xiana said. "Being different is keeping you alive. And if that's the case I don't want you to leave my side."

"Why?"

"Because special people have got to stick together," Xiana said quietly. "We're the only chance any of the others have of surviving this."

Taris leaned in so their faces were practically touching. Now she was getting somewhere. Maybe she wouldn't have to be trapped in Hammerhead Hold for very long after all. "Why is that?"

"The more different you are, the better you're treated. The Hammer likes the different ones. If the Hammer likes you you'll live. If the Hammer deems you ready, you get to leave."

"The Hammer," Taris said slowly. "He's the one in charge. What's he like? I mean, can I request to see him or does he come to meet me?"

Xiana scoffed. "Who do you think you are, the bloody queen of Sector One? No you don't get to meet him. He directs everything from his lofty watchman's Eye in the yard."

"So you never see him? Do you even know what he looks like?"

"No one sees him," she answered. "But everyone gets to meet him as soon as they are scrubbed."

"Scrubbed?"

"Yeah," she flicked a finger at her collar. "That thing on your collar in the back? The little color key box? That's your scrub box. Once your box gets to green you get to meet the Hammer."

Taris fingered the back of the collar awkwardly. "This thing is a meter? What's it metering?"

Suzy put her hands on the table. "It determines how long you have to be here. Every day they subject us to chemicals. Every day. The more chemicals you get, the more it changes color. When your color gets to green you go see the Hammer and your scrubbing is complete."

"So that's it?" she asked, touching the box in the back reflexively. "I just have to get this thing to green and then--"

"Game over," Xiana finished for her. "That's it. Everyone who goes to see the Hammer is never brought back down here again. Of course, it's longer for some of us than for others. I knew a Fynn tribesman who was only here a month, the lucky bastard, before his collar went green. And here I am, two years in and no green. I've been stuck on blue for bloody ages."

"So what happens when you meet the Hammer?" she wondered. "Does he...kill us?"

"I don't think so," Xiana said. "If he wanted to kill us, why go through all the trouble of keeping us locked up? You know what I think? I think it's measuring our ability to assimilate to the chemicals. Like we're lab rats or something. When we're green, we're done to them. Fully cooked."

Taris frowned. "Yeah, but what's the point of that?"

"Well," Xiana said, leaning on her arms, "I heard that they are working on an integration project. You know, putting Grays into the societies of humans so we can all coexist. Can you imagine? Living in a house with human neighbors? Anyway, everyone wants to be scrubbed. It's the only way to get out of here. Alive anyway."

"I don't think it's going to be that easy," Taris said suspiciously.

"Maybe not, but it's all we've got." Xiana looked around to make sure no one was listening. "I bet you'd be willing to stretch the limits to get it, too. I heard you talking to the lord guardian. You were having a pretty interesting discussion."

Lord guardian. She must mean Vale. "You heard that?"

"Yeah. I heard what you said about the time you fought with the rebels. With the humans. How you fight for causes you believe in."

"Oh that part," she said. "Yeah."

"Is it true?" Xiana asked her.

"Well yeah of course it's true..."

"Well," she said, lowering her voice, "how would you like to make good use of your rebel skills? How would you like to get out of here?"

348

She really wanted to. More than anything, but something about this didn't ring true with her. Something seemed suspicious. "What do I have to do?"

Xiana's eyes rippled with excitement. "All you have to do is say the word and I'll get you out of here. There's a lull, in the guard cycle, just before dawn. I have special privileges to go out on the courtyard twice a day. It won't be so hard to sneak you off and out before anyone's the wiser. You can even take the lord guardian if you'd like. Now, you'll have to find a way to get your own collars off, but I can get you out of the door."

Taris folded her arms in front of her and leaned back. "So that's all I have to do, eh? Just make small talk with you and suddenly you're my best friend?"

"Hey, I have a soft spot for us special types," she said flippantly. Her calm reserve was starting to fail.

"And, I suppose you have a brilliant reason as to why you haven't done this yourself?"

Xiana looked down. "Oh, you know, I am so close to green anyway. What's the point if I leave now?"

"Uh huh," Taris said. "Well that's convenient I suppose. And you're going to do this all out of the kindness of your heart I presume?"

"I told you, I have a soft spot for you," she spat out in hushed tones. "Now, are you going to accept my offer or not, because I'm sure there are hundreds of other Grays looking to break out of here that would love to take my deal."

"Grays," Taris repeated. "You just called your own people Grays. It's unusual to hear an Adulo refer to their own people as 'the Grays'."

Xiana's eyes widened. Taris knew that look. It was the look of a liar who'd been exposed. *Gotcha*, she thought. "Slip of the tongue," the woman rationalized.

"Why are you doing this, Xiana?" she asked. "What benefit would you possibly have?"

"Um...The lord guardian is a good guy to have on your side," she said, fumbling for an excuse.

"I don't think getting him thrown in a crate would be the best way to do that," Taris countered.

Xiana's eyes dropped. "Oh. So you know about those, do you?"

"I know they're nothing I want to mess with," Taris countered. "And that's where we would have been headed, am I right?"

"I don't know what you're--"

"Let me just stop you right there," Taris said, holding her hand up. "I'll spare you the lies. I know what you're trying to do here. No, don't shake your head, honey. I do. I know what a camp rat looks like."

"Camp rat?" Xiana asked, confused.

Taris leaned her elbows on the table. "Yeah. Camp rat. One of the inmates paid by the staff to weed out problems. Get them to admit to plots or attempt to escape so they can punish them. Keeps the prisoners in fear, keeps the jailors gainfully employed, keeps the investors investing."

"How did you know?" she asked, confounded enough to drop the façade.

Taris shrugged. "Oldest trick in the book. This isn't my first ride on the prison camp train you know. So tell me, what's in it for you, huh? Money? Reduced time? Couldn't be the food choices." She thought about it, and then it came to her. "Oh. I know. It's your freedom isn't it?"

Bingo.

"Nerais are the hardest to scrub," Xiana blurted out. "Everyone knows that! It could take years! They said if I could get the new Grays to attempt escape they'd let me go! Do you have any idea what that means?"

"I know what it means for me," Taris retorted. "It means a scrathe beat down and doing time in the crates. Neither of which sound like they would be worth the risk."

"It's just a night in a crate!" Xiana exclaimed in as hushed a tone as she could manage. "I've been here two years! You've been here less than a day! Who cares? It doesn't even hurt that much!"

"That is not true, Taris," Vale said, sliding into the seat next to her. Taris felt an unexpected sense of relief when she saw him. Xiana recoiled when she saw him, like a child caught trying to set fire to the family pet.

"Hello, lord guardian," she said to him, bowing her head.

"You are not telling the truth, Xiana Nerais," he said, unwavering. "The crates are more than just a cage. They are constant, boiling pain. The metal used to make those boxes is amalgamated with scrathe fibers. It sends constant shocks through the entire body of the captured person. It's terrible unblinking agony. You cannot sleep. You can barely move. There are Adulos who go mad after only hours in a crate. Many die."

Taris turned to Xiana. "I told you. Camp rat. I knew it."

"How very deceitful, Xiana," Vale said reproachfully. "You've learned to manipulate like a human. I'm displeased."

Xiana raised her eyes. A ripple of anger flashed through them. "I don't care if you're displeased, Guardian Vale. I don't care at all. This place, it changes you. It makes you cold and bitter and angry. Three hundred and six human years I lived without those feelings, and now they are all I care about."

His eyes scanned her. "There is something dark in your soul. You are tainted, Xiana."

"It's not my fault!" she protested. "Those drugs they give us, they corrupt the Adulo soul. I'm miserable. I'll do anything to get out of this place. I'm tired of waiting, lord guardian. I can't suffer for two, three more years here. I just can't. I'm taking my destiny into my own hands for once. You'd be smart to do the same."

Vale stood up and walked around the table. Without explanation or prompting, he took Xiana into his arms. She resisted at first, but finally relented, allowing herself to fold into his chest. Small silver tears dripped down her face and dripped onto Vale's gray sleeve. For a moment they just stood there in the quiet embrace. Taris could feel the despair and desperation of Xiana's plight. She knew the woman was desperate, but she couldn't help but feel inexplicably jealous at the fact that Vale was comforting and embracing her, a woman who so obviously didn't deserve it.

"I'm so sorry, lord guardian. Please forgive me. I just…I don't know what I'm doing anymore," she said, her tone honest and tender. Taris relented in her anger somewhat. But not much.

"Sometimes I feel like I don't know who I am," Xiana whispered. "I'm starting to forget things. Memories, places from home, and the dreams. They're intolerable." She pulled back and stared into his eyes. "They're changing me. They're changing all of us. I'm becoming less of myself. I think it's killing me."

He reached down and cupped her face in his hands. *I know, but not for much longer. Have faith, young Xiana Nerais. This will end very soon.* Taris heard his words, so comforting, so determined. Xiana seemed calmed by that, assured even. It made Taris irrationally irritated. She didn't like it one bit. He should be scolding her for trying to trick them, not comforting her. She was about to say as much when she heard a noise coming from the guard booth. The HALO was rapping on the glass with his scrathe baton.

"Hey!" he yelled, his voice muffled through the barrier. "No physical touching! Suzy, get back to your cell."

Xiana nodded and stood up quickly, brushing the liquid mirror tears from her face. With a sideways look at Taris, she walked off, gliding toward the cells with no more thoughts or explanations. The Grays who were watching went about their quiet business as though nothing had passed.

"So do you comfort all women by hugging them," she asked with a bite in her tone, "or just the ones with exciting hair?"

He cocked his head to the side. "You're mad at me."

"Well obviously," she said, keeping her arms folded. "That woman tried to sell us out and what did you do? You hugged her. You made promises to her."

"She did what she did out of desperation," he argued. "Why have I upset you? I don't understand."

"Oh that's such crap," she said angrily. "How do you not know why I'm mad? Everyone here is desperate. She was the only one who decided to use it to her advantage."

"Taris," he said. There was that tone again. "You can't harbor resentment for everyone who seeks personal gain. For in that resentment you become more loathsome than the ones you despise, blinded to your own hypocrisy."

She sighed heavily. "Oh look, the lord guardian wants to preach to me."

Vale furred his brow. "Why did you call me lord guardian?" he asked, sliding down on the bench next to her.

She shrugged. "Everyone else was calling you that, why can't I?"

"Because that title holds no significance to you," he said.

"Exactly. So why don't you explain it to me instead of telling me how wrong I am for being spiteful?" she shot back, turning away from him. She felt him scoot in closer to her. *No,* she told herself, *don't let him charm you down. Stay mad. Stay strong.*

With the guards no longer looking, in the dim lights of the room, Vale slipped his arm around her waist and pulled her close to him. With his other hand he reached up and clasped her hand, tracing the lines of her scar with his thumb. His touch was electric. She turned to face him, and as soon as she did every angry thought she had in her mind dissolved. His face was alight with emotion. He clasped her hands, wrapping her fingers with his. Gently, ever so discreetly, he pulled her hands to his lips and kissed the edges of her fingers. If she had been a lesser woman, she might have swooned. She wasn't so sure that was entirely beneath her.

"Whoa," she breathed. "I hate when you do that."

He looked at her. "Kiss you?"

"No," she said, looking down. "Win the argument. Sneaky."

He stifled a laugh at that. "Perhaps I'm actually right."

"Perhaps," she said with a little smile.

"You perplex me, Taris Leigh Bodil," he said affectionately. "Sometimes you're such a mystery."

"I know," she responded. "But you like it."

"I think I truly do," he said, watching her eyes absorb his. She stole a look at the HALO. He was eyeing her suspiciously. With great regret she detangled herself from Vale's embrace and scooted slightly away from him. "So, did you find out anything about our friends? The situation?"

"Nothing of too much consequence," he said, "but I am not disheartened. The gods have not failed me yet, and they will not now."

"You have a strange concept of success," she said, taking a good look around the dungeon. "And I'm not the type who likes to place trust in gods I don't serve."

"Put your trust in me, then," he said gently. She felt his arm brush up against hers. It was the tiniest of touches, but it was enough.

"And what makes you think I'll trust you?" she asked. "I didn't trust your lady friend back there." He might have won the argument, but that didn't mean she was willing to let it go just yet.

"You'll trust me," he said confidently. "I can see in your thoughts that you will."

"This whole energy reading thing that you do? It's really creepy," she pointed out.

He raised an eyebrow. "You have a lot to learn about not being human, Taris. That involves a lot more than just energy reading."

"Oh goody," she grumbled. "I can hardly wait to find out what *that* means."

Chapter Twenty-four

They slept on the floor like dogs.

All they were given were a few blankets and a hard cement floor. When the guards called for lights out, everyone filed into the different cells that corresponded with their number groups. Taris and Vale were in room ten together, along with half a dozen others. The barred gates closed, sectioning them off for the night. The Grays were spread out on the ground, scattered like silver-haired birds in a poorly kept cage. At first Taris refused to sleep. Vale tried to convince her to sleep, that it was for the best, but eventually he gave up and dozed off. Taris leaned against the wall with her arms wrapped around her knees. She was furious as she watched the sleeping Grays, scattered all over the floor. No warmth, no comfort. Not even a pillow. It was so inhumane for so many reasons. She didn't want to join the sleeping herd. She didn't want to lie down and just accept her fate. She refused on principle…but even principle has physical limitations. Eventually the exhaustion overtook her. She was dreaming before she even realized it.

It was the reoccurring dream she always had, but strangely, this time Vale was in it. He was standing outside of the circle, directly behind her, and his hair appeared to be glowing. He was speaking to her, but she couldn't understand the words. She was still holding the sword with her bleeding hand, but something was different. Looking up, she realized that she was being watched. By many. The hills, so dark and unremarkable in all of her other dreams, were filled with the reflective liquid eyes of Grays. There were everywhere, staring at her. Whispering things that she couldn't quite make out. Hundreds of them, just standing there, staring in awe. She wanted to turn and ask them what they were doing there, but something distracted her. The blue fire that glowed in the middle of the rocks started to expand. It cracked with raging power as it grew. Curiously she reached out and tried to touch the fire. Her fingers extended toward the blue flames. She could almost feel the heat of it on her skin. Suddenly she felt a hand clamp down on her arm, stopping her. It was Vale.

"No," he said sternly. "Do not touch the noticulus. It is not time."

"Time for what?" she asked. The power that raged in him was white hot and ever-growing. His hair and eyes seemed to glow with incandescent strength.

"The Star of Gray must be protected," he said. "Now is not the time."

"What? What does that mean? Vale? Vale!"

"*Get up, get up, get up*!" screamed the intercom, startling her out of her dream. "Rise and shine silverbacks! It's time to face another day! You have fifteen minutes to make yourself presentable and get in line to your respective groups. Get up, get up, get up!"

She sat up promptly and rubbed her eyes. The transition from dream to awake was jostling to say the least. She rolled her shoulders and adjusted her stiff back. She had fallen asleep while leaning against the wall, and that position was not one of the more comfortable ones. The cell doors opened with a loud metal grinding noise as she braided her hair down her back. Vale, who had slept next to her, sat up stiffly and stared at her. The look on his face was neutral as ever, but his eyes were flowing with movement, liquid and intense. Irritated, she narrowed her eyes at him and yawned widely. She had not had a good night's sleep. She was in no mood to tolerate his severe spiritualism after so terrible a night.

"I don't suppose they'll give us a cup of coffee for breakfast, will they?" she asked with a sarcastic smile.

"Taris," he said quietly. "Do not touch the fire."

She blinked. "What?"

"The fire in your dream," he said quietly. "Don't touch it. You can't do that until the time is right."

The realization hit her like a splash of water. "You mean...oh my god. You were in my dream. That was you in my dream, wasn't it?"

"Yes," he answered plainly.

Her mouth dropped. "How do you do that?"

We were all in your dream, actually, thought a Gray standing next to her. He looked younger than he probably was, with the face of an impossibly beautiful teenager. He was staring down at her with a scowl. *You need to learn to filter yourself.*

We're not supposed to know who the three pillars are, said a woman with sickly pale skin and saucer-shaped eyes. *It's forbidden.*

They belong to the Star of Gray, pointed out the young male.

"What?" she asked, feeling overwhelmed. She hated when they all thought at her at once. Especially in that angry, frustrated tone they all seemed to take with her.

The Star alone is the only one who can declare the faces of the pillars. Why did you do that? demanded the woman.

You, of all Adulo, should know better, chastised a large and extremely muscular Gray with floor length hair. His tone, and dubious expression, implied that he was extremely old.

But now you know the face of one, Vale chimed in, coming to a stand with a serious face. *You all know, and now you know what must be done.*

But what if she dreams and brings us in again? the first Gray teenager asked.

What if we see the faces of the other two? the old man wondered. *The gods will frown on us if we betray their decree.*

I agree, thought the woman. *We cannot abide by our laws if we are dragged into a dreamscape against our will.*

This was involuntary for everyone, Vale pointed out. "It will not happen again." *She will not reveal the other two. She doesn't know them. She doesn't even know who she is.*

But she took us into her dream, the woman protested. *All of us.*

That was a powerful threspinning, the man with the floor length hair thought, staring at her with interest. *I've never seen the likes of that before.*

It was an accident, Vale clarified. *She doesn't know how to control that.*

Then you had better teach her, lord guardian, or she will endanger more than just herself, said the teenager Gray with a dark look.

"Oh my god, please stop," Taris said bitterly. She stood up groggily and put her hands on her ears. "You're all screaming at me. It's too much."

What, she can't control her thoughts, either? the boy asked Vale incredulously.

Well that's rude, thought the woman, folding her arms.

"Can you all stop talking about me like I'm not here?"

"Well this is an unprecedented experience," the younger male Gray said. "We did not expect to share your dream. Especially not *that* dream."

She frowned. "Wait a minute. Are you telling me all of you were actually in my dream?"

Vale swung around to face her. *Yes. Every Gray in the complex.*

She rubbed her eyes. "What? How is that even possible?"

Shh! The long-haired man thought at her. *Why are you speaking, child? Do you want to get us all killed? Do not betray the thoughts of our people!*

"By talking?"

YES! She heard at least a dozen Grays think in unison.

The woman scoffed as she braided her silver hair into two braids. "Hmmhpm. Doesn't know herself indeed."

"And *she* is supposed to help us?" the teenager said dubiously. "Gods save us all. I thought we were in enough trouble here."

"Oh well you can just go to hell, guy," Taris retorted. "I'll not be judged by a kid with a bad attitude."

"I'm ninety-two years old, *leathchea*," he said, putting his hands on his hips. "I am not a kid. Not by your human standards, anyway. And it appears we just might go to hell." *If you're one of the ones meant to save us.*

She scoffed. "What made you think I'd want to do that?"

"Hello? Pillar number one?" *It's your duty, or hasn't the lord guardian explained that to you yet.*

She raised her eyebrows. "No..."

The ninety-two year old teenager looked at her and laughed. It was a desperate, nervous laugh that was meant to be insulting. And it was. *Oh gods*, he scoffed. *We're all doomed now.*

"*Enough!*" Vale said, uncharacteristically raising his voice. His tone was so strong that every Gray - possibly in the whole complex - froze to listen to him. Even the young Gray stopped moving. Taris looked around and realized that the Grays' eyes had glossed over. It looked almost like they were standing at attention. Her gaze travelled to Vale. *He's commanding them,* she realized. All of them.

You all were privy to a scene you should have never seen. Vale's words were strong, unwavering. Resonating with authority. *This can be undone. For the sake of our own kind, and the existence of our race, you will forget. You will all forget. Forget the dream, forget the three, forget the scene you just witnessed. As lord guardian, I command you to erase that dream from your memory. Understood?*

Understood, lord guardian. She heard the sound of hundreds of voices all speaking in union. If it had been out loud, their response would have shaken the ground in its power.

Thank you, my tribesmen. By the will of the Five, it is so forgotten. Fight for freedom with valor. His tone was proud, powerful.

By the will of the Five, they responded.

There was a stale moment where the entire world seemed to cease movement. Taris watched as every Gray in her cell closed their eyes. In the span of a breath, it seemed as though the world had shifted ever so slightly. In that one moment, something small and significant had changed. Then the Grays opened their eyes and everything went back to normal. They all started moving about, brushing their hair and teeth, going about their business as if nothing had happened. The teenager looked at her and smiled.

"Hello there, Teag. Sleep well?" he asked genuinely.

She was shocked. Wasn't she just fighting with this guy? "Not really," she replied honestly.

He laughed. "I know. It's hard the first time, sleeping on the floor, but you get used to it."

She nodded, unable to think of a response. With a shrug the young Gray moved on, walking into the main room to chat with some friends. *He forgot all about me*, she realized.

Confused, Taris moved into a corner in the back of the room and pulled Vale into it. No one seemed to be paying her any mind anymore.

"What the hell did you do?" she demanded.

"I commanded them to forget," he explained plainly. "And they did."

"They forgot what? My dream?" she asked. "Why did you tell them to do that?"

Vale ran his hands through his hair. He held her by the shoulders and lowered his voice so it was barely a whisper. "Taris, the dream you shared with everyone. You should not have done that."

"Okay, why is that?" she asked. "And why are you acting like I just released some big Adulo secret?"

"Well," he said, wincing. "You did."

"What? No I didn't!" she protested. "I don't know any Adulo secrets! How could I have done that?"

"It was a surprise to me as well," he admitted. "But it's the truth. Your dream contains a secret. A secret that only the Star of Gray has the authority to reveal. You just shared that secret with everyone here."

Guilt rose to the surface, even though she had no control of it. "So, what does that mean? Are we in danger here?"

He shook his head. "No. Thankfully I was here. No Adulo, no matter what tribe they are from, is allowed to resist a proclamation from a lord guardian. The matter is forgotten. Literally."

"So you just…tell them what to do and they do it?"

He nodded. "That is the truth. I have the power to do that. I told them to forget and they did. Except for you and me, none of them will recollect the dream from last night."

"Wow," she breathed. "I didn't know you could do that. So you can just choose to forget something and then it's forgotten?"

"That's correct," he said, as though she was overacting to that fact.

"Wow," she said. "That's amazing."

"Like I said, Taris, there is a lot about Adulos that you do not know," he said with the ghost of a smile on his face.

"So, how often do you just order them around?" she wondered, looking at him with newfound appreciation. "I mean, how many times have you just commanded people like that? It must be great for crowd control."

He gave her a reproachful look. "That's not why I have this ability. It's used only in extreme emergencies. And, since you ask, that was my first time."

Her mouth dropped. "First time?! Aren't you like six hundred years old? How can this be your first time?"

"I'm seven hundred and eight human years old," he corrected, stroking the back of his hair thoughtfully. "Although that's hardly something to be proud of when you don't have the hair to show for it."

"And you only used your authority over people once?" she asked, astounded.

"Power is not given to people who would misuse it, Taris," he said in a lecturing tone. "Not for the Adulos anyway. The humans haven't quite mastered that yet. Perhaps this concept hasn't translated very well."

"Speaking of translate," she said, relaxing a little. "Why do you speak to each other in English? I mean, not speak but...well you know."

His eyes twinkled with amusement. "Oh! No. It's not English. It's Caleum, our nonverbal language."

"No it isn't," she argued. "I've heard it myself. It was English."

"You hear Caleum," he said. "Your brain translates it to the language you prefer. You hear English because that's what you understand."

Taris yawned widely and shook her head. "Ugh. It's too early for me to try and understand that stuff, Vale. Whatever you say. So what about my dream thing? Are you going to, I don't know, teach me to block out my thoughts or whatever?"

"One step at a time," he said gently, pushing her braid off of her shoulders with a light touch. "Let's see if we can get through today in one piece."

"And if we do survive today, then what?" She wasn't about to let the matter go. "I don't want to wake up every day with disgruntled Grays complaining about the bad seats they got to the dream show."

Vale sighed. "Taris, trust me. I'm a dream walker. I can block prying eyes - intentional or otherwise - from entering your mind. Not just for your sake, but for mine as well."

"You?" she said, smoothing down the front of his prison uniform, if only to feel the hard muscles underneath. "What's this got to do with you?"

He frowned. "Your dream revealed something to me that I should not have known."

She stopped at that and looked up at him. "Really? What was it?"

"It's better that we not discuss it," he said quickly. "Not yet. Contextually, doesn't make any sense to me. I think it needs to stay that way."

"Are you going to…forget or whatever?" she asked. For some reason the thought of that made her a little sad.

"No," he said after careful consideration. "I choose to remember, but not to seek out the answer as to why."

"But," she protested, a little groggy and frustrated. "I still have so many questions. So many things still don't make sense to me. I'm tired of feeling like I'm in the dark all the time."

"Taris," he said, intensity in his tone. "I will help you to understand your dream, but not right now. Not here. It is not safe."

"Why?" she prompted. He looked really uncomfortable, like he had no interest in continuing the conversation

"It's too complicated to explain," he said. She was not about to accept that as an answer. Before she could force him to tell her things, a warning bell whooped a couple of times, distracting her from the flood of questions she was prepared to ask.

"They're ringing the breakfast alarm," he observed stiffly. "We had better go. I'm told that ignoring the bowl of mush gets you scrathed."

"Fine," she agreed begrudgingly. "We can finish this later. And we will, too."

"I hope so," he said.

"Now come on," she said, taking his hand and leading him out of the cell. "We don't want to be late for the morning gruel. I hate to say it but I think I'm starving. Hungry enough to eat that crap they call food anyway."

He smiled widely at that. She loved to see him smile, but she didn't say so. She had a feeling she didn't have to.

In the main area, Grays were either eating listlessly or filing into small groups. Taris and Vale sat across from one another on an isolated table, spooning gruel into their mouths mechanically. He looked sick, like the act of eating in itself was a burden. He pushed the mush around with his spoon with a look of dispassionate frustration. Taris was hungry enough to consume the bland porridge without too much complaint. Finally she finished her bowl and stared longingly at Vale's untouched portion. He followed her gaze and then looked up at her in disgust.

"Would you...care to take my food?" he asked, confused as to why she'd even want it. She nodded and he spooned the contents of his bowl into hers. She ate hungrily while Vale observed her with curious interest. He kept staring at her like he wanted to say something, but he couldn't quite put the words to it. Finally she looked up at him and raised an eyebrow.

"Something on your mind, Vale?" she asked with a mouthful of food.

"You confuse me beyond words, Taris Leigh Bodil," he said, watching her spoon up the remaining contents of the bowl into her mouth.

"Why?" she asked, licking her fingers. "I was hungry."

"How can you eat this way?" he asked, truly repulsed at the idea. "Food tastes like ash in my mouth."

"I dunno," she answered. "I like breakfast. I always have. You know, it's the only meal I ever need in a day."

"You only eat one meal a day?"

"Yep, just one. It's like…I don't know, like that's all my body can handle."

"Hmm," he mused, leaning back to observe her. "Interesting."

"You always say that," she said, wiping her face clean with her sleeve, to the open disgust of several other Grays in her line of sight. "Besides, you have a stomach, right?"

He narrowed his eyes at her. "Yes…"

"Well, what's it do then?" she asked. "If you don't eat, what's the point of it?"

"To consume and process liquid," he said. "On my planet, nutrients are produced in liquid form."

She laughed. "Sounds like my kind of planet."

"Fermentation is not what I meant, Taris," he said in an exasperated tone.

"You don't make alcohol on your planet?" she asked.

"Oh we do, it just isn't so flagrantly misappropriated like it is here by *some* people," he said wryly.

"Oh, taking a stab at my drinking, are we lord guardian?" she said, leaning in on the table. "Maybe I should have made you eat your breakfast."

"No," he said with a little push of emotion. "I surrender."

She laughed at that. "So wait a minute. If you only drink nutrients, and you don't get anything to drink, do you like, starve to death?"

"No," he said patiently. "We do, however, become malnourished. It makes us sickly and irritable and weak. Easy to manipulate and control."

"Irritable and easy to control eh?" she asked, thinking of Xiana. "I think you might be right about that."

She looked around the room, which was quickly being divided into ten groups, and she noticed a pattern. There was a descending level of attitude in the grouping. The tens were like most of the Grays she'd ever seen. They were serious, composed, unruffled people. The number ones, however, were erratic and nervous, chatting away in hushed worried tones. Their composure was awkward, their eyes were suspicious and they all seemed perpetually unglued. She saw Xiana, standing in the row of ones, looking hopeful and desperate, standing on her tiptoes to see over the others in front of her, fiddling with her hair as she waited to go into the elevator.

"There's something not right about this, Vale. I can feel it."

He nodded. "So can I."

"This system of colors and groups is strange," she pointed out. "I think it's a pattern."

"I agree," he said. "Some of these Adulos seem *incorrect* somehow. Their thoughts are hard to hear, their emotions are bizarre."

"There's something going on here that's way beyond your typical prison torture, Vale. Something really bad."

A light above their heads started to blink. The voice that woke them up came over the intercom and barked orders, telling them to get into their group. Immediately.

"Well…we're about to find out," he said with a hesitant tone.

Chapter Twenty-five

The HALO led Taris and Vale into a small, dark room. Three other Grays were already there, looking listless and apprehensive. The guard shoved them in and closed the door without so much as a grunt. For a moment, they all stared silently, unsure of how to speak to each other in such a strange situation. There were no chairs or tables, only one door, and a glass mirror on one wall. A mirror that she knew was a window. A window where others could look in, but she could not look out. She'd seen them before, when she was interrogated for her involvement in the rebellion. Taris walked the length of the room twice, inspecting everything thoroughly.

"This is pretty solid," she said, rapping lightly on the wall. "Solid concrete all around. The glass is probably three inches thick. The door is made of that scratchy metal stuff."

"Sidus," Vale offered. "The metal is sidus."

"Yep; that's it. Strong stuff. And itchy, too." She scratched her neck instinctually. The skin that touched the collar was tender and starting to get severely irritated. "Man I cannot live another few years like this. It's killing me."

"You say that," said a familiar male voice, "but you don't know the half of it yet."

Taris turned and saw a young-looking Gray standing in front of her. His hair was long and shimmering as he walked toward her, blanketing his shoulders in silver waves. He was as tall as Vale and walked with an elegant grace, like a snake on the water. His almond shaped eyes were shimmering silver and he had dimples on either side of his smooth cheeks. Those dimples, those eyes. She knew those eyes. She knew those dimples. She knew that blue tattoo that snaked its way up the side of his neck.

"Hey, you're that Gray," she said slowly. "From Boone Hooper's house. You were the bartender."

He nodded, genuinely pleased to be recognized. "That's correct. You're the woman who ordered a lot of whiskey."

"That's me!" she exclaimed. "Oh my god! Steve right? Well what the hell are you doing here?"

"The emissary removed all branded workers from his house after the accident," he explained softly. "He thought we were a threat to his life. He sold most of us, but there were a handful of us who came here. The ones he thought were in most need of 'cleansing'. I tried to run, but they caught me before I could truly get away. And my name is not Steve. It's Kyran Ato."

"Kyran Ato," she repeated with a smile. "That's a nice name. It suits you much better than Steve."

"Thank you," he said kindly, trying to mask the worry in his tone. He was being intentionally careful with his words. They all knew they were being watched. That didn't need to be said. "I don't mean to be intrusive, but I'm genuinely interested in what brings you here, madam."

"Taris," she said, offering him a hand. "My name is Taris...Teag."

Vale gave her a curious sidelong look at that, but she pretended to ignore it. Kyran shook her hand politely and cocked his head to the side. "Taris Teag? Is that so? Last I recall you were not of the Adulo persuasion."

She heaved an exasperated sigh. "That's a long story, Kyran. Needless to say I'm sort of grappling with my own sense of self right now."

"I see. And you're not one for want of good company." He turned to face Vale. "Lord guardian. Good to see you are still alive."

"And you, Kyran Ato." Vale touched his first two fingers to the middle of his forehead, and then extended his pointer finger out toward him. Kyran duplicated this gesture, bowing his head slightly to Vale in a sign of respect.

"Wait, you two actually know each other?" she asked.

"We do, yes," Kyran responded, eying the one-way glass carefully. "My tribesmen have known his tribesmen for generations. But the real question is, how do *you* know him?"

Oh god, where to begin? "If live through this, remind me to tell you all about the worst week of my life. Bartenders are good listeners, right?"

"Sounds like an enchanting tale to be sure," he said with a charming smile. "I hope I will enjoy that story."

"Have you met any of our friends since you've arrived, Kyran?" Vale asked politely. It took Taris a minute to figure out what they meant. *Oh, the secret greeting.* Two lines across and one vertical. *Kyran is part of the Silencium*, she realized.

"Some, lord guardian, but not many. I'm worried for them," he answered. He turned to Taris. "I'm worried for you as well."

"Me?" she asked. "Why?"

"Because," he said, looking up at the ceiling. "This is your first time in the chamber. The first time is always rough."

A series of sprinkler heads were strategically spaced out on the roof tiles. Each one was a different color she noticed, and they all looked well used. She did not like the look of that. Suddenly a thought struck her. She had seen places like this before, in the war. She knew the look of this all too well.

"Wait a minute," she said. "Are they going to gas us?"

Kyran nodded. "Yes. I'm afraid so."

"Oh my god!" Taris exclaimed. "They can't do that. That's immoral! It's illegal! It's inhuman!"

"We're not human," Vale pointed out. "Do you really think they care what they do to us?"

"Oh we'll see about that." She stormed over to the window and pounded on the glass. *"Hey! HEY! What are you doing to us?! What kind of poison are you making us breathe? Hey!"*

"We don't know what kind of gas it is," Kyran said. "We only know it's quick, the effects are painful and lingering, and when it's all over you feel...different."

She spun around. "Different? How?"

He frowned, searching for the words. "It's hard to explain. There are more emotions. You feel hurt and confused. Like you're not yourself anymore. Your skin burns. Things become fuzzy."

"Well that shouldn't be too bad," Taris said sarcastically. "I've been drunk more than a few times. I know a thing or two about confused and fuzzy thoughts."

Kyran shook his head. "It's not like that. It's something much deeper than that. It strips you of something. A layer of yourself. I've been through this twice and it's been the same each time. It gets worse every time. It's hard to put words to it. There are *other* ways to explain it, if you would prefer."

"No thanks," Taris said quickly, knowing he meant telepathy. "I think I've got it."

"Grays, prepare for treatment," the male intercom voice commanded.

Taris had the distinct urge to flee. She walked to the door and tried to jiggle the handle helplessly. She considered giving into the panic when she saw the Grays, one by one, bow their heads and open their palms to face Vale. She wanted to ask what they were doing, but there was something that stopped her. Something that told her she was witnessing something intimate. Something she didn't want to interrupt. She watched as they communed together, mentally connecting in a deeply spiritual and genuine way.

She'd seen people pray together before, but this was something wholly different. It was something that transcended mere religion. It was a connection of souls.

A connection of souls who were all focused on Vale. He was, in some strange way, a purveyor of hope for them. Vale stood in front of each one, making the effort to touch each forehead to his own. Taris found herself feeling like she had intruded on some private ritual. She felt a little awkward, like it wasn't her place to be a part of that ceremony. Vale looked in her direction and reached out to her. Wordlessly, she took his hand, grasping it tightly. His touch was warm, resonating with a powerful sensation.

"Brace yourself, Taris," he said, gripping her hand. "I have seen what we are up against and it will pain you worse than ten scrathes. Be strong."

"I will do my damndest," she said. She gave him a wistful smile and then turned to the glass reflective window.

"All right you bastards," she said. "Give it your best shot."

Taris took a deep breath and braced herself for the worst.

With a little click the sprinkles turned on, filling the room with orange smoke in a matter of seconds. She held her breath for as long as she could, but she could feel the smoke swirling around her. She heard the sounds of coughing. The Grays around her started gasping.

Then they started screaming.

Vale let go of her hand and collapsed into a little ball. The Grays started to wail in abject horror. The sounds of painful torture echoed through the room as all the Grays screamed in agony in their native language. Still holding her breath, she looked around the room wildly, but it was filled with orange smoke so thick that she could barely see in front of her. The Grays in the room were sprawled on the floor, wailing hysterically. They sounded like they were dying. Perhaps they were. Eventually her lungs could not take it any longer. She let out the breath she had been holding, closed her eyes, and tensed every muscle in her body. She braced for the pain to consume her.

It took two large, orange-smoke filled breaths for her to realize that nothing was happening. She wasn't in pain. *I'm not affected*, she realized. *Oh my god it doesn't hurt me.* Surprised, she opened her eyes and looked around. The smoke was starting to clear. Her fellow prisoners were curled up in balls, whimpering or praying. Pools of silver tears saturated the floor next to their anguished faces.

"Grays, prepare for decontamination."

Taris acted quickly. She laid down on the floor and pulled her face next to Vale. His body was shaking and his breaths were quick wracking gasps. He was in far more pain than he let on. She could see him struggling to control his emotional reaction it as much as he could. His face was splotched with red marks and his eyes were circled in red. She touched the side of his face gently. For a moment he flinched, almost as if he didn't know who she was. He opened one hooded eye and looked at her.

"Taris," he said through clenched teeth. "Are…you…okay?"

He could barely move and he was worried about her. Vale never ceased to amaze her. "Better than okay," she whispered. "Vale, that stuff, it didn't do anything to me. I'm fine. I'm fine and I have a plan--"

"Decontamination in three, two, one...go."

The sprinklers went off and doused them in water for only a matter of seconds. The Grays screamed again, pain giving way to sorrow. She watched Vale gasp and stifle screams in his throat as the waters poured over him. It might as well have been acid. The sprinklers turned off, leaving them as nothing more than defeated bodies on a wet cement floor. The water started to travel to the drain in the middle of the room, sliding off of their shivering bodies in slow, trickling motions. She saw the steam rise from their skin, snaking up and dissolving into the stagnant air like a freshly extinguished match.

She had never heard the sounds of pain and torture like that. She thought of all the Grays she'd met in the complex, and how they have surely had to endure years of this pain day after day. She thought about Xiana, and the desperation in her voice when she told them how badly she wanted to escape. She thought about all the faces of the scared and confused that she saw in the jail cells. She thought of the humans, so many of them who didn't see the Adulos as people. Maybe they couldn't. She thought about the scrathe burns, and the pain and the betrayal she felt every time she was shocked with one. She thought of all of this, and a fire started to burn inside her. Taris was mad. Very mad. More furious and unforgiving than she had been in a very long time. She heard the door open, and the rage boiled to the surface.

Closing her eyes, she pulled herself into a ball, curled up against Vale and kept her head down. *Show time.*

Chapter Twenty-six

It had been almost two weeks since she was first sold to the complex, and every day was the same. Get up, get ready, eat gruel, get scrubbed, walk around outside for an hour while the chemicals seep in, spend the day in the cell block, sleep. Aside from the usual fake screaming in the gas chamber, most of her days were spent in silence. Well, not in complete silence.

Okay Taris, she heard Vale say as they slowly walked a wide figure eight in the courtyard, *let's try this again.*

She frowned. "I don't want to."

Not with your voice, Taris, chastised Kyran. *Think and express your thoughts in your head.*

"But it's just such a strain on you two," she protested, grasping for any excuse she could find. "You're weak from the scrubbing."

Not today, Vale pointed out. *You know that. You can feel it.*

She could, damn him. She knew they were better today than they had been in over a week. The scrubbing chemicals had been surprisingly mild the last few days and the Grays in her group seemed to be doing better. Usually they had to be dragged out of the cell and hauled into the mud until the HALOs threatened them with scrathes to stand up and start walking. Sometimes not even that would get them on their feet. It was killing them, she knew. Every day it killed a little bit of them, stripped more of them away. Made them weaker.

All except Taris.

Every day she went into the chamber and pretended to be injured. They would mock her and drag her into the mud like everyone else, but it was nothing more than a little wet and uncomfortable for her. She didn't want the guards to know that, though. She let them keep on believing that she was just as poor and helpless as the next Gray. She wasn't sure how yet, but she knew she could use that to her advantage someday. In the meantime, Vale and Kyran had been spending their days trying to perfect what they called, her "horrible excuse for Adulo knowledge and skills" by making her perfect the art of telepathy.

Naturally, she fought them on it every step of the way.

Stop procrastinating, Taris, Kyran said, walking a few paces behind her. *Give it a try.*

"Fine," she agreed.

Taris...

FINE! she bellowed mentally, startling the both of them. She laughed under her breath. *Ha, ha.* She thought. *Scared you.*

Well I'm glad to see you're taking this so seriously, Vale complained, walking beside her with his hands behind his back casually. She was about to stop and pout on principle when she looked up. Above her head was a large white sign that read CHEMICAL AIR-INFUSION CENTER. NO STANDING ALLOWED. *Even signs are against me today,* she grumbled, continuing to scuffle through the grime. Vale and Kyran had perfected the art of not looking at each other when they talked. They could stroll casually though the mud, appearing as though they were simply pondering their own thoughts, and have an entire discussion. No facial expressions, no gestures, just words and emotions and meanings. It was driving her crazy.

I'm so bad at this, she thought, feeling the embarrassment rise to her cheeks. *You've had literally hundreds of years to perfect this and you're giving me two weeks. It's not fair.*

You're a fast learner, Vale thought supportively, *and unfortunately you don't have the benefit of time. You need to learn this now.*

She blew a strand of her hair from her face. *Fine,* she thought. *Let's go through the drills before our time in the courtyard is up.*

Kyran, in his surprising brilliance, had created a system of questions and answers for her to respond to telepathically. The repetitive nature of the questions would make the responses - and

387

eventually the telepathy - come naturally. At least, so he had
said.

Okay, Kyran started as they rounded the bend slowly,
weaving in and out of crates with healthy room to spare. *Let's
start with the basics. Who are you?*

I'm Taris Leigh Bodil, she said mechanically. *From
Earth. No matter what some Grays might say...*

Taris, stay on topic please, Kyran instructed. *Next, what
is your position?*

She focused her answer intently. *I am the captain of the
Starship Intrepid. I am also the warrior pillar of Adulo*, she
thought.

Very good, Vale responded. *This time that went only to
the two of us and not to everyone.*

Vale had chosen Kyran to be a confidant in this matter,
allowing him to know that Taris was one of the pillars. Mostly
because the first few times they had tried this exercise she'd told
him anyway. And everyone else in the courtyard. Vale made
them forget, much as it pained him to do so, but he allowed
Kyran to remain aware of it. Apparently, as lord guardian, he
was authorized by whatever higher authority he served to pick
and choose that sort of thing. Kyran, as it turned out, was some
sort of protector of his realm - a warrior in his own right - and
one rank down from Vale in the Gray's strange system of

leadership. That made Kyran the second highest ranking Gray in the complex, so the two of them spent a lot of time going over strategies. Currently, they were focusing all their strategic attention on getting her to focus her thoughts on only one person at a time. Two weeks and a thousand accidents later and she was finally getting a grip on it.

Tell me about the pillars, Kyran prompted, reciting the next question in line.

She sighed. She rarely got through this one without doing something wrong. *There are three pillars,* she recited from memory. *Once there were many and now there are three. By the will of the Five we are chosen, above all others, at a time of need to serve the Adulos. I am the warrior. The other two are the wanderer and the witch.*

And what do you possess?

We each possess a piece of the noticulus, she said slowly. *The noticulus is the blue flame of the Adulo people. This flame is hidden in three pieces, in our three souls. Together we are the key to the Star of Gray.*

And what do you do with your noticulus?

She swallowed. This part was always her favorite. Vale had indeed explained her whole dream to her. The dream coincided with his fabled three pillars, which he found fascinating and she found ironic. *We three, at a unanimous time, must willingly combine our noticulus in the Shadow Valley, in the circle of floating stones. There, Star of Gray will unleash his power and save the Adulo people.*

By the will of the Five, Vale thought.

By the will of the Five, Kyran echoed. That was the traditional response. It was the closest thing the Grays had to the word "Amen".

And do you fight for freedom? Kyran asked. It was the last question in the repertoire.

I fight for freedom with valor, she responded. It was the motto of the Adulo people, more or less, and used frequently by the Silencium.

Kyran and Vale stopped walking, causing her to stop short in her tracks. Vale turned and clasped her hand. *You did it,* he thought, staring deep into her eyes. *You went through all the drills without messing up once.*

"I did?!" she exclaimed. "Well that's great!" She leapt up and wrapped her arms around Vale's neck, completely forgetting where she was. The shock of the collar reminded her, throwing her down into the mud with electrical pain.

"*No touching, silverbacks!*" shouted one HALO, holding a scrathe remote with a sneer. "And no talking either!"

Damn, she thought. *So close.* Taris wiped the mud from her face and stumbled to her feet.

Well you did make it through the drills without getting scrathed, Kyran thought encouragingly as they continued their walk. Taris wiped her muddied hands on her already soiled prison jumper in defeat.

Yes, she thought in a whiny tone, *but now I'm covered in mud, and we only get one change of uniform a week!*

Vale tried to act as though he wasn't amused by her, but she caught the corners of his mouth turn up. *Fortunately, you get a change of uniform and a shower today*, he pointed out. *It's Thursday.*

Well lucky me, she thought, shoving her dirty hands in her pockets. *A clean pair of clothes and a six-minute cold shower. The worst part is that this is truly going to be the best part of my entire week.*

It could be worse my warrior, Vale said gently. *You could have gotten mud on yourself on Friday. Then you would have had to wait an entire week.*

Always a silver lining with you, Vale, she thought, shaking her head.

Well...a gray one anyway, he said kindly.

The alarm rang, indicating that their time in the courtyard was at another end. Kyran bid them goodbye as he always did, with the two-and-one finger salute of the Silencium. Mechanically he turned and followed the guards who herded him into his cell block. *Fight for freedom with valor*, he said with a proud nod.

By the will of the Five, Vale and Taris responded.

Vale looked down at her, a small smile on his face. *You're getting much better at this my warrior,* he said. *We might make an Adulo out of you yet.*

She shook her head and kissed him lightly on the cheek. "I wouldn't bet on it."

The scrathe collar shocked her to the ground again, but she didn't care. It was worth it.

Back in the cell she was told to call home, Taris was shoveling dinner in her mouth, appreciative for the clean new uniform and her freshly washed body. All the prisoners craved even the smallest creature comforts, whether it was a blanket, a ponytail holder, even a new pair of fitting shoes. With little else to look forward to, the moods of the prisoners seemed a little higher on Thursday nights, right after the laundry swap. Most of them were bold enough to smile, and she'd even heard laughter from time to time. Everyone seemed in better spirits. All except Vale of course, who preferred to brood over the situation rather than find reasons to enjoy it. They were sitting at a surprisingly crowded dinner table as Taris spooned food in her mouth, much to the open disgust of her fellow inmates.

How can you eat like that? Breth'a Nerais asked. He was the old man with the long hair she had seen on her first night.

She shrugged. "It's not so bad if you don't think about it too much." She was learning to be comfortable with telepathic communication with Vale and Kyran, but for the others she found it was too much noise. Without asking, she picked up Vale's bowl and dumped its contents into her own.

This act was so shocking that she actually heard audible gasps of disapproval.

You cannot take the lord guardian's food! protested Breth'a.

He is sacred, the woman with the dual braids named Ona Fynn chimed in. *He is the lord guardian of the Star of Gray. Elected by Elias himself. You must ask before you can touch the lord guardian's things.*

Taris looked at Vale, and then back at the horrified onlookers. "Why?" she asked, reaching up to tousle Vale's hair. More gasps echoed through the crowd. "It's just Vale. He's not going to bite."

Lord guardian, whined the annoying teenage-looking Gray named Travisayon Fynn that Taris couldn't stand, *why is she allowed to break our sacred vows? You must stop her.*

"My friends," Vale said quietly, "she is *aruna*. She can touch whatever she likes."

That seemed to end the argument. Without further complaint the Grays went about their business, pretending to eat and acting like they were still not staring at her. She finished her bowl of gruel and stacked the empty bowls on the table.

"So what's aruna?" she asked.

A smile crept across his face. "Sure you want to know?"

"Yes," she said. "Now more than ever."

"It means you have a death wish," he said calmly. "You see, on my planet, we do not die from age."

Her mouth dropped. "You live forever?!"

"I said we do not die from age," he pointed out. "I did not say we do not die. In spite of this fact of our biology, there are very few Adulos who live beyond a thousand human years."

"Really?" she asked, leaning on the table with interest. "Why is that?"

Vale frowned, thinking about it. "Disease, accident, injury, tragedy, loneliness, betrayal, loyalty, depression. All the things humans can die of, only we have to live with the possibility of them for much longer than you do."

"You make living forever seem like a bad thing," she said, folding her arms.

"It's a curse to many," Vale said seriously. "Think about it, Taris. With humans, death is a certainty. Something they must all accept. They know it's coming for them. It's an absolute. For the Adulos, it's only a possibility. Just another thing we can't control or predict. It's maddening."

"Spoken like a true immortal," she grumbled. "Do you have any idea what you sound like right now? 'Woe is me, I get to be beautiful and young and smart forever and none of my loved ones are going to die'. Sounds tragic."

"My loved ones died long ago, Taris," he said in that Taris-tone of his, "and it is quite tragic. Many of us take our own lives."

She stopped at that. "Really? The Grays kill themselves? I never knew that."

He nodded. "They do. Quite a few of them. Sometimes we intervene, if it's a person we can get to in time to help. We assign a religious person to help the unstable one through the hard process. This time period is called *aruna*. It means 'around death'."

"So, the only reason those people let me eat your food is because they think I'm crazy, and that you're my religious guide?" she asked, pointing her spoon at him. "Why Vale Teag, I do believe that was a bit deceitful of you."

His eyes grew wide. "Isn't that the case?" he asked. "Are you not a woman bound to kill herself with alcohol, trying to escape the world? And am I not trying to guide you through this hard time? I don't think I hear a lie in that."

She threw the spoon at him playfully. "You know, you're starting to become more and more like me every day," she said with a small grin. She watched his face contort as he tried to come up with a response that wouldn't be insulting. He appeared to come up with a diplomatic answer but before he could voice it he was interrupted by the sound of the bedtime bell.

"Hmm. You lucked out, mister lord guardian," she said, standing up slowly. She handed their bowls over to the receptacle and then made her way to their designated cell. She started to walk over to her corner when she felt him press against her. In the shadows of the room, for only the fraction of a moment, she felt the warmth of his chest on her back, the feel of his hands on her shoulders. The gentle touch of his lips on the top her head. It made her stop. She trapped herself in the moment, just enjoying the connection between them. It was always brief, it was always dangerous, but it was always perfect.

"See you in your dreams," he said gently.

In order to keep the eyes of others out of her unconscious mind, Vale and Taris had been sleeping hand-in-hand. According to Vale, it was the only way that he could teach her to keep from threspinning out of control and dragging everyone into her nightmares. She wasn't sure how necessary the hand holding was, but she never argued. It seemed to work. He said she was getting better at controlling her thoughts. Still, there was a part of her that hoped she would never perfect the art of controlling her dreams. Otherwise she'd have no reason to hold his hand at night, and frankly that was the only reason she had to keep living some days.

They always chose a dark corner so they wouldn't be noticed. Taris would press up against the wall and Vale would face her. He would take her hand, she would fall asleep and together they would enter her dream. She was still scared, but having him there made the dream easier to manage. Every night, Vale would stand by her, no matter where the dream took them. She didn't always see him, but she knew he was there. Through the fields of the destroyed rebel moons, to the space battles, to her mom's funeral, to the incoherent violent nightmares involving open flesh and screaming flayed men. When she would wake up screaming and shaking he would hold her until she calmed down, or until the HALOs scrathed them apart. He never faltered, he never pressed it, and he never asked for an explanation. And she adored him for that.

As she was spreading out the one blanket she'd managed to acquire by trading a hair tie with a young Nerais girl, Vale laid down on the floor and stared up at her, a strange look on his face. "Something is different," he said quietly.

"What do you mean?" she asked, looking around. They had only gotten a couple of new faces in the cell block, but no one in the last few days.

"I don't know," he said slowly, furring his brow. "I can just tell. Something has changed here. The feel of this place has changed."

"Maybe that's a good thing," she said, pulling the blanket over her. "Maybe they'll serve pancakes instead of goop for breakfast. Maybe they'll permit the use of alcohol in the complex. Maybe the Intrepid will come and rescue us and I'll be elected president of the world."

He rolled to his side and reached for her hand, sliding his fingers in between hers. Gently his thumb traced her scars on her palm, while her finger traced the burned brand on his hand. His touch always sparked fire in her heart, even when she was on the verge of sleep.

"Maybe tomorrow is the day we leave this place," he suggested.

"Mmm," she said, smiling as her eyes drooped closed. "That sounds nice." She felt the touch of his lips on her forehead, and then she was in the dream again. As usual she had company. Only this time, it wasn't Vale.

Chapter Twenty-seven

The boy seemed as surprised to be there as she was. He could not have been more than nineteen at the oldest, with shock-white shoulder-length hair that glowed with strength and power. His face, for all the wisdom it possessed, was impossibly young. He was muscular and tall, with a strong jaw and deep-set silver eyes that seemed to emit their own light on command. His wide lips held a placid smile on his face. He was standing in the circle, staring at the blue noticulus flames like he was looking at a favorite piece of artwork.

"Who are you?" Taris asked, looking for Vale. She couldn't see him. She knew he was somewhere near her, she could feel him, but she couldn't see him. She couldn't see the other two pillars either. They were all uncharacteristically absent. It was just her and the strange teenager.

"Hey!" she exclaimed a little louder. "Who are you?"

"This is for me," he said softly, looking around at the Shadow Valley. "But I will never live to see it in person." He looked down at her hand. "You're bleeding."

She didn't need to look down to know she was bleeding. Every time she had the dream she was bleeding. It was nothing new. She shrugged it off. "Why are you here?"

"You brought me here," the boy said, walking around the floating blue fire with interest. His robes shimmered as he walked, like sunlight dancing on a river. He was the closest thing to a celestial being that she had ever seen. Maybe he was one.

"What do you want?" she asked.

He looked up at her. "The same things you do. I want freedom. I want peace. I want to be happy."

"I don't want to be happy," she said.

"Yes you do," he responded gently, reaching down to pluck a small white flower from the ground. She looked down in confusion. Since when were there flowers on the ground? "I have a message for you," he said.

"Okay," she said slowly. "What is it?"

The boy thought about it. "I'm here to tell you that the worst is yet to come."

"Oh great," she said sarcastically. "The harbinger of doom with the face of an angel. Lovely."

"Not just for you," he said, gently smelling the flower, "but for all. You can stop it, though."

"How?" she asked. "How can I stop it?"

"You need the other two pillars to make the noticulus burn bright enough," he said, gesturing to the flame.

"Yes. I know that," she said. "Vale told me."

The boy's eyebrows raised. "Vale Teag still lives? By the will of the Five, that is good news."

"Yes," she said quickly. "Vale's fine. Happy and healthy. Well…not really, but he's alive. Now tell me how to stop the end of the world, kid."

The boy smiled at her and pointed. "Ah, I like you Taris Leigh Bodil."

"Good," she said urgently. "Then tell me what I want to know."

The boy smiled and sat down on a fallen floating stone that was hovering only a foot off the grass. Taris had never noticed it there before. Was this guy accommodating himself in her dream? She wondered how to do that, and if maybe Vale could teach her.

"The three pillars walk the think gray line," he started. "They belong on two paths, not one."

"Well that doesn't make a lot of sense," she grumbled. "I hate when Grays became strangely spiritual and vague in their responses."

"It means they are all like you, Taris," he said. "And when you know what that is, you will know what they are and it will all make sense."

"Like I said, I'm not a big fan of poetic Gray vagueness." She sighed, rubbing her temples out of habit rather than dream headache. "Okay, so how do I find them?" she asked. "The others I mean."

The boy frowned. "The man with the device you need. He knows. He will tell you."

"Ah," she said, "so this whole conversation is to be a riddle thing."

"You'll figure it out," the boy said kindly. "You will know the other pillars when you see them. They will be strangers until you see them, and then you will know each other."

"Well that's handy," Taris said with a sigh. "So is that it? Anything else?"

The boy jumped off the floating stone and walked up to her. "There are three things you need to know, Taris Leigh Bodil. Things that will make sense to you someday. Things that you will need as you embark on your long and difficult journey."

She rolled her eyes. "It's always three, isn't it?"

"One, the fallen one is still alive," the boy said, staring at her intently. "Two, the witch pillar is trapped in time, and three...and three..." He hesitated.

"What? What's the third one?" she demanded, surprised by her own urgency. The boy turned to her and his eyes caught fire with light.

"Vale Teag will fail."

Her heart stopped. "What?" she said. "Fail at what? What do you mean?" Breathless, she dropped the sword in her hands and gripped him by the shoulders. "Fail to save Elias?"

The look on his face spoke stronger than words ever could. Devastated, she shook her head. "Oh no. There has to be something I can do change that. That's why you're telling me, right? To avoid that from happening?"

"When the time comes," he said slowly, "you will make the right choice."

"You're damn right I will," she said, feeling the dread and the panic flooding her thoughts. She felt her grip on the dream starting to fade. She was waking up and she knew it. *Wait! Not yet!* she protested, trying to fight her conscious mind from winning.

"Who are you, kid?" she asked. "Are you a real Gray? Someone from the complex?"

The walls of the dream were staring to fade away. She reached out to touch him but felt nothing. She was losing the dream, and with it the answers she was dying to know. "Please!" she pleaded. "Tell me who you are!"

The boy cocked his head to the side and smiled. "You know who I am, Taris," he said plainly

"Elias?" It was him. She knew it the moment she laid eyes on him. He was right in front of her, talking to her, and yet she could not touch him. Could not save him. "But how can that be? Where are you?"

"Oh Taris," he said with a gentle tone, "I'm right under your nose."

"Get up get up get up! Friday morning, silverbacks! Get up! Breakfast time!"

"Elias!" Taris exclaimed, startled from her dream. Her eyes popped open and she looked down at Vale. To her surprise, he was still sleeping. She touched him gently, and found him unresponsive. In her sleep-induced confusion, she had a momentary lapse in reason where she thought he might be dead. Panicked, she started shaking him violently.

"VALE!"

"Aaah! Gias, tremunsa aha tarischa!" he exclaimed, startled. Disoriented, Vale backed up several paces from her. His eyes were wide and confused, like an animal trapped in a cage. Then reality seemed to settle in, and the calm reserve of his usual face replaced the scared and irrational one.

"Tarischa," he said in a shaky, suspicious tone. *"Yies dreathis etii."*

She rubbed her tired face with her hands. "English, Vale. English."

He stared at her like she didn't make sense, like she had done something very strange. Then his mind seemed to wake up

404

and his senses returned to him. Slowly he ran his hand through his silky silver hair and crawled back to her. "I'm so sorry, Taris," he said, taking her hand. "I'm afraid I was unable to connect to your dream last night."

"It's okay," she said excitedly. "Someone else did."

"I was afraid of that," he said reproachfully, as though chastising himself. "How many did you take with you?"

"Oh no!" she said excitedly. "It wasn't a whole crowd, it was just one guy! There were no innocent bystanders this time."

Vale's eyebrows raised, and did she detect a twinge of jealousy? "Oh? And who was this dream walker who joined with you? Without your permission, I might add."

The excitement of telling him bubbled to the surface. "Elias," she blurted out, staring into his eyes. "It was Elias who was in my dream."

Vale's mouth dropped. "You are serious. By the will of the Five…"

"Yeah, yeah," Taris waved him off. "Be spiritual about it later. Right now we have bigger things to worry about."

She filled him in on the dream in as much detail as she could remember. She told him everything Elias told her, except for one part. The part about him failing. She couldn't do it. She couldn't bring herself to tell him. It was too much for her to believe that she wasn't willing to even acknowledge it. Besides,

Elias had practically told her that she could prevent it, so why get Vale all worked up over nothing? By the time she had finished, he was beside himself with joy. Well, as beside himself as any Gray could be.

"So he said he was right under your nose?" he said, pondering that. "What do you suppose that means?"

"I don't know," she said, spooning breakfast into her mouth. "The term he used is an old Earth phrase. My dad says it sometimes, but I never know what he means."

"Perhaps it means he is in close proximity to us," Vale supposed. "I thought for sure that Boone Hooper was keeping him hostage, but I guess he must have moved him to Hammerhead Hold."

Boone. Hammerhead. Elias. Suddenly it all made sense. "Oh my god!" she exclaimed, forgetting entirely where she was. She leaned back on the bench so far she nearly fell off. Alarmed, and he reached over the table and grabbed her arm to steady her.

Taris, are you okay? he asked, instantly alarmed.

I know where Elias is, she realized. *He's in the cleansing cells.*

Vale's eyes grew wide. *How do you know this?*

Telepathically, she explained the footage she saw the first time she met with Natsumi. How Boone made a call during Vale's message that included the words Elias, cleansing and

Hammerhead. Vale stared at her, his attention undivided, hanging to her every word.

"Why didn't you mention this sooner?" he asked, a mix of joy and utter frustration splashed across his face.

"Well, you were the enemy back then," she pointed out. "Why would I?"

"And now?" he asked, discreetly running his finger over her knuckles. "Am I still the enemy to you, Taris?"

"No. Of course not. Things have…changed…since then," she said, scratching under the collar. She'd managed to shove her uniform between the collar and her skin, but every now and then it escaped and caused massive itching. "Besides, we have the information now, don't we?"

"Yes," he said in a strained tone. "And now we can do nothing about it. If Elias is here, then he is as trapped as we are."

"That doesn't give you the right to give up," she said gently. "You owe him the benefit of a try."

Vale's expression flushed for a moment. She saw the sadness in his eyes. It was so apparent and so strong that for a moment, just a moment, she felt the sadness herself. It entered her mind, filling her with overwhelming grief and despair. Noticing this, his expression changed, and the feeling left her as quickly as it came.

"You're right. I must do something," he said, balling his fists. "So much is at stake. I cannot fail Elias. Not like this. Not when I am so close to saving him."

"*We* must do something," she corrected. "Not you, *we*. We're a team now."

"Taris," he said in that tone he always used with her, "I can't ask you to risk--"

"No, no, no," she said, holding out her hand to stop him. "None of that nobility crap. I'm coming with you and you don't have a choice. Got it?"

He nodded, knowing she was not going to let him win that argument. "Got it."

"Good," she said. "So…got any ideas about that?"

He scowled at the thought. "No. Not really."

"Well, what do we know about this place?" she asked. "The Hammerhead. What do we know?"

He thought about that. "Well, from what I learned there are four underground sections in this facility. Each one holds about fifty Adulos, so there are approximately two hundred tribesmen here."

"Good to know," she said. "Anything else?"

"There are also four levels." *The first is the courtyard level where they process the prisoners,* he said, switching to telepathy. *The Eye is where the Hammer's office is located, and* it oversees the courtyard and surrounding areas of the complex. The second and third are holding cells, like the one we're in, and the fourth level is called the cleaning chamber.

"Okay," she said. "That's all good info." *And the cleansing chamber is where we think Elias is being kept.*

"I agree," he said. "But the question is, how do we get there?"

"I talked about this a little bit with Xiana yesterday," she said. "She said that the cleansing was the last step in the scrubbing."

They weren't the best of friends, but Taris found Xiana's company to be tolerable. Well, Vale told her to play nice with the other inmates and she had begrudgingly agreed. After all, they could be living together for a long time and she had to make the best of it. Aside from the fact that she tried to have Taris thrown in a crate, Xiana did know a thing or two about Hammerhead Hold.

"So how do we get to the cleansing chambers?" he asked. Giving up, Vale pushed the barely eaten bowl of mush toward her with a disgusted look on his face. She ate his food happily, ignoring the stares of protest from her fellow inmates.

"I have a plan," she said with a mouth full of mush. "It's a little bit crazy, but I think it just might work."

"Aren't all your plans crazy?" he asked with a small smile. She pointed her finger at him.

"Oh look, the Vale humor everyone enjoys so much."

"Only when you're around, Taris," he said, brushing his hand against hers surreptitiously. "So what is it you have in mind?"

"Oh, I have a couple of tricks up my sleeve." *Including the fact that I'm not burned by the scrubbing,* she thought to him. *It's time to use that to my advantage.*

He turned and looked at her, eyes wide with uncharacteristic excitement. She actually felt the pride swell in his heart. *Taris,* he said, *this is the first time you ever initiated a nonverbal conversation with me.*

"Well don't get used to it," she said with a smile. "I still think it's creepy."

"I'll keep that in mind."

"Speaking of mind," she said with a mouthful of mush, "where was yours this morning? You weren't in my dream, and then you woke up and acted like I was going to kill you."

His expression glossed over, going Gray in a second. "Oh. That was nothing."

"So the defenses are up I see," she said with a frown. "And that wasn't nothing. I've had enough combat nightmares to know that your reaction wasn't just nothing." He pursed his lips.

He looked like he really didn't want to talk about it, and she really didn't want to let it go. She raised her eyebrows. "Oh, so I can bear my soul to you but you can't explain a little outburst to me?"

She watched his eyes wash over a sea of emotions until they were gone like footprints on the beach, washed away by the surf. "There are things that I have experienced that give me bad dreams, Taris," he said, avoiding her gaze.

"Haven't we all?" she asked, reaching for his hand. He allowed her to take it, but he still wouldn't look directly at her. He struggled to explain himself.

"Not like mine, Taris," he whispered. "Not like mine."

"So is that why we never go into your dreams when we sleep?" she asked gently. "You're afraid that I'll see your nightmares?"

He looked up at her, and she almost recoiled. She felt the terror, the emotional hysteria, the confusion. The overwhelmingly evil fright that consumed him. It was fear itself. Raw, uninhibited, petrifying fright. There was nothing as terrible or as paralyzing as what she felt right at that moment. As soon as the emotions surfaced they were gone, and she was left reeling. He'd given her a little taste, she realized. A preview of his nightmares to illustrate his point. If that was but a fraction of what he felt, she was horrified. There wasn't a word for the level of scared she had experienced, only that she hoped she'd never have to feel it again.

"My god, Vale," she gasped. "*That* is how you feel in your dreams? How can you stand it?"

"Oh Taris," he said sadly. "I do not have dreams. I have terrors. The things nightmares are made of. Those things that humans are too scared to even imagine. The things that fear uses to control people. The truly terrible and grotesque, that's what I see when I sleep. I have *those* kinds of dreamscapes." His voice dropped to almost nothing as she clung to his every word. "That's why I became a dream walker," he said tenderly. "To escape my own mind. To travel with the thoughts of others. To never have to sleep though my horrors. I do it to keep myself sane."

Her heart was beating in her chest, her thoughts still racing. "Oh my god Vale. I am so sorry. I had no idea."

"And you never will," he said, "and for that I shall be grateful."

Gently his hands stroked her shoulders up and down. He looked in her eyes, the want in his expression evident. Passionately, the grip on her arm tightened. She could feel the need to touch him, to be close to him, to connect to him. For a moment, he was so vulnerable, so perfect, so deliciously honest that all she wanted to do was kiss him. She pushed her body toward him, desperate for the softest of touches. Their faces reached the middle of the table. She felt the caress of his breath on her skin, the moistness of his pink lips welcoming her.

She could almost taste the sweetness of his kiss when--

"*Hey! No touching!* And no kissing, silverbacks! Back off!" The guard rapped on the glass, holding a scrathe remote in one hand and a mean expression on his face. "Any more shit like that and we'll separate you two into different cell blocks, got it?"

With the fiercest of regrets she pulled away and glared at the HALO, slamming down on the bench with a pout. *Oh, we are sooo breaking out of here today*, she thought.

The warning alarm whooped, signaling them that it was time for the scrubbing. Vale's body became rigid, knowing what was about to come. *Well I hope you think of something soon*, he thought in a worried tone.

Trust me, she responded, standing up slowly, *it's already in motion.*

Chapter Twenty-eight

"Jeez, it smells like a rat's ass in here," one of the guards said as they stepped into the chamber. She heard several men laugh at that. The sounds of boots on wet cement slapped all around her. The scrubbing was complete, and it was time to be dragged out to the courtyard. She could tell that today's dose was particularly painful. Vale could hardly keep his thoughts straight. *It's almost over*, she said to him, gently stroking his hand. *We're getting out of here.*

"Rat's ass? More like wet dog," a man retorted with a guttural chuckle. She recognized that voice. It was Charlie York, the HALO who scrathed her at the gate. *How convenient*, she thought sarcastically. She gritted her teeth and kept her head down.

"Well, well, well. Would you look at Snow White," she heard him say. "Even this feisty little bitch can't defend herself against the scrubbing."

The other guard laughed. "None of 'em can, Charlie. That's the point."

He walked over to her and kicked her with his boot. "Hey. Hey princess, the bath's over. Now come on. Get up.

We've got to get you all outside and walking around. Let the chemicals seep into your skin."

She watched as the HALOs dragged the other Grays to their feet. They were weak. Each one had to be supported as they were led out of the room. She caught Vale's eye for just a moment. He looked drowned and beaten. Furious, she watched them drag him out of the room like a sack of flour. The guards "escorted" the other Grays out of the chamber until she and Charlie York were the only ones left. She felt the fury overcome her, and she welcomed it. She would need it.

"Come on, princess," he said, grabbing for her arm. "Get the hell up. This room smells like shit. I don't want to stand in here any longer than I have to so let's go. Come on."

"Leave me here," she said quietly.

Charlie laughed. "I don't think so. You don't get to stay in the chamber. We've got several more groups coming in here soon and we have to prep for the next scrubbing. Now come on. Get up."

She looked up at him and squared her jaw. "No."

Charlie York scoffed. "No. No? Are you freaking crazy? You don't get to tell me 'no'!"

"Well live with it," she responded. "I said no. I'm not going with you."

He bent down to her level, grabbed a handful of her hair and yanked her face up. She saw the coldness in his bland eyes, the unfeeling snarl that curled his lips over discolored teeth. He yanked her face close to his and licked the side of her cheek with his scratchy tongue. His hot, disgusting breath prickled the fine hairs on the side of her face. Cringing, she yanked away from him in utter disgust.

"Ahh. Tastes like meat," he whispered wetly into her ear. "I see you still need to be whipped, silverback. I think I need to teach you a lesson. A personal lesson."

"You'll get in trouble," she said, pointing to the window. "They'll see you. They won't let you do this."

He shook his head. "Sorry princess, but there's no one there. No one to hear the screams. No one to come for help. So go ahead, bitch. Go ahead and howl, because no one's coming to save you. It's just you and me...and all the weapons on my belt."

She reached into the back of her throat and spat right in his face. He recoiled instantly and backhanded her as hard as he could and her face hit the cement with a wet, slapping sound. It hurt like hell, but she didn't care. It only fueled her rage. Charlie screamed obscenities and wiped his face. Gruffly he grabbed her hair again and dragged her toward him.

"You'll regret that. You're going to regret the shit out of that," he threatened. He reached down and started unlatching his belt. His cold eyes locked on her as he tried to unfasten his pants.

"I wouldn't do that if I were you," she said.

"Ha! Nice try silverback," he said. "Now turn over."

"Go fuck yourself," she responded.

That's when he saw the gun. The barrel of the resonator - his own pistol - was in her hands, pointed directly at his stomach. He looked back at her and then down at it in disbelief. "How the hell did you get that?"

"I snatched it when you were wiping my spit from your ugly face," she responded smugly. "Now who's regretting things?"

Charlie stared at her incredulously. "But...you were scrubbed. I watched you go down! That stuff knocks the crap out of you people. After the scrubbing you Grays are barely able to walk! How the hell did you get my gun?"

She smiled and drew her arm back, pistol whipping him in the temple. Hard. He yelped in alarm as blood trickled down the side of his face. Before he could recover she jumped up, keeping the resonator pointed directly at his head.

"I told you, Charlie York, you got the wrong girl," she said. "I'm not what you think I am."

"But you *are* a Gray," he protested weakly. "I scrathed you myself. I watched you get scrubbed just now. You registered as a Gray on the infoscanner. Your brand on your hand! I mean for Christ's sake, your eyes!"

"You shouldn't believe everything you see," she pointed out. "But really, that's the least of your problems."

"I don't care what lies you try to feed me," he said. "You're a Gray. You're just playing a trump card to try and save your skin. I've seen this before. I know I'm in no actual danger."

"Oh?" she said, charging the resonator to full blast. "And what would you call having a gun to your head? Foreplay?"

"Ha!" he said, wiping some of the blood from the side of his head. "Not hardly, but a Gray with a gun is no threat to any human. That's the first thing they teach us here; that you won't fight back."

"Well it's good to know that," she said. "It will make killing you people so much easier."

Charlie shook his head in disbelief. "I don't think so. You might panic and cry and even make threats, but in the end you won't shoot me. You couldn't live with yourself if you did."

She kicked him as hard as she could in the stomach. He doubled over and fell down, slamming his head on the ground. She kicked him a couple of more times for emphasis until she thought he wasn't in a position to talk back anymore.

"I don't know what I am," she said, "but I know that I'm not the type that won't fight back. I'm not alone in that, either. These people that you treat like animals? They're fighting back.

The Adulos will not be treated like a second class race anymore. None of them. They will no longer stay dormant while their race is enslaved, beaten and brutalized into extinction. It's going to be stopped."

"Oh yeah?" he said defiantly. "And how the hell are you gonna do that, Snow White? With your seven Gray dwarves? You gonna look for your prince charming to come save the day?"

"Okay enough with the fairy tale metaphors. I get it. I have black hair and I'm a girl. You're so god damn clever. Now shut up," she ordered, putting a foot on his throat. "Besides, who needs a prince charming when you have a lord guardian."

"What? What the hell does that mean?"

"That Gray I'm with? He's the leader of an army," she said defiantly. "An army of Adulo fighters called the Silencium. They're people who fight against oppression and slavery. People who will no longer stand in the shadows and allow their people to be treated like this. The reign of man over the Adulos is coming to an end. Vale Teag is leading the way, and I'm standing beside him."

She realized the words were true after she said them. Strangely, it filled her with a sense of pride and purpose. Vale's cause had somehow become her cause. A noise distracted her from her thoughts. Charlie York was cackling. It was a low, guttural noise that sounded menacing and revolting.

"What's so funny?" she demanded. She kicked him and he fell on his back on the wet floor. He made a stifled groan and she pointed the resonator directly at his temple.

"Oh the end is coming all right," he agreed. "But not the way you think. This chamber you're in? It's a scrubber."

"So? You're poisoning people. I figured that out already, actually. That's going to stop. All of it is going to stop."

"No, you're not getting it, princess. Scrubbing is not poisoning; it's genetic cleansing. We're rewriting the Gray genetics. From the inside out."

"What? What the *hell* does that mean?" she demanded. She pressed the charge on the side of the resonator pistol. *"Tell me what that means!"*

Charlie York stifled a laugh. "It means that we're reprogramming Gray genetics. Takin' out all their genetic crap and filling it with human DNA. Slowly stripping them of all that is Gray and making them human."

"What? But that's…that's impossible."

He shrugged. "Apparently not. We've released hundreds of scrubbed Grays into the population. All of them have no memory of what they used to be, and all of them show no traces of their old genetics. It's a clean, *human* slate for all of them. As soon as we perfect this process we're taking it to their stupid ass planet. We're going to scrub every single silverback until the entire population is humanized. Talk about a conversion, eh?"

"But why?" she asked, horrified. "Why would you do that?"

"Why not?" he asked casually. "Grays aren't people. They're not even human. Oh sure you walk like humans and talk like humans but you're not. You people are an infestation. Your planet is filled with nothing but a race of creepy parasites. You don't eat, you barely talk. You don't even believe in god."

She was stunned. "You can't possibly tell me that a guy like you is doing this for religious reasons, Charlie."

He narrowed his eyes at her. "Of course not. I'm doing this for the money. I hear Boone's looking to make trillions upon trillions on this deal, and what's good for the goose is good for the gander, you feel me, princess?"

Taris was stunned. She reached with her open hand and touched the gage interface on the back of her collar. "So that's what this is. You're reprogramming them to be human. You're taking everything that it is to be Adulo and you're changing it."

Charlie nodded. "Yep, and you're along for the ride too. When the panel on your collar turns green you're ready to go. The scrub's complete."

"Yeah, but why?" she demanded. "I mean, we're really talking about the extinction of an entire race of millions of people! Who in god's name even sanctioned this?"

"That," he said with a wicked grin, "is something you're going to have to take up with the Hammer."

"Fine," she said. "Take me to him."

He shook his head. "Oh I don't think so. See, you might be able to withstand the chambers now, but eventually you'll break down."

"I wouldn't count on it," she said confidently.

"Even if you don't you'll never make it out of here," he said. "You won't last ten feet in the hallways before you're captured. They'll lock you in the crates for a week when they catch you. Most silverbacks can't last a day."

He was likely right. She might make it through a few hallways, but the moment they saw her collar they would scrathe her and lock her up. It wasn't worth the risk. She thought about what she needed to do and what she wanted to do. Then she thought about what Vale would do. She frowned and leaned in closer, keeping the resonator pointed directly at his chest.

"Then help me," she said in a gentle tone. "I'll give you the chance to help me. If you help me I'll let you live. Do the right thing, Charlie York, for once in your life."

"The *right* thing?" he asked with a little laugh. "You think *this* is the right thing? Holding me at gunpoint? That's rich, bitch."

"What you should do is decide what matters here," she said, trying very hard not to pull the trigger. "Think about it. Is killing millions of people really the right thing to do? You're going to have to ask yourself that, Charlie."

"I don't have to do shit," he said, spitting on the floor. "I'll tell you what I'm *going* to do, though. I'm going to wait for you to leave me in here and then I'm going to hunt you down. I'm going to hunt down every single Gray you care about and I'm going to personally see to it that they pay for *your* crimes. And your short haired buddy? Well, gosh, I don't think you'd be too happy if something happened to him, would you?"

Her blood started to boil. She felt her resolve crumbling. She was blinded by hate. Consumed by it. "Don't you dare touch one strand of silver hair on his head, do you hear me? Don't you dare."

"Oh struck a nerve there did I?" he said with a menacing smile. "Well I tell you that I'm going to do, then. I'm going to torture the shit out of him and then you know what? I'm going to put him up against a wall, and I'm gonna execute him myself."

"I take it that's a 'no' to the helping me thing, then?" she said.

"No I'm not going to help you," he snarled. "You can burn in whatever hell you believe in for all I care. So go on, fight your cause, get captured. Enjoy your next few minutes of freedom because they're about to be your last. Say goodbye to your silverback boyfriend, princess."

"Taris," she said sternly. "My name is Taris."

"I don't give a damn what your name is," he said bitterly.

"One last chance, Charlie. One last chance to join me and make a difference. One last chance to do the right thing."

He looked up at her with his beady, unfeeling eyes. "*Fuck* you, Taris. You'll never be able to stop the scrubbing, you'll never save your people and you'll never be able to pull the trigger. Never."

She straightened her back and released three rounds into his flesh. Two in the chest, one in the head. Charlie slumped back against the wall and slid down to the ground, dead. Small streams of blood flowed out of his body, snaking their way to the drain in the middle of the room.

"Never say never, Charlie," she said quietly.

Chapter Twenty-nine

Taris had to pull Charlie's HALO uniform high over her neck so it would cover her collar. The blood, water, and chemicals made it the worse for the wear, not to mention the two resonator burn holes in the middle which she cleverly hid with her rifle. Lucky for her, the hallways were dark. The lights were marginal at best and provided only a shadow of luminescence, so her disheveled appearance went by relatively unnoticed. She pulled her hair back in a slick bun and put on a pair of dark, wide sunglasses that she found in Charlie's pocket. The last thing she needed was another human drawing attention to her eyes, or any part of her for that matter.

She walked through the hallways with a sense of military purpose. No one seemed to pay her any mind. Every now and then she got a couple of nods or hellos from the other guards, but for the most part she blended in well. For that she was relieved. She tried to tell herself that she belonged there; that she was stationed there and not an imposter. It always helped her to try and almost believe the lie while undercover; it made her act that much more believable. She had to believable, and she had to be quick. It was only a matter of time before they found Charlie's body in the storage closet just outside of the gas chamber.

After about fifteen minutes of wandering around the dark, identical hallways, she finally managed to find a staircase. She reached for the door handle, but it was locked. After a momentary jolt of panic, she remembered that she was wearing Charlie's identification badges. She reached up, grabbed his ID card and pressed it against the door's interface. The panel blinked for a moment and then turned green. She climbed several flights of stairs before she came to the top. There were two doors, one to the left and one to the right. The one to the right said "OFFICES - MAIN LEVEL" on a plaque by the door. The one to the left said "COURTYARD - WEST ENTRANCE". *Jackpot*, she thought. Using Charlie's ID badge, she unlocked the courtyard entrance and opened the door.

The sky was overcast. The gray early morning felt still and the air clung close to the ground. Outside she saw dozens of Grays all milling about, walking numbly in loping circles around the unkempt and mostly muddied courtyard. With their silver hair and drab uniforms, in the pale light of an overcast morning, they looked almost like ghosts. Wandering, aimless ghosts with hollow expressions and drooping limbs. They drifted through the courtyard as though the world around them didn't even exist. She could see HALOs posted at different positions on the outer wall of the facility. Blast turrets swiveled from the three smaller guard towers as the black electronic Eye rotated slowly, observing the courtyard with the feel of bitter indifference.

Slowly she made her way toward the group of HALOs just to the right of the Eye. A couple of them looked in her direction, but they didn't seem too interested in what she was doing. She scanned the courtyard cautiously. Most of the Grays were moving around mechanically. Some of them looked sad, others worried, tired and even cold. A couple of faces were familiar to her; the young boy from her cell block, the woman with the braided hair. She spotted Kyran with his blue tattoo, wandering around in aimless circles. She didn't see Vale, though. She searched for him for several minutes, but she didn't see any sign of the short-haired guardian in the courtyard. That made her nervous. And suddenly very scared.

Damnit Vale, she thought, trying out her wobbly and newfound telepathy skills, *where the hell are you?*

Gone, she heard Kyran think. *He tried to fight them when you didn't come out of the room. They took him away.*

HE DID WHAT?!

Her outburst so startled him that Kyran physically jumped and took several steps backwards. Taris had to keep herself from confronting him. Keeping her breathing slow and deliberate, she tried to calm down.

That stupid man, she thought. *He never raises his fists and suddenly he picks a fight? What did he do that for?*

Kyran stared forward, but she saw the muscles in his neck tense. *They told us, as we were being dragged out of the chamber, that the HALO who was left behind with you was going to…give you extra punishment.*

Oh no, she thought.

They taunted him with it. She could feel the hated, the anger, in his tone. *The lord guardian would not suffer to hear of it. He fought them until they scrathed his neck black, Taris. Until he could barely breathe.*

She was heartbroken. *So, he risked his life…to save me?*

Kyran looked at her out of the corner of his eye. *Unstoppably. And apparently pointlessly, since you are here now. So, I take it you were able to fight off your attacker?*

Eh…in a sense. She walked along the side of the courtyard, keeping her distance but close enough to speak to him. He turned to look at her and his eyes grew wide. *Taris, how did you acquire that outfit?*

I killed the guy who was wearing it, she answered honestly, instantly nervous that he would be appalled by that. Instead he have her the smallest of nods.

Good, he thought.

Where did they take Vale? she asked, trying to look HALO-like and hating herself for it. She wanted to rip the circled H right off her bullet-riddled vest.

To the lowest level on the floor, he responded. *That's what I heard. He told me if you returned that you are not to try and save him.*

She scoffed. *Yeah right. Like I'm just going to let him die down there.*

I told him you would not heed his warning, Kyran responded with a shrug. He looked up and his eyes caught a HALO in the back corner. A small Latina woman standing in the back, as far away from the Eye as possible.

You need to blend in, he said, *go speak to that guard.*

Why? she prompted

That guard has access to the lower level, Kyran explained. *She'll take you there.*

How do you know that? she demanded, stopping short.

He swung around and glared at her urgently. *Just trust me*, he begged. *Go. Now.*

Fine. She walked around to the furthest edge of the courtyard and sidled up next to the female HALO as casually as she could. *It's time to play my part,* she thought wistfully.

"Hey," Taris said nonchalantly. "How's it going?"

"Not bad," the woman responded.

The HALO was slight in height but muscular. She had broad shoulders and curly hair that was pulled back in a tight bun. Her skin was tanned and she had dramatic eyebrows that made her look more serious than her oval, pleasant face did. She was smoking a blue cigarette, resting her hand on her weapons belt casually. Plumes of dark blue smoke puffed out of her pouty mouth. It reminded her of Dave. She thought about all of them. The people on her ship. The ones she was forced to leave behind. The ones she never got to apologize to, say goodbye to. She hoped they were all still alive. She hoped they hadn't given up.

"Hey. Hey I know you," the guard said to her. Taris felt her heartbeat quicken. *Oh no, please don't make me shoot you,* she thought.

"Oh yeah?" she said carefully. "How?"

"Boone Hooper's party," the woman said. "I saw you on TV! You got drunk and beat up the viscount of acquisitions for Sector Three, right?"

Relief washed over her. Then embarrassment. "Oh yeah. Yep, that was me."

"I thought that was you!" she said, snapping her fingers together. "Oh man, that was hilarious! That thing with the bow tie and the guards? How long did they chase you?"

Taris felt herself blush. "Ah, well I'm not sure. I think I ran around for about twenty minutes before anyone caught up with me, and even then they cheated because they used hover bikes and…I'm sorry, who are you?"

"Oh!" the HALO said, shaking her hand excitedly. "I'm Sergeant Angie Joplin, Thirty-Ninth Division, Sector One Protection Squad," she said proudly.

"I'm Taris. Captain Taris Bodil." She paused at using her real name, but it didn't seem to matter. The woman already knew who she really was, it seemed pointless to lie now.

Angie smiled. "Captain, huh? So you're in the fleet?"

"Yep," she said, casting a shadowing look at the guard tower. "I work on a spaceship and everything. Usually." *Even though it's currently under the command of a mutinous xenophobic psychopath*, she thought to herself.

"Huh," said Angie. "This is a strange post for a fleetwoman."

Taris thought quickly. "I'm um…filling in for a friend. As a favor."

"Favor?" Angie asked amiably. "Not much of a friend if they asked you to pull complex guard duty for them as a favor."

"Well you know," she said dismissively. "I work for Captain Philip. He sometimes offers our crewmen…to fill in here at the complex…you know…if there are high interest cases. It's hard to turn him down, you know?"

She hoped to god that was believable. Usually, military protocol would have made that scenario highly improbable. However, since it seemed her erstwhile captain was involved in things which were anything but in keeping with protocol, it was at least moderately likely.

Angie took the bait. "Oh, Captain Philip! Well that makes sense now. He's sent you guys to do rounds here before, right? There's that tall engineering female and, um, the big Italian. What's his name?"

"Tyler," Taris said with a disapproving frown. "Lt. Vinny Tyler."

Angie snapped her fingers in agreement. "That's the one. Yeah, he usually does this complex duty. How did you end up with it?"

Taris shrugged. "Lost a game of cards to him, had to take his next shift. You know how it is."

Angie snorted. "Yeah I do. Hey, I hate to tell you this but you know Lt. Tyler cheats, right? He probably tricked you into this."

"Yeah," Taris said slowly. "Boy do I ever know that now."

She stood there for austerity's sake for a few seconds, trying not to look as desperate to flee as she felt. Finally, after what she felt was an appropriate amount of time, she cleared her throat and Angie looked up at her.

"So hey, sergeant. Got a question for you."

"Something wrong, Captain Bodil?" she asked.

"Yeah. We brought in a couple of Grays a couple of weeks ago. One of them was high profile. Said to be real valuable. I was instructed to keep an eye on him but I don't see him out here," she said casually.

"Oh? Hmm. Well, what do they look like?" she asked, scanning the courtyard.

"Well the high profile one is a tall Gray. Very tall. Handsome face, quiet voice. He has short hair. That's the most unique thing about him," she said. "He was just, er, scrubbed...and he was supposed to be sent out here but I don't see him."

"Hmm. That is strange. What about the other one?" she asked.

"The other what?"

"The other Adulo. What was the other one like? Maybe they got sent to some special group thing or something," Angie explained.

"Oh. Um..." *She looks exactly like me* didn't seem like a good answer. "It was a female. Not very remarkable, really. You know these Grays; they all look the same..."

Angie nodded. "I know what you mean. I don't know how they can tell each other apart. Anyway, I am not sure about the female, but I heard a couple of HALOs say that they were taking a short hair to the cleansing cells."

"Cleansing cells, hmm?" she said, trying not to panic.

"Yeah the cleansing cells. You know, the final destination? Usually they don't like to skip steps, but in high profile cases they go directly to the brain washing before the genetic cleansing is complete."

Taris's throat felt dry. "Brain washing?"

"Yeah. Apparently they think he's some sort of leader. They need to aggressively neutralize him before he creates an uprising or whatever. I bet he's your man."

Sweet lord, she thought, *they're going to turn his brain into mush.* "So that's on the lower level, then?"

Angie looked at her. "What, they didn't give you a tour before you went on duty?"

"Nope," she said, hoping to sound casual. "Apparently not. That big woman was the one who helped me. She wasn't very helpful though," Taris explained weakly.

"Oh, that's Jade. She's not very nice. Or helpful."

"So I noticed," she said. "Anyway, my captain's orders are pretty clear. I really need to send my updated report soon, so if you would just point me in the direction of the cleansing rooms I'll just be on my way…"

Angie gave her a strange look that made Taris tense. If someone scrutinized her thoroughly - like what Angie was doing right now - they would see the resonator burn holes in her

434

uniform. They would know something was amiss. Taris looked over Angie's shoulder. They were standing away from earshot of the other HALOs, but not out of gun range. If she was going to have to shoot this guard, it was not going to be good. She'd be outnumbered and overrun in a matter of seconds. *Last resort*, she told herself. *Shooting her is a last resort.*

Angie peered up at her closely. "Captain, can you take off your glasses?"

"Excuse me?" she said, feigning indifference. "I don't have to take orders from you, sergeant."

"It's not an order, ma'am. It's a request."

"Look," she said sternly. "If you don't want to help me I can go find someone who will."

"No you won't," she said, lowering her voice. "You have nowhere to go. You're not supposed to be here. Take off your glasses, captain, or I'll shoot you were you stand."

Taris looked down. Angie's sidearm resonator was aimed right at her chest. Directly in the burn hole where she shot Charlie. Taris looked around. None of the other HALOs seemed to notice them talking at all. Some of the Grays were giving them sideways glances, but the hollow expressions of defeated pain told her that they would either be unwilling or unable to help. Taris gulped and clenched her jaw.

"You don't want to do this, Sergeant Joplin," she whispered.

"I wouldn't be so sure about that," she said in the same tone. "Apparently this won't be the first time you've been shot today, either."

"It's not the first time this *uniform* has been shot," Taris corrected uselessly. Angie's resonator clicked, indicating that it was charged.

"Either way, captain, you're not who you say you are."

"Well actually that's not true--"

"Take off your glasses. Now."

Taris hesitated for a moment to evaluate her options. There were no exits, too many armed guards and watchful eyes. Even if she found Vale, she was in a reinforced fortress guarded by countless armed HALOs. Angie had her up against a proverbial wall, and the look on her face said she had no qualms about shooting her right there in the courtyard. She wouldn't be doing Vale any favors if she got herself killed. She sighed heavily. *Show's over.*

"I only ask that you not harm my friend," she said quietly. "What I did here, it's not his fault. He doesn't even know."

"I'm not going to ask you again. This resonator is charged to kill."

"Okay, okay." She reached up, grabbed the bridge of her glasses, and pulled them off. She squinted a little in the new light. In that moment, she knew that her cover was blown. Her eyes, so alike to the Grays, would be reflecting the light around her. The way they always did and she denied. The way she never accepted to be truth, and told lies about, and never believed herself. The eyes that showed what she really was at the core of her being.

"All right," Taris said quietly, staring at her. "Go ahead and get it over with."

She stood there for a moment, bracing herself for the resonator burst. She heard the click of the weapon, but not the discharge. Confused, she looked down at Angie.

"Taris," she said quietly, *"camme sans supre Adulo?"*

"Something like that, yeah." She exhaled slowly. *Well isn't that a bit of irony? I'm finally able to admit that and now I'm going to die for it. Awesome.*

For a moment the two of them just stood there, studying each other. Taris raised her eyebrows. "Well? Aren't you gonna shoot me?"

"Look at me, Taris."

"I am looking at you."

"No...I mean *look at me.*"

Angie's brown, unremarkable eyes suddenly transformed, glossing over to reveal a liquid silver. Eyes that were distinctly, unequivocally, and totally Adulo. Taris gasped. A couple of Grays turned in her direction. One of them was Kyran. He cocked his head to the side and a smile crept across his face. Ever so discreetly he raised two fingers to his forehead, extending his pointer finger outward, and Angie discretely repeated the gesture. The sign of the Silencium. The symbol of an ally.

I told you she'd help you, Kyran said with a smug smile. Taris looked back to Angie at a loss for words. As soon as her eyes had transformed they changed back, returning to a dull brown again. Angie uncocked her resonator and returned it to the holster.

"Put your glasses back on," she whispered. "You're going to need to go unnoticed if we're going to go get Vale back."

Taris mechanically shoved the glasses back up the bridge of her nose. Her mind was running faster than her mouth could move. "What did you just do? How can you do that? You know Vale? How do you know about Vale? Wait. Adulo. You called them Adulos not Grays. Of course. Of course!"

"Vale sent me here," she explained. "I was looking for you. The black haired one they called Snow White. He told me to find you. Didn't realize you'd be in uniform, though. I've

438

been scanning the courtyard for the last fifteen minutes in a panic. I thought they took you to the cleansing chambers, too."

"Why did Vale send you for me? *How* did Vale send you for me?"

"Don't worry, Taris," she said with a wink. "I'm a friend and I'm here to help." Angie led them to an exit on the east side of the building. They walked unnoticed through the courtyard to the far entrance. She unlocked the deadbolt and the door swung open. Quietly they slipped inside.

"Who are you?" she whispered again. "I mean really. What's your name?"

Angie had started down the steps. Halfway down the first flight she turned to face her, a smile plastered on her mysterious face. "I'm Jyrisa Ato-Teag. I believe you were looking for me."

Chapter Thirty

By the time they reached the cleansing floor Taris felt slightly claustrophobic. The cleansing chambers were in a small alcove deep underground. The hallway was just one long corridor - about a quarter of a mile long - with closed metal doors on either side. The hall was dank and smelled like stagnant water. It was empty of traffic but occupied by four HALOs at the other end of the hallway who were guarding two separate doors. Taris and Jyrisa were standing by some storage containers in a small alcove out of earshot, pretending to be cataloging items for storage.

"This is the lowest level of the complex," Jyrisa explained quietly. "This is the brain washing department, if you will. It's the last stop here before the captives are released into the public."

"What does that mean?" she asked. "This cleansing process. What does it all do?"

Jyrisa ticked off an item on a fake checklist and placed a box of god-knows-what into the container in a perfunctory manner.

"Cleansing is what they do when they rewrite the memories," she explained. "The Adulos who come here have already been stripped of their natural genetics, but that's not enough. They need to be stripped down *mentally*. The cleansing removes the thoughts, memories, identity of any kind. So they go into these chambers and the machines wipe their mind clean. Erase them entirely. Then they program whole news lives into their heads."

Taris's mouth dropped. "Oh my god. That's unbelievably awful."

"Agreed," Jyrisa said, casting a dark look at the cleansing cell doors.

"I mean, it doesn't even seem real," Taris mused, fixated. "How do they even do that, anyway?"

Jyrisa shrugged. "The science is a little beyond my understanding, but they have this device that drills into the brain and sort of downloads memories into it. It turns the mind into a giant computer, erasing the thoughts of the Adulo and replacing them with whatever they want. After this is completed, the subject is considered neutralized. Thus the process is complete. The once normal, harmless Adulo is turned into a sleeper agent."

"Sleeper agent?" she asked. "Like with the trigger words and the mind control and all that?"

Jyrisa looked up at her and frowned. "I don't think so. We know they're programmable but I don't think they're deadly walking automatons."

"Okay," Taris said, reeling her imagination back in. "Regardless, that process has to take forever."

"Anywhere from several months to a couple of years," Jyrisa explained. "I hear the Nerais are the hardest to neutralize. Go figure, right? Those people are so stubborn. Anyway, using hypnotic inference technology, the science team 'reprograms' Adulos to be and think any way they want. They remember nothing of themselves before, none of their former thoughts."

"Blank slate," Taris said quietly.

"Exactly. Oh, and that collar on your neck? It's a gage. It determines how far along you are in the process before the scrubbing is complete and you're ready to be cleansed."

"Yeah I figured that out," she said, touching the outside of the collar instinctually. "I was told that the plan is to wipe out the entire Adulo race eventually. Is that true?"

Jyrisa's jaw tightened. "Yes. Yes that is the plan in the end, but they're not ready yet."

"Why not?" Taris asked. Jyrisa was fiddling with several small metal parts, attaching them together from memory. *What is she building?* "I mean, not that I'm complaining, but what's the hold up?"

"We really don't know. I'm sure they have their reasons. Maybe to place their sleeper agents in strategic positions? They could program them to be suicide bombers, or to be the heads of pivotal corporations, or to lead the military."

"Sweet fancy Moses," Taris swore under her breath. "Putting them in charge of everything. Taking control of whatever they want."

"That's my guess," Jyrisa said, screwing what looked like a metal washer on top of a ball full of wires. "It's terrible but it's also brilliant. This facility is spearheading the whole neutralizing project. They have been for years."

"How many years?" Taris wondered.

"Over thirty we think."

"Thirty *years*?" she gasped. "That's insane! Do you have any idea what kind of damage must have been done in the last three decades?!"

Jyrisa's expression fell. "Yes. More than you know."

Taris brooded over that. "So, is there any way to reverse it? Is there any way to retrieve the old memories of the scrubbed Adulos? Any way to get back what was taken from them?"

Jryisa shook her head slowly. "To our knowledge, no. It appears to be irreversible."

Taris was taken aback. "Never? How terrible."

"Yes. It really is. So really, anyone you meet could easily be a sleeper agent. They wouldn't even know it. They're just fulfilling the preprogrammed suggestions of their neutralizing, but to them, their thoughts and feelings and emotions are as real as the next human's. I don't think they ever know what they really are, honestly. Maybe it's better that way."

"And there's no real way to tell?" she asked cautiously.

"Not really," Jyrisa answered, fishing deep to the bottom of the storage container and pulling out some metal clamp, affixing it to her device. "They even surgically remove the brands from their hands usually, or they must come up with a damn good excuse for their existence. I mean, I suppose there would be irregularities."

For some reason that gave Taris pause. She felt nervous the more the conversation continued. "Irregularities?" she asked, trying to sound casual. "Like what?"

"Dreams, they say," Jyrisa said, attaching two wires together delicately. "I've been told sleeper agents have powerful dreamscapes, even after they've been scrubbed. Oh! And sometimes they're still susceptible to scrathes, just like us. No one knows why that is, either."

Taris felt like she'd been punched in the gut. The dreams. The brand on her hand. The scrathing. The eyes. Everything that she hated about herself, everything that indicated a sleeper agent, she had all of that. *But it couldn't be*, she thought, *it's impossible.*

Jyrisa had stopped working on her device and was glaring at her. "What's impossible, Taris?"

"N--nothing," she stammered, pushing the thoughts from her mind. *Stupid telepathy.* "How do you know all of this?"

Jyrisa opened the last small container and inspected its contents gingerly. "The Silencium order I belong to had aspirations to take this facility down. We've been watching this place for months. Knowing the guard shifts, putting agents into the staff, learning the inner workings. After Boone Hooper captured the Star of Gray it was clear we had to strike. We had to make a move before any more of those awful neutralized sleeper agents were released."

"Awful?" Taris repeated. "But it wasn't their fault. They're still Adulos."

Jyrisa looked up at her in the dark. For a moment, her eyes shifted to the reflective silver, glinting in the shadows. She saw anger in her eyes. Resentment. Resignation. "Once they're neutralized they're not Adulos, Taris," she said in a strange, very Gray tone. "The Adulo is dead. The only thing left is a shell with an enemy inside. That's all."

Taris swallowed hard. *Not now*, she thought. *You shut up and keep your thoughts to yourself, Bodil. Do it.* Jyrisa was waiting for her to respond, but she couldn't form the words. Finally, with an altogether entirely Gray motion, Jyrisa shook her head and a calm look fell on her face. Her eyes went back to brown, her face unreadable, and she went back to building her little round device. Taris turned around and wiped the sweat from her brow. Time to change the subject.

"So which room is Vale in?" she asked, pushing her paranoia from her mind.

Don't know," Jyrisa said, struggling to twist a particularly stubborn part on the top of the device she was building that was starting to look more and more like a metal egg with a stem. "We're just going to have to take out all the guards and go through the rooms one by one. We have to hurry, though. We don't have much time."

"Why?" Taris asked.

Jyrisa looked up at her. "The cleansing, it's meant for fully scrubbed Adulos. If it's done too early, if the Adulo is not ready it will kill them. Painfully."

"What? Why the hell didn't you say that in the first place?!"

"Because I needed you to stay with me until I was done," she retorted. "Otherwise you'd have gone in there, guns blazing, and killed us both."

She was right, of course, but Taris didn't say so. "It's not going to happen," she said, cocking her weapon. "I did *not* go through all of this with Vale just to have him die now."

"Then you're going to need this." Jyrisa handed her the little device she had been building. Upon closer inspection, Taris realized it was an old fashioned blast grenade.

"I recognize this. From the war. The rebellion used them when the pulsar burst rounds ran dry," she whispered.

I stashed the parts in the container over time. Rebuilt it from memory, Jyrisa thought with a smile.

Impressive, Taris responded, nodding appreciatively. Jyrisa nodded at the compliment. Down the corridor, in a sound so quiet it seemed muffled and distant, she heard the screams. *Not today*, she thought. *So help me god Vale, you're going to live.*

"Okay, go ahead. Throw it."

Taris held the cold, heavy explosive in her hand and pulled the top pin. She gripped the end, released the hammer, and tossed it down the hallway.

"Hey what the hell is that?"

"Grenade!"

The explosion rippled through the corridor and knocked Taris and Jyrisa to the ground. She heard the rumbling from the walls, the smell of burned flesh and ripped metal. It took several moments for her to regain her bearings. When the ringing finally stopped she managed to sit up, dragging herself to her feet awkwardly. Through the red flashing lights and smoldering debris, she searched for Jyrisa. She called her name a few times before she found her, still alive and covered under two large crates. Taris pushed the crates out of the way and helped her up.

"Whoa," Taris said, surprised. "Jyrisa. You look...different."

Jyrisa's hair was no longer brown and curly, but long and rippling silver. Her skin had transformed into the ashen color of the Grays and her eyes were shimmering in the dark. She had also managed to grow about a foot, and her clothes strained to contain her new frame. Jyrisa looked down at herself and sighed.

"Oh yeah. Sorry about that. My concentration was broken. Give me a second." She closed her eyes and her body started to change. Within seconds it morphed back into the small Latina woman that she had been before. Taris' mouth dropped.

"You can shape shift?" she exclaimed. "I didn't know you Grays could do that! Oh my god!"

Jyrisa frowned. "Yeah. Of course. I'm half Ato. All Atos are morphers."

"Really?" she asked, pulling her weapon out from under the crates. "Holy shit no way! You have to tell me how that's even possible!"

"Some other time I assure you," she said in a strange tone. "Now let's go."

The two women started cautiously toward the doors at the end of the hallway. The explosion covered the ground with rubble, metal, blood and debris. Weapons at the ready, Taris led the way. The explosion center was pretty torn up. All four of the HALOs were dead, completely ripped apart. Flesh and bone scattered over the walls and floors. Taris stepped lightly over the rubble and body parts, making her way through the mangled hallway in the dark, the angry red emergency lights guiding her eyes.

"So," she said as she made her way carefully through the a tangle of hanging exposed wires and jagged pieces of concrete. "Can you, you know, morph into anything?"

"Not anything," she answered. "And not for extended periods of time. I'm only half Ato, so my longevity is somewhat limited. The reconstruction of one's own physical matter is not an easy science to master, Taris."

"Wow. How cool," she said, genuinely impressed. "So, how come we've never seen that before? How come humans don't know about this I mean."

"Because that knowledge would give them more of a reason to hate, fear and kill us, Taris."

"Oh." She peered slowly into the first room. "Well that makes sense I guess."

"Wow. Vale told me that you were raised on Earth, but he didn't go into detail about your ignorance of our people," Jyrisa mumbled.

"I was rather pressed for time, Jyrisa," said a small voice in the corner. "Explaining Taris to you mentally would have taken a lot longer than the three seconds I had when I was passing you in the hallway. A lot longer."

"*Vale!*" Taris exclaimed.

He was chained to the wall, slumped over, held up only by the shackles around his wrists. Attached to his head was a helmet filled with needles that had been drilled into his skull. The needles fed into some sort of mechanical device that had been, until the blast stopped it, pumping drugs directly into his brain. His face looked gaunt and flushed. He was sweating profusely, he was injured, he was in pain, but he was alive. She jumped over a small pile of debris and fell to her knees in front of him.

"Good god Vale, are you okay?" she asked, cupping his face in her hands.

"Careful," he said, pointing to the device on his head. "I think it's still plugged in." He pointed to the spherical device around his head with a weak grimace.

"Don't worry," she said intensely, staring directly into his eyes. "I'm going to get you out of this. You're going to be okay, trust me."

"I always have, *tarischa*," he said, giving her a weak smile.

She followed the trail of cords that led to a round metal base against the wall, walked around the electrical column and found the panel interface. She thought about trying to figure out how to turn it off, but smashing it with the butt of her rifle seemed much quicker. And more effective. The device powered itself down and she heard Vale gasp in relief. Taris found the keys to the chains inside the pocket of the dead scientist who had been performing the cleansing. He was crushed under the weight of one of the unused cleansing devices, likely toppled over by the force of the blast. Taris and Jyrisa shoved the column to the side, retrieved the keys from the crushed man's pocket, and released the shackles around Vale's hands and feet. Carefully she removed the helmet, plucking the needles out one by one. Little droplets of blood dripped down his head from where they had penetrated his skin, trickling down his face in small red streams.

"That device is called the crown of thorns," Jyrisa explained. "It's what cleanses the brain and reprograms it. It's terribly painful."

"I'm acutely aware of that, Jyrisa. Thank you." He rubbed his face gently with a shaking, shackle-burned hand.

"Lord guardian, did they damage your mind?" Jyrisa asked in a soft tone. "Have they erased you irreparably?"

Vale leaning against the wall and Taris for support, laboriously lifting his reflecting eyes up to her.

"No," he said. "It was not permanent, and I am able to purge the poison before it sets in."

"Are you sure?" she asked cautiously. Taris noticed that Jyrisa's hand was hovering over her weapon. Vale, undaunted, stood up a little taller.

"*Yii, difila tibus,*" he said in his feathery tone. Jyrisa relaxed instantly at the sound of their language on his tongue. "That being said," he continued, "if you had hesitated more than a few more minutes, I could have lost a great deal of my memory, yes. More likely my life. For that I am in your debt. The both of you."

He reached out and touched the side of Taris's face affectionately. His skin was not as warm as it usually was, but the fire of his soul danced in the tingle of his touch. They stared at each other in the dungeon, but even in the darkness she could see Vale as clear as day. She always could.

"Yes," he said, though no question had been asked.

"Yes what?"

"Yes your eyes gleam in the dark as well," he said with a little smile. "I could tell that you were wondering, so I thought I would tell you."

She stifled a laugh. "I thought I told you to stay out of my thoughts, alien."

"And I thought I told you that you need to accept yourself for who you are, Taris," he said gently. That stopped her. Slowly, and not without a regretful expression, she moved his hand and cradled it in her own.

"I don't really know what I am anymore, Vale."

"Well you're about to be dead if we linger here any longer," Jyrisa said urgently, keeping her rifle pointed down the hallway. "We all are. So let's just get the other Adulo and get out of here."

"What other Adulo?" Vale asked quizzically.

"There was another person down here," Taris explained, helping him to a stand. "They are being held in the cell across from yours."

Vale frowned. "Are you sure of this? I felt no others of our kind in my presence here. I always feel the presence of others. Surely you're mistaken."

"It's no mistake," said a strangely adolescent voice. "And together, we are in very real danger."

Taris looked into the doorway. Standing in the hall, with the glowing white hair and the strangely smiling face, was the young Gray man from her dream. He looked just as he had in the dream. Childlike eyes, smooth skin, shoulder length white hair, hands clasped politely in front of him. Jyrisa and Vale took one look at him and fell to their knees, touching their fingertips to their forehead and bowing in reverence. Taris's mouth dropped.

"You!" she exclaimed.

He looked at her, the fire of life itself emblazoned in his white eyes. "My name is Elias Ohn," he said in a quiet voice. "I am the Star of Gray. It's nice to see you again, Taris Leigh Bodil."

Chapter Thirty-one

"Elias!" she gasped. "So that *was* you in my dream, wasn't it?"

He nodded. "It was, yes. And thank you for that," he said kindly. "I haven't been threspinning in a long time. It was a lovely experience."

"Why are you here?" she prompted. "I mean, in the cleansing cells."

He smiled. "I was brought here, as were you, to atone for my fictitious crimes against humanity. I am glad to have found you, Taris. I thought I might not find you before my time on this plane ended. It seems I was wrong."

"Me?" She clasped her hand to her chest. "Why me? What am I? I'm nothing. Just a starship captain with a gun and a drinking problem. You're the one that's important here. Vale has been moving heaven and earth to find you, Elias!"

"I know this," he said, cocking his head to the side. "And for his dedication and sacrifice my lord guardian shall be rewarded."

"You hear that, Vale?" she asked, genuinely excited. "You get a reward!"

"However, you are mistaken in your initial declaration. You are not a nobody, Taris. You are far from nothing."

"What? What in god's name makes you think that?" she asked.

Elias stepped lightly toward her. His hand came up and reached out, cupping her face. In that one touch she felt the power of his being. The light inside him grew brighter and he closed his eyes. She felt him enter her mind unobtrusively, like he was entering a room. She thought about protesting, but she didn't resist him. She couldn't resist him. After the most brief and glorious of moments he retracted his hand gently. The fire of his skin still echoed on her cheeks.

"Glorious," he said with a bright, uninhibited smile. "You are indeed as I suspected you to be, Taris. You are one of the three. We have waited for this day for a very long time."

"Oh, you mean because you think I'm one of the destined ones or whatever?"

"One of the three pillars," he corrected. "Many believe you not to exist, but there are those of us who never lost hope. We knew you would find us. Vale's suspicions were right; the warrior of the three has returned. You walk the thin gray line."

Taris put her hands on her hips. "Why do people keep saying that?"

"Star of Gray," Jyrisa said in a voice filled with reverence. "Pardon my intrusion, but my sources tell me that they can no longer stall the oncoming reinforcements from above. If we are to get you to safety then we must leave now."

"Very well," Elias said, bidding them stand. "We must leave. Warrior, where do we go next?"

It took her a few moments to realize he meant her. "Huh? Me? You're calling me 'warrior' now?"

"I am, yes," he said calmly. "You are the warrior who fights with righteous valor. You kneel only to honor. Your hands bleed with the fate of two worlds."

She shook her head. "Holy mother of moly. And I thought I was finally getting used to that prophetic stuff with Vale. And, since you asked, I have no idea what to do now. Jyrisa led us here, she probably has a plan."

"Well actually I don't," Jyrisa admitted a little sheepishly. "The only exit is now blocked by incoming forces."

"What?" Taris exclaimed. "So we're trapped here? Oh great. I don't suppose we have any more grenades we can use, do we?"

Jyrisa shook her head. "We only thought we needed the one. Didn't want to waste resources."

"No," Taris said, rubbing her temple. "Wouldn't want to do that. Well hell. So much for going out with a bang."

"What do you propose we do, warrior?" Vale asked her seriously.

Sighing, she scratched her neck from under her collar and looked around. "Okay. Well I gotta say, now would be a great time to have my wristband. That thing has about a million different things on there that we could have used at this moment."

"Where is it?" Jyrisa asked.

"In the Hammerhead Eye I presume," she said bitterly. "I don't suppose you happen to have teleportation abilities, do you?"

Jyrisa frowned. "Is she serious?"

"Frequently," Vale responded, "and always at the strangest of times."

"Okay, enough," she said, becoming Captain Bodil. "We need my wristband and the keys to the collars. I need to get to that Eye."

"That can be arranged," said a voice down the hallway.

Taris turned her resonator rifle at the source of the voice. She found herself facing at least a dozen rifles and one unarmed man standing in the middle. She'd never seen him before, but he seemed somehow painfully familiar to her. He was tall and very thin, but by no means a small man. His stern chiseled face was framed with frantic brown hair and his angular, high cheekbones were shadowed with a dusting of dark facial hair. He was wearing an expensive black striped suit that made him look out of place, especially considering the surroundings. His accent was very Scottish, which made him sound more aggressive than he meant to be.

"Hello. Snow White, is it?" he asked, resting his hands in his pockets casually. "I see you're here with your three fairy godmothers, although they don't look very magical to me."

"You're confusing your fairy tales," she countered, keeping his head directly in her resonator's sights. "And this princess is armed, so don't try anything stupid."

"Oh come now," he said lightly. "Really, there's no need for that. We're just here to chat. Just like old friends."

"I don't know about you," she said, feeling the sweat trickle down her temple, "but I usually don't have conversations with my friends at gunpoint. Do you?"

"I try not to have many friends," he said. "They make things complicated. You should know. After all, you wouldn't even be in this mess if it weren't for your poor choice of companionship, would you?"

She was stunned into silence. He knew who she really was, that was obvious. "Oh yes Taris Leigh Bodil," he said as if reading her mind. "I know who you are. Good to see you again."

"Again? Sorry bud, but I don't think I've had the misfortune of meeting you the first time." She narrowed her eyes at him.

"Oh no?" He seemed genuinely surprised. "Well that is interesting. Okay then. From scratch it is. Ugh. You're not much fun when you meet people for the first time. It's like you're hoping they'll dislike you and leave you alone."

"You're doing a pretty good job of making me dislike you," she said. "I'm desperately hoping you'll leave me alone. And what makes you think you can talk to me like you know me or something?"

"Oh Taris," he said, shaking his head affectionately. "I know all about you."

"Really?" she questioned. "Then you'll know I'm a great shot. Right now, I'm aimed directly at your forehead. How do you like that? I never miss, you know."

"I know. And you should know that I never come unprepared to a party. Ever." He reached into his pocket and pulled out a scrathe remote activator. *Shit*, she thought. *He's got me there.*

"Do you know what this is?" he asked lightly, holding it up for her to see.

"Yes of course I know what that is."

Find out what his intentions are, she heard Vale convey to her telepathically. *If you provoke him, and he uses that device, we will be powerless to fight against him.*

"What makes you think I'm going to provoke him?" she responded.

"What's that?" the man asked.

"Nothing," she said quickly. "Okay. So you have a scrathe remote. Well, what are you waiting for? I'm surprised that wasn't your first move, quite frankly."

"I told you Taris," he said. "I'm here to talk. How about this? You lay down your rifle and I'll put this remote back in my pocket and we can talk like civilized people."

"Or I could shoot you right here," she suggested, charging the resonator to full.

"Taris," she heard Vale say behind her, "perhaps we should hear what he wants to say." *If he wanted to scrathe us he would. He wants something. Let him speak.*

She groaned but eventually relented. "Fine," she said loudly. "We put down our weapons - all of us - on three. Are you ready?"

The man nodded. "We're ready."

"Okay," she said. "One...two...three."

Quickly, and before she had a chance to second guess herself, Taris pulled her weapon back and uncharged the chamber. To her relief - and surprise - the HALOs uncharged their resonators as well, withdrawing their aim on command. The man in the middle clasped his hands together in appreciation and ran his fingers through his lustrous hair.

"Well that was very good, then," he said appreciatively. "Thank you. We're starting to trust each other already."

Taris snorted. "Hardly."

"Let's start with me introducing myself," he said, ignoring her. "*Again*, it would seem. My name is Simon Finnegan. I'm the caretaker of this facility. They call me the Hammer."

"I'd say nice to meet you, but that would just start off this whole conversation with a lie," she said bitterly. "So you're the big man in the black Eye, huh? The one who makes this entire god-forsaken facility possible. Your mother must be so proud."

Simon laughed. "Too true. How clever you are. I heard you were still funny. I'm glad to see that was not a lie."

"I'm only funny when I'm pissed off," she said dryly. "Anyway, you already know who we are, so no need to dance around that. What do you want from us?"

The man put his hands in his suit pocket and raised his dramatic eyebrows. He genuinely did look disarming, but she knew he wanted to come off that way. It was a well-played tactic on his part. He was a man of authority. One who was used to getting his way. One who wasn't easily fooled by side-stepping conversation.

"Information," he said. "I want to know everything that you know about the Neros Effect, Taris Leigh Bodil."

"The what?" she said, confused. "The Neros Effect? You mean that project my dad worked on?"

Simon nodded. "That's the one, lassie."

She shrugged. "Ah. Well I guess I'm about to disappoint you, because I don't know anything."

Simon clucked his tongue in disapproval. "Oh come now. Surely you had to know something. Why else would you be here, poking your nose where it doesn't belong, hmm?"

"Hey, I didn't come here for the fun of it," she pointed out. "This wasn't some fun little trip I planned for me and my friends or anything."

"My reports tell me that the Intrepid - your ship if I'm not mistaken - landed on our airstrip a couple of weeks ago. Is that not true?"

She clenched her jaw. "Yes. That is true, but it is not what you think. I was not in control of my ship at that time. The landing coordinates were preprogrammed."

Simon's eyebrow raised. "Preprogrammed? A z-class stealth ship was preprogrammed? By whom?"

She exhaled heavily. She knew he was baiting her, but she had to keep the dialogue going. They were severely outnumbered. A gunfight would likely end badly for them, and she was not about to lose Vale. Not when she just got him back. Well, that and he would be extremely upset with her if she managed to get herself killed. She had a feeling that not even death could keep that man from holding a grudge.

She took the bait knowingly. "Our systems were…hijacked by a Caleum-language code."

"Ha!" the Hammer exclaimed. "Well now, that's a first, isn't it boys?" he asked the HALOs, who chuckled on command. "And I'm assuming that your short haired companion was the mastermind behind that little *coup de gras*. Isn't that true, lord guardian?"

Vale said nothing. He was standing at his full height in front of Elias, shielding him from the line of armed guards. The Hammer took his silence to be admission and whistled in approval.

"I see," he said smugly. "And then you just decided to stroll on up to the Hammerhead and get the inside tour, did you?"

"No," she snapped. "Then I was scrathed, collared and corralled like an animal for slaughter. But you already knew that, obviously."

"True," he said, "but I like to hear your perspective. From the horse's mouth, if you will."

She tightened her fists and glared at him. The anger over her situation surged inside her, boiling in rage. She hated him, she hated the military, she even hated humans for allowing places like this to exist. Suddenly the idea of talking it out with the Hammer didn't seem worth it. Quickly she raised her rifle and pointed it at him before the HALOs could react. They all pointed their rifles at her, but the Hammer raised his hand to keep them from firing. She didn't know why. He was only about thirty feet in front of her and they were outnumbered. It wouldn't be so hard to take her down. Not hard at all.

"You know what?" she yelled across the hall. "This show's over, Hammer. I'm done with this. I'd rather get scrathed than dance around for your amusement."

Simon sighed and pulled his hand out of his pocket, his thumb on the scrathe remote. "Suit yourself."

The shock brought her to her knees. The blinding lightning bolts of pain shot through her head with angry intensity. She screamed and threw herself to the floor, ignoring the rubble and debris at her feet. The electricity shot through her collar, reaching all parts of her body like a wildfire.

When the pain finally abated she attempted to right herself up again, but when she put her palms on the ground to steady herself she felt a sharp pain. She looked down at her hands and realized she was bleeding. She'd cut them on the broken glass and metal scattered on the ground. Swearing profusely, she managed an unsteady stand and leaned against the wall, panting. The Hammer looked inconvenienced.

"Well. I hope we're done playing the brave little rebel," he said snidely. "Are you ready to be a big girl now?"

"Do I get a choice?" she grumbled.

"Oh? Aren't we sarcastic? Even in your pain you make jokes. You know I think I like this new you."

"Ha. Well I don't like you," she said, spitting out a mouthful of pain-induced saliva.

"Well that's a shame," he said, frowning in earnest. "I had hoped to forge a friendship after this is all said and done with."

She could hear Vale trying to protest in her head, but she shoved him out. She knew he would try to stop her from saying stupid things, but she didn't want to be stopped. She stood up and glared at the Hammer.

"Friends? You and me? Not going to happen, buddy," she said in even tones. "Now what do you want?"

His hard brown eyes looked up at her, steely gaze unwavering. "I want information," he said. "I want you to talk."

Warning lights went off in her head as he stood there, waving the verbal banner of peace, his HALOs at the ready.

Taris, Vale managed to get through. *Don't do this. Don't let him win.*

I know what I'm doing, she lied.

Taris, don't--

Before he could finish, she pushed him out of her head and stared the Hammer down. "Interrogate away, Hammer."

"Brilliant," he said as a smile spread widely across his face. "Right then, back to the topic at hand. Why did you come back? Really? Is this another rebellion scheme, or are you on a trigger mission for the United authority?"

"Come back?" she repeated. "I've never been here before in my life! What the hell are you talking about?"

He tapped the scrathe remote lightly with the tips of his long fingers. "Taris, don't make me use this again."

Her eyes widened. "Hey! I'm serious! As long as I have lived I have never set foot in this hellhole."

He tilted his head to the side. "Are you sure?"

"Yeah. Positive. I would have remembered that. Look, maybe you have me confused with someone else, but I swear I've never been here!"

Simon nodded and rubbed his stubble chin thoughtfully. "Well, I have to say, I'm surprised. Your memory truly doesn't appear to recall this place at all."

"What the hell do you mean by--"

"However," he continued, talking over her. "Now that you know, it's going to take a lot more work to remove it from your mind. I just don't see any other way around it."

"See any way around what?" she asked cautiously.

"Scrubbing you," he said. "Well, cleansing you, more like."

"Huh. I'd rather be shot here," she said without thinking.

"I'm sure you would," he responded, "but I'm afraid you're too much of an investment for that sort of thing. And don't think you'll get off as easy as you did before. That is to say, in the gas chambers. Poor Charlie. Didn't stand a chance against you, now did he?"

The guards started to advance on them. Taris pulled her rifle up quickly, but before she could pull the trigger her collar activated. The shock incapacitated her and she fell to the floor, screaming incoherently. By the time the pain finally dissolved, she was being held up by two HALOs, who were not doing a good job of supporting her weight. Vale, Elias and Jyrisa were all being held by guards as well. The Hammer strolled over to stand in front of her.

"Oh Taris. You didn't actually think it was going to be that easy, did you?"

"I don't know what you have planned but I swear to god I'm going to stop you," she threatened. "Swear to god."

Simon laughed under his breath and traced the rim of her collar with his finger.

"Still the fighter I see. Well good for you. I like a challenge." He turned to the guards who had Vale, Elias and Jyrisa in custody. "Take the Grays to the courtyard and put them in a crate." He looked over at Jyrisa, still in her human form. "And take this female defector with them."

"What?! No!" Taris screamed, writhing against the strength of the HALOs holding her. "Don't do this! Don't take them! Take me!"

The Hammer looked at her. "What did you say?"

"I said take me!" she screamed. "Put me in the crates, not them. I will take their punishment, just please don't hurt them!"

"Oh look at you?" he said, his snide smile curling into a frown. "Noble even at the risk of your own life."

"These people don't deserve to be tortured," she said. "They're good people."

"They're not people," the Hammer snapped. "Grays are not people. You're not a person, Taris. You're a freak of nature. A beast. A cancerous flaw in god's great design and if I had my way I would crush every last one of you into dust. You and your precious guardian. I gave you a chance once before, but it seems it was not enough, was it? No. Obviously not because here you are again, causing trouble in my life for no bloody reason."

"What the hell are you talking about?" she demanded, struggling against her captors. "I've never met you before in my life! Why are you talking to me like you know me? You don't know me at all!"

She looked up at him. She saw the hatred in his brown eyes. The angry, distrustful aggressor that lingered just under his cool facade. She could see that he meant every word he said, and he was careful with every word he chose. Simon Finnegan was a dangerous man, she knew, and he held her life - and Vale's - in his hands.

"You know, it's times like these when I wish I had the opportunity to kill you, Taris," he said cryptically. "It would make my life so much easier."

"So why don't you do it then?" she taunted. "Kill me now and get it over with."

"Oh it would be my pleasure," he said with ferocious honesty, "but I'm afraid I cannot."

"Why?" she asked.

"Because I promised a very dear friend that I would bring you to him safe and sound. Again. He's very anxious to see you."

"How accommodating," she quipped.

"Well I am a man of my word," he said, smoothing his suit down in the front with a self-assured smile.

"Only when it suits you."

The Hammer threw his head back and laughed. "So charming. Taris, forever the unwilling Gray. Well it was fun watching you writhe, but I have a deadline to keep. HALOs, take these silverbacks away."

"No!" she screamed, struggling with all her strength. "No. *No*! Don't you hurt them!"

The guards yanked her back and held her head down as they dragged Vale, Elias and Jyrisa away from her. Jyrisa looked terrified and defeated. Vale looked fierce as he struggled against the chains being wrapped around his limbs. Elias looked unperturbed. Calm even. He willingly allowed his captors to chain and drag him away without so much as an objection.

"No! You can't do this! They didn't do anything! It wasn't their fault. Oh my god, please. Please don't kill them!" she begged.

Please do not fear for us, she heard Elias say. *You have not failed us. We all owe you a debt of gratitude.*

"*Cespecula modici luach,*" she yelled down the hallway.

By the will of the Five, she heard three voices respond. The guards dragged them into the stairwell and out of sight.

Defeated, she hung her head, refusing to let the Hammer see the tears fall.

"HALOs, take our old friend Taris here to the Hammerhead Eye, please. There's someone waiting there for her who is just dying to see her," he said with a smile. "Oh, and take the lift please, will you? She might try to throw herself down the stairs. And, of course, we couldn't have that."

"Yes sir," said the nearest guard, grabbing her by the arms.

"Good," the Hammer said, touching the ends of his hair with his fingertips. That's when she saw it. A strange, sad expression flashed across his face. It was only there for a moment, but she knew she saw it. If she didn't know any better, she would have mistaken that look for one of longing.

"I don't know who this friend is or what he means to you," she said evenly, "but I swear to you I will break his neck if I get the chance."

The Hammer ticked his finger back and forth patronizingly. "Don't make promises you can't keep, Taris."

"Don't underestimate me, Simon," she snapped.

"I never do," he said. "Never."

Chapter Thirty-two

The office inside the Hammerhead Eye was fittingly dark and quiet, blinking with the lights of mechanical equipment. The room rotated slowly, observing the grounds of the complex through tinted windows. Covered with computers, boards of lights, switches and security cameras, there were HALOs watching the movements of the entire compound. They sat, unwavering, as Taris was dragged into the room. In the middle of the space was a large illuminated table filled with papers, coffee mugs and a holographic projector screen. Standing in front of the main circular table was a man she knew very well indeed.

"Well, well, well," said Boone Hooper with a snide tone. "We meet again, Taris Bodil."

She rolled her eyes. This was the guy she was so afraid to face two minutes ago? "You're wrong, Hammer," she said, keeping her eyes deadlocked on Boone. "Killing Boone is a promise I can absolutely keep."

"Oh ho! Big talk coming from a muzzled mutt," he said with an arrogant grin.

He was dressed like a rich cowboy, or maybe what a rich man thought a cowboy ought to dress. A white leather suit, tailored to stretch around his generous midsection, complimented by tassels and even spurred boots. He capped the ensemble off with a large matching cowboy hat and an unlit cigar that he was gnawing on like a cow chews cud. He was clearly proud of this outfit.

"You look ridiculous," she said just to be petty. "Like a fat cartoon sheriff."

He scoffed. "Oh, as if *you're* some sight for sore eyes. Please."

"I should have known you were behind all of this," she said angrily. "You must have known where Elias was all along didn't you, Boone?"

He frowned and took his hat off, folding the crease in the top between two fat fingers. His white hair was combed well, but the scowl on his face had replaced the usual smile. It occurred to her that the clothes might allude to more than just poor fashion sense. Most likely he didn't want to be recognized. That was strange, too. She knew him well enough to know that he liked to be acknowledged when he went anywhere.

"I knew I should have detained you the night of the attack," he said dismissively. "You are such a hindrance on my life, Taris Bodil."

"You're not exactly my little ray of sunshine, emissary," she replied sarcastically.

Boone stifled a laugh and took a long drag from his cigar. "Ooh! Listen to you! You're feistier as a Gray than you were as a human. You've got your hands full with this one, Hammer. I might not be paying you enough."

"Nothing I can't handle, sir," the Hammer said. He walked around to the front of the table and stared at her. "Besides, you know I like a challenge."

"Hmm. Indeed."

"What the hell do you want, Boone?" she demanded impatiently. "Christ on a cracker, I am not going to sit here and listen to you play the superior slave master for your own amusement."

He crossed the room in two large steps and backhanded her as hard as he could with his club-like hands. She groaned. She'd been backhanded twice in one day and that was enough to last a lifetime. The force of the impact swung her around and she fell roughly to her knees. She looked up and felt him grab a fistful of her hair, yanking her face up to his. She could see the sweat dripping from his pink, clammy brow.

"You don't get to call the shots here, silverback. I do," he hissed wetly. "You wanna know why I'm here? I'm here to slaughter some of my cattle."

He yanked her across the floor and to the foot of the nearest guard. The man was sitting in front of a series of large monitors displaying different parts of the complex. Boone pointed to one of them with his fat finger.

"Show her the courtyard. This silverback needs to see what happens when my dogs misbehave. Show her!"

Wordlessly, the HALO obeyed and brought the courtyard camera into view. Boone yanked her up by the hair and forced her to an awkward stand. Taris watched in horror as the guards dragged Vale, Elias and Jyrisa into one of the crates. The moment their skin touched any part of the box they recoiled. She could see the anguish, feel it in her soul. The suffering, the fear, the pain was so tangible. The last face she saw was Vale's. It was strained as he attempted to stand in the box without touching anything. He was more readable and visibly pained than she had ever seen him. Defenseless, she could only watch as the HALOs left them in the torture box, sealing the door shut. They were trapped. They were all trapped.

"They'll never survive in there," she said, swinging around to face Boone. "Let them go."

Boone chortled. "Well now, making demands are you?"

"Let them go," she said evenly. "Or you'll regret it."

"And elevated to a threat already?" he said, shaking his head. "Oh honey, we need to teach you the art of negotiation."

She kicked him in the genitals with all her strength. Surprised, Boone released her hair and doubled over in pain.

Taris kicked him again, sending him down for the count. She jumped on top of him, yanked the knife from his holster and pressed it against Boone's neck. The razor sharp edge started cut into his pale skin as small trickles of tears pooled in the corners of his eyes.

"How's this for negotiation?" she asked darkly. "Call off the guards or I'll split your throat right here." She pressed down on the knife for emphasis. "You know I'll do it, too."

"Stop, guards, stop! Stop!" Boone yelped. The HALOs held their ground, but they stayed within close distance. She knew she didn't have much time. She had to make every second count.

"Okay here's the deal," she said, tightening her grip on the knife, "let my friends go or I kill you."

"If you kill me you'll be shot down where you stand," he said in a strained tone.

"And you'll still be dead," she said. "Now do it."

He looked at her, trying to decide whether or not she was serious. To emphasize her point she dragged the knife against his neck, slicing a sliver across his doughy skin. His eyes grew wide. "Okay okay! Hammer, release her friends!"

"All of them?" the Hammer asked, displeased.

"All of them," she said, "or your generous benefactor will bleed more than just money onto this place."

The Hammer sighed. "Fine." He reached over and picked up an earpiece. "HALOs on ground, stand down. That's right, take the prisoners out of the crates. Why? Because I said so. Look, just do it, okay? Keep them in the courtyard, though. Well, you never know. Minds can be changed."

"Happy?" Boone asked. "Will you let me go now?"

She clenched her jaw. "Not hardly. We're not done here, emissary. Why do you want Elias?" Boone looked like he was going to hesitate, but she wasn't in a mood to allow that. She pushed the tip of the knife harder against his neck. A trickle of blood appeared and slid down the blade like a tiny red stream. Startled, Boone yelped in alarm.

"Okay okay! Stop, stop, stop. I wanted him because he is the Star of Gray. I want it, okay?"

"Want it how?" she asked suspiciously.

"I wanna get it," he said seriously. "You know, for myself."

"And how are you going to *get* it? I thought the Star of Gray was metaphysical or something."

"It is," Boone said stiffly. "It's the ultimate power of the people of Gray. A real source of supremacy. A genuine superhero strength, wasted on that shiny, obnoxious boy."

"Right, and you can't just take his 'power' or whatever," she chided. "I don't think a spiritual sense is something you can just shrug off and pass on, idiot."

Boone's face was stern and his expression unwavering. "Don't you dare joke about this, Taris. You have no idea what you're talking about. The Star of Gray is greater and mightier than your little brain could possibly understand."

"So educate me. Quickly."

"You don't know this story?" he said, genuinely surprised. "Good lord woman, where have you been?"

"Busy," she said, pushing the knife harder against his skin. "Explain."

"Okay, okay!" he conceded. "So, ne'er as I recall it, all Grays had power once. Some kind of energy-harnessing power. I guess we would call it magic, for lack of a better word. Anyway, this magic was wonderful and useful, but it led them to war. They become corrupted by their own power. They killed each other over this magic stuff for centuries. Then - and now this is according to legend, mind - the elders of the five tribes got together and asked the spirits for help."

She sighed heavily. "This is starting to sound an awful like a Gray bible lesson, Boone. Get to the point."

He frowned at her. "Well I would if you wouldn't *interrupt* me. Rude. Anyway, the elders offered to take the corrupting power of the Grays and put it into a living vessel to be protected by one of their people. The Star keeps the power safe and this keeps the people from killing each other. Allegedly, this led to the end of all war for their people. It's why their folk seem so friendly all the time I guess; the power-rage is all contained into that one tiny person. They don't have the fight in them anymore."

"You mean to tell me that Elias - young, passive, peaceful Elias - is the most powerful being on the planet?" The notion was almost laughable.

"Possibly the most powerful being in the universe," he said dramatically.

"So you're after the power of the Gray," she said pointedly. "And how do you presume to take this star power, Boone? I don't think asking nicely is gonna cut it. I also don't think you're capable of that."

He frowned and jutted his chin defiantly. "I have my ways."

"Ha!" she said. "Oh don't try to be mysterious. You're trying to cleanse it out of him, aren't you?"

Boone didn't answer. She shook her head in dismay. "Oh emissary…grasping for straws are we?"

"It's a new process," he said defiantly.

"How pathetic," she said, pushing the knife down so hard she found his adam's apple under the layer of fat. "The hell do you care about a magical Gray prophet, anyway? Don't you have enough money to keep yourself busy?"

"That's just it," he said. "I am a wealthy man, Taris. A very wealthy man. There ain't nothin' that I can't buy, but this...this is something so much more. Something that my money can't touch. It's the only bonafide superpower in the known universe. And I want it."

"And we'll do anything to help him," the Hammer added. "For a price, of course."

She looked up, having forgotten he was there. That was a mistake. In that one moment, she let her guard down. It was only for a second, but it was a moment too late. She didn't even have time to scream as her collar roared to life. It sent the pulses of pain rippling through her body. Recoiling and incapacitated, she was thrown to the floor. Defenseless, controlled and out of options, she yanked on the collar helplessly as she screamed for mercy. She was practically sweating blood before her collar finally turned off.

"Well you sure took your sweet damn time with that scrathe remote," Boone said to the Hammer, holding a handkerchief to his throat delicately. "That wretched little thing could have killed me!"

"Yes, she would have," the Hammer said in an irritated tone. "And if I had pressed the remote button while she was pressing that knife to your throat, her muscles would have tensed and she would have jabbed that blade right into your neck."

"It hurts," she groaned, feeling the residual effects of the collar subside. She coughed and rolled to her side, when she noticed a large black box under the table. It was locked with a panel interface, but was otherwise unremarkable. She remembered what she was told when she first arrived, about how the keys to the collars were kept in a box in the Hammer's office. She tried to reach out and touch it, but as soon as she extended her fingers she felt them being kicked away.

"Give me that thing," Boone said, snatching the remote away from the Hammer like an obstinate child. "It's my turn."

"No," the Hammer protested sternly. "I promised I'd keep her alive. You know that."

"Hey, who pays you?" Boone responded angrily. The Hammer sighed and relented.

"Very well, sir," he said with strained patience. "But don't kill her. At least, don't make a mess about it."

"No--"

Her words were choked by pain. It surged through her, scorching her blood. Her thoughts turned to mush, her voice rasped with screams. Her muscles were weak and uncontrollable as she flopped like a fish on the floor of the Eye. Boone was unrelenting. Every time she thought she had a respite, he pushed the button again and she screamed in agony. She started to shake violently. She began to fade in and out of consciousness, her screams drowning in her own thoughts. Her heart started to slow.

She heard the shouting, but she couldn't understand it. The pain wouldn't stop. It just kept coming. She prayed for death. She wanted it. She couldn't take it any longer. She closed her eyes and let the tears drain down her face. She sucked in her last wracking breath, waiting for the end.

"That is enough!"

A booming, authority-driven voice echoed through the room. The voice sounded familiar, but her mind was so muddled that she could not place the origin. At that moment, the pain stopped. Well and truly stopped. Void of logical thought or reason, Taris started laughing. It was an empty, toneless laugh that registered barely over a whisper. In truth, it sounded like she was whimpering, but she didn't care. She was just so damn grateful to be free of the pain. After what seemed like an immeasurable amount of time, she finally drew the strength enough to roll herself onto her back. She heard three men arguing in low, muddled tones, then a blurry face peered over her body.

"I don't know who you are," she said hoarsely, "but I'm so damn grateful for you. Thank you so much for stopping him."

"Taris…it's me. Jeazus, what have they done to you? Are ye all right love?"

She knew the tone. She knew the voice. She knew the inflection and the lift of the vowels. She'd known it all her life. Choking back the sobs, she looked right into his pale blue, worried eyes.

"Dad?"

Chapter Thirty-three

Her father and a guard helped her to a seat. Taris had to move slowly, and her teeth were chattering, but she managed to sit upright at least.

"Dad," she said weakly. "You have to get out of here. I don't know how you found out where I was but you can't be here. This place...it's not safe."

Her father shook her off and dabbed her bleeding head with his handkerchief. "Never you mind about me, Taris. It's you I'm worried about."

She looked around at the HALOs who seemed unperturbed, at the Hammer who seemed no longer interested in her, at Boone Hooper, who was straightening his appearance in the reflection of the glass. Not one of them had stopped her father. Not one of them had shot him. He had just walked into a heavily armed, heavily guarded facility without so much as a second look.

"Something...something's not right here," she said, trying to shake the fog from her mind. Even the motion was excruciating. Wincing, she reached up and felt her throbbing neck. The touch was so painful it made her want to cry. Her father lifted her hair to the side and gasped in horror.

"Sweet mother!" he exclaimed. "Your neck is blackened the whole way around! Good god, Taris. How did this happen?!"

"I'm allergic to this metal," she said, tapping the collar. "That, and they keep scrathing me half to death."

Her father's wise face turned an angry red. "Simon Finnegan," he barked, "you bring me the key to her collar now."

"But sir," the Hammer protested politely, "the regulations clearly state--"

"*Bollocks* to that," he countered furiously. "You're in enough trouble as it is, Finnegan. You should have brought her to me the moment she arrived."

"She didn't register on the infoscanner database, sir," the Hammer protested. "We didn't know for sure who she was."

"You knew *damn well* who she was," he countered angrily. "I could have your neck for this Hammer, and you know it. Now shut your trap about regulations and rules, you duplicitous bastard, and bring me her *bloody key now*!"

The Hammer moved quickly. He bent down, pressed his hand against the panel on the black safe and pulled out a little black key. *So I was right*, she thought through the haze, *that's where he keeps the keys*. The Hammer handed her father the key and he affixed it to the back of her collar. With a small click, the device unlatched, releasing itself from her neck. Breathing a sigh of relief, she yanked it off and threw it at Boone Hooper's feet.

"Don't be mad at *me*, honey," the emissary said, gnawing on his cigar indifferently. "I didn't do this to you. I'm only here for the execution of that dead body puppeteer, Vale Teag. Which seems to be taking forever, I might add."

"Keep yer shirt on, emissary," her father said sharply. "Let me talk to my daughter first."

Boone sighed. "Whatever you say, Murphy. Try to hurry it up, though. Lyn's having the cooks prepare ribs for dinner tonight, and you know I don't like to miss rib night. No sir."

"I said be patient," Dr. Bodil countered. "One thing at a time, Boone."

"What?" she asked, stunned. Why was Emissary Hooper talking to her father like that? "Oh…Oh my god." *He's in on it,* she realized, devastated. *My dad is in on it…and he has power.*

Defeated, she turned her weary, blackened eyes from him and stared numbly at the floor. She sat in stunned silence as her father bandaged her throat. He worked mechanically, inspecting her for damage and treating her wounds while chastising the Hammer and Boone intermittently. Finally her father finished bandaging her and stood up, his hands on his hips.

"There, that ought to do it," he said appreciatively. "You're not in great shape - well that's obvious - but you'll be right as rain in a few days or so."

"No, dad. No I won't be," she looked up at him with hooded eyes. "What's going on here? How do you know these horrible people?"

Dr. Bodil frowned. The expression made him appear older than he was. He looked around and spotted a small office by the door.

"Simon," he said, keeping his eyes on her, "we're going to use your office for a moment, if you please."

"Sure thing, boss," he said, barely giving them a second look.

Her dad led her into the small office with no windows. Taris limped herself into a chair, refusing help, although the action of walking was agonizing. Her father turned slowly to face her, the look of sadness glossed over his face. She was the first one to speak.

"So you're in on this." It wasn't a question. "Christ Dad, are you really *working* with these people?"

Her father's eyes fell to the ground. "Yes, Taris."

"But everything?" she asked. "The collars, the torture? Good god, the genetic manipulation and sleeper agents? Did you know about all of that, too?"

He nodded slowly. "I knew. I've known for a long time."

"Oh Dad." Tears of betrayal and defeat filled her eyes. "How could you?"

"Taris, the Grays are not what they seem," he said in a quiet tone. "There are things about them that you don't know. Dangerous things. Things that threaten the life of every man, woman and child on this planet. I know it looks bad, but really we're doing them a favor."

"That's total bullshit," she growled. "You're stripping them of everything that they are. You're taking their very being and changing it. That's monstrous."

"We're taking the wickedness of their genetics and we're giving them life. A real life. A human life. We're liberating them, Taris. Ye have to believe me."

"Why? Sounds like you've managed to justify genocide all on your own."

"Taris, don't talk like that," he chastised. "You're just sympathetic for the Grays because you've spent the last couple of weeks with them. It will fade."

"Yeah, well right now I'm more Gray than human," she spit out. "Which means you have some explaining to do since I'm pretty sure you and mom were both human."

"Oh, that." He sighed. "You should never have even been scanned, let alone had yer results show up Gray. If they had told me sooner I would have been over here immediately."

"And just cleared up this misunderstanding?" she asked, sarcastically. "I've been scrathed, dad. A lot. This is a little beyond a paperwork error."

"Well," he said, rubbing his hands together. "I'm sure you've noticed this already, Taris, but you're not like other people. You're different. Special."

"Dad," she said, looking up at him with probing, serious eyes. "I can't dance around this so I'm just going to ask. Am I a Gray?"

He crossed his arms and turned to her. She saw the years of thinking that creased his forehead. She was literally holding her breath as she waited for him to respond.

"No." He leaned down and faced her directly. "You're not a Gray."

She let out the breath she had been holding. She was surprised to feel disappointed in that revelation. "Really?"

"Actually...You're a hybrid."

"A *what*?"

"You're a half human, half Gray hybrid," he said proudly.

She scoffed incredulously. "Dad, come on. That's not possible. Everyone knows that our genetics are not compatible. We can't breed with the Grays."

"That's true," he agreed. "But I didn't say ye were *born*."

She blinked. "Maybe I'm just slow on the uptake, what with the scrathing and all, but *huh*?"

He sighed heavily. "Okay. You were grown in a lab using human genetics and Gray genetics. So many said it would never work, but I kept at it because I knew it would work. I just knew it. And it did. It worked for ye. Fighting in defiance of all odds, it worked for ye."

Her mouth dropped. "I was born in a lab? Well that's charmingly horrifying."

"I was heralded as a scientific genius amongst my peers," he said, genuinely enthusiastic. "If it wasn't such a closely-guarded national security secret I'm sure I would have received the Nobel Prize or something. Eh, that would be a treat, wouldn't it?"

She rubbed her face with her hands. "Oh my god. You're serious. You're really serious."

"I am, that," he said.

She looked down at her hands. The triangle scar with the slash marks in the box. "What about these?" she asked, holding her palms up. "Did you brand me?"

He looked at her hands like he had forgotten all about them. "Oh yes, those. Well there is a good reason for that...sort of. Okay no, there isn't. We branded ye."

"*I knew it*," she said, furious. "I knew it. Damn you, dad. Wait...you are my dad, aren't you?" A horrible thought struck her. "Do I even have biological parents?"

"Of course!" he said with a strange smile. "And one of them is me! Your father unit properties were contributed by me. All members of the project contributed, but it was a proud moment, I must say, to discover that my genetic material broke through the reproductive barrier."

"So, you really are my father?" She was surprised to find herself so relieved.

"Yes, Taris. Of course," he said as though her questioning that was utter lunacy. "Ye couldn't tell by the genetic similarities between us?"

"You just told me I was *grown in a lab*, dad," she countered. "I don't know what to believe anymore. So who...who was mom?"

His expression changed for a moment, his eyes filled with sadness and loneliness. "Nancy was my wife. She knew what ye were, but she raised ye like a daughter anyway."

"So I was like a pet to her, then." She folded her arms, trying to hide the hurt she felt. "Something she inherited when she married you."

"Don't think badly on your mother, Taris. She loved ye with all her heart. To her, you were as good a daughter as any she would have given birth to herself."

"Except that I wasn't born," she said, realizing the absurdity of that statement after she said it. "Except even *she* kept things from me. So who is my real mother?"

He shrugged. "Her eggs were harvested from an unknown Gray. I do know that she was a Teag, though, if that helps."

"It doesn't," she quipped. "Dad how could you do that?"

"I wouldn't be complaining if I were ye," he said, folding his arms. "Ye wouldn't be here otherwise."

"That isn't the point. And why didn't you ever *tell* me this?" she demanded.

"On top of wanting to avoid the meltdown you're in the midst of having, it was a matter of national security, Taris," he argued. "Too many lives were at stake. I was sworn to protect ye and the identities of the others."

The blood drained from her face. "Others? Did you say 'others'? Does that mean that there are *other* hybrid people?"

"Yes. You were not the only successful combination," he explained. "Although the rate of return is a little low, I'll admit."

"How many? Dozens? Thousands? Millions? Is that refugee colony on Mars just some encampment for genetic monsters that you're holding hostage?" she asked, coming to a shaky stand.

He shook his head. "No. It's not like that. Genetic splicing, well it's not an exact science. Almost impossible, actually. Hybrids like you are extremely rare. In the thirty-five years we've worked on the Neros Effect project we've only managed to create four living specimens. Four, out of the millions of attempts."

"Four," she repeated. She reached up and touched her neck cautiously. It still stung, but she didn't care. The pain made her feel real, and she needed to feel real.

"Are you...Oh god, I can't believe I'm even asking this, but are you their father unit as well? Are you just breeding genetically-mutilated offspring for yourself?"

He looked taken aback. "Oh. Oh no! No, nothing like that. The four of ye weren't even created in the same lab! Each one totally unique."

Unique. She didn't feel unique. She felt isolated and confused, but not unique. She looked down at her hands. They looked human. They felt human, but they weren't. They were some experiment that someone had created. Even her skin felt foreign.

"So who owns me, then?" she asked, tracing her scars on her palms. "I mean I'm branded and paid for I assume. Who footed the bill?"

"The United authority funded the project," he said. "But don't think of it like that, Taris. Yer not property to me. You'll never be."

"But I am to the United authority, right?"

"Taris, don't be like that--"

She shook her head. "Don't. Just don't." She was in no mood to listen to his excuses, and she would not be calmed by anything he had to say. "So where are the other hybrids?"

"Living their normal lives," he said casually. "For the moment."

"Living lies, you mean."

He sighed. "Each one of you has a sponsor who monitors you, but for the most part you're totally normal people leading normal lives."

"Yeah. I think I proved the flaw in that thinking when a simple infoscanner revealed my Gray DNA, dad."

He frowned. "Yes. I heard about that. Were ye wearing your wristband, love?"

"Yes," she said quizzically. "I was actually. Oh but it wasn't working right. I think some system might have been corrupted. The clock was blinking all strange and stuff."

"Hmm. That must have been what happened," he mused.

She raised an eyebrow. "I don't think it's the *wristband's* fault that I got scrathed, dad."

"Your wristband is a utilitarian device," he explained. "It serves many purposes, but it also serves as a dampener. As long as ye wear the wristband your genetic information will only show your human side."

"Oh." That was pretty clever, she had to admit. But she didn't have to say so.

"You know, of all the hybrids created, you looked the most human," he said with an appreciative smile. "You are also half of me. That's why I'm always trying to make your wristband safer."

"Well they took it from me," she said, touching the bare space on her arm where it used to be. "I suppose it's been destroyed by now."

"Oh! That reminds me." Her father reached into his pocket, fumbled around, and pulled out a wristband. The black leather looked soft and expensive, and the metal interface gleamed with that brand new look. Even the buckle looked new.

She hadn't realized how much she missed having a wristband until she saw it in his hands.

"My special project," he said a little sheepishly. "It was gonna be a gift to ye for Christmas, mind, but then I thought…you'd need it now. It will be more comfortable than the old one. The new leather is really nice. There are a couple of new features and enhancements, so that whole infoscanner glitch shouldn't happen again." He handed it to her expectantly. "Here, take it."

"I don't want it," she said, unmoving. "I don't want anything from you. Ever again."

"Taris," he said, pushing the wristband toward her, "I know you feel like that now, but you're going to want this wristband. No, don't shake your head. I'm serious. You can hate me all you want, but you know you will need this someday. Please take it."

She stared at it like it was going to bite her. She wanted to throw it in his face. She wanted to scream at him for lying to her, to throw things at him and tell him she never wanted to see him again. She wanted to refuse him, but she couldn't. Sighing, she took the wristband from his hand and shoved it in her pocket.

"Okay, but this is the last thing," she said sternly, folding her arms tightly. The strength in her muscles was returning with force. "I want to know about the others. The other hybrids. Who are they?"

Her father hesitated. "I…I don't think I should say…"

"I don't care," she said in an icy tone. "Tell me. Who are the others like me?"

"Now it's not as simple as that, Taris. You see, ye all used to know each other. You were all very close, actually. Then there was this conflict, and we chose to divide ye. So then we decided--"

"What are their names?" she interrupted. "I want to know their names so I can find them."

"I'm so sorry, Taris," he said softly. "Really I am. But I can't tell you that."

"Hmm," she said, narrowing her eyes. "Well that's just not acceptable."

"That's the way it is, I'm afraid," he said with equal stubbornness. "And don't think you'll be able to find them on yer own. The two of 'em would be strangers to ye now."

"Wait," she said. "Two? We're missing one. Where's the fourth guy?"

"The second male unfortunately perished two years ago. Massive spaceship accident. Everyone died. Terrible tragedy." He spoke as if he was reflecting on the waste of equipment than the death of a person.

She absorbed this slowly. "Three hybrids. The only ones in existence." In the infinite whole of the universe, there were only two other people like her. That was it.

"But what about...OW!" She fell out of the chair, grabbing the sides of her head.

"Taris, are ye okay, love? *Taris!*"

She couldn't answer. She was beleaguered with feelings of scorching pain. Torture. It washed over her like a tidal wave. *Vale*. It was him, she knew it. He was calling out to her. He was in trouble. He was hurting. His emotions were reaching out to her like they had before, only this time it was so much worse. Then, as quickly as it came, the pain abated, ebbing from her like water drying on sun-scorched pavement.

Disoriented, she looked up and met her father in the eye. "They put them in the crate," she gasped, struggling for air.

"Taris, what happened?" He offered her a hand up, but she refused him, using the chair to steady herself.

"I have to help them," she said feebly as she struggled to regain her composure. "They're in trouble."

"Hold on," her dad said. He opened the door to the office. "Simon, what the hell is going on out here?"

"Could ask you the same question, Murphy," the Hammer responded dryly. "Your daughter was screaming like a banshee. Thought you might have been killing her."

"Huh," Boone through his cigar. "It's a shame he didn't."

"You put them in the crates, didn't you?" she demanded, trying to keep herself from shaking. "Vale? My friends? They're being tortured in one of those stupid boxes, aren't they? *Answer me, you son of a bitch!*"

Boone glared at her. "Well, we were not gonna wait around all day for you and your pops to work things out. I have a schedule to keep."

"*NO!*" she screamed. She started out the door but found herself blocked by two HALOs, scrathes at the ready. "You can't!"

"Aw, ye couldn't have waited until *after* I'd neutralized her ta do that, Hammer?" her dad complained. "Come on, now."

She stopped fighting and turned slowly around to face her father. "I'm sorry. After you'd *what*?"

The Hammer's dramatic eyebrows raised at that. "Looks like you've got some explaining to do, Daddy Bodil."

Her eyes grew wide and she shrunk back into the office, pressing herself against the wall farthest from him. "What is he talking about, dad?"

Casually, he walked over and shut the door behind him, exhaling slowly. It was a heavy sound, filled with the resignation of a man about to relieve himself of a hefty secret. "Do you remember the resistance?"

"Yes," she said. "I remember every part of that."

"No…you don't." He looked up at her with sad pale eyes. "You remember the parts we *wanted* you to remember."

"Oh my god," she breathed. "Please don't tell me what I think you're telling me…"

"You were a sleeper agent that we placed inside of the resistance," he said, ignoring her horror-stricken face. "You were put there to gain the trust of the leaders. You were oblivious to this, of course. We couldn't have you realizing your true self or anything. So by day you were a freedom fighter, but by night you worked for us."

She shook her head. "No. No that's not possible. I would have remembered something."

"No ye would not," he argued gently. "Your programming is very specific. We used a trigger. A symbol that you would only see when we wanted you to see it. When the trigger was activated, you would carry out your mission for us, whatever that was: gathering intelligence, getting the names of resistance fighters. On many occasions, killing."

She reached into the recesses of her mind, trying to recall a single part of her time in the resistance that would indicate he was telling the truth. She recalled nothing, yet in spite of this, she knew he was telling the truth. She could feel it. Taris felt like her world was crashing down around her. There was a lot she could forgive about a person, but not even she could find it in herself to forgive a double agent. Even an unwilling one.

"The fall of the resistance was my fault," she realized. "We lost because of me."

"Och, don't be so hard on yourself, Taris. It wasn't just you. It was all of the hybrids. Ye worked as an incredible team."

The horror of his words sank into her soul. All the things she stood for and believed in…and she had been the reason it all failed. She was a robot, controlled and armed. She'd never felt more used in her life. Now she was really angry.

"What was the trigger?" she asked, almost scared to know.

"It doesn't matter now," he said gently. "We had to scrub your mind after the fall of the resistance and disposed of the trigger. It's better to change out triggers so a sleeper doesn't become too familiar with one."

"Well isn't that convenient?" she answered bitterly. Her mind was spinning, but in spite of this all she could think about was getting to Vale. She had to find a way. She inched herself closer to the door. "Good god, dad, how can you live with yourself?"

"Because, I genuinely believe this is the best thing to do," he retorted. "These Grays that you see, they are a dying breed. They are joyless, unhappy creatures."

"No!" she protested, positioning herself with the door to her back. "That's not true! How can you have studied these people for decades and not seen them for what they really are? They're kind, gentle, loving people and you're killing them!"

"They're dangerous unto themselves and everyone else," he protested, unwavering. "I know you're heartbroken now, sweetie, but in time you will come to know that this is a good thing for everyone."

"Why do you even care what I think?" she asked.

"You're one of the hybrids," he said simply. "You're designed to be the best of both human and Gray. You were created to bring judgment upon our enemies. Enemies that swore a blood oath to protect and defend their own."

She realized what he was saying and it made her sick. "You made us to kill them...because you knew they would never kill us."

"You're strong, fast, brilliant, and your life span is tenfold that of a human," he said, swelling with sickening pride. "You're the closest thing we have to a living god, and we have total control over you. You're the greatest weapon we have."

"No," she said darkly. "You don't control me. I won't let you."

Her father rubbed his forehead frustratingly with his fingers. "Taris, I hate when you do this. You always do this.

You know, I've tried scrubbing it from you, but this rebellious nature of yours just keeps coming back."

"You tried to scrub away the parts of me you don't like? What kind of father does that?!"

"A smart one," he said, as though it were meant to be a joke. "And besides, it's not like I'm keeping you here and scrathing you into submission."

"I hope you don't expect me to be thanking you for that."

"As a matter of fact I do, Taris," he said sternly. "Believe me, there are those within my organization who would relish the chance to make you squirm."

Things were getting complicated. She had enemies she didn't even know about? "How many people know about me?" she asked cautiously. "How many people know what I am?"

Her father thought about it. "No more than a handful. It was a well-kept secret. The Hammer knows, obviously, because you worked for him."

That thought made her sick. "I worked for the Hammer? When I betr-" She couldn't even bring herself to say it. *Betrayed the rebels. Murdered them. Destroyed the rebellion because I was a traitor.*

"You did what you were ordered to do, Taris. The Hammer was a great ally to you. Considered ye a friend, even."

"A friend? Well he has a funny way of showing his friendly affections. I have the scrathe burns to prove it."

"I think he was trying to get back at ye. The two of ye had a falling out before you were neutralized last time. Guess he hasn't forgiven you yet. Oh but that doesn't make it right. He'll pay for that, I assure ye," her dad said sternly.

"So now what?" she asked. Her fingers wrapped around the door handle. "You're going to neutralize me? *Again*? You're just going to turn me into a totally different person and that's it?"

"It has to be done, Taris," he responded. "I'm afraid it's the only way to minimize the damage done here."

"So you're going to make me forget everything that happened here? The memories, the people, everything? It's all going to be gone and I'll just, what? Wake up like nothing happened?"

He nodded. "More or less. You'll feel a little dizzy at first. Maybe disoriented for a couple of days, but you'll wake up none the wiser. A whole new life. This time, I think we're going to avoid the military. Initially we thought it would be a good idea - you know, keep up the training, perfect your war fighting skills - but now I'm thinking it's just too dangerous. Maybe we'll do something a little more low-key, like teaching anthropology in a mid-level college or--"

"No," she said, interrupting him mid-sentence. She'd heard enough. "Not this time. There might have been other Taris Bodils in this world - better, faster, stronger more obedient ones - but this Taris Bodil is not going to be wiped out of history. It's not going to happen."

"Taris, honey," he said in a patronizing tone. "I love you. I know you don't think so, but I do. That's why I have to do this. It's for your own good."

"You can't strip someone's personality down and rebuild from the ground up when you don't like something!" she exclaimed. "It doesn't work that way!"

"But it does, Taris," he said softly. "That's what the Neros Effect is; genetic reconstruction."

She shook her head. "Well not for me. Not anymore. Not as long as I have a breath in my body. Not as long as I have the will to fight. You can take my memories, my mind, my personality even, but the core of who I am fights against this with every fiber of my being."

"Taris--"

"No. *Don't* interrupt me," she said. "Now it's *your* turn to listen. You can't do this to people. You can't make a person and then turn them into your own little soldier. And scrubbing the Adulos? Turning them into humans and taking away every part of them that makes them who they are? How dare you. *No one* deserves to have their thoughts taken from them. *No one* deserves to be enslaved."

He stared at her silently, arms folded. They stood on opposite ends of the room, eyeing each other. Waiting to see who would make the next move. The hybrid and the scientist. The daughter and the father. The rebel and the authority. Standing on different sides of the same war. Both believing in their cause. Both unrelenting.

"What do you want me to say, Taris?" he asked stiffly.

"I'm going to give you one last chance to do the right thing," she said quietly. "One chance to walk out of here with me and join my cause. The Adulo cause. Walk out of here with me, dad, and help me save these people."

"I'm sorry, Taris," he said finally. "Truly I am, but I can't. I just can't. My hands are tied on this one. I can't join your ever-present rebel cause, and if I don't neutralize ye then you'll be labeled a liability and the United authority will have you killed."

"I'd like to see them try," she said viciously.

"I would not," he said. "Which is why I have to do this, love. Just trust me."

She shook her head. "No. I'll never trust you, father. Never again."

It was clear to the both of them that the conversation was over. Taris thought about arguing her case more, when she realized it wouldn't amount to anything. She wasn't going to talk him out of neutralizing her, but she wasn't about to let it happen, either. That only left one option.

Run.

Before her father could think to react, Taris yanked the door open, punched the nearest guard and made a beeline for the stairs.

"Guards!" her father yelled. "Grab her! Don't let her escape!"

She made it to the door before she was tackled by one young and particularly energetic HALO. He pinned her down, but to her surprise he didn't scrathe her. She struggled under his weight, desperate to get away.

"Get off me you jackass!" she spit out, trying to wriggle free.

"Shut up," he whispered, but it wasn't an angry tone. It was a warning, and that accent sounded familiar...

She stopped struggling and looked up at him. His tinted helmet was pulled over his face, but something about him seemed distinct. "Do I know you?"

"Just do as I say, Taris," he whispered to her. For reasons she couldn't understand, she relented and allowed the guard to hoist her up, arms behind her back. He didn't scrathe her, he didn't bind her wrists. What was this guy doing? She could have snapped his neck if she wanted to, but something stayed her hand. Something was so familiar about him.

"I've got the prisoner in custody, sir," he said to the Hammer. "I'll just pop her into the cleansing chambers then, shall I?"

The Hammer turned and also looked at that particular guard, scrutinizing him with interest.

"Oi, guard!" The Hammer cocked his head to the side. "Your accent sounds familiar. Are you from Sector Two?"

"I am sir," the guard replied amiably.

The Hammer snapped in recognition. "Aha! I thought so. Welsh, correct?" he asked.

The guard nodded. "Born and raised in Cardiff, sir."

"Good lad," the Hammer said appreciatively. "Nice to see someone from my area of the world for a change. How long you been in this Sector?

"Three years now," the guard responded. "Three years, two months and oh, twenty-seven days I guess. Give or take a day."

"Gareth?" she squeaked out.

He lifted his visor and smiled widely. "Hello captain. Did you miss me?"

The Hammer's mouth dropped. "Who the bloody hell are you? What are you doing here? HALOs!"

"Lights out, Hammer," Gareth said in his thick, brilliant Welsh accent.

With that, the entire complex went offline. The Eye collapsed into chaos.

Chapter Thirty-four

In the pandemonium of darkness, it was clear that Hammerhead Hold was not prepared for contingencies. The blackout crippled the whole operation. She heard the Hammer yelling at people, and the scuffle of boots scrambling blindly. She heard Boone screaming over the noise that he was going to make sure someone was held responsible. He threatened legal recourse, utter destruction, and even a few ass kickings. When that had no effect he defaulted to the old hellfire and brimstone to anyone within earshot. He sounded scared. Taris was thrilled about that. Elated, she reached out and grabbed Gareth's blast-proof vest, pulling him into a hug.

"Gareth! Oh my god, how did you find me? How did you get here? Is everyone okay? Is the Intrepid still under Vinny's control?"

He grabbed her by the arm and led her to the stairwell. "It's a long story. I'll tell you on the way. Now come on!" He yanked her out of the door and down the stairs before she could object.

"Where are we going?" she asked as they thundered down the stairs.

"Outside," he said over his shoulder. "We have to get everyone out there. The troops should be taking over the courtyard now."

"Troops?" she asked. "What troops?"

"HALOs, get them!"

Taris turned around and saw two guards thundering toward her. Gareth grabbed her arm and put something into her hand. It was her knife, the one she usually kept sheathed in her boots. She smiled. It was bizarrely empowering to have something she owned in her hands again. The first HALO advanced on them, pointed his rifle at her, and pulled the trigger. She braced for impact.

Nothing happened.

The second guard pulled the trigger. Nothing happened. "What the hell?" the first guy said, pressing the trigger several times.

She smiled in relief and gripped the knife tightly. "Bad luck, boys," she said. Before they could get their bearings, she grabbed the barrel of the first guard's gun and shoved it back, forcing the butt directly into his face. She heard the crack of bones and he jerked back, reeling as blood spilled from his nose. She clocked him on the side of the head, hitting him directly in the temple. The HALO slumped back, unconscious.

"Good shot, mum," Gareth observed approvingly.

"Thanks," she said, yanking the rifle from the unconscious guard's hands. It was completely off. There wasn't even a power light on the side. "So how did you escape Rage Vinny, anyway?" she asked. The second guard charged at them. Taris grabbed the HALO by the collar and yanked him back, swinging the rifle like a club. She hit the guard in the face as hard as she could and he jerked back, screaming.

"Well it's a good thing you didn't shoot Dr. Tomas," Gareth said casually, as though nothing were going on around them. "He turned out to be quite helpful."

"Christian? Helpful?" she asked. "I'm interested already." The guard charged her again and she swung at him, hitting him in the eye. He stumbled and toppled backwards over the railing, tumbling down the stairs. She heard an abrupt scream followed by a fleshy *thump*. Taris and Gareth looked down and saw a bloody mass crumpled at the bottom of the staircase. They looked at each other, shrugged, and continued down the stairs.

"Well, while Vinny was busy selling you and Vale to the complex, Natsumi was busy regaining control of the ship," Gareth explained. "She was trying to translate the controls when she accidentally released the doctor from his cell."

"It's an easy mistake to make," she said with a smile. She heard the sound of a door opening below them and footsteps quickly approaching.

"Oh it was an accident well worth it," Gareth explained. "He ran out of the brig and tried to escape through the hanger deck, when he ran into Matt and Dave. They were tied up there, you remember."

Three more guards ran up the stairs. They all tried to fire on them, but like the HALOs before them, nothing happened when they pulled the triggers. *None of the weapons seemed to be functioning*, she realized. The first HALO realized this quickly and dropped his gun, reaching for a knife. A really, really big knife.

"So what happened?" she asked, dodging a quick jab. The knife guy was flashy with his stabbing movements, which made her think he didn't really know what he was doing. He thrust the end toward her gut but she avoided it, slashing his forearm deeply with her blade. The guard wailed in surprised pain.

Gareth was un-phased. "Well, Mat and Dave told Dr. Tomas what happened, and Dave, if you can believe it, managed to talk Christian into helping them. As a team, like."

"No kidding?" she said, swinging a rifle like a bat at the head of the second guard.

"Yes. So the doctor waited for me and Vinny to return, and when we did, he ran up and attacked Vinny with a huge piece of metal framing! I mean it was enormous! Knocked him right out! It was pretty impressive, mum, I'll admit."

Taris laughed and forgot herself for a moment. Enough for her to get socked in the jaw by an enormous HALO. He yanked the disabled resonator from her hands and raised it over his head. She took the opportunity and shoved her knife into his armpit, slicing the artery. The HALO wailed and fell back, thundering down a couple of stairs and slamming his head against a metal box on the wall. Taris righted herself and started down the stairs when the first knife guy charged her, fists flying.

"So what happened next?" she asked Gareth, connecting her left hook with knife guy's eye.

"Well, then the doctor was going to shoot Vinny see, but Matt and Dave talked him out of it."

"They did? Why?" He swung at her with his knife again and she dodged it, slicing his neck deeply. Knife guy dropped his weapon and grabbed his throat, sputtering until he collapsed.

"Tsk," she said to the guard as he choked on his own blood. "You never show your blade off in a knife fight, dummy. That will get you killed."

Panting, Taris reached down and snatched his hunting knife, only to be hit square in the back with something metal and hard. *Oh right, the third guard.* The female HALO was standing above her, holding a fire extinguisher of all god damn things. Taris rolled to her back, hooked her feet around the guard's ankles and yanked her down. The fire extinguisher clamored to the ground.

Gareth maneuvered around the melee so he could continue speaking. "They said it was your call to make - not ours - as to what happens to Vinny. You're the captain, they said, and you need to make the punishment."

"How...considerate," she said, grunting as she struggled with the female HALO. "So what...did you do...ow! What did you do with him?"

Gareth leaned against the railing next to her and shrugged. "We threw him in the brig. But that still didn't solve the problem of you being trapped, right? Well the doctor told us about a rebel Gray base camp not far from here, and Natsumi, brilliant Natsumi, managed to fly us over there. The Grays were really distrustful at first but they knew the doctor and trusted him. Eventually they let us into their rebel camp."

"Really?" she asked, feeling slightly jealous. She managed to gain the upper hand and pinned the female to the floor, punching her several times in the face before the HALO struggled free. "What was it like?"

Gareth made an excited noise in the back of his throat. "Like nothing I've ever seen. These Silencium fellows, they have mastered the art of living under the radar I'll tell you that. And they make the most phenomenal tea. I think it is called *ka'rah*? In any event, it was delightful."

The female guard reached for the fire extinguisher again but Taris leapt up and shoved her down the stairs with all her strength. The female tumbled down a full flight before her head hit the wall with a wet-sounding crack. The woman stopped moving. Taris spit a wad of blood out of her mouth and picked up the extinguisher.

"Hmmphm. I'm glad you had fun with your new friends while I was imprisoned in a torture chamber fighting for her life," she grumbled. They started back down the steps.

He ignored her. "So the Grays, they already had this plan to take down the complex. They said they would be ready to make their move but they needed a really big distraction. Something that would knock out any electrical impulse, including scrathe coil detonators. It can't be done, we argued. No one knows how. Well lucky for us we have Matt and Dave, right?"

"Stop right there or I'll shoot!"

"Oh good lord, how many of them *are* there?" she whined, side stepping one of the bodies. She grabbed Gareth and continued down the stairs, running directly into the guard, stopping her short. Holding his rifle like a club, he reached up and swung directly at Gareth.

"Gareth, watch out!" she pushed him to the side. The rifle hit the side of the wall with crushing force. She pushed Gareth into the alcove behind her and swung the fire extinguisher, connecting with the guard's head and smashing his skull into the wall. He slid down the side of the cement, leaving a trail of wet blood as he went down.

"So…hmm, where was I?" Gareth said, frowning.

She looked up, panting and covered in sweat. It took her a moment to catch her breath. "You were about to tell me about Matt and Dave."

He snapped his fingers. "Oh right! Sorry, I got distracted."

"*You* got distracted?"

He waived her off and continued back down the stairs. "So the mad scientists, they say they can create an electromagnetic debilitation bomb that will knock out anything with an electrical pulse for three miles. Great, we say. Hop to it. So they fight and work, and complain for days. They're up for days and nights on end, with Dave smoking like a chimney and Matt drinking his weight in coffee, but they don't give up. Tirelessly for two weeks they worked, fought and tested and built, and then one day they crawled out of their lab on the Intrepid with this little ray gun thing."

The next HALO jumped down a full flight of stairs to them, but she was in no mood to dance around this time. With one decisive stroke she sliced him cleanly across the neck. Blood splashed the front of her uniform, and the guard slumped down in front of them. Taris kicked him down the stairs to join the pile of bodies and turned back to Gareth. "Wait a minute, Dave and Matt made themselves a lab on my ship?"

"Oh yes," Gareth said. "It's right by engineering. They converted the whole A storage section into an office."

"What? I didn't authorize that!"

"There they are!"

Two more guards were climbing up the last flight of stairs. Taris shoved Gareth into the corner and stabbed the first one in the side of the neck before he could take a breath. The other guard was quicker and dodged her attack. He swiped at her knife with his rifle, knocking it from her hands. She rolled out of the way of his next attack and jumped up, boxing him in the ears as hard as she could. Startled, he dropped his rifle and held his head in his hands, moaning.

"Anyway," Gareth said to her as she swung the rifle at the guard. He managed to dodge the attack swiftly. "So the Silencium guards gave us these uniforms and we set the plan in motion. Then it was all a matter of finding you and Jyrisa and Vale and getting you all out. Hey, did you know Vale was like a prophet or something? Anyway, finding you wasn't too hard, once we heard that half the basement had been blown up."

"I do like to leave an impression," she admitted. The guard jumped at her, knocking her to the floor. He wrapped his arms around her neck and started squeezing with all his strength. Taris looked up at Gareth wildly.

"Fire...extinguisher..." she gasped.

Gareth looked at her like he didn't understand at first, then it came to him. "Oh! Right." He ran up a flight of stairs and returned with the extinguisher. He stood there as though he was waiting for her to take it. *Oh hell and a half,* she thought. With one snap motion, she shoved her knee directly into the HALO's groin. He paled and released his grip on her. She shoved him off of her, stood up awkwardly, yanked the fire extinguisher from Gareth's hands and smashed it on the HALO's head several times. He crumbled, falling back onto the other bodies that had already collected at the bottom of the stairs.

Laboriously, she supported herself with the blood stained extinguisher, leaning against the wall. Taris and Gareth reached the bottom floor and she saw the sliver of daylight under the door. She heard the sounds of screaming and shouting both above and below her. She was covered in grime and blood, she was bleeding in a couple of places and her hair was scattered all over her head.

"You look a right mess," Gareth said with a little smile.

She laughed loudly, pushing her hair back behind her ears. "Yeah I know, thanks. Oh, and thanks for the fire extinguisher. You were a big help."

He tilted his head to her respectfully. "Here to help you, mum. No matter what."

She looked at him and squeezed his shoulder gently, her eyes saying all the things she didn't need to voice. "Thank you, Gareth. For everything."

He grinned widely at that and nodded politely. "It's always my pleasure to serve you, Captain Bodil. Now, are you ready for round two?"

She could hear the noises of combat outside. The screaming of the dead and dying, of metal clashing and flesh hitting flesh. It was all the familiar noise of combat, but what she didn't hear were the sounds of pulsar explosions and resonator bursts. "Wait," she said, stopping him in his tracks. "Why are none of the rifles working?"

"No electronics anywhere," he said. "Unless they had an incredibly strong protection shield - and I mean very strong protection shield - nothing with an electronic charge will work within a three mile radius. That includes scrathes, by the way."

She leaned forward on her knees and wiped her face with her sleeve. "Well I don't know if I can keep fighting like this," she said, looking down at her knife. "I was swinging those things like a cavewoman and they are not light. I'm exhausted. I need something else to fight with."

Gareth laughed under his breath, pulled a weapon out of a sheath that she hadn't noticed before, and placed it in her hand. She stared at it in shock.

"Where did you get a *sword*?" she asked, flummoxed. It looked three hundred years old if it was a day. She knew nothing about swords, but what she did know was that it was metal, it was heavy, and it didn't make her palm itch. Not sidus metal, then. She tucked the knife in her belt and gripped the sword awkwardly with both hands.

Gareth smiled. "Dave's father, the sword collector, let us borrow his cache. Major Schuler wasn't exaggerating, by the way. His father's entire basement is filled with weapons. It was utterly bizarre. Not that I'm complaining. I mean, what good fortune that we happened to know a guy with a technology-free armory? Truly a stroke of luck, that."

Her eyes grew wide. "You *met* Dave's family?"

Gareth laughed, taking the large knife she obtained from one of the HALOs. "That's a conversation for a different day, mum. Now, go put that thing to good use."

With a heaving push, the two of them opened the door and spilled into the overcast chaos. All around her she saw the metallic flash of swords being swung. HALOs were screaming, attempting to use scrathes and swinging guns, unprepared and untrained to fight without their strongest defense. The Grays were everywhere, liberated from the threat of the scrathe, dancing with fury. They moved like snakes on the water as they fought, their actions liquid and precise.

"You're bleeding," Gareth said, pointing to her hand. She looked down and realized that her hands were, in fact, bleeding. She was holding a sword and she was bleeding. She'd seen that before. Every night for a decade, as a matter of fact.

"Oh my god," she said. "It's just like my dream."

Gareth swung around. "What? What did you say?"

"I said it's just like my dream," she said a little louder. "I am the warrior who walks the thin gray line."

He gave her a strange look. "Geez, what did this place do to you? You sound just like one of them."

At that moment a guard flew at her, holding a cinder block above his head like a caveman. Caught off guard, she shoved Gareth out of the way and ducked, rolling to the side just in time to watch the cinder block crash down on the wall behind her. She staggered at an awkward stand and held the sword in her hands. Her movements were choppy as she swung at the guard furiously. He dodged her thrusts without much effort and pulled out a large knife discreetly. To her dismay, this one looked like he knew what he was doing with it. Her eyes grew wide.

"Let's see how well you fight now, silverback," he taunted.

His gestures were quick and methodical. The knife moved like a serpent's tongue. He was better with the knife than she was with the sword. That was bad. She acted quickly. He reached for her throat but she moved out of the way. The knife landed on her arm, slicing a red line on her shoulder. She fell to the ground, positioning her feet in front of her. When he came at her again she kicked him in the chest with all her might, knocking him back. Quickly she swung her legs around and tripped him, forcing his body to the ground with a muddied *thump*. Before he could regain his bearings, she leapt on top of him and stuck her sword right into his gut. She had forgotten how easy it was to penetrate human flesh. She watched the life drain out of his body and then yanked the sword from his belly. The blood slid off the metal like silk. She turned and helped Gareth to his feet, ignoring his wide-eyed horror.

"Well that was a little less organized than I would have expected for a soldier of your er, experience," Gareth said dubiously, staring at the bloodied mess of the guard at her feet.

"Yeah well I'm a little rusty on my sword fighting skills," she said defensively, staring at the heavy metal broadsword in her hand. "Now come on, we have to get to Vale."

She looked up and her eyes caught the nearest Gray in the middle of a melee. His silver hair flashed in the light of day as he came down for a kill. It was Kyran Ato. His long, thin sword sliced right into the neck of a guard, killing him instantly. The blood dripped off the blade as Kyran stood gallantly, muttering some type of prayer it sounded like. He looked up and caught her eye, running over to meet them.

"Warrior," he said, bowing his head slightly and making the symbol of the Silencium. "The fighting continues everywhere. All the prisoners are revolting. Without the threat of the scrathe we are empowered. We will take this complex in short time."

"Very good," she said. "Where is Vale? We need to free him."

"There's two of them!" In seconds they were surrounded by five HALOS. Two of them were using chains as weapons, one of them had a knife and the other two were using their rifles as a blunt object. On instinct, she pushed Gareth against the wall and out of harm's way. Kyran pressed his back against hers and raised his sword.

"I'm not very good with thing," she said to him. "I'm just warning you now."

Then I will teach you, he responded. *Watch my movements.*

The chain gang brothers swung first. One of them whipped his links at her, striking her in the leg. She yelled in pain but kept her feet planted. She swung heavily at them, and missed both by several feet. Kyran swung his sword with precision accuracy, lobbing off the head of the first chain-bearer in one swift motion. The disembodied head rolled to the ground at her feet, pouring out blood. The body fell into the mud in front of the HALOS, landing with a slick *splat*. The guards hesitated, staring at Kyran with open hesitation. One of them took one look at the headless heap and fled.

Her mouth dropped. "How did you do that?"

Let the sword work for you, he instructed. *Grip it where the weight is distributed evenly. No, that's too high. Right there,* he said, nodding in approval. The knife-bearer, recovering from his initial shock, slid away from Kyran and advanced on Taris. She dodged his first thrust, but he sliced her protective vest almost to her skin.

That was a close call, she thought, startled.

Bend your elbows and use your shoulder muscles for levity, Kyran instructed, shoving the end of his blade into the gut of one of the rifle-holders. *Now, when he reaches for you, bring your blade down on his arm at an angle. As hard as you can.*

She did exactly what he told her to do, and with a jarring and direct stroke she took his knife hand off completely. The HALO's eyes grew wide and he dropped to his knees, grabbing his bloody stump and wailing hysterically.

"Ha!" she said, sticking the end of her sword in the mud. "I did it!"

"Captain!" Gareth screamed. "Behind you!"

She reached for her sword, but it was stuck in the mud. She had just enough time to duck to avoid the other chain bearer. He missed her head but made contact with her arm. She screamed and grabbed the chain with her good arm, yanking on it with all her strength, knocking him off his feet. She wrapped the chains around his neck and yanked on them. He struggled under her grasp but it wasn't enough. Eventually he stopped struggling and his body went slack. Exhausted, she shoved the body to the side and accepted Kyran's hand up.

"Well that could have gone better," she said, nursing her injured arm.

"You'll gain the skill in short time," Kyran assured gently.

"Captain," Gareth said, jogging up to her, "are you okay? It looks like your arm is hurt."

"I'm fine sergeant," she said quickly.

Gareth looked Kyran up and down with surprise and not a little appreciation. "And who is this Gray swordsman who just saved your life?"

"Oh. Gareth, this is Kyran Ato. He's a Silencium protector...and a trusted friend." Kyran nodded at Gareth respectfully.

"Hello human friend of the warrior," he said politely.

Gareth peered at him. "Hey, don't I know you from somewhere?" he asked.

Kyran frowned. "I highly doubt it." He reached into the mud and yanked her sword out of the ground. "Don't stick it in the mud point down," he chastised her. "It will become dull that way."

"Okay, Kyran. Whatever you say." He handed it back to her with the smallest of appreciative grins, pushing his hair behind his ears. He held his head higher than she had ever seen it, the metal of his collar splattered with the blood of his enemies. Seeing this, a thought struck her. "Kyran, I need you to do me a favor."

"Anything, warrior," he said respectfully. "I am yours to command."

She looked up at the Eye. "Can you get in there? I need you to retrieve something for me. A box. It's very important."

"Silverback bitches!" A guard was flying at them, carrying two daggers that looked like they'd been ripped out of a display case. He swiped at them and jabbed right for Gareth. Kyran blocked it deftly and shoved his blade straight through the HALO's neck. The guard sputtered and fell forward, dead before he hit the mud.

"You…you saved me," Gareth said softly, looking up at Kyran. "Thank you."

Taris rolled her eyes. "I saved you like ten times and you never thanked *me*. You are totally worthless." She said with an exasperated smile.

"So what is in the box, warrior?" Kyran asked, wiping his blade clean with his sleeve.

"It contains the keys to all the scrathe collars," she said.

Kyran's eyes rippled with excited interest. "And you are sure of this?"

"Positive," she replied, showing her collar-free neck. "Kyran, we have to get that box."

"Well he can't go in there all by himself!" Gareth protested. "There are still dozens of HALOs in there!"

"Exactly," she said. "Which is why you're going with him."

"Me?" Gareth exclaimed. "But I'm no good at this! I'll get us killed! Kyran needs someone who can actually fight to go with him. You should go, mum, not me."

At that moment, the body of a HALO guard fell off the top of a crate in front of them and landed with a *splat*. Taris saw the hilt of a dagger buried in his back. She looked up at Gareth and cocked one eyebrow.

"You sure you wanna stay here, sergeant?"

Kyran turned to Gareth and gripped his shoulders. He bent down and peered into Sergeant Hoble's eyes intently.

"Gareth Hoble, I have all the faith in my heart that you and I will triumph in whatever mission we perform. I would be honored to fight at your side."

Gareth's nose turned bright red. "Okay then. I'll go with you."

Taris hid a smile. "Okay. Well the box is a big heavy black one that's under the large table in the middle of the room. Can you get it?"

Kyran nodded and raised his sword to her. "We will do this for you, warrior. We will retrieve the keys, and we will be triumphant."

"Yes," Gareth said, mimicking the motion with his knife. "What he said. Triumphant."

"I have all the faith in the world that you will be," she said. "Both of you. And thank you."

"*Cespecula modici luach*," Kyran said, touching two fingers to his forehead, extending one out to her. She repeated the gesture, swelling with pride. That was the first time she'd ever done that. It seemed fitting that it should be with Kyran.

"By the will of the Five," she responded. A smile crept across his face. She saw the joy dancing in his eyes when he looked at her. It was hope, lighting the face of the recently liberated. It was a beautiful thing for her to see. Kyran clasped Gareth on the shoulder, then the two of them slid through the stairwell door in one swift motion. Not wasting time, she raised her sword and ran through the courtyard as fast as her muddied shoes could take her. She only had one thing on her mind: to find Vale.

She turned the corner to an open clearing. That's when she saw them, and her heart stopped.

Chapter Thirty-five

"Dave!" she screamed, running toward them, dragging her heavy sword behind her. "Dave Schuler!"

He was standing by Matt, using his diffuser on the crate that held Vale. Christian was standing beside them, his fingers locked with Jyrisa's as they stuck out between the bars. Christian turned to her and grinned, nodding to her slightly. Matt waved frantically like he was trying to direct air traffic. Dave looked up, and his entire face transformed into a smile.

"Taris!" he shouted. "Oh my god, you're alive!"

"Captain Bodil!" Matt Conner screamed, scanning her as she ran up to them. "Your vital organs are all still intact!"

She laughed. "Well that's good to know!"

She started toward them when a female HALO charged her, knocking her down. She hit the ground on her injured arm and yelped in pain. The woman raised her hand up, a bloodied rock in her hand. She brought it down, but Taris dodged quickly, narrowly avoiding having her skull caved in. Her sword was too far away for her to grasp, thrown out of the way by the force of the blow. The woman started swinging the rock at her head hysterically. Taris shoved the HALO off of her and pulled out her knife. She backhanded the woman with her good hand and swung herself to her knees. She grabbed the HALO woman's hair and sliced her throat open in one motion. Taris released her hair and the woman fell back, choking on her own blood to a sputtering death.

Slowly and gracelessly, Taris dragged herself to a stand and glared at the HALO's body. "You know, I am getting really sick of being tackled," she complained.

"Taris! Are you okay?!" Dave asked.

Before she could respond, he handed his diffuser to Matt and ran her, wrapping his arms around her waist. She buried her face into his chest, overwhelmed with joy. He smelled like clean laundry and Cobalt cigarettes. She inhaled strongly, just soaking up the moment. It was the first time she'd felt safe in as long as she could remember. Finally, she pulled back and looked into his smiling face, running her fingers through his red curly hair.

"Took you long enough," she said with a smile.

His smile turned into a sarcastic scowl. "Hmmphnm. Some gratitude. How about a 'thanks for saving my life, Dave'? Do you have any idea the kind of hell we've gone through to get you back? This has been the worst two weeks of my life! Good god, we thought you were dead, and I ran out of blues four days ago and I haven't slept in days and--"

Before he could protest any further, she cupped his face in her hands and kissed him squarely on the mouth. The look of startled, red-faced surprise on his face was enough to make it all worth it.

"Thanks Dave, for saving my life," she said. His wide-eyed surprise was the only reaction she got, but it was enough.

"I got the box open!" Matt exclaimed. Christian, Taris, Dave and Matt pulled the heavy metallic door open. Jryisa, in her natural Gray form, leapt onto her husband, wrapping her arms around his neck. Christian swung her around and buried his face into her hair, his strong arms wrapping around her slender frame. They seemed suspended in time, grasping each other silently, just as the rain started to fall.

"Hey baby," he said in a velvety voice. Christian pulled her face to his and kissed his wife passionately. Taris wanted to turn away out of respect, but she could only smile. Jyrisa started speaking to him in Caleum, wiping the tears from her husband's face and whispering words of love and encouragement. She grinned, brushing the rain from her face. *So the doctor finally found his wife*, she thought. *Today really is a victory.*

Vale.

She turned just in time to see him walking out of the crate, stepping into the drizzling day. He was limping, his skin blackened by scrathe burns, his forehead spotted with the holes the crown of thorns left behind. He was weakened, tired and anguished as he observed the battlefield with squinting eyes.

Then he saw her, and his expression transformed.

The private impression of a smile - the one that he reserved only for her - formed on his lips as he reached out to her. It made her blush, which embarrassed her, and only made the red of her cheeks grow hotter. She looked at the doctor and Jyrisa, wrapped up in such beautiful and uninhibited love. When she looked back at Vale, she realized that she didn't know how to act publically with him. She'd never had to before. Awkwardly she shoved her hands in her pockets and tried to avoid his sizzling stare.

"Hey," she said, clearing her throat. "Are you...okay?"

He brushed the wet hairs off his forehead and looked at her with an amused expression. "I have suffered worse. Although I'll admit I was worried you might not come."

"Oh, right," she said, offering Elias a hand out of the crate. "Sorry it took so long. There was this thing with my dad, and these HALOs, and then Gareth told me about this electro-knockout thing that the mad scientists made, and there was a fire extinguisher...and stuff. But I'm here now, so that's good, right?"

Elias evaluated her with a worried expression. "You are bleeding, warrior."

"Oh this?" she asked, gesturing to the blood splatter on her uniform. "It's nothing. It's not my blood. Well, a little bit is mine but not all of it. Mostly not mine…I'm fine is what I'm saying, thank you Star of Gray." *Well that came out well, Bodil,* she grumbled to herself.

Vale scrutinized her thoroughly and hid an amused smile. "How did you manage to get so damaged? Were you unarmed while you fought?"

She glared at him. "*No*, I wasn't unarmed, lord smarty-pants. I didn't have access to my usual weaponry is all." She dropped her sword heavily in front of him for emphasis.

"Is that a human-made sword?" Vale asked with genuine interest. "Where did you acquire that?"

"They're my dad's," Dave interjected, looking at the sword with a worried expression. "Hey, you're being careful with those, right?"

She waved him off, nudging the weapon toward Vale. "Hey, do you know how to use a sword? Because Gareth gave me this one and I just suck with it--"

"*HYBRID!*"

The voice from behind her was so dark, so terrible, and so menacing that it made her freeze. Vale looked over her shoulder and then back at her, eyes wide. Danger, they said. Fear. Run. Slowly she turned and faced the owner of the voice, and her eyes grew wide in horror.

"Sweet mother of Jesus," she cursed, looking up.

Standing in front of her was the biggest, most formidable giant of a man she had ever seen. He was seven feet if he was an inch, with unnaturally engorged muscles strained under tanned skin. His face was angry, with a long nose separating two black, beady eyes, his brown beard almost as long as his hair. He was wearing the uniform of a HALO, and she found herself wondering how they found a uniform in his size. In his hands were two enormous swords. A lesser man would have needed both hands to hold one. *This must be goliath*, she thought, slightly horrified.

"What do you want?"

She reached for her sword and knowing it would do her no good. She was terrible with that thing. As if he knew this, Vale reached down and grabbed her sword from the mud, holding it like he was made for it. The beast advanced on them, his giant footprints sinking into the slick mud. There was fighting and dying everywhere, but no one challenged him. He stood ten paces from her and raised one of his broadswords in her direction.

"*You!*" he bellowed. His thundering, heavily accented voice carrying over the chaos like the drum of a cannon. "You are the hybrid? Answer me!"

She didn't answer, but slowly reached for her knife. She had size and speed on her side. If she could manage to slide under the man and slit an artery, she could luck out. Vale stood beside her, sword at the ready. She knew her friends surrounded them, all eyes on her. Vale's eyes on her. She could not falter. Could also not lie. Too much was at stake.

The beast growled in irritation. "I said are you the hybrid, little girl?" he demanded.

She squared her shoulders. "Yes," she said with as much strength as she could muster. "I am." She wouldn't turn back to witness the reaction - or the judgment - of her friends. She wasn't ready to face *that* beast just yet. "And who are you, gigantor?"

The humongous man smiled. "I am Rowan."

"What do want with her, Rowan?" Vale asked. The rain was pouring harder, drenching their clothes.

"I want the hybrid's blood on my hands!"

Vale stepped forward, raising the sword. "You will not get to her!" he called back. "You will never get past me."

Rowan let out a rumbling laugh. "I will not have to."

Within seconds they were surrounded by HALOs, a dozen or more at least. Christian and Jyrisa stood back-to-back, ready to strike. The mad scientists jumped up on top of the crate, holding small - and ironically matching - machetes. The guards advanced on them quickly. Three of them charged Vale instantly and knocked him to the ground.

"Vale!"

The moment she turned her head she was backhanded with the force of a battering ram. The impact sent her flying across the courtyard, sliding to an aggressive stop against a crate. Before she could gather her bearings, Rowan kicked her as hard as he could in the gut. It was so forceful that it knocked the wind from her. Wheezing and desperate, she reached for her knife, only to realize that it was about three feet from her, sinking into the mud. *You've got to be kidding me*, she thought bitterly.

Something was coming down on her, and she moved her hand just in time to miss the razor sharp blade. Rowan cursed and swung for her again. Wheezing, she rolled out of the way and reached for her knife. As soon as grabbed the hilt, his boot came down on her fingers, crushing her bones. Taris screamed in agony. Desperate, she grabbed his tree-stump calf and bit down until she tasted blood. Rowan wailed in pain and yanked his leg away, releasing her crushed hand. All of her fingers were broken and throbbed in pain.

"Taris!" She looked up and saw Vale, pinned against the crate, fighting to get to her. One of the HALOs swiped at him with his knife, drawing a red line down the side of Vale's face. He responded by sticking his sword right through the man's midsection. The guard fell to the ground and Vale took a step toward her, only to be attacked by two more HALOs. They were keeping him from her, she realized.

Rowan grabbed her by her hair and yanked her across the mud, slamming her head against the crate. She saw the sword come at her and raised her arm up defensively, kicking her legs with all her strength. The sword came down on her forearm, almost cutting to the bone. She felt the blood, hot and fierce, begin to pour out of her. Rowan took that opportunity to smash her face in a couple of times with his massive fists. She was drenched, she was blinded, and she was bleeding badly. She was absolutely certain this guy was going to kill her, and there was nothing she could do about it.

Taris, she heard Elias say. *Stand and fight, warrior.*

No, was all she could think. She could barely think. She wasn't even sure her limbs would work if she commanded them to. Rowan slammed her head against the crate so hard she lost consciousness for a second. He stepped back, laughed, and wiped the grime off of one of his giant steel swords.

Fight, Elias instructed her, *or Vale will never survive.*

She looked over at Vale, slashing through the HALOs to get to her, a pile of bodies collecting at his feet. His face was cut and covered in blood, there were enemies everywhere, and in spite of that he was only looking at one person. Her. They kept coming and he kept killing because he was trying to get to her. If she gave up, so would he, and she wasn't not about to let that happen.

Okay Bodil, she told herself, *get your shit together. Time to slay the giant.*

She forced herself to her feet and Rowan smiled, showing a mouth of surprisingly straight white teeth. "Good," he said, raising his sword. "Face me, unholy half-breed. I will take your head off with a clean stroke."

"No way, goliath," she responded weakly. "You haven't beaten me yet."

"Ha!" he burst out. "That's not what I see, little girl."

"Well, we'll have to fix that, won't we?"

Rowan laughed and swiped his sword at her. Instead of backing up and getting her head chopped off, she launched forward. She jumped on him, wrapped her legs around his huge midsection and shoved her good thumb directly into his eye until she felt it pop. White mush and blood spurted out and he screamed, throwing her off of him. Rowan's socket dripped with the goop that used to be his eye and he swung around to face her. She was weak, shaking from pain and losing blood, but she managed to pull herself to a stand.

"No more of this," he said. "I'm killing you now."

"Wasn't that what you were trying to do before?" she asked, reaching for her knife with a shaking hand. He charged and she tried to maneuver out of the way, but the mud made her slip and she fell to the ground, taking Rowan down with her.

Acting quickly, she rolled to her side and jabbed her knife directly into the meat of his bicep. Rowan shouted and clamped his paws down on her hand, ripping the knife from her grasp. She reached up to kick him and he blocked it, punching her in the throat with all his strength.

She rolled on to her back, choking for breath. Rowan jumped on top of her and pinned her hands down in the mud. His weight was crushing the life from her as she gasped for the tiniest of breaths. The beast looked down at her, his remaining eye filled with hatred.

"Kill the hybrid," he said as though reciting a mantra, "kill the hope."

She stared at him, sucking in painful gasps. "What?"

Rowan wrapped his mitt-sized hands around her neck and started squeezing. "The Hammer. He said to tell you 'goodbye', hell-bound crossbreed."

His hands were crushing her neck. No matter how hard she struggled, she couldn't fight it. No more air. *No more air!* She tried desperately to pry his hands off, but they were rooted to her neck. She flung her arms wildly, grabbing for something, anything to save her. She was losing the ability to think. She started to get dizzy and her arms fell to her sides. That's when she felt it. Metal. Leather. Familiar. She grabbed it and held it up.

There, in her muddy, broken hands, was her wristband.

She had only seconds left. The world was starting to spin. Frantically she touched the screen and started pushing buttons with her broken fingers. She saw holographic processions of clocks and land maps, random noises and music, but nothing useful. Frantic, she started smashing her fingers against it, begging for a grenade, a loud noise, anything. Nothing came.

With the last of her strength, she pressed the wristband panel one last time, and gave way to the darkness.

Chapter Thirty-six

She never saw the laser beam, but she absolutely heard it.

It shot through the air with a resonating *zap!* Instantly Rowan's vice-like grip released on her, and the air poured back into her lungs. She strained to take desperately needed breaths, only managing to squeeze out terribly painful ones that grated her throat as she breathed life back into herself. Rowan, still poised on top of her, slumped down. A hole the circumference of a cork had burned straight through his skull. His remaining eye blinked mechanically in shock, as though the mind couldn't understand what had happened. Then he collapsed onto her, pressing her down into the mud. His head loped over the side of her shoulder and blood dumped out of the wound, soaking her uniform. She lacked the strength to move him so she just laid there, sucking in aggressive little breaths, pointing her broken and beaten face to the sky. The rain had settled to a light misting and she closed her eyes, letting the droplets kiss her skin. There wasn't a part of her body that wasn't in pain.

"Taris!"

She heard her name, but she didn't respond. She was beyond moving, beyond talking. She heard the sound of someone screaming in a language she didn't understand, and then the feeling of an excessive weight being lifted from her chest. She opened one swollen eye as Vale rolled Rowan's body off of her, letting it slop heavily into the mud. He looked at her and his eyes grew wide with alarm.

"*Tarischa*," he said, his voice strained with uncharacteristic emotion. *"Gias, es finis yii! Tarischa!"* He sat on his knees and wrapped her in his hands. Silver tears streamed down his face as he continued to mutter in his native language, rocking her back and forth gently, clutching her to his chest.

"Tarischa, ei sadah. Gias, ei sadah…"

"Vale," she croaked, her throat raw and stabbing. "English, please."

He pulled back and stared at her in open shock. "Taris!" he exclaimed. A surprised smile spread across his lips. "You're alive!"

"Ow," she responded. He released his grip on her and cradled her gently in his arms.

"I thought you had died," he said softly.

She tried her best to smile, but only managed more of a grimace. "Almost. Not quite."

Vale's face was filled with more light and life than she had ever seen. Unrestrained in his joy, he almost seemed like a completely different person. A happy person. He stroked the side of her face with his hand, brushing her muddy, drenched hair to the side of her face. His face was still streaked with silver, snaking like metallic rivers down his cheeks.

"Hey," she said gently. "You're still crying."

"Yes," he said, perplexed. "This has never happened before. I am filled with an emotion that I wholly lack the strength to control." He seemed pleasantly confounded at that. "I will admit this is a strange sensation for me."

"You'll get used to it." She reached up and gently wiped the tears from his face. "Wait a minute, I thought Adulos weren't allowed to cry in battle."

"Oh? And why is that?"

She tried the smallest of shrugs. "Bad for morale. It grays the mood."

He laughed - truly laughed - at that. It was the most beautiful, natural, precious thing she'd ever heard.

"See?" she said with a painful chuckle. "I told you that you'd come to appreciate my sense of humor."

"Oh Taris," he said kindly. "Shut up."

He wrapped his fingers around her hair, tilted her face to his, and kissed her.

He kissed her, and with all the fire, all the passion, all the uninhibited emotion she had inside her, she kissed him back. He tasted like starlight; power and passion and strength and mystery. Nothing else in the world mattered. At that moment it was just them and the rain and the perfection of it all. When she thought she could take it no more, she felt him plunge himself into the kiss with dizzying ardor. His passion consumed them both.

Oh gods, Taris, she heard. *I yearn for you.*

With more restraint than she possessed, Vale pulled back gently and pressed his forehead to hers. She could still feel the burning of desire in her heart. The taste of his touch still lingered on her lips, begging for more.

"You're...I don't even know if there are words for what you are, Vale. Amazing," she said, looking into his preternatural eyes. He laughed and kissed the top of her forehead. The touch was so light and delicate it was almost painful in its restraint.

"And you, Taris Leigh Bodil," he said gently. "You are everything."

"Uh...did I miss something?" Dave's voice rang from above. Straining, she craned her neck and saw the two mad scientists staring down at her. Matt looked giddy. Dave looked inconvenienced.

"Oh, hey guys," she said sheepishly as Vale helped her to a stand, keeping his hand wrapped around her waist. Both mad scientists gave her looks that demanded explanation. She had just been making out with the guy she originally threw in jail. There were bound to be questions. "How's it going?"

"Well, we won the battle," Dave said in a disgruntled tone. "Which you would have noticed if you would stop kissing people for two seconds."

She took a good look around. Black uniformed bodies were scattered everywhere, dead in heaps upon heaps. There was no shortage of Gray casualties too, she noticed, but the majority of the bodies were HALOs. A few of the Silencium fighters had rounded up the HALOs who had surrendered and were corralling them in the corner. Many of the Grays, Silencium and prisoner alike, were covered in blood, many badly wounded, but they were alive. Alive and liberated and happy. Their faces didn't show it, but she could feel it. And that made it all worth it.

Matt touched his glasses, scanned her and frowned. "Hey Christian!" he yelled across the courtyard. "Can you come here for a sec, buddy? Taris needs medical help."

"It's going to take more than medical attention to get Taris the help she needs," Christian yelled back.

"Oh ha ha. Nobody likes a sarcastic doctor, you know," she shot back.

"I doubt that!" He quickly finished what he was doing and jogged up to her, carrying a medical bag and a playful grin on his face. Vale lowered her to a relatively dry spot next to the crate, and the doctor crouched beside her.

"I must go, warrior," Vale said gently, kissing the top of her forehead. "You're in good hands."

"Where are you going?" she asked, reaching out to him.

"I need to speak with my tribesmen, but I will return to you," he said, kissing the palm of her hand. "I'll come back for you, Taris."

"You always do," she said, kindly shoving him away from her. "So go. Go be the guardian. I'm not going anywhere."

He gave her one last look before he took off, gracefully bounding toward Jyrisa who was, at that moment, trying to shove half a dozen HALO prisoners into one crate. Taris stifled a laugh at that.

"Hello again Taris," the doctor said with an amused look.

"Hello doc," she said wryly. "Well isn't this familiar? I'm bleeding and you're suddenly by my side with a bunch of medical stuff."

He laughed. "Yeah. Déjà vu. Except this time there aren't any talking corpses."

"God I hope not," she said.

"I guess I just have a knack for being there when you need me," he said, assessing her injuries with his medical scanner.

"Oh yeah? And where were you *before* goliath tried to crush my throat with his mallet-sized hands?"

"Okay, not always." He took out a series of devices and made short work of repairing her, starting with her neck. As soon as the warm device was pressed against her skin, her throat instantly felt better. He finished with that surprisingly fast and started working on her gaping flesh wound. "You're lucky," he said, sewing her arm back up with laser sutures. "Most of your injuries aren't too severe, considering the circumstance."

"Luck would have been not getting my head crushed in the first place," she said dryly.

"It would have been worse if we would have had to use a neuroreconstruction device on you," he said, looking up at her with a knowing expression.

"That is lucky I guess," she conceded. "I would not want to become a hot mess like Vinny."

Christian cocked an eyebrow at her, setting her broken fingers. "*Become* a hot mess? Who said you're not there already?"

"Hmphm. Shouldn't you be in a brig somewhere?" she asked ironically.

"Shouldn't you be getting scrubbed right about now?" he retorted.

"Ha!" she said, pointing her stiff, newly repaired finger at him. "The scrubbing doesn't work on me. So there."

"That's because you're a hybrid," Matt chimed in matter-of-factly. "Your genetics already have human in them. Scrubbing you is pointless."

She felt her heart sink at his words. So they hadn't forgotten that, then.

"How, erm, how do you know about the scrubbing?" she asked.

"The rebels," Matt said with a shrug. "They know a surprisingly large amount about these complex places. Including the horrible things that are done in them."

"We know all about it Taris," Dave said in his gentlest tone.

"So…about that hybrid thing…what do you think about that?" She cursed herself for not being more verbally diplomatic. *They taught me to fly spaceships and kill people but they couldn't have programmed clever speech?*

"Oh...that," he said slowly. "Well..."

"What?" She was almost scared to look at them, of what they might think of her.

"Yeah," Dave said running his hands through his red curls. "We sort of…already knew. That you are a hybrid, I mean."

She blinked. "What? You *knew*? How do you know?"

"Your readings were really strange when we first met," Matt explained, tapping his glasses. "When I scanned you it came up as human *and* Gray. We didn't know exactly what you were--"

"I did," interrupted Dave.

"Anyway," Matt continued, "we didn't know exactly what you were, but we knew it wasn't human."

"I didn't know," she said quickly, feeling defensive. "That is, I just found out. I wasn't trying to cover anything up I swear."

"Oh," Dave said. "We figured you just didn't want to tell anyone about your half-Gray side. You know, because of the scrathing and the prejudice and all that. I didn't blame you for not bringing it up."

"No matter how many times we tried to provoke you to tell us," Matt added.

"What? What do you..." Suddenly a thought struck her. "Oh. The blueberries from the Stargazer?"

Matt nodded. "The blueberries from the Stargazer."

She couldn't help but laugh at that. "Oh, you're real evil geniuses. Flushing me out with the scent of pancakes."

"Hey, it was the best we could think of on short notice," Dave said gruffly.

She hid a smile. "So...you don't care?"

"Why would we care?" Dave said, shrugging. "You're still Taris, aren't you?"

She smiled at him. It was like a weight lifted off her chest. In those cantankerous words, every doubt she had evaporated. "Oh David," she said strongly. "I really am."

At that moment Jyrisa ran up to them, bounding like a deer over the debris and dead bodies. "Christian love, I just got word. Natsumi says it's time to go."

He shot his wife a wide smile, seemingly grateful for her mere presence. "Thanks, baby." He turned to Taris. "You ready to go?"

"Guess so," she said, looking down at her blood and mud caked clothes. "God, I need a drink. And a shower."

"We have to move quickly," Matt explained as he and Dave helped her to a weak but no longer excruciating stand. "That electro-blast machine we built can't hold off electricity forever. Eventually it will wear down and everything will turn back on."

"Oh great. Well let's not be here when *that* happens," she said. They started toward the exit, Matt and Dave assisting her every step, when suddenly she stopped. Something told her not to go. To stay. That she was needed. Dave turned and looked at her.

"What?" he asked gently. "Is something wrong?"

"No, nothing's wrong," she said, wincing from residual aches. "Uh…you all go on ahead. I just have to get Vale."

"You sure, captain?" Matt asked suspiciously.

"Yep, I'm sure. I'll meet you all there."

She bid them farewell and then turned to look for Vale in the crowd. He was walking up to Elias, who was standing silently in the drizzling mist, eyes closed, hair glowing like the embers of a fire. He looked like he was praying, but his expression was etched in sadness. She had the strange notion that she did not want to disturb the hallowed Star of Gray.

She touched the side of Vale's arm and he turned, his face lighting up at the sight of her. "Vale, the ship's preparing to leave. You ready to go?"

He nodded. "Absolutely. Let me just get Elias."

Vale reached out to touch Elias, but he didn't seem to notice. Vale frowned. *Elias?* he called out to him. *We are preparing to leave, Star of Gray.*

I'm not going with you, guardian, Elias responded, unmoving.

You needn't fear for your safety, he said. *We have a safe haven we can take you to. A new place on the Lucian moon. They will not find you this time, Elias. On my life I swear it.*

No, guardian, Elias responded. *I am not coming.*

Elias turned to them. His eyes blazed with light, his hair electric and charged. His skin emitted incandescence, casting his own brightness in the bleak light of day. His face was as unreadable as any Gray, but his emotions surged and rippled over his body. It was so strong that Taris unconsciously stepped backward, awed and intimidated by his light. Vale's expression was solemn, but his emotions were heartbroken.

Star of Gray, he started, *please. Come with us. I have to protect you. It is my duty.*

No, Vale Teag, Elias said, holding out a palm in protest. *Your mission for me ends here. I have seen it. This is where it is meant to happen.*

Taris had no idea what that meant, but it appeared to mean a lot to Vale. Silently, he dropped to a knee and bowed his head. Elias touched the top of his head and Vale raised his eyes to him.

Is there no other way? he asked, his tone pleading.

Elias shook his head. *This is the end, faithful servant. As it always was. As it was meant to be.*

Taris was about to ask what they were talking about when the door to the Hammerhead Eye opened. Vale jumped to his feet and reached for his sword. Taris reached into her pocket for her knife, realizing that she'd had lost it somewhere in the melee. She found the wristband and held it at the ready, just in time to see Gareth walk out of the door carrying the black box of keys with a proud grin.

"Good job, Gareth," she said, relaxing a little, shoving the wristband in her pocket.

Gareth's face was alight with excitement. "Oh it was amazing, mum! Kyran took on upwards of fourteen men all his own! Even sliced a line down Boone Hooper's fat stomach before he emergency teleported out, the coward."

"And...my father?" She was almost afraid to know.

"Gone," he said. "Don't know where, but he wasn't in the Eye that's for sure."

She breathed an internal sigh of relief. As much as she hated him at the moment, she didn't not wish him dead. "So Kyran really laid waste to the place, did he?"

"Oh it was a sight, mum! Nothing was going to slow him down, I'll tell you. He ran over tables and jumped over things like an acrobat!"

The thought of Kyran vaulting off of bodies like he was gymnast was utterly hilarious to her for some reason. "And where is the conquering hero?" she asked. "I want to thank him myself."

Gareth turned to the door. "Here he comes now, mum. And he's brought us some company."

The door swung wide and out strode Kyran Ato, soaked in the blood of countless enemies, dragging a prisoner in chains unceremoniously through the mud. He reached the feet of Elias and Vale and came to a knee.

"Lord guardian, Star of Gray," he said. "I have brought you the wicked one to face his judgment."

At the end of the chains, beaten and bloody, was the Hammer. And he looked pissed.

Chapter Thirty-seven

"Gareth?" Taris started slowly, keeping her eyes deadlocked on the Hammer. "Can you please take that box to Matt and Dave on the Intrepid? After they get it open, please make sure every single Gray has their collar removed."

"Yes mum. It would be my pleasure." He started to walk away when he stopped and turned to her. "Are you not coming, then?"

"Not just yet," she said with a forced smile. "I'll be right behind you."

Gareth looked like he wanted to argue, but simply pressed his lips together and nodded. "Right then. See you back at the ship. And Kyran too, I hope." He gave the Gray a small smile and then spun on heel, propelled by purpose. Taris waited until he was gone before she felt comfortable enough to speak.

"Rowan is dead," she said, folding her arms triumphantly.

The Hammer looked over at the body of the gigantic HALO, an unmoving fleshy hump in the mud. "Hmm. A pity."

"Not really," she said dismissively. "Guess you'll have to try harder the next time you want me killed."

The Hammer stifled a laugh. "I'll keep that in mind."

"Star of Gray," Kyran said, coming to a respectful stand, "it would be my honor to kill this human for you."

Elias held out his hand and gently placed it on Kyran's head. *Thank you, Kyran Ato, the protector. You are a champion amongst soldiers.*

Kyran's trademark stoicism broke ranks for a moment, just enough to let a proud smile transform his face. *Star of Gray, I am honored. Thank you. Shall I kill him, then?*

"No," Elias answered verbally. "But thank you."

Kyran looked perplexed and slightly disappointed. Taris was a little confused herself. "I'm sorry but I agree with Kyran," she said. "Why aren't we going to kill him?"

The Hammer snorted. "Dissention amongst the ranks?"

"Shut up," she said, shooting him a look.

The Hammer laughed. "Well don't fall apart on my behalf or anything. Wait, on second thought, that's fine."

Elias cocked his head to the side. Lightly he stepped over to the Hammer as Kyran yanked him awkwardly to his feet.

"You have tortured Adulos with pride," Elias said softly, studying the Hammer's face. "You were callous and unfeeling in your methods. You neutralized hundreds of my people without so much as a thought of what you were truly doing."

"I was performing my duty," he said with bravado. "This is what I am good at. This is what I do."

Elias shook his head. "You were a pawn in this game, Simon. An unwilling pawn in a game that you couldn't possibly understand."

"Which again, is why we ought to kill him," Taris said, wishing she knew what button she pressed to make the laser come out of her wristband again.

Elias turned to her. "We have all played parts in this that we did not want to play. Isn't that right, Taris?"

Her mouth dropped, but she quickly closed it. "I guess so," she said, embarrassed. Does he know? she wondered.

"Yeah Taris," the Hammer taunted, "don't want to hypocritical, do we?"

"That's different," she said quickly before he could explain himself. "I had no control. You do."

"True," he admitted. "But at least I can live with myself because of it."

"You taunt us like you want us to kill you," Elias said. "I can see it in your soul. You think it's hatred but it isn't. It's guilt masked as anger. A sadness you cannot explain."

"Bollocks," the Hammer responded. "I don't care about your spiritual bloody sense, silverback."

Elias leaned in close to him, studying his face intently. "You have dreams, don't you Simon?"

The Hammer's face drained of color. Elias struck a nerve. "I don't know what you're talking about."

"Yes you do," said Elias gently, touching the top of the Hammer's wild brown hair. "There will come a time when the atrocities that you have done here will come to light in your mind. When this day comes, it will pain you greater than any punishment I could inflict upon you."

The Hammer jerked his head away from Elias's touch. "What kind of religious dribble is this? What are you getting at, silverback?"

"The humans were wrong," Vale added, his words swelling with pride. "Our living cells regenerate. And they are fighting back."

"What's this got to do with me?" the Hammer asked, feigning indifference.

"Your time is almost up," Elias said. "The nightmares will continue and they will get worse. I pity you, Hammer, for you knew not what you did. Yet still, you must answer for it."

"Well. That was...prophetic I suppose. In truth, I really don't want to know what any of it all means. Not a tick." The Hammer glared at him. "So what are you trying to say, you long-winded Gray? And can you make it quick? This mud is going to ruin this suit."

Elias crouched in front of the Hammer and placed a radiating hand on his shoulder. The Hammer seemed to respond strangely to Elias's touch and stared at him in confused anger. Elias brushed the Hammer's face with his palm affectionately.

"I'm here to tell you, Simon Finnegan, that I absolve you," he said with tender honesty. "In the presence of those with whom you have wronged, with the eyes of the unfairly treated, the Star of Gray does hereby pardon you of your sins. You are absolutely and completely exonerated for your actions, and it will be thus from this day forward."

The Hammer glared at him. "I don't want your absolution."

"No," Elias said softly. "But you will." He reached out and grabbed a fistful of the Hammer's dark brown hair. He yanked quickly, holding several strands in his fingers as the Hammer yowled in protest.

"Hey!" He complained. "What the bloody hell did you do that for?"

Elias smiled. "You're going Gray, Simon."

The Hammer looked down. In Elias's hand, surrounded by several long, silky brown follicles, were several very strange gray hairs. No, not gray. *Silver.* The strands shimmered, reflecting light in the muted overcast day. Taris gasped.

"Oh my god," she breathed. "But that means that the Hammer is…" *An Adulo.*

The Hammer swung his head around and glared at her, his eyes wide in petrified shock. She clamped her hand on her mouth. *Oh my god,* she thought. *Did he hear me?* She looked at him, staring into his furious brown eyes. *Are you an Adulo?*

At that moment, Simon Finnegan lost it.

"No! I'm not going to listen to this anymore! *Stop it! Stop your lies*!" He struggled against his captors with all his strength. "Release me! I'm not going down like this! *Let me go*!"

Taris reached up to hit him, but it was Elias's hand that stopped her.

"No," he said, gently lowering her arm. "Do not strike him."

"What? Why? He's a torturer and a murderer! He's a danger to all of us!"

"He was used," Elias argued. "He's angry."

"So am I!" she exclaimed. "Elias, Star of Gray, whatever. Listen to me. We can't keep him here. We can't take him with us. This man has to die!"

"If you attack him, warrior, you become no different than your enemies." He stood between them, protecting his own enemy against her. "There will come a time in everyone's life when they will need forgiveness, and a time when they will need to give it. The measure of morality is weighed in those moments, Taris. If you have the will to fight, you can find the strength to forgive."

She looked into his kind eyes, smiling in spite of herself, when she caught a strange movement. By the time she realized what it was, it was too late.

The shot rang out through the courtyard, echoing through the walls. Elias stumbled back, clutching his chest. The Hammer held the smoking revolver in his long fingers, wide-eyed horror splashed across his face. The metal bullet penetrated Elias's heart, a direct shot. A giant pool of dark red blood poured over the front of his prison uniform. He looked up, his face blanched in shock.

"I…I believe I've been shot."

At that moment, the power inside Elias exploded.

Chapter Thirty-eight

His whole body erupted with light, eclipsing the overcast light of day. It was a blinding, powerful, raging incandescence. It rose in size and then exploded from him like a sonic boom. A lightning bolt of energy struck everyone in the area with aggressive strength. The Hammer was flung away from Elias with force. He hit the side of the crate and landed face down in the mud, unmoving.

Taris felt like she'd been struck by lightning.

She gasped for breath for a few moments before finally regaining control of her lungs again, painfully pulled herself to a stand. They were surrounded by a wall of fire. The entire complex was engulfed in flames, lapping up the cement like it was kindling. Stranger still was that there was now an audience. Surrounding them, shadowed by the fire, where the Grays. Hundreds of them, lined in rows, standing like a host in the chaos. They seemed to come from nowhere, materializing from the smoke of the flames. Kyran was splayed a few paces from her, still alive but unconscious. Several of his tribesmen lifted him from the ground and into the crowd without so much as a whisper of explanation.

Elias was curled in a ball in the spot where he had stood, shaking like a scared child. His head was down, his hair was no longer glowing, and a circle of blackened earth now surrounded him. Vale dragged himself down into the small crater and wrapped the Star of Gray in his hands. Taris stumbled over the mud and fell to her knees in front of them.

"He's bleeding badly," she said, pressing her hands against the gushing wound. "The Hammer penetrated his heart."

"Can Christian repair it?" Vale asked, his desperation palpable. "Will he live?"

She looked him in the eye, pressing against Elias's chest to slow the bleeding. Slowly, she shook her head. "I'm so sorry."

Vale's expression fell. *Oh gods, no.*

Lord guardian, Elias thought, looking at Vale with pleading, muted eyes. *Please lift my head up. I would like to address my people.*

The Adulos stood inhumanly still, watching the scene with a silent reverence. Though one did not touch the other, she could feel the unseen bond that strengthened them, joined them as a whole. She could not see it, but she knew it was there. She was not a well-woven part of it exactly, but she felt it. It felt like a current. She felt the movement, the fluid motion, the surging unstoppable force that surrounded her, but she was not swept away by it. She was an outsider, she knew, but not unwelcome. Walking the thin gray line.

Adulos who witness this day, Elias said with surprising strength, *remember this moment and commit it to memory. Keep your hope and hold it close, my tribesmen, for you will need it in the days to come. Have faith in yourselves, in your fight, and in your faith. Today you bear witness to the start of the Age of Pillars. In your memories, our history will live on. Do not let this moment be forgotten.*

For the Star of Gray and by the will of the Five, they recited, *it is so done.*

Taris had been trying to slow the bleeding, but no matter what she did the blood continued to stream in between her fingers. Elias was white as a sheet and starting to grow cold. She felt the panic rise in her throat, but nothing was working. She was losing him. Vale cradled Elias in his arms. The childlike angel with white hair was dying. She pushed back the tears, trying to give him as much time as she could. Elias looked at her and grabbed her wrist gently.

Warrior, he thought, his words tender, *you need not worry. This was meant to be.*

She shook her head, refusing to accept to defeat. "No," she said. "I can do this. You're going to be okay. Really. I…I've seen worse injuries than this." In truth she was surprised he had any blood left to spill. She started fumbling. "You know what's funny? Blood is the same color. I mean, Gray blood, human blood, it all looks the same…" She trailed off when she saw the look on his face.

Taris, he thought, his words draping like silk over her fears. *I have to tell you something.*

She swallowed the sobs back and looked at him. *What is it, Elias?*

He gave her arm a small squeeze. *When I'm gone, it will be up to you to save our people.*

She shook her head. *Uh… You mean Vale, right?* She looked at Vale, hoping for some sort of affirmation and finding only equal confusion. *Vale's the lord guardian,* she protested. *He'll know what to do.*

No, it must be you.

But… She searched for an excuse. *But I'm not ready for that. I wouldn't know where to start, Elias. I mean, I'm just getting used to the idea of being a pillar.*

Warrior, he said, *I am giving the Star of Gray to the three pillars.*

Her eyes grew wide. *What?!*

NO! Vale exclaimed. She looked up at him, confused.

Well thanks for the vote of confidence, she said, trying to be light. Her expression dropped when she saw the look on Vale's face. Utter devastation. It was as though Elias had just asked him to slaughter his whole family. She peered at him, confused. Vale's eyes filled with tears and he looked at Elias in open-mouthed desolation.

No, he begged in a tone so soft she almost didn't hear it. *Not her. Anyone but her.*

"Anyone but me?" she asked aloud on reflex. "Why anyone but me?"

He looked at her, the expression so intense she thought her heart would break at the sight. *Because I cannot bear that it be you, my warrior. I cannot bear it.*

Taris, Elias beckoned, distracting her from Vale's emotionally broken expression. *You will each have an even piece of the power of the Adulo. You must find the others and take them to the Shadow Valley. There you must all choose, at the same time, to combine your power. Do this, and you will save us all.*

Now she was panicking. *Elias, you don't know what you're asking here. I don't know the first thing about the Star of Gray power. I'm not even a full Gray. I don't even know the other two pillars!*

Patience warrior, he said gently, *all will be revealed to you in time. The witch is far from reach, but the wanderer is closer than you think. He will come to you on a starless night and trade you three truths for one lie.*

Well that didn't help her at all. *Elias, you can't do this,* she said, verging on hysterical. *You can't die. You can't put this on me. I can't handle that kind of pressure. I'm not what you think I am.*

And what do I think you are? he asked.

She hung her head in shame. *A hero.*

And you are not?

There was only one way to prove her words, but it would ruin her. Still, she couldn't let him give her any power. She couldn't fail the Adulos. She wouldn't let them put their trust in a traitor. She thought about what her father told her, about what she did. She carefully and deliberately recalled this, showing it only to Elias, even blocking Vale from her thoughts. She wasn't ready to show him her true colors. *Do you see?* she asked, looking down in shame. *You've got the wrong girl. Just give the power to Vale, Elias. He's the right one.*

Taris Leigh Bodil, Elias said slowly. *I forgive you.*

She looked up at him, thunderstruck. *No,* she said sternly. *Don't do that. Don't forgive me. I'm not worth it.*

He pulled himself up ever so slightly and she leaned in, her tears falling onto his blood-soaked uniform. With a shaking hand he pushed two fingers to his forehead, and then pressed his finger against her forehead. The salute of the Silencium.

I forgive you absolutely, his words whispered to her soul. *And so do our people.*

With the complete abandon of her composure, she lost herself to her grief and began to sob. The tears flowed, overwhelming her. Her shoulders shook from the force of her sadness. It had been inside her so long, eating at her for so long. She'd been trying to poison herself for years, hating every piece of herself for reasons she could never understand and now, after all that time, she felt peace. True, absolute, all consuming peace, and it was all she had needed all along.

She looked into Elias's dying eyes and returned the Silencium salute to him. "Thank you," she said softly, her sobs reduced to silent tears. *Thank you, Star of Gray.*

Fight for freedom with valor, warrior, he said, his eyes closing, *and you will discover the path to victory.*

She let go of his wound and pressed Vale's hand down in her place. Whatever Elias needed to say to him, they needed to be alone to say it. He applied the right amount of pressure as she stood up, her hands drenched in his blood. Vale cradled Elias in his arms.

Vale, Elias said, *I don't have much time.*

Star of Gray, he responded, *I am so sorry. I have failed to save you.*

No lord guardian, he said, *it was always going to be this way. The Five declared that my path ended here.*

Vale's eyes rippled in thought. *Star of Gray*, he said slowly, *if you split the powers, does this mean I am no longer the guardian? I only promised to protect you, but if the Star of Gray is divided…*His tone lifted with the smallest hint of hope. *Might I be released of my vows?*

Your mission to protect our people has not changed.

Elias please, Vale said, his disappointment apparent. *If that is so, you know what it means for me.*

You must protect the warrior, he said simply. *Protect the pillar of strength. She will find the others, she will release the noticulus. She will save us all. Protect her, and you protect the future of the Adulo race.*

Protect her, Vale thought cautiously. He looked up at her, his eyes filled with overwhelming grief. She hated that expression. Why was he looking at her like she was dying?

No, Vale said, not breaking his gaze with her. *Star of Gray, you can't ask me…Please don't make me do this.*

You know what is required of you, lord guardian, Elias said in a tone that sounded like a warning. *And you know what you may never do.*

Vale's overwhelming distress was heartbreaking. She didn't quite understand what they were talking about, but Taris knew that Elias was forcing to Vale to accept something horrible. Something he wanted to fight with every fiber of his being. Something that was apparently unavoidable.

She'll never understand, Vale protested. *She will despise me for this.*

Perhaps, Elias said, the sound of his voice growing weak, *but you will endure it. The Five have declared you lord guardian. You have no choice.*

Vale was nearly in tears. *I have walked the thin gray line for centuries. I have been a faithful servant of the Five in all aspects of my life, and it has brought me nothing but loneliness and grief. She,* he said, pointing to her, *she is the only one that could make my journey worth the pain.*

I grieve for you, lord guardian, but it is not meant to be. Elias was unwavering. *You are destined to fight beside her, to protect her, to guide her. Nothing more may come of it. You know that.*

Vale's face was painted with a deep, ever-growing devastation. His feelings were so saturating that she felt them weigh down her heart, burning with pain, with loss. *Is there no other way?* he pleaded, his voice soft. His will was buckling, she could feel it. *Can there be no other? Please...*

You know there is not, Elias responded. *I am sorry my friend, but this is the only way. You must uphold your duty to the Five. You must remain lord guardian.*

Vale, anguish evident on his face, tore his probing eyes from her and turned back to Elias. *I...understand. I will continue my mission, Star of Gray. For our people. By your command, and by the will of the Five.*

And so it is done, Elias responded. Simultaneously, they both exchanged the salute of the Silencium as the fires of the complex surrounded them. Elias gave Vale the tiniest ghost of a smile before his eyes rolled into the back of his head and his limbs fell at his sides.

On this day, in the presence of friends and flames, Elias said, *so begins the Age of Pillars. By the will of the Five...it has begun.*

She felt, rather than saw, his soul leave his body. In the span of a collective breath, he was gone. Elias Ohn was gone. The Star of Gray was dead.

The only sounds in the courtyard were the crackling of the wall of fire, and the soft sound of crying. No, she realized, it wasn't crying. It was humming. She looked around and realized that the whole Gray host was standing around them, humming a strange and unearthly melody. It sounded like a spirit dancing in the wind, twisting and knotting in a strange yet rhythmic way. It was somber and reverent, heavy with sadness and longing. Taris didn't need to ask Vale what they were doing. They were saying goodbye.

Farewell Elias, she said, kneeling as she reached out to close his eyelids. *Farewell.*

As soon as her skin touched his, the lightning shot through her. It surged through her body, lighting her insides on fire. A white scorching light consumed her. The terrible, crippling, blinding pain absorbed every molecule of her being. She felt it rip her from the inside out, the power of a thousand scrathes all at once. She screamed wordlessly, her voice lost in a wave of agony. It was just her and the light and the anguish. And the sorrow. And the suffering. And the torture of a million souls all screaming at her at the same time. Confusion. Betrayal. Pain. Fury. Emotions overwhelmed her. She remembered reaching out for Vale, screaming for help, and then she lost consciousness.

When she opened her eyes, she had no idea where she was, or how she got there. *Oh god*, she thought, *now I'm in trouble.*

Chapter Thirty-nine

She was standing in a white room, void of everything but her.

No windows. No furniture. Just her, white walls, white floor, and an open door. At first she thought she was dreaming, but she realized that it was beyond a dream. No, this was something different. Some sort of hyperconsciousness. It felt unreal enough to not be tangible, but not imaginary and nonsensical to just be a dream. There was no pain, there was no noise. It was calm, serene even.

Oh god, she thought, *I'm dead. That's what this must be. The afterlife.*

Taris found herself strangely amused with the thought that she wasn't burning in some sort of hell. She felt a smug sense of self-satisfaction in that fact. Then she thought of the pain she had endured and her smile faded. *Perhaps I had to go through hell to get here*, she wondered. *But where is here?* She looked down at her body, trying to evaluate the state of her ethereal being. She was no longer wearing her blood-and-mud-stained HALO uniform, but the gray ceremonial robes from her dreams. *Huh. That's strange. Maybe I'm not dead.* Her hands weren't bleeding she noticed, and she wasn't carrying a sword.

Taris…

She looked up, startled. She heard him. Vale. He called out to her from the hallway, somewhere far away. Somewhere she couldn't reach.

"Vale?" she replied, hearing the strange echoing emptiness in her voice. She peered out into the white hallway. "Vale?"

Taris…come to me…

She ran. She tore through the hallways, turning corners and running through corridors. Every wall, every room looked the same. *Vale!* she called out mentally, *Vale where are you? I can't find you!* She tore through the endless string of walls and rooms, but she couldn't find him. Every now and then she could feel him, would know he was close, and then the feeling would vanish.

Taris…don't give up.

"I'm not!" she screamed. "I'll find you!" Propelled by purpose, she flew around the nearest corner and came to a screeching halt. The hallway had led her to a large open room. On the side of the wall were numbers, formed in a circular motion like a clock, but not in the right order. And they were *moving.* Amazed, Taris walked over to the wall and reached out to touch a floating 8. When her fingers got close, the 8 backed away shyly, just out of her reach. She smiled at that and reached out for another number, when all of them floated away from her like a school of skittish fish. All the numbers were the same she noticed, except the 2 and the 0, which seemed to be blinking with a light that the others were not. She reached out slowly, so as to not scare them, and then snatched the 2 from the floating school of numbers before it could float away.

As soon as she had it in her hands she heard the screaming. A girl's voice, shrieking in pain. Startled, she dropped the 2, which joined the frightened collection of other floating numbers on the wall. The screaming stopped, but something was different. Taris had the strange feeling that she was no longer alone. She turned slowly to the doorway, and that's when she saw it. A girl in gray robes with curly red hair streaked with silver ran past her, crying.

It's coming, the girl's sad voice echoed through the walls. *The war is coming. The rivers will bleed with the lives of the innocent. The evil rises as the three are divided. The Star of Gray must be united or all is lost. All is lost, all is lost, all is lost…*

Taris's mouth dropped. The girl…it was the girl from her dream. She thought of a word. A title. Something she'd always known, but was hidden from her somehow. She reached into the earth of her mind and dug up the word she was looking for. *Pillar.* The girl with the red hair was the Spirit Pillar. When she thought of it, she knew it was true. She wasn't sure in what context, just that she was a pillar, and Taris needed to find her.

She tore out of the room and ran down the hallway in the direction of the red haired girl, but she couldn't find her. Then she saw her again, the red hair running around a corner.

"Wait!" she screamed, chasing after her. Every step she took seemed to bring her farther and farther from the girl. She'd see a flash of red hair, or the billowing of robes as they slipped around a corner, but she couldn't reach her. Finally, after what seemed like an endless amount of time, she slowed her running to a defeated walk. No matter what corner she turned or what empty room she found, the girl was nowhere to be seen. She couldn't even backtrack to the room with the numbers. She was lost in an endless labyrinth of nothingness. Taris had the vague idea that she ought to be exhausted by now, but she felt no fatigue in her body.

Taris...

There it was again. Vale, calling out to her from somewhere. He kept calling to her, but she could never find him. He was just a shadow of a voice, intangible and imaginary. She wanted to believe that there were people looking for her, but she was alone. Utterly and totally alone, with only the phantom of a voice and a ghost with red hair for company. She was starting to think that maybe she actually was in hell. Frustrated, she started crying. She turned a corner down another identical hallway, walked into the nearest room and started bawling.

That's when she realized the room wasn't empty.

He stood in the corner, the hood over his head, unmoving. She couldn't see his face, but she knew him. She'd always known him, somehow. His presence engulfed her and she stopped crying, wiping her face with the sleeve of her robes. The third pillar, her mind told her. The Pillar of Wisdom. As soon as she titled him he turned around, faced her, and slowly removed his hood. The moment their eyes met, she knew him instantly.

"Theo," she breathed.

He was her age, tall, with a thick neck and skin that had been tanned by light. His jaw was firm and square, framing a frowning mischievous mouth. His forehead was high and his eyebrows thick, hovering over round, questioning brown eyes. His dark wavy hair was cropped closely on his head and his ears sported several earrings. He cocked his head to the side and pointed to her with a large, masculine finger.

"Taris," he said in a questioning tone. His voice was rough and strong, soothingly familiar.

She nodded wordlessly. He furred his brow, as though remembering something long forgotten. Slowly, deliberately, he brought two fingers to his forehead, and then extended one finger out to her. She repeated the gesture, touching her finger to his.

The moment they touched, she felt the spark. The perfection of the both of them. The absolution of their power and their importance. It all made sense. Theo looked confused and overwhelmed, slowly dropping his hand to the side. His brown eyes, so human in color, shifted like liquid, just like the eyes of the Grays. Then his expression changed, as if he'd remembered something abruptly that he'd forgotten.

"Tabitha," he said slowly. "Where is Tabitha?"

Tabitha. The girl with the silver and red hair. She looked out into the hallway and back to him.

"Lost," she responded. "Trapped in time."

"Where?" he asked, folding his arms.

She thought about it, and the floating numbers on the wall came to mind. "Twos and zeros," she answered cryptically, unable to form an intelligible answer to his question for some reason. Stranger still was that he seemed to understand what she meant.

"Hmm," he said, frowning. "Well, we will have to get her, then."

She looked up. "Now?"

He shook his head. "No. I have to find you first."

"But, you have found me," she pointed out, confused. Theo smiled at that, transforming his face into disarming joy. He stifled a breathy laugh, and for a moment - just a moment - she thought she saw his hair turn gray.

"Not here," he said. "We need to leave this place."

"How?" she asked, casting a hesitant glance into the hallway. She was afraid if she walked out there that she'd lose him again.

Taris…please…come to me.

Vale was calling to her, or rather the ghost of Vale's voice. She didn't want to go to it. She was afraid of it. She wanted to stay with Theo and never leave. He seemed to read her thoughts and reached out, gripping her arm gently. His touch was like embracing power.

"You have to go out into the hallway, Taris," he said urgently.

"I don't want to go," she protested.

"You have to," he said. "Go to him. He will save you."

"I want to stay here with you, Theo," she said, feeling the fear start to consume her. Theo gripped her by the shoulders. His body shuddered, and suddenly his eyes and hair transformed into the glittering silver of the Adulo. She gasped.

"Taris, go into the hallway," he demanded urgently. "Follow the voice. If you don't we're all doomed, okay?"

"I'll get lost!" she protested. "I don't want to be alone, Theo. I don't."

He bent down and pressed his forehead against hers. The way Vale had done with her before. Theo's touch was different, less romantic but somehow more intimate. Suddenly she was overcome with strength and calm. "You're never alone, Pillar of Strength," he said in his raspy, authoritative voice. "I will be with you. I am always with you."

She believed him. Without further explanation or protest, she believed him. And it empowered her. She took a deep breath and pulled back. "Okay," she said.

Theo nodded and shuddered, his hair and eyes returning to the rich brown they had been before. "Go, Taris," he said, pointing to the door. "Go find the guardian."

"And then what?"

He smiled and pulled the hood back over his head. "When you find him, I'll find you. Now go."

He turned around and faced the wall, shutting off any further communication. Mechanically, she walked toward the door. She stopped in the doorway and turned back one last time, but when she looked back, he was gone. No trace of Theo remained. She felt the stab of loneliness piercing her resolve.

Taris…come to me.

She closed her eyes, stepped into the hallway, and let herself be led by the sound of Vale's voice. She walked blindly through the hallways, letting the unseen force guide her. She started to feel cold, heavy. Her steps felt laborious, her breathing more strenuous, but she kept moving on. She could hear more things now. The sounds of water, of people speaking, but it didn't quite make sense. She felt the presence of others, many others around her at one point, but then they dissipated.

Taris, you're almost there. Come to me.

She pushed herself forward, too scared to open her eyes. He was close. She could feel him around her. *Vale*, she said. *I'm here. I'm here!*

Take my hand, Taris.

She took three more deliberate steps and reached her fingers out as far as she could. Her fingertips brushed against something. A tangible feeling. No, more than that. A connection. A person. She gripped his hand with all her strength.

Vale!

Slowly, deliberately, Taris opened her eyes.

Chapter Forty

"Taris," Vale said, his voice thick with emotion. He was looking at her like he'd seen a ghost. He looked like one himself. He was sitting at the edge of her bed, drenched in sweat, gaunt, traces of hopelessness etched on his face. He leaned out of his chair and fell into her lap, wrapping his arms around her waist. "Oh Taris," he said softly. "You finally stopped running."

She was in a room that looked like it had been carved out of rock. No, she realized, it was rock. She was in a cave that had been converted to a room. There were a few chairs surrounding the bed, and a desk with an assortment of medical devices and bottles scattered on it. A small round window looked out into what seemed to be a forest, drenched in rain. The bed was small but warm and there were thick candles burning inside small alcoves that had been carved in the rock wall. For all intents and purposes, it was a very cozy crypt.

"Where am I?" she asked, her voice hoarse from lack of use.

He looked up and sat on the edge of her bed, pressing his forehead to hers. "*A tarischa*," he whispered. "You're safe. We're in the Silenecium compound, on the moon Lucian. They won't find you here."

"They?" she asked. "Who's they?"

Vale pulled away, the mirrors of his eyes shifting like a current. "The United authority," he said. "They're searching for you."

"Hmm," she said, slowly processing that. "They're already hunting me down? How long have I been asleep?"

"Forty-two days."

"Oh," she responded. Well that was enough time for them to turn the whole of human civilization against her, she figured. "And the others?"

"Safe," he said. "We were able to fly out of the atmosphere before the United authority caught us."

"Good," she said carefully, rubbing her temples in an attempt to reduce her horrible headache. She felt like someone had beaten a thousand years of thoughts into her head at once. Nothing was making a lot of sense. She remembered the white rooms, the floating numbers, the girl with the red-and-silver streaked hair, Theo telling her to find Vale. There was so much more, but it was like her mind was slowly processing it, evaluating it as everything trickled into the compartments of her mind. Vale sensed this and reached out, pushing her hair gently away from her face. She caught his hand in her own, her muscles weak and stiff.

"In that place," she said softly. "You were searching for me."

"I was," he said. "You kept running and disappearing. I couldn't get you to slow down."

"But I did," she said, tracing the outline of his face with her finger. "Thanks to you. You pulled me out. You found me."

"I'll always find you, Taris," he said, his tone uncharacteristically filled with emotion. "Always."

Vale, she thought. *Kiss me. For the love of god, kiss me.*

The fire of his soul surged in his eyes like the sea during a storm. He cupped her face in his hand, bringing her toward him, and kissed her with arduous abandon. Every part of her felt electrified by his touch. His tongue danced like the wind through the trees, soft and melodic. She could feel his energy flowing within him. It surged like a current; brave and fast and driven. She started to pull back but he drew her back in, wrapped his arms around her, and kissed her deeply.

Then, abruptly, he pushed himself away. Before she could stop him he stood up, embarrassed, and covered his face with his hands. *"Ah gias…*I'm sorry, Taris."

"Why?" she asked, reaching for him. "Why are you sorry?"

He looked at her, his eyes watery with silver tears. "Because I am the lord guardian," he said, slowly composing himself as only a Gray could. "And I made a vow. To put the protection of my people above all else."

She knew what he meant and her heart sank. Above all else. Above her. She tried not to let the horror of his statement show on her face, but she knew it did. "I…understand."

"No you don't," he said, leaning against the wall. She noticed, for the first time, that he was wearing blue robes, not unlike the ones he was wearing when they first met. The symbol of the Silencium was sewn on the front in silver fabric. He closed his eyes and held his hair in his hands. "I barely understand it myself, Taris. I have suffered in despairing silence without you. I thought it would be better when you woke up, but it's so much worse."

"Sorry to disappoint," she grumbled. "Next time I'll try to stay in the coma so you won't have to give me mixed signals."

"Taris," he said in his exasperated tone, "please do not do this to me."

"I'm not the one doing the pushing away, Vale," she retorted. Now she was angry. "You can't just wake me up and kiss me and then tell me we can't be. We did not just go through hell together for nothing."

He clenched his jaw and looked down at her. "A lot has changed while you've been sleeping, Taris."

"Oh, well that makes it okay, then," she said, wishing she possessed the arm strength to slap him.

"I know you're mad at me," he said quietly, "but believe me, there is no other way. I begged Elias to release me but he would not. I have prayed to the Five and they tell me--"

"Oh don't you bring religion into this," she said sternly. "Don't you dare."

"*Tarischa*, please. You don't understand."

"No I don't," she said, trying not to cry. "And nothing you say is going to make me understand."

"Taris--"

"No," she said, stopping him. "I don't want to talk about it right now. Believe it or not, we have bigger problems to deal with than your inability to handle your emotions."

He looked at her, his face composed into the neutral Gray expression, though his eyes betrayed his feelings to her. That almost made it worse. "What? Did you see something in your dream?"

She shifted herself into a stiff sitting position, trying to focus on anything except her feelings for Vale, or the way her lips still tingled from his touch. "I know the faces of the other two pillars," she said quietly. "And they know me."

"Truly?" he asked, his voice alight with hope. "What happened? Did you speak to them?"

"Yes. Well it's complicated," she said. "The wisdom pillar told me he would find me when I found you, and the spirit pillar said if we don't unite the Star of Gray soon people will die. A lot of people."

The wind picked up, scratching the trees against the window. It seemed like a bad omen. She shivered in spite of herself. Suddenly her thoughts burdened her beyond measure.

"There is a war coming, Vale," she said, staring out at the rain-drenched forest, "a big one. And we don't have chance of winning if we don't find the other two pillars. We have to find them before the war starts or we're going to lose."

"Taris," Vale said gently, taking her hands in his. "The war has already begun."

The lightning struck outside, lighting the whole room, shaking even the rock with its intense thunder. She looked at Vale, the sadness and worry peeking out of his eyes, hidden behind his unreadable face.

"Help me out of this bed lord guardian," she said sternly. "It's time I joined the fight."

As soon as her feet touched the rocky floor, the lightning struck the ground in surprise. *That's right,* she thought. *The warrior is up, and I'm here to win this fight. On my grave, we're going to win this.* The thunder rumbling in protest, but she welcomed it. It empowered her.

She took a deep breath, pushed her shoulders back, and took her first step as a Star of Gray.

Show time.

END OF BOOK ONE

About the Author

Hubbard J. Tozer is a science fiction and fantasy novelist. She has been writing in a professional capacity for ten years. She has produced news articles, horoscopes, short stories, blog posts, magazine articles, speeches for generals, and novels. She currently lives on the East Coast with her family.

To find out more, go to www.hubbardjtozer.com
Join the fight! Check out the Star of Gray series Facebook page

www.ingramcontent.com/pod-product-compliance
Lightning Source LLC
Chambersburg PA
CBHW030920020726
47498CB00001B/49